Necessary Decisions

GIACOMO GIAMMATTEO

Also by Giacomo Giammatteo:

Fiction:
Friendship & Honor Series:
MURDER TAKES TIME: Friendship & Honor: Book I
MURDER HAS CONSEQUENCES: Friendship & Honor: Book II
MURDER TAKES PATIENCE: Friendship & Honor Book III

Blood Flows South Series:
A BULLET FOR CARLOS: Blood Flows South: Book I
FINDING FAMILY: Blood Flows South: the Beginning (A Novella)
A BULLET FROM DOMINIC: Blood Flows South: Book II

Redemption Series:
Necessary Decisions
OLD WOUNDS (Coming late 2014)

Non-Fiction:
No Mistakes Careers
NO MISTAKES RESUMES: Book One of No Mistakes Careers
NO MISTAKES INTERVIEWS: Book Two of No Mistakes Careers

Sanctuary Tales (True Stories From An Animal Sanctuary)
WHISKERS & BEAR (Coming soon)

Necessary Decisions

A Redemption Novel

GIACOMO GIAMMATTEO

INFERNO PUBLISHING COMPANY

NECESSARY DECISIONS
by Giacomo Giammatteo

INFERNO PUBLISHING COMPANY

For more information about this book, visit
www.giacomogiammatteo.com

ISBN: 978-1-940313-02-3 (ebook)
ISBN: 978-1-940313-03-0 (print)

This book is a work of fiction. Names, characters, places, and events herein are either the product of the author's imagination or are used fictitiously. Any resemblance to actual persons, living or dead, is entirely coincidental.

Note to Readers:

Welcome to the Redemption Series, featuring Detective Gino Cataldi and his partner, Hector "Ribs" Delgado. This is not the first book in the series. The first book, Old Wounds, was supposed to be out earlier in the year, but I didn't like the way some of the plot played out, so I am re-writing the whole thing. The good news is that the Redemption Series is not a continuing storyline, so you don't need to read them in order.

This book is also written differently than my other books. I think it starts out a little slower. I realized this as I wrote, but it was necessary to have the effect I wanted. Stick with it, and I think you'll find it is well worth your time. If you don't think it's worth your time, let me know. I guarantee all of my books.

Giacomo

Lines are meant to be crossed. Laws are meant to be broken.

Gino Cataldi

CHAPTER 1

HIGH STAKES

While the dealer shuffled the cards, I checked the gun tucked in my waistband—a Beretta with a full clip. A snub-nosed .38 was strapped to my leg. My stakeout partner sat at another table across from me with a good view of the front door.

I squeezed the cards and stared at a pair of lovely ladies. Not a bad hand to start with, especially when the guy to my right, a notorious bluffer, just raised two hundred dollars. I was considering how much to raise when I heard a ruckus at the door.

"Nobody move! Stay calm. No one will get hurt if you stay calm."

I thought about going for my gun but couldn't see what was behind me. I looked over to my partner, Ribs Delgado. He shook his head. I wondered if he just wanted me to play it safe or if—

The feel of a gun against my head answered the question.

"Money and valuables," a voice said.

The barrel of the gun pressed into my temple. I could damn near tell the caliber.

"Money and valuables." The phrase was repeated by another guy at the table where Ribs sat. An instinctive analysis told me this was not a group of hopped-up druggies. I pulled out my wallet, showed him it was empty then laid my money clip and cash on the table.

"What else?"

"Nothing." I still hadn't even seen this guy, but I caught a glimpse of the guy going through the same process at Delgado's table. That one wore latex gloves and a mask.

"Your watch," the guy behind me said.

I looked at it—a plain black face with only a second hand showing. A button on the side lit the minute and hour hands. It wasn't valuable in terms of money, but Mary had given me this the Christmas before she died. "It's not worth anything. It was a gift from my wife."

"I'll decide that."

"You're not getting the watch," I said, and turned toward him.

The right side of my head felt as if it exploded. Blood ran down my neck and face. When I tried talking it ran into my mouth. He hit me again. The barrel of the gun opened another gash in my head, and the force of the blow knocked me off the chair. Sometime between chair and floor I heard someone yell, "Number Three," and then I passed out. The last thing I remember was grabbing my watch.

***

Number Three stooped to get Gino's watch. He found the gun in Gino's waistband then the badge in his pocket, and the second gun in a leg holster. Number Three stood, holding the badge. "Look what we've got here. Who's the partner?"

When he got no response, he pulled out a switchblade and slipped the tip under the upper lip of the man seated at the table in front of him. "I'm going to start cutting with him. I'll keep cutting until the other cop steps forward."

Delgado stood slowly, his hands in the air. "I'm his partner."

As Number Three reached for Delgado, a voice rang out from across the room.

"Number Three!"

He turned, glaring. "Yes, Boss?"

"There has been enough violence."

The man Number Three referred to as Boss went to Delgado, hand extended. "Guns and badge."

Delgado gave him what they wanted. "I need to look after my partner."

Boss looked at his watch. "You have five minutes."

Delgado got bandages from the guy who ran the game. He patched Gino up with a few gauze pads and a couple of Band-Aids. Within five minutes, Boss returned to him, having stripped the others of their valuables. It took another ten minutes to duct-tape everyone. Boss set the guns and badges on the kitchen table, and bowed as he exited the front door. "I thank you, gentlemen. It has been my pleasure."

***

I WOKE UP FEELING as if I'd been shot. My hands and feet were bound with duct tape. All of us were gagged. The pool of blood on the floor made me wonder how bad I'd been hurt. Delgado nudged me and managed to give the "okay" sign with his thumb. Guess I'd live.

It took almost two hours before our boss, Captain Gladys Cooper, suspected something was wrong. She sent a half dozen units to investigate. Damn embarrassing is what it was—Delgado and I robbed and tied up. We found our guns and badges in the kitchen, but not the watch.

Delgado took me to the emergency room, where a doctor fixed me up.

"Take good care of him," Delgado said. "He's my cuz."

"Only by marriage," I said, smiling at the doctor. She smiled back then put 18 stitches in my head and sent me home with a couple of pain pills. I'd have rather had a kiss on the cheek. Wasn't much for pain pills.

Instead of going home, I had Delgado drive me back to the station. Captain Cooper had a lot of questions; we had no answers. And the guys who hit the game had taken over 20 grand. And my watch.

"This is the third game they've hit in six weeks," Coop said. "Neither of the others turned violent. Why did this one?" She directed the question at me.

"They wanted my watch. I wouldn't give it to them."

She raised her eyebrows and gave Delgado one of those I-knew-it-was-him type looks.

"Mary gave me that watch, Captain. No way was I giving it up."

"But they got it, didn't they?"

I turned my head.

"Didn't they?"

"For now."

"You should have given up the watch, Gino."

"I'll get it back."

Coop eyed me the way only she could, and then she turned to Delgado. "Leave us alone for a minute."

Delgado left with a confused expression. It matched the one I wore.

"We need to get clear on one thing," Coop said. "I don't want any repeats of Rico Moreno."

So that's what this is about. She's afraid I'll go after this guy.

I swallowed hard. "You've got nothing to worry about."

She stared at me for about ten seconds. "Whenever you or your ex-partner tell me not to worry, it scares me." She held her gaze a few seconds more. "I don't give second chances, Gino. Don't fuck this up."

I offered Coop my best smile. "I won't."

"All right. Get out of here. Go home and rest."

I turned to leave but Coop said, "You know that watch will be gone by tomorrow. If they can get a few dollars for it, it'll be in a pawn shop by the end of the week. If not, you'll have to go dumpster diving."

I gritted my teeth but said nothing. The watch wasn't worth anything more than memories. I nodded. "I know."

Delgado offered to drive me home, but I told him I was good. The swelling had gone all the way to my eye, which hurt like hell, and my head throbbed so bad I wanted to just hold it and squeeze, but I was okay to drive.

As I drove home, I thought about a lot of things, but all I could focus on was the guy who hit me. *Number Three.* No matter what Coop said, I'd get Mary's watch back.

CHAPTER 2

HARD TIMES

Lonny Hackett grew up poor. Hard-working poor. The kind of poor that made a man proud because he'd worked all day and his muscles ached. The kind of poor that made him smart from scrimping to pay bills and haggling over prices.

Like most poor people, Lonny dreamed about getting rich. He didn't want a lot. Just enough to let him buy Lucia a new dress now and then. Or a new pair of shoes. Take her out to dinner on Friday nights. The kids too, if they'd go. Enough so he didn't have to pray *every single night* that his old truck would start in the morning and get him to work. Enough to stay home when he got real sick.

He dreamed about it a lot, especially during the winter months when construction was slow and Lucia had to take on extra work to help with food. His mama had always told him that money ruined everything. When he was young, he figured she was right. He still believed in what she said, that money could ruin him…but he wanted to try it out sometime.

Maybe in the next life.

Lonny quit daydreaming then finished striking the joints on the brick facing for a drilling rig company. It was the first nice job they'd had in months. *Thank God for the oil industry.*

As he moved to the spots exposed to the afternoon sun, he put away his iron striker and used a smooth, wooden one he'd made out of hickory. Wood wouldn't burn joints—an important consideration in Houston's climate—and hickory was hard enough to polish joints instead of stripping them.

Lonny stepped back and smiled. He might be down to half of his hours, but that was no reason to slack off or do shoddy work. He wiped sweat from the corner of his eye then got his coarse brush and cleaned the mortar off the brick. Occasionally he used the wooden handle to scrape dried cement from the edges. When he finished, he placed his tools in his canvas bag, slipped his level through the handles, slung it over his shoulder, and climbed down the scaffold to the parking lot.

Mr. Mattusek, the boss, stood off to the side, talking to one of the concrete crew. "See you tomorrow, Mr. Mattusek." Lonny waved as he headed to his truck.

When he was almost there, he heard his name called.

"Lonny, you got a minute?"

He tossed the tools in the back of the pick-up—a ten-year-old blue Chevy with a metal toolbox fastened to the bed—grabbed a bottle of water from the cooler then headed over to Mattusek. If he was lucky, he'd get more work out of this.

"You need something done, Mr. Mattusek? You know I need the work."

Mattusek turned his head to the side. "I hate this shit."

Lonny's gut lurched. He felt as if he might throw up.

"I've got to let you go," Mattusek said. "I don't know for how long, but I promise you'll be the first one I call back."

Lonny's voice cracked when he spoke. "What about the restaurant we were supposed to get? And the—"

Mattusek was shaking his head. "We didn't get the contract for either. The financing fell through on the restaurant, and we lost the bid on the other. Somebody undercut us."

Unable to talk at first, Lonny managed to keep his dignity. He shook Mattusek's hand and thanked him for the years they worked together. "Call me if you get anything. I mean *anything*."

"I will," Mattusek said. "Promise."

Lonny got in his truck and headed for home. *How am I gonna tell Lucia?*

As he thought that, the phone rang. It was her. "Hey, baby," he said. "I hope you have a few filets on the grill topped with my favorite mushrooms."

"How'd you know, old man? And just in case your dreams come true, stop and pick up some *real* milk to go with those imaginary steaks."

"You got it. See you soon." Lonny felt like running, getting on the freeway, and heading west, or south into Mexico. Anywhere to get away from his responsibilities. If it weren't for Lucia and the kids, he'd pack up and leave. Instead, he pulled into the corner store and slowly walked inside. He checked the price on a gallon of milk then counted his money. He grabbed a Hershey's milk chocolate bar for Lucia, a Heath Bar for Jada, and a bag of crunchy Cheetos for Mars.

May as well make them happy with my last few bucks.

Lonny set everything on the counter and yanked the crumpled bills from his pocket. "Dave, how's it going today?"

"Not bad. Business is slow, though."

"About to get slower, I imagine."

Dave rang up the order. It left Lonny with $1.08. "I'll tell you what, give me one of those Texas Lotto tickets. What's it up to?"

"Thirty-nine million."

"Thirty-nine million…I could use that."

"Cash option?"

"Regular's fine. I get the cash option, I'd spend it all at once."

Dave handed Lonny the ticket. "Good luck."

"Thanks." Lonny clutched the ticket in his hand.

Come through for us, Lord. My family needs this.

CHAPTER 3

THE PROM

Jada Hackett walked down the long hall, her head hung low. It was the beginning of May, and no one had asked her to the prom. If it didn't happen soon, it wouldn't happen at all.

Alexa was cramming books into her locker when Jada approached.

"Well?" Alexa asked.

Jada sighed. "Nobody. Not even Kenny, though I'm kinda glad he didn't ask. I might have been tempted to say yes."

"You just broke up with him last month. Regretting it already?"

"Not hardly. Kenny was nice but he…just didn't have it."

"And you *know* you won't have that problem with Jason."

They both giggled, finished putting their books away, then headed toward English Lit class. Halfway through *Great Expectations*, Jada realized she was dreaming of Jason Rules instead of Pip. She sat up straight, cleared her thoughts, and got back to reading. Two hours later, on her way to the bus, she felt a tap on her shoulder. When she turned, she almost gasped.

"Jason! You scared me."

"Enough to go to the prom with me?"

Jada couldn't believe she was hearing this, but she played it cool, soooo cool. "What, nobody else would have you?"

He leaned in real close, his breath warming her cheeks. It sent goose bumps up her arms.

"You *know* that's wrong." Jason brushed his fingers against her neck, tucked her hair behind her ear. Kissed her. "So what's it gonna be? I can't be making my boys wait on me."

She cocked her head, as if she hadn't said yes a million times in her heart already. "I guess we'll make a good couple."

"You got that right, girl. We'll couple for sure."

A horn beeped. He flipped them the finger. "Gotta go. We'll catch up and figure things out."

Jada waited until he was out of sight then held her hands in front of her face and screeched. Then she giggled and laughed, running for the bus. Alexa was already there.

"Girl, was that Jason Rules I saw you talking to?"

Jada jumped up and down, screeching again. "Jason Rules—he *rules*."

"Jason Rules has got the *tools*."

Alexa and Jada laughed more, hugged each other as they got on the bus, and almost danced their way to a pair of empty seats.

Kenny approached Jada, hands in his pockets, head hung low. "You going to the dance?"

"Jason asked me," Jada said, her head halfway to the clouds.

"Jason Rules?" Kenny shook his head. "You could do better."

"Like you?"

"Yeah, like me, but by the time you figure that out, you'll be messed up. Forget I asked."

"I already did."

Alexa put her hand on Jada's arm. "Don't worry about it. He can't ruin this day."

"You're right about that. *Nothing* can ruin this day."

Half an hour later, after riding the bus to Alexa's house, Jada caught a ride home with a friend. The houses in her neighborhood were three-bedroom ranch homes built in the fifties or sixties. Most didn't have a garage. She waved to old Joe out sprinkling his lawn, and to Mr. Cobb tending his gardens, but mostly she thought about how to tell her mom that she wouldn't be going to the prom with Kenny. Her mom liked him.

Jada got out near the end of the street, walked up the short driveway and into the house. The door opened into the living room, which shared space with the eating area.

Her mother was folding clothes from a basket on the table. "How was your day?"

Jada tried containing herself but didn't do so well. "I got asked to prom!"

Her mother continued folding a towel but glanced in Jada's direction. "Kenny?"

"Another boy asked me first. I couldn't say no, not this late; besides, he's *adorable*."

Her mother kept folding towels.

"Mom, you don't understand. It's Jason Rules, the most popular guy in school. And he asked *me*. Aren't you happy?"

Her mother finished the last towel, and then set the laundry basket down and hugged her. "Of course I'm happy, but…"

"But what?" Jada pulled back, staring, afraid of what would come next.

"What will you wear?"

"We'll have to get something."

Her mother's face grew rigid, almost stern. "You know the situation. Nothing's changed."

"Don't we have *any* money?"

"Where do you think we'd get money? Did *you* bring any in this week? Your father's work is down by half." She grabbed a dishtowel and tossed it to Jada. "You dry. I'll wash."

Jada dried a few dishes, setting them on the counter. "What about Mars? Is he still going to jiu-jitsu?" She tried taking the anger from her voice.

Her mother's glare made Jada feel ashamed. "His classes have been paid for since the beginning of the year. And we *don't* get refunds for canceling." She washed the pan they'd cooked asparagus in and handed it to Jada. "Believe me, if we could get a refund, we would."

"How come I get shafted? You knew the prom was coming up."

Her mother turned off the water, set down the washcloth, and stared at her. *Glared* was more like it. Again. "Yes, I knew the prom was coming up, but I *did not* know that your father's boss would cut his hours in half, or that he wouldn't be able to find more work." She looked ready to cry, but held it back. "And I did not know that *every damn* thing we need to live would go up in price. If I *had* known, maybe I would have found time to save money for your precious prom."

Jada cringed and looked away. She ran the towel across the bottom of the pan and wiped the inside. "I'm so sick of seeing dog hairs. I can't wait till Scooter goes."

Her mother turned on her with fire in her eyes. "I *know* you don't mean that. Tell me it was one of those stupid, *stupid* things that come out of a young girl's mouth."

"I'm sorry, Mom. I didn't mean to upset you." She leaned over and kissed her on the cheek. "I love you." When her mother didn't say anything, Jada repeated it. "I really am sorry. And I really do love you."

Her mother stared at her for a moment then nodded. "All right. And about that prom, don't give up yet. We may find a way. I can still sew a mean dress."

"It's okay. I don't need to go."

"What, and let poor what's-his-name take a lesser girl to the prom?" They both laughed. Her mom wrung out the dishcloth and wiped the table. "He'd never forgive me."

"You're the best, Mom. And by the way, his name's Jason."

"You mean I'm the best mom *if* I figure out how to get you a dress?"

"Either way, but that would make you the bomb."

She laughed. "I don't know if I *want* to be the 'bomb,' but thanks."

"Did you go to prom with Dad?"

Another laugh. "No. I went with Roger Mattens. At the time, I was certain I was going to marry him."

"But?"

"But I met your father." She sat in a chair and stared at a wall filled with pictures of pigs—a baker, a chef, a butler. More pig ornaments dotted the shelf hanging on the side wall. "I met him at prom. All night I pestered Roger to dance. And all night I watched your father tear up that dance floor." She sighed. "He must have noticed me watching him. At the first chance, he asked me to join him. I looked over at Roger. He shrugged, so I went with your father." She laughed. "We danced the rest of the night together. He took me home afterward."

"I bet you stopped for a little something, huh?"

"Jada!"

"Don't act so innocent. I can count. I was born seven months after you were married."

Her mother tried to hide her blushing face. "Shame on you, Jada."

Jada rubbed her fingers together in a taboo signal. "Shame on you, Mama."

They laughed together like two girlfriends then hugged.

"I'll find some way," her mother said. "You'll have your prom."

CHAPTER 4

THE REAL WORLD

Lonny pulled into the driveway. Before entering the house, he washed his hands and arms at the outside spigot, then brushed the cement from his clothes. His back ached, and his fingers were split and cut, but Lucia didn't tolerate cement dust in her house. He mustered optimism from somewhere and wore it like a mask when he opened the door.

"How are my favorite girls tonight?"

Jada ran to him, hugged him and gave him a kiss on the cheek.

"Whoa! Something's going on. I don't get this kind of greeting unless someone needs something, and badly."

"Daddy, I got asked to prom today by the cutest boy in the whole school. Maybe the whole *world*."

"That's great." He hugged her and patted her back. "I'm tickled for you. Who's the lucky boy?"

Lucia walked over. "I hate to interrupt this moment of joy, but what your daughter *isn't* telling you is that she needs a prom dress."

Lonny had used all of his willpower on the fake smile. Nothing but frustration remained. "Jada, you *know* we don't have money."

"Sorry, Dad. I didn't know if—"

"You didn't know, or you didn't *think*? Or maybe you just didn't care."

She cowered. "Dad—"

"'Dad' *my ass*. Did you bother to think how it makes me feel not being able to afford a dress for my only daughter? Your brother would never do that, he—" Lonny stopped. He went to his chair, where he sat, head buried in his hands. When Jada came to him, he got up and almost ran to the bedroom.

***

JADA TRIED FOLLOWING BUT stopped short of going in. She backed up and went to her mother, falling into her arms. "I think Dad's crying."

Her mother hugged her back. "Men cry too, dear. They just try not to let others know."

"What's going on? Why is Dad crying?"

Lucia led Jada to the kitchen. "Your father's a proud man. Proud men have a lot further to fall when something goes wrong."

"What's wrong?"

"I don't know yet."

***

LONNY SAT ON THE on the edge of the bed and stared at the floor. For years, he'd taken care of his family—but now he couldn't. He didn't know how he would feed them, let alone pay the mortgage or electric bills. He was already one month late on the mortgage. Now, with no work...*I can't lose this house. I* won't *lose this house.*

Then he remembered a conversation with a guy named Willard who arranged jobs for people. The problem with his work was that if Lonny got caught, he'd spend time in jail. Still, he had to feed his family.

What the hell am I gonna do?

He thought about his old truck, with dents in the back quarter panel and front fender, an engine that sputtered. How long could it last with 155,000 miles on it? Willard drove a two-year-old Mercedes, which got cleaned and waxed every week, at least from what Lonny heard.

He was about to say no when he thought of Jada and how excited she was about that prom. His little girl all grown up. Then he thought about how Jada and Mars would feel if he lost the house. Where would they live?

A big battle raged inside of him, and when it was over, Lonny had his decision. No matter what happened, his little girl was going to the prom, and she'd be picked up at *this* house.

I'm keeping this house if I have to kill someone to do it.

CHAPTER 5

DESPERATE TIMES

All night, Lonny fretted over his decision. Sometime between his third or fourth trip to the bathroom, sick to his stomach, he decided he wouldn't call Willard after all. He'd find work somewhere, even if it meant doing odd jobs or cutting lawns. He'd shovel shit if he had to.

Dilemma resolved, he finally got to sleep. It was late, maybe five AM when he nodded off, but he got up at six and smiled as he made his way to the kitchen. Looking for a job was as difficult as doing one, or so they said. He hadn't done it for a long time, so he didn't remember if the old saying was true. What he *did* know was that he had to get money before next month's mortgage payment was due. It would be tough to dig out of this hole, but he was glad he'd decided to do it the *right* way.

"Good morning, ladies." He kissed Lucia and rubbed Jada's head then playfully punched Mars in the arm. "You too, tough guy."

"Be careful, old man. I'll take you down."

"Don't even *think* you can come close to that."

"Ha! Did you see my take-down at the last competition? It had your name all over it."

Lonny laughed then went to get his coffee.

"Sit down, Dad. I'll get it," Jada said.

"This smells like bribery to me."

"It *is* bribery. I figure if I make you breakfast every morning and send you out healthy, you'll be able to find more work in time for the prom."

Lonny grabbed his coffee and sipped it. "We'll see. Don't give up yet."

"I can quit my lessons," Mars said. "I can go back later."

Jada leaned down and hugged him. "Little brother, nothing means more to me than this prom, *except* seeing my baby bro win competitions. But thanks for offering. You're the best."

Lucia brought an omelet to the table and scooped some on each plate. "This is all there is. Enjoy it."

"Where's yours?" Lonny asked.

"I'm on a diet."

Lonny got up and grabbed another plate, scraping half of his onto it. "You'll eat this, or I'll throw it away."

Lucia stared at him, but when he didn't back down, she smiled and kissed him. "All right, mister. Now sit and eat before it gets cold."

Lonny joked with the kids during breakfast then grabbed his boots and headed out the door. He drove to a new construction site they had just broken ground on to build a new school. He got there half an hour before the gates opened, first in line. When it was time, a man came to unlock the gates.

"Foreman here yet?" Lonny asked.

He pointed to a trailer. "Over there, but we're not hiring, if that's what you're here for."

"What's his name?"

"Mitch."

Lonny started off toward the trailer, praying all the way. He knocked on the door, his gut roiling, turning that omelet over and over.

"Come in."

Lonny stepped up and opened the door. Once inside, he removed his hat. "I'm looking for Mitch."

There was only one guy in there, a tall blond-headed guy with a face full of freckles. His hardhat lay to the side, holding down one corner on a set of blueprints. A large glass ashtray held down the opposite side, cigar butts mounded high on thick, gray ashes.

The man never stopped what he was doing, and he didn't look at Lonny. "I'm Mitch. What can I do for you?"

"I'm looking for work. I can do—"

"Not hiring."

Lonny hesitated. Took a deep breath. "I can do concrete, brick, block, stone. Just about any masonry you got. I've even done a little stucco."

"I'm full, pal. Sorry."

Lonny's hands moved along the rim of his hat, pressing it, squeezing. He *had* to get work. "Listen, Mr....Mitch, I'll do *anything* right now. I'll do labor, and..." He got the feeling he was about to be cut off again, so he hurried. "If you got *anything*, I'll jump in and do it. All I need is a chance. I'm not like these kids today. I *work.* Tell you what, I'll work a day for free, just to show you what I got."

"I'd like to help, but like I said, I'm full." The guy still didn't look up.

Lonny started toward the door, but then stopped and turned back to Mitch. "Mr. Mitch, I know you said you're full, and I understand that, but I...I'm gonna lose my house if I don't get work. My kids..." He stopped before he embarrassed himself.

Mitch put his pencil down, took his glasses off, and looked at Lonny for the first time. "What's your name?"

Lonny stood straight and put his hands at his side. "Lonny Hackett, sir. I been a bricklayer for sixteen years, and I—"

Mitch stopped him. "I wasn't kidding about not having any work, but keep checking back with me. Come by once a week and ask to see me personally. Tell them I said so." He reached into a drawer next to the table, pulled out a business card, and handed it to Lonny. "In the meantime, go see this guy—Brian Robinson. He's running the new office project on Tomball Parkway. You know where that is?"

"I know exactly where it is. I'll go see him now."

Mitch held his hand out. "Tell Brian I suggested you see him."

Lonny shook his hand. "Thanks, Mitch, I really appreciate it. You can count on me being by every week if I don't hook up with Brian."

Mitch smiled. "You do that. Good luck."

Lonny took the half-hour drive to Tomball Parkway, where he waited an hour to talk to Brian. He had no work for Lonny but referred him to another friend, who did the same. By noon, Lonny had talked to four superintendents and gotten the same story at each site—no work. When he ran out of places to go, he stopped at a few fast-food joints. He couldn't even get a job there. Frustrated and desperate, he turned off the road into a parking lot of a closed-up restaurant. He opened his phone and took out a piece of paper with a number written on it. For a moment he just stared at it. Then he punched in the numbers for Willard.

"Hello?"

"This is Lonny Hackett. I'm looking for work."

"I don't know what you're talking about."

"Is this Willard?"

"Ain't no Willard here, and I've had this number six months or more."

"Sorry. I must have dialed wrong."

Lonny checked the number on the paper versus what he'd dialed. It was the same. *Shit!* He stopped at several corner stores he'd heard Willard frequented. They said they didn't know him. About an hour later, on the way home, Lonny got a call.

"Hello?"

"Are you willing to do anything?"

"Who's this?"

"I heard you been lookin' for work."

"Willard?"

"I don't know Willard, but I hear you're looking for work. I'll ask one more time. Are you willing to do *anything?*"

Lonny paused for a deep breath. He searched his soul for a reason to say no, but all he could think of was Lucia trying to give him her share of breakfast. And not being able to pay next month's mortgage. "Yeah, anything."

"I know a guy, but the thing is, you can't fuck with this guy. If you tell him you're in, you better be in all the way. Know what I mean?"

"Give me the number."

"It doesn't work that way. If you're in, tell me."

"Why the runaround?"

"Are you in or out?"

"In," Lonny said, and received his first instructions. He drove to another corner store and checked with the clerk inside, who told him a disposable phone was in a bag in the dumpster. Lonny got it and wiped it off, disgusted at what he was doing already, then waited in the truck. He waited for almost half an hour before it rang. "Hello?"

"I heard you want work."

"Yeah, I need work."

"Here's what you do. And don't write this down. Nothing gets written down, got that?"

"Okay."

"Go to the coffee shop at Louetta and Kuykendahl Road. Be there at 9:00 AM. *Do not* be early. Park in the lot behind the shop next to a green van. The door will be unlocked. Get in the passenger side, put on the mask that will be on the seat and slip through the curtains into the back of the van. Talk to no one. Bring this cell phone with you."

"Is this a joke? You must be nuts."

After a short delay, the man spoke again. "Deal is off. Put the phone back in the bag. And remember, we know where you live, Lonny Hackett."

Lonny panicked. *How the hell do they know my name? And where I live?* "No, wait. I'm sorry. I'll do it."

"Any more arguments, and you're finished. Clear?"

There was something about the way the man said *clear* that both grated on Lonny, and frightened him. "Clear," Lonny said. He asked for the instructions again, then got in his truck and headed home. He kept telling himself he was doing this for Lucia and the kids, but he knew differently. This was an easy, cowardly way out of a tough situation.

God forgive me for whatever I'm about to do.

CHAPTER 6

EASY PICKINGS

Lonny woke with a queasy stomach. He got dressed, sat on the edge of the bed and said a prayer. Then he stood, straightened his shirt, took a handkerchief from the drawer, and tucked it into his back pocket. Not many people carried handkerchiefs these days, but Lonny's father had taught him that it was something gentlemen do. Lonny always made sure he had one.

Coffee waited for him in the kitchen, compliments of Lucia. Lonny drank the coffee, and managed a piece of toast but gave his eggs to Mars. The way Lonny's stomach felt, he didn't think the eggs would stay down for long.

A few minutes before nine, he got to the coffee shop. At exactly nine, he pulled alongside the green van. The door was unlocked. He hesitated before getting in, searching for a reason not to do this, but his desperation had him open the door. A wool cap with a dark nylon stocking mask lay on the seat. Lonny looked around to make sure no one was near. His hands shook as he slid the mask over his face. He moved the curtains aside and got in back. Five minutes later, the driver's door opened and the van started. Lonny never saw the driver.

After a drive lasting about twenty minutes, the van stopped. A tap on the ceiling signaled Lonny it was time to get out. He exited through the side doors into a small room resembling a two-car garage, but it was industrial, not a home. A door to his left was open. He walked into a large room. He noted the metal walls, concrete floor, and lack of windows. *Warehouse,* he thought. Fluorescent lights shone from about twelve feet above. At the far side of the room, a man sat behind a laminate desk. He wore the same kind of mask as Lonny.

"Come in, Lonny."

His deep voice matched his lumberjack size. Probably weighed 240. Lonny didn't like that the guy knew his name.

"Have a seat," the guy said. "I'm called Boss."

Lonny endured an intense interview with Boss, who explained the process to Lonny—what he didn't know already—and more than once reminded him that mistakes were not tolerated.

"We never take our masks off," Boss said. "*Never.*"

"I got that from this morning."

"That's another thing. *No one* is to know where you meet. The meeting place will change every time. No personal information is to be shared. All instructions must be carried out immediately. Clear?"

The word *clear* shook Lonny's nerves. *So this is the guy?* "Clear," Lonny said.

"The person who drives the van is called Driver. No one sees Driver. No one talks to Driver. Clear?"

"Clear," Lonny said.

"You will go through several days of training before your first job."

"I need work right away. I—"

"I know you need money. You'll be paid for the training."

Lonny nodded. "What do I do?"

Boss stood, walked to a door at the back wall, and knocked. Another guy with a mask came in. He wasn't as tall as Boss, and not as big, but still had Lonny by an inch or so. "This is Number Three," Boss said. "He'll teach you what you need to know."

For the next few days, Lonny went through the same routine. Meeting the van—at Starbucks, or Denny's, McDonald's, or a donut shop—anywhere that drew a lot of morning traffic. Afterward, he was driven to an unknown location where Number Three put him through the paces. On the fourth day, they went out, receiving instructions from Boss on the way to a job. Lonny had no idea what kind of job until they were halfway there.

"This is a home invasion," Boss said. "If we follow procedure, no one will get hurt, and we'll make good money."

Lonny swallowed hard. *Home invasion! What the hell have I gotten myself into?*

They got to the house by mid-morning, driving past it a few times to check that all was in order. Just before noon, Driver pulled to the side of the street and tapped on the ceiling to let Boss know it was clear. Boss waited while Driver got out of the van, and then Boss moved to the front seat, closed the curtain, and removed his mask. He exited the van and approached the house. He was dressed as a telephone repair man; it wouldn't do to be seen wearing a mask in this neighborhood. He rang the bell. By the time an old woman answered, Boss had his mask on and gun drawn.

Number Two got the call to come in. Driver pulled up to the garage. Everyone exited the van and entered the house through the back door.

The wife was the only one home. It didn't take much time to gather the jewels, a little cash, and a stack of negotiable bonds from a safe hidden in the bedroom closet. Lonny's job was to watch the street from the front window. Number Three got the safe, and Number Two watched the wife. Boss checked the house for things they might have missed. He found a few pieces of art that would bring good money.

Boss looked at his watch as he came back to the living room. "Number Three, time to go."

Thirty seconds later, they were in the van and headed back to the base. Boss paid everyone then sent them home. "I'll call when the next job comes up."

Lonny's cut was a little more than two thousand. Not a fortune, but enough to keep his mortgage paid and put food on the table. He hated what he'd done, but Boss said the wife's insurance company would cover everything. That made it seem less like stealing.

For two nights, Lonny threw up, cursing his weakness, ashamed of what he'd done. The only things that kept him going were the money and the knowledge that no one got hurt. He didn't give a *shit* about insurance companies. Still, when the call came from Boss about the next job, he got sick all over again.

***

BOSS PARKED A BLOCK down the street from the Marshalls' house, fastened a leash on the dog, and started off on his daily walk. He'd been doing this for a week, ever since he chose this house as the next target. He didn't like home invasions, but they produced big scores with less risk than banks, which didn't bring much more than a good convenience store. The poker games had been a good gig, but they had gotten too hot since Number Three hit that cop. Boss should have killed Three for doing that. Next time he would.

Boss walked slowly, taking time to case the house and make note of the Marshalls' routines. The dog path ran past a wooded section of the backyard that bordered a golf course, a perfect spot to gain access. After he finished the walk, he loaded the dog into the car and headed for home, calling Dispatcher on the way.

"It's me."

"Tell everyone it's tomorrow night. I want them to meet me an hour early."

"They'll be there."

Boss sat in a folding chair, going over the plans one final time. A door creaked open, and he stirred, pulling his mask down as his hand slipped to the gun in his waistband. The mask was nothing more than a dark nylon stocking, but it sufficiently disguised his face.

"Number Two coming in."

Boss relaxed, focused on the door. Number Two took a seat next to him, studying the plans.

"We're certain of the times?"

Boss nodded. "Double-checked and confirmed."

"And the neighbors aren't home?"

"Not on the side we approach from," Boss said. "The others won't be able to see us."

"Good," Number Two said. "That's why I like working with you...Boss."

Before long, Numbers Three, Four and Five arrived. They went through the details one last time, and then Boss looked at his watch and stood.

"Remember your stations. And remember protocol. No one has to get hurt. No one *should* get hurt. Clear?"

"Clear," everyone answered.

"How much time do we have?" Number Two asked.

"From entry to exit, twenty-five minutes." He looked around. "Any questions?"

"How are we going to drive with a mask on?" This question from the newcomer—Number Five.

"Driver will drop us off and pick us up. None of us will *ever* be unmasked in front of anyone. Any more questions?" No one answered. "Let's go."

Driver parked half a block from the house, where an access road to the golf course cut through the houses. As they approached the Marshall house from the rear, Number Four went around to the front, keeping close to the bushes. He stepped onto the front porch and rang the bell.

Boss checked his watch. "Ten more seconds," he whispered, then continued the countdown. "Five...four...three...two...one...go!"

They stepped quickly across the Marshalls' backyard, moving to the sliding door and making their way inside. A young girl was at the kitchen table. Her mother was answering the door.

Number Three moved quickly through the house and grabbed the mother. He held a knife to her throat. "Don't make a sound."

Number Two had the girl. "Don't scream," she said.

Boss walked quickly to the living room. Number Four had the servant under control.

Boss turned to Number Two. "I'm going upstairs. "Five, come with me."

Marshall was still in the shower. Boss entered carefully, yanked the door open. A knife was in his hand. Knives scared people more than guns. The man screamed. Fright does that to people.

"Try to keep quiet, sir. We have your family in the other room. We don't want anyone to get hurt."

"What do you want?" He panicked, grabbing a towel to cover himself.

Boss took it from him. "No need for that. We're all family. Come with me."

"What do you want?"

Boss pressed the knife into the man's stomach, just enough to draw a little blood. By the time they got to the living room, Number Two had the son naked too.

"I want all the jewelry and cash. And any valuables that will fit in these bags." Number Three handed two bags to the mother and daughter. "If you try anything, the men die."

"Don't hurt us," the mother said. "Please don't hurt us."

"Do as I say, and it will be fine." Boss nodded to Two and Five, a signal to accompany them. "We don't have much time."

They returned in a few minutes. Judging by the smirk shining from under Number Five's mask, it must have been a good haul. Boss turned to the father. "Where's the safe?"

"There is no safe."

Boss nodded to Number Three, who struck the boy on the knee with a tire iron. He was a big kid, almost as big as his father, but he went down screaming. Three kicked the boy in the stomach until he gasped for breath.

"No!" the mother screamed. She broke from Number Four, rushing toward her son. Four grabbed her. Number Five held the servant and daughter.

Boss looked to the father. "If you want him to ever play football again, you better tell us where the safe is."

The mother screamed, "Tell them, Charles. It's only money."

Charles Marshall lowered his head, embarrassed, but whether by his cowardice or his greed, Boss didn't know.

The boy grabbed Number Three's ankles and yanked, bringing him down. Number Three scrambled to his feet. He struck the boy's face with the tire iron repeatedly.

"Number Three!" Two yelled.

"That's *enough*," Boss said.

"The safe is in the bedroom!" the father screamed. He tried going to his son, but Boss stopped him.

"Your wife can bandage the boy while you take me to the safe." Boss grabbed an empty bag and followed Marshall, returning in less than five minutes. He nodded to the others. They used duct tape to secure all five of them in a circle on the floor. "Let's go," Boss said.

They left through the back door, moving along the path at a leisurely pace. Near the end of the trail, Driver picked them up.

As Driver pulled out of the neighborhood, Lonny screamed at Number Three. "Why'd you do that? You hurt that boy."

Number Three reached for him, but stopped dead when Boss' gun pressed against his head. "Sit back, Three."

Three hesitated. Boss cocked the hammer. "Your share of the money can pay for cleaning the van. Your choice."

Three leaned against the wall of the van, glaring at Boss.

Boss turned his attention to Lonny. "Four, if you ever question what was done on a job again, *your* share will go for cleaning up. Clear?"

Lonny gulped. "Clear."

CHAPTER 7

NEW CASE FILE

I got the call around 10:00 PM. I was seldom asleep, but if the phone rang late at night, I worried if something was wrong with my son.

Did he fall off the wagon? Did he overdose?

I'd been living with this nightmare for a year, though it seemed like ten. I grabbed the phone, anxious. "Hello?"

"Gino, it's Chief Renkin. I hope it's not too late."

Chief Renkin! What the hell?

"Not a problem, sir. What can I do for you?"

"We have another home invasion, but this one escalated; they beat the son pretty badly."

"Where?"

"Champions Forest. You live close by, don't you?"

"Not far at all, Chief. You think it's the same group?"

"It sounds like it."

"I assume you'll clear this with Captain Cooper."

"Already done." Renkin hesitated, as if he was going to hang up, then, "I know this doesn't make any difference, but the Marshalls are dear friends of mine."

"I understand, sir." *Doesn't make any difference, my ass.*

I grabbed my gun and headed out. Home invasions were bad enough; these people being "dear friends" of the chief compounded the situation. During the twenty-minute drive to the crime scene, I thought about my new job—Special Crimes. Sometimes I liked it, and at other times, it was a pain in the ass. Tonight would fall into the latter category.

A few minutes later, I turned off Champion's Forest Drive and into a circular driveway that looked as if it led to a country club. Why did the chief bother with an address? He could have just said look for the house that's as big as a factory. The place stretched for half a block, all brick and windows, and enough rooflines to put a cathedral to shame. I rang the doorbell and waited, wondering if a nap was in order before they could answer.

While I waited, I thought about what Marshall might look like based on what I knew—his name, and that his son played football. Damn good football, according to about every paper in Texas. A man who appeared to be in his mid-forties with signs of gray in his hair greeted me. Marshall fit everything I'd imagined. He was big, my guess was linebacker in college, and from the ring on his finger that anybody in Texas would recognize, he had played for A&M.

"You must be Detective Cataldi."

His accent had me guessing he was from East Texas, maybe up by Tyler. I shook his hand. "Chief Renkin told me what happened, Mr. Marshall. How's your son?"

"Not good. My wife is still at the hospital. I came back to meet with you." He stepped aside. "Come in, Detective."

I stepped into a marble foyer that looked half as big as the first floor of my house. It boasted a double-spiral staircase that resembled something from the *Gone with the Wind* era of mansions.

Marshall led me through several rooms, all large and all decorated as if *Interior Design* or *Architectural Digest* would be there in the morning for photographs. We ended up in the kitchen, a place I could have retired in. It was the first time I felt truly comfortable since entering the house, but then again, kitchens had a way of doing that to me. They sparked images of food and good wine, although the good wine part was only in my dreams. My kitchen was stocked with cheap, or should I say, *inexpensive* Chianti. Anything over ten bucks a bottle had to wait for a Saturday night.

"Would you like a glass of wine?"

I was tempted to refuse, being on the job and knowing he was a friend of the chief, but curiosity got the better of me. "I'd love some. Thanks."

"What do you prefer?"

"Whatever you have is fine, sir."

"I'm guessing you're Italian by the name. How about Brunello?"

"Brunello would be wonderful."

I expected him to turn to his servant or butler or whoever had been trailing us and issue an order, but he didn't have to say anything; the guy took the cue and disappeared.

"What happened to your head, Detective? That looks rather nasty."

"I got it while working undercover. It's mostly healed."

Marshall sighed. "Good God, what is the world coming to?"

I was about to say something when the butler returned. While he poured the wine, I took out my notepad. "Tell me what happened, Mr. Marshall, and try to go through it slowly. No detail is too small or too insignificant."

From the intense look in his eyes, I got the distinct feeling he understood. "I was in the shower when they came in. Roger, my son, was in his room showering. I'd picked him up from football practice and we came home and, as we always do, went to shower." He sipped his wine and stared at me. "It's almost too much of a coincidence that they chose *that* moment to come in—when both of us were showering. Don't you think?"

I made notes as he talked. "Who answered the door?"

He shook his head. "My wife, but I know the details. One of them rang the bell, which she answered. The others came in through the sliding door in the back." Marshall rose from the table and walked into the next room. "As you can see, there is easy access from the golf course, with plenty of cover from the foliage."

From the periphery, I saw the butler nodding. I wondered if he had warned them previously of what I was thinking.

Keep the fucking door locked.

"The door wasn't locked?"

He scoffed. "It never is, except at night. My wife checks the doors and sets the alarm before going to bed."

I walked outside and took a look around. We hadn't had rain in weeks, so the ground was too hard for footprints, even with sprinklers. "Did they wear gloves?"

The butler stepped forward. His accent wasn't British, as I expected, but it was eloquent. "All of them did, sir. Surgical gloves."

I made a note and turned back to Marshall. "What happened next? Did you hear them?"

He shook his head again. "I didn't know anything had happened until one of them came into the bathroom. He opened the shower door, wielding a knife, and ordered me out." He flushed before continuing. "For God's sake, Detective, they wouldn't even let me dress. They forced me out naked in front of my daughter."

"I wouldn't say it's common practice, sir, but a lot of professionals do it. It makes people feel helpless. Naked victims are less likely to resist." I wrote down what he said, then continued. "What did they do next?"

"They took our jewelry and cash then the one who seemed to be the leader asked where the safe was."

"You say *the leader*. Is there a reason why you say that?"

"He ran the show. There were five of them, four white and one black. The tall man I'm talking about was white. He gave the orders."

"Is there anything else you remember about them? Take your time."

The butler spoke. "One of them seemed…feminine."

"You mean gay?"

"No. A woman. She spoke only once. When the man struck Roger, she yelled 'Number Three.' After that, she never spoke again."

I sat upright, muscles tensed. My fist clenched involuntarily. "She said 'Number Three.' You're sure?"

"Positive," the butler said. "I thought it odd at the time. It stuck in my head."

I looked to Marshall. "Did you hear it?"

He seemed to give it thought. "I honestly can't say. I was focused on Roger."

The butler spoke again. "After she said that, the lead man hollered 'That's enough, Number Three.'"

My pulse quickened. My heart raced. This was the only lead I'd had to the mysterious Number Three since that fucker knocked me out and stole Mary's watch. I was so damned nervous, I couldn't think straight.

I turned to the butler. "You said one was a woman. What makes you think that?"

"Her voice sounded feminine. She was slight of build, and the way she moved shouted female. I was close enough to see her skin, too. It was smoother than the others'."

"I thought they wore masks."

"They did, but her arms were exposed. Or perhaps I should say her forearms were."

"That's very good. That may help." I turned back to Marshall. "What happened with your son? Why did it turn violent?"

He lowered his head. "It was my fault."

I let him keep the silence, not forcing the issue.

"As I said, after they'd taken the jewels and cash, the leader asked where the safe was." Marshall looked up at me. For a minute, I thought he'd cry. "I told him I had no safe."

I waited, but he said nothing more. "What happened then?"

"He didn't give me a second chance. The boss nodded to one of the others, and they took a…a tire iron, and swung it at Roger, beating his legs and kicking him." Marshall *did* cry now. "Roger…screamed and grabbed the man's leg. Then they hit Roger's face. And they kept hitting, and hitting, and hitting." Marshall closed his eyes briefly, as if recalling the incident. "I thought they'd killed him. Jesse screamed 'Tell them, Charles. It's only money.'"

Marshall wiped tears away. "After that, I told him where it was, Detective. I told him where everything was, but I had waited too long." Marshall got up and walked around the kitchen. "The thing is they *knew* we had more. Someone must have told them."

"Did you have insurance? Who else knew where you kept things, or that you even had a safe?"

"Of course the jewelry was insured. As far as who knew, all of us have safes."

"'All of us'?"

"I'm sorry. All of our friends, the people we associate with. But none of them know where our safe is."

"And neither did the robbers."

"Detective, honestly. You can't think our friends had anything to do with this."

"Right now, Mr. Marshall, I'm just asking questions. Let's go over everything again. What they looked like. How tall they were. Their build. How they talked. What they said. Any accents? I'm going to need everything I can get if we hope to catch these people."

And I wanted to catch these people more than Mr. Marshall could ever know. That watch was my last gift from Mary, and that scum-sucking fucker named Number Three was going to pay for taking it.

I got back to focusing on their answers. The butler said the one in charge was maybe 6' 3" or even 6' 4". Marshall swore he wasn't that tall.

"I'm 6' 2"," Marshall said. "And he was about my height. No taller."

I made note of that. "What about build. Big and bulky? Thin and wiry?"

Marshall thought. "Big, I'd say."

"He was bigger than Mr. Marshall," the butler added.

"How did they talk? Did anyone have a recognizable accent?"

"They were from Texas," the butler said. He seemed positive about that.

Marshall agreed. "They didn't say much, but when the leader asked about the safe, I detected a Texas accent."

I finished my notations, took a moment to focus, and started again. "Let's go through the whole event one more time. I know this is difficult, but it may help."

Marshall gripped the wine glass as if it were a life jacket. "I'm ready. Go on."

For the next hour, we went through the details. The butler had an excellent memory. When we were done, I gave them both my card and said I would be back to ask more questions.

Marshall walked me to the door. "Do you think there will be more invasions?" He paused. "Do you think you'll catch them?"

"It's difficult to say, Mr. Marshall. These cases are tough. If they quit now, the chances are not good for us catching them. We normally only catch them if they start making mistakes." I knew that wasn't what he wanted to hear, but I hated to give victims false hope. Nothing worse than promising to catch who did them wrong and not deliver.

He nodded, probably expecting no more.

As I left, I thought about what I'd learned tonight. I knew without a doubt that there would be more of these break-ins, or home invasions, and I knew that the next ones would be more violent. Once violence entered the picture, it always escalated. I had to catch them, and fast. I wouldn't say it out loud or promise anything to the Marshalls, but I swore right then and there that I'd get these fuckers.

CHAPTER 8

THE SUN SHINES IN TEXAS

Morning sun broke through the mini blinds, a harsh awakening for Lonny. He hadn't slept much, worrying about that boy. Now he felt like he needed a shower—on the inside. He took the money out of his nightstand drawer and counted it again. *$3,400 for hurtin' that boy.* The money would have to last a long time, because Lonny vowed he would *never* work for those people again. Damn redneck crackers is what they were. As bad as anybody from the hood ever was.

He almost wanted to turn that money in to someone and tell them where it came from. *Almost.* He knew he wouldn't. He'd use it for food, and electric, and gas. And if he had enough left over—for a prom dress.

Shame on me, Lord, for what I done.

As he dressed, he worried over what to tell Lucia. He'd have to lie to explain the money, and that meant pretending to work during the day to maintain that lie. After all these years of loving her, it was a bad time to start lying. The irony struck him. Their life together started at a prom eighteen years ago, and now it was taking a horrific turn on another prom.

Lonny told Lucia he'd lost his job, but that he had a lot of prospects for new work. He was still lying, but for some reason, he felt better.

"No need to tell the kids yet," he said. "Let's wait and see if I get some work."

Jada tried cheering him up at breakfast, joking and making not-so-clever remarks about her new beau, Jason, a boy Lonny hadn't even met. He finished his coffee and eggs, kissed Lucia, then snuck Scooter a treat from his leftovers. "See y'all tonight."

"Bye, Dad. Have a nice day," Jada said.

"Get strong, old man," from Mars.

Lonny smiled at Mars' jab then got into the truck and headed out.

One of the prime spots for day work was only a couple of miles away. He was almost there when his phone rang. He answered on the first ring.

"Lonny, how's it going?"

He recognized the voice. The guy who got him the job. "I decided I don't need any more work."

"What, you found something?"

"Not yet…but I got a few prospects. It won't be long."

"Our friends aren't gonna like this."

"Can't be helped. Tell them I'm through."

"I'll tell them, but they don't take 'no' very well."

"Tell them anyway." Lonny turned left and soon was standing on the corner of an empty parking lot with sixty or seventy Latinos—Mexicans, Guatemalans, Hondurans, all hoping to be picked for a day's work. Lonny missed the days when he had a job to go to every morning. He and Lucia never had much money, but at least he didn't have to worry about feeding his family.

A guy in a truck pulled up and offered $50 for a day's work. Five of the men jumped at the opportunity. Lonny opted to wait for better pay. He had a good shot at being picked since he spoke English and had a truck. This was one of those few times when being black paid off. Forty minutes later, Lonny wished he'd taken the earlier offer. Fifty dollars would buy a few good meals. He finally got work digging footings for a concrete pour. Not much money, but it lasted the rest of the day and might stretch for a few more.

When Lonny got home that night, he was more tired than normal. The physical work he was used to, but not the stress of fighting inner battles all day. He put on a good face, though, determined not to let his family suffer for his sins. After kicking off his boots, he walked in the front door. "Guess who's home and hungry."

From the kitchen he heard Lucia's voice, sweet as the day he married her. "Must either be Scooter or a man who found more work." She came around the corner, wiping her hands on her apron. "I guess you found something?"

"Not much," he said then took money from his pocket and threw it on the table, "but enough for a little girl's prom dress, I imagine."

Jada almost dropped the plates she had in her hand. She ran to hug him. "For real? I can go?"

"Not until I meet this boy…what's his name?"

"Jason," Lucia said before her daughter could answer then she kissed her husband warmly. "I'll be seeing you tonight," she whispered, a sultry tone if he ever heard one.

"What kind of work did you find? Permanent?"

"No, but it might last a week or two. And it's good pay." He bent down to pet Scooter as he said it, not wanting his expression to give away the lies.

Jada was still counting the money when her mother smacked her on the butt. "I hope that dress is a bright one. We're gonna need it when the electric gets shut off."

Lonny showered. Then, as he was dressing, he saw the lotto ticket on his counter. He brought it to the kitchen. "Where's the paper?"

"On the chair," Jada said. "Right where you like it."

He laughed. "You can stop being nice. I already said you could go." He opened it up to see the results from the lotto. "The lotto is $39 million. Maybe we hit it."

Lucia and Jada came to the table. "Get Mars in here," Lonny said. "If we're gonna be rich, I want us all here to share in it."

"Mars, get in here," Jada hollered. "Dad thinks he's gonna hit the lottery."

Lucia huffed. "Wouldn't that be something? A new dishwasher is the first thing we'd get."

"New *dishwasher*?" Jada said. "How about new *house*."

"Jiu-jitsu school for me," Mars said as he came in.

Lonny sat at the table, heart pounding, chest on fire. He could barely speak just thinking of the possibilities.

Lucia grabbed a broom and started sweeping the floor. "Lonny, you brought in mud again. I hope that imaginary lottery ticket will buy a maid to clean up after you."

"After we hit this lottery, you won't need to sweep the floor."

She huffed. "Nobody hits those things. I don't know why you waste your money." Lucia smiled. "You *could* have bought me another chocolate bar. That would have gotten you a lot more than that lotto ticket."

"Oh my God, Mom. Cut that talk out."

"It really *could* be us," Lonny said. "It happens all the time."

"Hurry up and look!" Jada said.

"Lucia, come here, baby."

Lucia stopped what she was doing and rushed over. "What's the matter?" she asked, leaning over him.

He handed her the lottery ticket and pointed to the paper. "Check these numbers. See if I'm wrong."

She looked at him funny, but bent over and gaped, first at the ticket, then the paper.

Lonny pinched her arm and whispered, "Pretend we won."

Lucia's eyes popped wide open, and her hand flew to her mouth, gasping. "Lord in heaven. *Praise* the Lord in heaven!"

Jada came over. "What's the matter? Did we hit it? For real?"

Lucia grabbed Lonny, kissing all over him, then hugged Jada, squeezing her hard. "The Lord has smiled down on us again. I *knew* if I kept praying, it would do good."

"Don't kid me, Mom."

When Jada said that, Lucia fell onto Lonny's lap, laughing. Lonny kissed her and smiled. "We were rich for a few seconds."

"That was cruel, making us think we were rich." Jada wore a spoiled pout. "I was already dreaming of a house like Alexa's. And a pool."

"You sure can dream fast, girl." Lucia turned to Mars. "What about you? You get a chance to dream up any crazy notions?"

They all laughed and then hugged each other in a big circle.

"And I thought we were gonna be rich," Jada said.

"We *are* rich," Lucia said. "And now we need to say our thanks before supper. The Lord has blessed us with good health and a wonderful family." She folded her hands. The rest of the family joined.

"Lord, I know we've all done wrong from time to time, but we've seen our way through it with your guidance." She put her hand on Lonny's arm and kissed his cheek. "You surely know how much this man deserves a break, working like he's done all these years and never complaining. I'm only gonna ask for one thing. Give this man a break. For all of us, Lord, I thank you. Amen."

Lonny's smile was genuine, but his heart was heavy. Every word of praise from Lucia was like a dagger. Would the Lord would take away the things he had?

Please don't, for my family's sake. If you have to administer punishment, take it out on me.

CHAPTER 9

A NEW LINE OF WORK

Dispatcher answered the phone on the second ring. "Go."

"I'm looking for more help, and I don't want Number Three on the next job. Did I tell you how bad he fucked up?"

"You've told me several times." Dispatcher waited a few seconds, then, "I have a replacement for Number Three available. When do you need someone and what kind of job?"

"Send him over right away. I want to check this one out first. As far as the job, I'll let you know."

"One more thing," Dispatcher said. "Number Four is no longer available."

"Fuck! All right, send the new man as the new Number Four. I'll use the old Number Three for now."

Boss waited at the meeting place, going through options for the next job. They had been happy with the take from the Marshall house, but the heat would be on with that kid getting hurt. Cops looked for robbers when it was a home invasion, but when someone got hurt, they looked a lot harder.

If only that damned Number Three hadn't gotten out of hand.

Boss heard the van pull into the garage and got his mask on. A moment later, the door opened. Number Two walked in with a new companion.

Boss looked up. "Number Four, I presume?"

Number Four tugged at the mask. "Why do we have to wear these when we're inside?"

"If you don't like the rules, leave now. These rules will never change."

"It's hot."

"Prisons are hotter," Boss said. "Almost every partnership among criminals ends with one of them ratting out the others. *That* is why we wear masks. I want no one to know who I am, or who anyone else is." Boss looked to each of them. Number Two nodded. "This is for all of us. If I get caught, I can't tell the cops who you are, because I don't know."

"What about Dispatcher?" Number Four said.

Boss got right up in his face. "Have you seen Dispatcher?"

"No."

"That's right. None of us have. All I have is a phone number."

"So how does he get his cut?"

Boss sneered. "Worried you're getting cheated already?"

"No, it's just—"

"Bullshit. Don't worry. I send Dispatcher his cut when the job is over. And just so we all keep with the rules, let's not refer to him at all. Dispatcher is my problem. Clear?"

He waited until Number Four acknowledged, then continued. "First rule is no names, only numbers. I am Number One, or Boss." He pointed to the left. "That is Number Two, and I believe I hear Numbers Three and Five coming in now. Any questions?" He waited, then said, "Good. We've got work to do."

"What do you have in mind?" Number Two asked.

"Kidnapping," Boss said, as Three and Five entered.

Number Two seemed to disapprove. "Kidnapping is dangerous. And we don't have a target."

"I like it," Three said.

Boss listened, absorbing it all. "Targets are easy. There are plenty of rich people in this city. All we have to do is look for the easiest mark."

Number Two paced. "I don't like it. Might as well kill someone as kidnap them. The penalties are almost the same."

"That's an idea, too," Number Four said. "But I don't go for unnecessary violence."

Boss pretended not to hear what he said, but he took note, and he liked the part about not liking violence Number Three seemed to like it too much. "Kidnapping carries stiff penalties, true, but if we get away with it, what do the penalties matter?"

Boss waited to see if anyone raised objections. "If we decide to go with a snatch, anyone have problems?"

Silence.

"You, Number Two?"

"If everyone else is in, I'll go along."

"Good," Boss said. "Let's go over this." They discussed the possibilities for another half an hour or so then left, leaving Boss alone. When he was certain they were gone, he called Dispatcher.

"Go."

"I'm looking for a mark to snatch."

"I don't have to tell you how dangerous that is. Very few succeed. If they do, it's usually because the mark is killed."

"All I need is a name. Any other information would help, but a name will suffice."

"I'll get back to you."

"And don't forget to keep your eyes open for a new Number Three. I'm not convinced this one will work out."

"I never forget."

Number Two poked her head back into the office. "We good?"

Boss nodded. "That worked well, you raising objections. We had to test the new member. Good idea, Number Two."

"Tell Dispatcher to get us a mark with a lot of money."

***

WHEN DISPATCHER HUNG UP, he returned to reading the paper, checking on the sports results and his investments. As he scanned the business section, a headline caught his eye.

"Biotech Firm from The Woodlands About to Go Public. Offering Expected to Set Local Record"

The article went on to describe how Scott Winthrop, the CEO, stood to make almost eighty million dollars, assuming the shares held at the projected offering price.

Eighty million dollars is a lot of money, Dispatcher thought, and leaned back in his chair to reflect on that. *He won't be able to cash it out just yet…but he could borrow on it. And I couldn't ask for a better mark.*

CHAPTER 10

A WONDERFUL LIFE

Scott Winthrop woke every day to ecstasy—not the drug, but a wonderful feeling of joy that accompanied a perfect life. Despite being agnostic, he had been blessed beyond the fortunes of fate. At forty-two, he was CEO of a hot new biotech company and had a stock position translating into many millions now that their IPO was in full swing.

Scott wanted to take a company public, and his startup was poised for a phenomenal IPO, with a new drug showing a promising treatment for diabetes. His stock options would catapult him into the high eight-figure range. Perhaps the best part was living in a 9,000 square-foot house tucked into a wooded community on a golf course, and being only five minutes from work. Life didn't get much better than that.

He had problems, though. The first two clinical trials showed positive results, but a new trial hinted at bad indications. If the results weren't good the IPO could go sour, and his fortune with it. On top of that, alimony was draining him.

Scott shook off the blues before they settled in. He rolled over, his hand rubbing against the soft, smooth skin of a goddess. "Good morning," he whispered into her ear.

She stretched and slowly turned over. Her eyes went wide when she saw him. "Oh God! Did I...did we..."

Scott sighed. "Unfortunately, no. You passed out before I could work my charms on you."

She composed herself, reached over and kissed his cheek. "Thanks. You're a gentleman."

"I don't know about a gentleman," he said, and slid his hand down her side.

She kissed him, while removing his hand. And then she got out of bed. "Let's save something for tonight. Besides, I need to shower."

"Through those doors," Scott said. He ogled her body as she walked away. "I'm cutting you off at two drinks tonight," he said as she closed the doors.

A few minutes later, she came out of the bathroom wrapped in a white towel. "I might reconsider waiting until tonight," she said.

Scott was reaching for her when a knock at the door startled him.

"Time to get up, lazy. You told me to remind you of your meeting."

"I'm up," Scott said.

"We're off to school, Dad. You better be up."

God, the joys of fatherhood. "Goodbye, dear. Have a nice day."

"It's *dear* now? You don't even remember my name?"

"Goodbye, Jada, or is it Monica?"

"Go to…you know where."

"See you tonight."

"Are we going to dinner tonight? You promised." Her voice had the pleading tone Scott hated.

"Can't do it. Maybe tomorrow."

Scott didn't hear her answer, but he heard the front door slam. An answer in itself. He turned back to Jennifer, still wrapped in the towel. "And what was *your* name?"

"You *better* remember my name."

Scott pulled her closer, kissed her nose, then her lips. "I can't seem to remember if it was Jennifer, Venus, or Aphrodite."

She kissed him back, ran her fingertips down his side. "Putting me in some lofty company, aren't you?"

"A well-deserved ranking," he said, and kissed his way down to her stomach.

Jennifer stopped him. "You didn't tell me you had a daughter. Are you…"

"Married? Not for six years. But Alexa's mother remarried, and Alexa can't stand the new husband, so…my once carefree nights are now filled with responsibility."

"I think it's sweet your daughter wants to live with you."

Scott laughed. "I want to be flattered, but I think I was the lesser of two evils. And perhaps more importantly, the most lenient."

"I'd like you to pick up where you left off," she said, "But I have to get to work."

Scott looked at the clock sitting on the nightstand. "You never told me what you do."

"Nothing nearly as exciting as you." She dropped the towel and reached for her clothes. "How am I getting home?"

"Where's your car?"

"At the club, remember? You swept me off my feet and right into your car."

"I'll send a car for you when I get to work. Or you can stay here until I get home, but it may be late."

"I think I'll take the car. I *do* have to work."

"I'm taking a quick shower," Scott said. "You can put coffee on if you feel like it."

A few minutes later, he stepped out of the shower, drying himself. Jennifer wasn't around. He went to the top of the stairs. Pots and pans sounded in the kitchen. "There's plenty to eat if you want to make breakfast. Just lock the door when you leave."

"I'm waiting for a car, remember? Do you want coffee? Or something to eat?"

"No, I really have to run, but fix something yourself."

Scott was down the steps in a few minutes. He kissed Jennifer on the cheek and headed for the door.

"Don't forget your phone," she said. "It's in the charger."

"Thanks," he said. "I'll call when the car is on its way."

"Don't bother. I'll get a cab."

"Suit yourself," Scott said, and closed the door.

He parked his Lamborghini in the space marked CEO less than twenty feet from the entrance. He got out, brushed off his suit, and walked into the lobby.

"Good morning, Mr. Winthrop."

He nodded to the receptionist. "Any calls?"

"Several, sir. Michelle has them."

He continued on with a fast pace through the lobby. "And sir, they're waiting for you in the conference room."

"On my way."

Scott walked in, set the briefcase on the table, and opened it. "Coffee?"

Michelle jumped to get him some and as she did, he looked over the group seated around the table. "I don't see a lot of smiles. Is everybody in a sour mood, or am I in for a surprise?"

Chris Reynolds, Vice President of R&D, lowered her head as she spoke. "We just finished going through Sanjay's report."

Scott took his coffee from Michelle and sipped it. "And?"

Chris found the courage to meet Scott's gaze. "We may have problems with the clinical data."

Scott studied the gloomy looks; obviously they all knew. "Explain."

"If Sanjay's right—and he feels certain he is—the drug is barely more effective than a placebo."

"Fuck!" Scott pounded his fist on the table and glared at Sanjay. "How did you miss this?"

Before he could answer, Chris got her hackles up. "Because we *rushed* it. Remember?"

"I said rush it, not screw it up," Scott said.

"When dealing with drug development, 'rush it' and 'screw it up' are synonymous."

Scott paced. "How certain are we? When will you know?"

Sanjay spoke up. "It will take a few weeks to verify."

Scott sipped his coffee, wrinkled his brow, and stared at Chris. "I thought this was a blind trial. How do we know what the data will show?"

Chris lowered her head, then spoke in a low tone. "Sanjay…knows someone at the CRO. They called him privately."

"So no one knows but us?"

"That's right, but we…"

Scott held up his hand, interrupting her. "All right, listen. This doesn't go outside this room. And I mean you tell *nobody*. Not wives or husbands. No one else in the company. Sanjay, keep this to yourself until we verify the data. And make *sure* everyone understands the importance of keeping it quiet."

"Scott, we are required to report this. If the—"

"Fred, I know you're CFO, but if you breathe one word of this to *anyone*, you will no longer be with us. And while we are on that subject, let me remind everyone that if this gets out, our IPO is sunk. Those new houses you dreamed of, the new cars, the vacations all over the world, early retirement…kiss them all goodbye."

Chris stood. "I don't intend to ruin my career—"

"Whoa!" Scott said. "Listen up, everyone. I am *not* suggesting we cover this up. *If* the data confirms what Sanjay suspects, we *will* report it. I don't intend to cover up anything. But we can't afford to let something like this slip out and ruin our position until we *know* we are wrong. Does everyone understand?"

Silence greeted him.

Scott put on one of his big smiles. "Right now we don't *know* anything. This was a blind trial. We have no access to the data. How *could* we know?"

"But we *do* know," Chris said.

Scott thought for a moment and cast a sideways glance to Sanjay. "Maybe the person who told Sanjay is wrong. Maybe the data is corrupt. A lot of things could be wrong. All I know is we have an IPO coming up, and we need to be prepared for it. Let's get busy."

He waited for objections, but none came. "All right, good." He raised his voice and put a lot of enthusiasm in it. "Come on, people, we have an IPO to prepare for."

An hour later the meeting officially broke up. Scott waited for the others to leave but asked Sanjay to stay. After the room cleared, he turned to Sanjay. "How did this leak?"

Sanjay didn't stutter, but his voice was hesitant. "Sir, I warned you about this. You knew."

"And I told you to keep it quiet. I said no one could know." Scott slammed his fist on the table. "If you want your family to ever get over here, you better make sure this stays delayed for a while."

Sanjay lost all his former boldness, lowering his voice to a level below meek. "Yes, sir. I will."

CHAPTER 11

DREAMS OF THE RICH

Lonny got dressed, shaved, and made his way to the kitchen. The kids were at the table and Lucia was busy cooking. "Breakfast is going to taste a lot worse this morning," Lonny said.

Lucia scraped the eggs onto a big plate then turned to hug him. "Why would breakfast taste worse?"

"I woke up half a dozen times dreaming about that lottery we didn't hit."

"I could have gotten whatever prom dress I wanted," Jada said.

"I was gonna buy a jiu-jitsu school," Mars said.

"In the thirty seconds you thought you were rich, you decided on that?" Lonny said.

"Shame on all of you," Lucia said as she meted portions of eggs and peppers onto their plates. "Jada, you'll get the same dress you thought about when we couldn't afford it." Spatula in hand, she looked threatening. "Even if we won the lottery, the Lord wouldn't want us squandering our money."

Mars shoveled eggs into his mouth, but he found time to talk between bites. "Don't worry, Dad. I'll get my black belt, win some competitions, and make us all money."

Lucia rapped Mars on the head. "Focus on your *real* school, young man. Not jiu-jitsu. I'll not have an illiterate child because you think you have talent."

Mars scraped his plate and carried it to the sink. "Would you have stayed here, Dad? I mean in this house?"

"Of course not," Jada said. "With all that money, we could have moved anywhere. I'd have gone to The Woodlands, where all the rich people live. Right next to Alexa."

"Yeah," Mars said, "A huge house with a swimming pool and a pool table."

"And a tennis court," Jada said. "And a dance floor in the party room."

Lucia shook her head. "Listen to yourselves. I'm glad we didn't hit the lottery."

"Mom…"

"Mom nothing. All your father did was throw away a dollar's worth of eggs, gambling on that lottery nonsense. And fill your heads with silly dreams." Lucia turned to face Jada. "What, you think those people over there would be waiting with cookies and milk, greeting us when we moved in, huh? You got a lot more to learn if you think that."

"Those days are over," Jada said, getting up from the table in a huff.

"Sit down and let me tell you something. Just because the law says there isn't prejudice, and just because we got a black president, don't *ever* think that prejudice is over. It flat out ain't true." She looked at Jada and Mars both. "I'm not talking about black and white here; I'm talking about a prejudice that goes a lot deeper than that—the one between rich and poor. That's been going on a lot longer than any black-and-white thing." She shook her head, mumbling, "The one thing rich people hate more than anything is poor people getting rich quick."

She looked as if she'd stop, but then she turned to Lonny. "And shame on you, husband, for letting this talk go on so long."

Lonny's smile had long since disappeared. He didn't know what he'd done to deserve her ire, but there was no sense in arguing when Lucia got like this. He imagined it was nerves eating away at her, which he couldn't much blame her for. "Your mother's right. We're simple folk, and we need to remind ourselves of that."

Lucia grabbed her plate and coffee cup from the table and put them in the sink. "Help me with these dishes, Mars. You too, Jada."

Mars grabbed a dish towel and started drying. "I didn't want to be rich anyway. It would have taken me too long to write down all I needed to buy."

Lucia stopped doing dishes and laughed, though it seemed to be mixed with tears. "Don't you worry, children. The Lord won't let anything bad happen to a good person like your father."

Lonny choked down the last of his coffee, cringing at her words. The Lord was certainly ashamed of him right now, and he had to do something about it.

CHAPTER 12

GINO GETS A PARTNER

I left the Marshall house feeling like I had nowhere to go on this case, and a night's sleep hadn't improved my outlook. Whoever the hell these people were, they were doing a good job of maintaining control. In the morning, I called Coop to see about getting help. I *had* to catch these bastards.

"Captain Cooper's office." Cindy's long drawl came across with a pleasant tone.

"Hi, Cindy. Where's Gladys?"

"She'll be all over your backside if you keep calling her Gladys."

"So where is she?"

"In the office."

"You know what Delgado's working on?"

"Why don't you come right out and say what's on your mind?"

"I need to know who's available before I ask Coop for help. I don't want to get stuck with just anybody."

"I think Delgado can be spared."

"Okay, put me through to the sweetheart."

Cindy was still laughing when she switched me over.

Coop picked up a few seconds later. "What do you need?"

"I need help. Delgado available?"

"Since there was a long delay between the time Cindy's phone rang and the time I got the call, I presume you know he's available."

"Coop, you're too damn smart for me."

"I know that," she said. "What's new on the case?"

"The father was pretty torn up, as you might guess. The wife was at the hospital. From the sounds of it, she's even worse off."

"Was he any help?"

"Maybe. But I need Delgado. We need to find the people doing this before somebody dies."

"I'll have Cindy tell him…unless you already did that."

"I didn't, and if you don't mind, I'd like to be the one to tell him."

"What kind of sick game are you playing now?"

I dialed Hector "Ribs" Delgado's number. He earned the name Ribs when he was young and so skinny his ribs showed, and because he loved eating ribs more than anything. Give Hector a choice of what to eat on any day, and the choice would be ribs.

"What's up, Gino?"

"I just got a call from Coop. She wants to see us right away. You know anything about this?"

"See us? What for?"

"That's what I asked. You don't know anything about it?"

"Fuck no, man. What the hell did you do now? Did you get me in some kind of trouble? Does this have anything to do with that poker-game robbery?"

"Nothing I can think of. Meet me at the station, and we'll go to her office together."

I knew he'd be sweating. For some reason, Ribs was terrified of Captain Cooper. I didn't blame him; she was one of the toughest cops I knew, male or female.

Ribs was waiting in my office when I got to the station.

"Hector, how's it going?" I asked.

"Depends on why we're being summoned. And quit calling me Hector, asshole."

I slapped him on the back. "Let's find out. I'm sure it's nothing to worry about."

"You dirty fuck," he said. "What's she really want us for?"

"I really don't know." I headed toward Coop's office, but he didn't follow. When I turned around, he was laughing.

"Hear we're going to be working together again, cuz."

"That lousy shit Coop. She told you, didn't she?"

He laughed more.

"And quit reminding me that we're related," I said.

"You didn't say that when you first met Mary."

I laughed, recalling that day. Mary's whole family had come to her house to meet me, all of them armed with questions and hard-eyed glares. "Yeah, I know. That was a fun day."

"So what do you need my brains for?"

"We got the same sons of bitches that hit the game." I pointed to the stitches in my head. "Same ones who did this."

"And took Mary's watch," he said.

"Yeah. But this time they did a home invasion and hurt the son. Bad."

"You sure it's them? You're not—"

"When the guy was beating the son with a tire iron, one of the others yelled 'Number Three!'" I stared at Delgado. "That proof enough?"

"I'm ready," he said. "Fill me in while we drive."

We stopped for coffee on the way. "I'm sure these are the same guys who did the house in Memorial, the one where the lady was home by herself."

"What makes you think they're connected?"

"Same approach. One guy went to the front door, the rest of them went in the back. Everybody wore masks and gloves."

"How many people are we talking about?"

"Four at the Memorial job. Five on this one. I talked to the husband and their butler. Both said there were four whites and one black. When I was about to leave, the husband said that maybe the black was Latino."

"So that's the way this is gonna play out. Blame the Latino."

"You know how it works, Ribs. I only asked for you in case we need an interpreter."

"What else you got?"

"Well-organized. Methodical. Barely talked at either job." I looked straight at him. "Except for the 'Number Three' remarks. In and out in less than thirty minutes." I sipped coffee, and continued. "Both were huge houses in neighborhoods with limited views of the front doors, and both backed up to a golf course."

"Sounds like these guys did their homework."

"At Marshall's they came in while he and the son were in the shower. And they knew he had a safe. The back door wasn't locked. They wore latex gloves, just like at Memorial. And before they left, they tied everyone with duct tape."

"*Dios mío*. The poker game!"

"Like I said, the poker game." My blood pumped harder at the thought of catching these guys. I wanted the fucker who hit me. Wanted to get him alone, with no witnesses. Even more, I wanted to get even for Mary's watch.

Delgado finished his coffee and stared at me. "You know I love you, but don't go gettin' wild on me."

"I'm fine. I—"

"You're *not* fine. I see what's working in that sick mind of yours."

I wanted to be pissed, but he was only doing this for me. "Ribs…"

"I know you've been fucked up since Mary died, but you still got Ron." Ribs poked at me with his finger. "Don't go fuckin' things up where he's got to visit you in jail, man. If I see you headin' in that direction, I'm out."

"Let's just solve the case."

Ribs stared at me, looking for the truth. "Maybe we should interview some neighbors. See what they didn't see."

I tossed my cup in the trash and headed out. "Let's do it."

CHAPTER 13

NEW PLANS

Boss spread the chart on the table. Across the top were six spaces. The first read "Driver," followed by spaces for numbers One through Five. He pointed to the slots beneath each one.

"These are your duties. Memorize them. Memorize the others too. Everyone needs to understand the whole operation. Clear?"

"Clear," they all said.

"Number Two has surveillance. We need to know when the girl goes to school. When she gets home. We need to know what time he leaves for work and gets home."

"Clear," Number Two said.

"Number Three has muscle, *if* it comes to that. He does the grab."

"Clear," Number Three said.

"Number Four will be our intermediary with the target. Number Five will be the primary watcher."

"Clear," they both said.

"The rest is on the chart. I'll take care of the equipment: electronic sweepers, chemical tests for the money, disposable cell phones. Everyone has extra gloves and masks. Clear?"

"Clear," they all said.

"Okay, we need to be quick and clean. Understand? *Quick and clean.* We grab the girl then make the call. Number Four, *do not* stay on the phone too long. The more contact we have with them, the more chance we have of getting caught. Follow the script." Boss looked around. "Any questions?"

"Won't they want to talk to her?" Number Four asked.

"We let them talk to her *after* they get the money. We want them worrying at first."

"You know they'll call the cops. Or the FBI."

"We have plans for that," Boss said.

"When are we grabbing her?"

"When it's right. We still have to rent the other hotel rooms, get more equipment, do other preparations, not to mention more surveillance."

Boss waited through the silence. "Everyone ready for this? This is the big league, people. If you're not in, now is the time to say so."

"We're in," Number Three said. He was joined by Numbers Two and Four and Five.

"Okay, any fuck-ups and somebody dies. Clear?"

"Clear," they all said.

CHAPTER 14

WHERE'S THE CONNECTION

Delgado and I walked the street in front of Marshall's house. All the houses were huge, with lots of trees.

"Damn trees block the views," Delgado said.

"Not much activity on the street, either."

"Not like my neighborhood," Ribs said.

"That's what happens when you have thirty relatives on one block."

"Nice, isn't it?"

I smiled, remembering the times Mary and I joined Ribs on weekends, partying and eating and laughing. "Sure is nice. It's the way every neighborhood should be."

"Where do you want to start?" Ribs asked.

I nodded across the street to a sprawling ranch that looked like a hacienda, all stucco with at least a dozen arches. "How about this one?"

"Sure, maybe one of our relatives lives there."

The guy who answered the door looked old, with remnants of dark brown hair hiding within the gray. He was thin and walked with a cane. "May I help you?"

I had my badge ready. "I'm Detective Cataldi. This is Detective Delgado. We're investigating a break-in across the street."

"Break-in? I didn't know there was one." He turned toward the kitchen. "Margaret, did you know there was a break-in across the street?"

Margaret looked about the same age as her husband, but with a lot more zest. She set a quick pace into the foyer. "Break-in? Where?"

I leaned in a little, hoping to get invited. "The Marshalls' house, ma'am."

Her hands flew to her mouth. "Oh my," she said, then, "Robert, invite the gentlemen in, for heaven's sake."

We followed Robert and Margaret to the kitchen then took seats at the table.

"How about some tea, Detectives?"

Before we could refuse, she started brewing it. There apparently wasn't an option for coffee, or anything else, for that matter.

"When did this happen?" Margaret asked as she pulled teacups and saucers from the cabinet.

"A couple of nights ago," Delgado said. "Right after dinner. Maybe seven o'clock."

Robert said he was watching TV at that time. Margaret was on the phone with a friend. "I'm afraid we won't be much help, Detectives."

"Do you know the Marshalls well?" I asked.

"Only to say hello," she said. "I don't even know what church they belong to." She turned to her husband. "Do you, dear?"

"The church of football."

"Be nice, Robert." Margaret served the tea and took a seat opposite me.

Delgado smiled and took a sip of his tea. Delgado hated tea. "Have you noticed anything unusual on the street in the past few weeks?"

"In what way?" she asked.

"Strangers walking or jogging."

"Maybe couples," I said, recalling that Marshall's butler had insisted that one of them was a woman. A couple wouldn't attract attention.

Robert shook his head, lip curled up. "Nothing I've seen."

Margaret, though, seemed busy with thought.

"You remember something, ma'am?"

"It's probably nothing, but there was a man walking a dog several nights last week."

"Did you recognize him?"

"I don't think I've seen him before. What made me remember him is the dog. I know most of the dogs in the neighborhood, but I'd never seen it before. I wanted to make sure this one didn't mess on my lawn."

"Can you describe the man?" I asked.

"I don't recall, but the dog was a beagle. A big, fat beagle."

"You're sure it was a beagle?" Delgado asked.

She huffed up. "I know my dogs, Detective. It was a beagle."

We asked more questions, but got nothing of value. At the next house, we got a vague memory of a van that might or might not have been seen in the neighborhood. We did get coffee, though. The rest of the block gave us even less information. When it was all said and done, we had an invisible stranger walking a big, fat beagle, and a vehicle, which possibly was a van and either blue, tan, or white.

"Got some observant people around here," Ribs said. "If I take up burglary in my next life, I know where I'm going."

"Yeah, just don't shit on Margaret's lawn. She'd ID you for sure."

We drove to a small restaurant in a strip mall down the street and rehashed what we had. I'd written it out on a pad.

Came in while Marshall was in shower. Coincidence?

Knew they had a safe. Coincidence or educated guess?

Door wasn't locked. How did they know? *Did* they know?

Wore latex gloves. Same as Memorial and the poker game.

Marshall and son were naked. Why? To embarrass them or keep them under control?

Took jewelry and bonds. At Memorial they took artwork too.

Butler swears one of them was a woman. Was it a sister? Girlfriend?

There were five at Marshall's house. One was Latino or black.

"They have to sell this stuff," I said.

"Which means they'll need a fence," Delgado said. He made a note to get Fat Charlie checking on that.

I looked at Delgado. "Where's the connection?"

"That's what I've been wondering. How do they find their marks? They've hit poker games all over town, a house on Memorial, and now a place way up here in Champions."

"We need to tear their lives apart until we find out what connects them. See who they work with, bank with, socialize with."

"Who held the insurance policies," Delgado said.

"Exactly. Somebody is feeding these guys information. And we've got to find out who it is before they kill someone."

CHAPTER 15

THE GRAB

Jada spent the night at Alexa's house. They were up half the night talking but still got up early. "Prom's almost here," Jada said. "I can't wait."

"Spoken like a girl who has a date."

"Finally!"

"Get ready, Jada, I've got to wake *Romeo* again."

Alexa rushed down the hall, listened at the door then knocked, hard. "Time to get up, Dad."

She walked back down the hall into her bedroom done in pink and white. Jada sat in the dressing area of the bathroom in front of a mirror, which stretched eight feet across. The left and right sides had optional magnifiers for applying make-up.

"This is bigger than my whole bedroom," Jada said as she applied eye liner.

"It's too big for just me."

"So, did you *disturb* him?"

"Not today. I think he was alone, believe it or not. But the other day, he wasn't."

Jada laughed. "Remind me to remind us to be more quiet when we're parents."

"Or to not have kids."

"No way. I *want* kids. I'm going to have five."

"Five! You're out of your mind."

Jada pursed her lips and applied the lipstick. "Don't forget. I'm going *shopping* with Jason. *Do not* call me."

"As long as you fill me in on all the details. Especially the juicy ones."

"Won't be any *juicy* ones."

Alexa huffed. "All day and half the night with Jason Rules. Come on. There are *gonna* be juicy details."

Jada giggled. A little at first, then full-blown laughter.

Alexa slid onto a stool beside Jada, brushing her hair. "That's what I'm talkin' about," she said, and they both laughed some more.

Fifteen more minutes of preparation and they were ready to go. As they walked down the hall toward the steps, Alexa banged on her father's door again. "Get going, lazy. We're off."

***

BOSS REVIEWED THINGS WITH Number Three before he left. Driver waited in the van. Number Two was already in position.

"You know where you'll grab her?" Boss asked.

"Two said there is a spot just before the girl gets to the bus. Driver can pull up behind her."

"Number Two does good work. And remember to—"

"I know," Number Three said. "Keep watch for witnesses."

"Then you're set."

"All clear, Boss."

"Good, get it done."

***

NUMBER TWO DROVE TO her position. The windows were heavily tinted so no one would recognize her face, not even Driver. She pulled to the side of the road. She only had a few minutes to wait before the girl came. Number Two got on the phone. "There are two of them. Repeat. There are *two* girls. If they don't split, we have to abort."

"I see them," Three said. "Which one is the target?"

"The one with long hair."

Less than two minutes passed. A car stopped, picking up the short-haired girl.

"Go," Number Two said. "We've got less than a minute."

Driver pulled the van down the street, slowly. As they approached the girl, Driver slowed even more, coming up from behind. Number Three got the pillowcase ready. He checked to be sure his knife was where it should be. At ten feet, a smile came to his face. At five, Number Three slid the side door open. He reached out and covered her head with the pillowcase, dragging her inside. She screamed. He held the knife to her throat.

"Don't make me cut you."

She shut up. Driver shut the door remotely, then put the car in gear and moved out slowly. Number Three gagged her and tied her hands behind her back. Three blocks away, the call came from Number Two. "Clear."

Number Two drove to the designated spot and got in the van, keeping to their mask ritual so no one's face was recognized.

A short while later, Driver pulled into the garage, waited for the door to close, and then got out and tapped on the side of the van. "Clear."

Number Two held the girl while Number Three opened the side door. "Don't try anything. You can't escape, and we don't want to hurt you. Nod if you understand."

She nodded.

"Good. Let's go."

Number Two took her inside, untied her hands then removed the blindfold and gag. "You can scream all you like now. No one will hear you."

The girl stared at her and nodded, scared, like a small animal caught in a trap.

Number Two smiled through her mask. "There are no windows, and the doors are bolted. No way to escape, so don't try. The others aren't as nice as me."

"I feel sick."

"You'll get over it. Try not to think about it." Number Two looked at her watch. "It's early yet. You'll get fed around lunchtime. By then the sick feeling should fade, and you'll be hungry."

"I feel like I'm going to throw up."

Number Two got close to her and gritted her teeth. "Don't think because I'm being nice that I won't hurt you. If you try to take advantage…"

"Okay, I'm sorry."

"Sit down. This will be over soon."

"How soon?"

"As soon as we get your daddy's money. As long as he does what Boss tells him, nothing will happen."

"You don't have to worry about that."

"Glad to hear it. I would hate to hurt a child."

Number Two checked the room one last time then closed the door and bolted it. As she walked away, she dialed the phone and waited for Boss to answer. "She's all yours."

CHAPTER 16

EARLY-MORNING CALL

Boss hung up, kept busy for half an hour then turned to Number Four. "In fifteen minutes, make the call." He reached over and patted Number Four on the back. "Stick to the script, and we'll be okay."

"Clear, Boss." He set the script in front of him, hands shaking, as he prepared to make the call.

***

SCOTT WINTHROP SAT AT the kitchen table, eating breakfast. He had planned on Jennifer spending the night, especially after the text she'd sent, but he couldn't find her at the club last night, and she wasn't answering her phone. He figured he'd pissed her off. He seemed to do that a lot with women.

The doorbell rang, and then the door cracked open. "Scott, are you here?"

He got up, confused over who it could be. He walked to the foyer then smiled. "Jennifer! What are you doing here?"

"Didn't you get my text?"

Now he was really confused. "I got a text last night, but all you said was 'Had a great time. See you.' I expected you at the club."

"Oh God, I must have cut it off or something. I'm not very good at texting. I meant to say, see you in the morning." She laughed. "And look, here I am with breakfast." She held out a bag filled with kolachis and coffee.

Scott reached in and grabbed one. "You're just in time. The breakfast I had planned is nowhere near as good."

"I'd have been here sooner, but traffic was atrocious."

He kissed her on the cheek. "I'm glad to see you. Sit down and eat."

She set the coffee on the table, got two plates, and put the kolachis on them.

"I ate one on the way over." She kissed his lips, lingering a while. "I think after breakfast I'll take a shower. I hope you have time."

He got up and wrapped his arms around her. "I should get to work, but…"

Jennifer pulled her top off, draped it over his head. "I'll make it worth your while."

Scott stared at her taut body. "I might have to join you in that shower. Are you staying the night?"

"That depends on what you have in mind."

"Dinner at Artista, perhaps a play, followed by a magnificent night in bed."

"I'll be here."

Scott rushed breakfast, his mind racing, fueled by the promise of sex. He wanted to take her upstairs and lie in bed all day, but he had to get to work. He was amazed Michelle hadn't called. He helped Jennifer clear the table and rethought his decision to go to work. If it wasn't for that clinical trial problem…

"I'm going to shower," Jennifer said. "I'll be here when you get home."

He kissed her goodbye, admired the view as she climbed the steps, and thought again about staying home. But then he shook his head and returned to the kitchen. As he reached for his briefcase, the phone rang. He looked at his watch.

Late again. Must be Michelle.

He grabbed the phone and said, "I'm on my way, Michelle."

***

Number Four stared at the script, already confused by the start. He hated to improvise. "This isn't Michelle. Listen closely. We have your daughter."

"What? Who is this?"

"I said, we have your daughter. So listen."

"What the hell are you talking about? Is this you, Ted?"

"This is no joke. Get a pen and paper and write this down."

"Mister, I don't know who you are, but—"

"Shut-up. Do you hear me? Shut the fuck up, or I kill her."

Scott pulled a pen and pad from his briefcase then checked to make sure the recorder was on. "Okay, I'm listening."

"Do you have something to write with?"

The voice sounded calmer now. Scott fought for control of his emotions. "I'm set. Go ahead."

"You are to get seven million dollars and—"

"What? I don't have that kind of money."

A long pause. "Mister, we know you don't have it yet, but you can borrow on it." The man on the phone paused. "I'm not going to say it again. Shut up and let me finish."

"Okay. Sorry."

"Seven million dollars in non-sequential serial numbers, hundred-dollar bills, no tracers on the money or in the money. We'll know if you try to track us. Have it ready in forty-eight hours. We'll call tomorrow with instructions on the transfer."

"Wait! I need to talk to my daughter."

"The next time we call, you can talk to her."

The line went dead. Scott stared at the phone. He dialed Alexa's cell, certain she would answer. After three rings, worry began to build. "Come on, Alexa. Pick up." When she didn't answer, panic set in.

School. He had the number for the principal's office in his contact list. A woman answered right away.

"This is Scott Winthrop. My daughter, Alexa, goes to school there. I need to speak with her."

"Hold one second, Mr. Winthrop. I'll call her classroom." She came back on a few seconds later. "No one is picking up. I'll have to send someone down, Mr. Winthrop. Give me a number, and I'll call back."

"No! I need you to check now." He got hold of himself. "Please, this is an emergency."

"Of course, sir. Hold on."

The few minutes it took for her to get back to him seemed like an hour. "I'm sorry, Mr. Winthrop, but Alexa didn't show up today."

He hung up without saying goodbye then dialed 9-1-1.

"Nine-one-one operator. What is your emergency?"

Scott breathed deeply before speaking. "My daughter has been kidnapped."

"Sir, did you say she has been kidnapped?"

"Yes, they just called. What do I do? Who should I call?"

"Hold on, sir. I'll patch you through to someone who can help."

Scott spent no more than five minutes on the phone before they said they would send someone over. He got off and called work. "Michelle, I won't be in for…I don't know, probably the whole day."

"Is something wrong, Mr. Winthrop? Anything I can help with?"

"No, it's personal, Michelle. Anything urgent yet today?"

"Nothing we can't handle, Mr. Winthrop. I'll call you if necessary."

Scott hung up and walked around the kitchen. He called Alexa's cell three more times but got no answer. "Where are you, Alexa? Where the hell are you?"

CHAPTER 17

A NEW ASSIGNMENT

My phone rang as I drove down the freeway. "Gino Cataldi."

"Gino, it's Coop. Where are you?"

"Almost at the station, why?"

"See me as soon as you get in."

"What's up?"

"Just stop by. We need to talk."

Ten minutes later, I pulled into the station parking lot and went to see Coop. "Hey, Cindy, she in?"

"And waiting."

I walked in, surprised to see Chief Renkin. I nodded to him. "Chief." Then to the captain, "Coop, what's up?"

Renkin got up from his chair and shook hands with me. "Are you getting anywhere on those home invasions?"

Is that what this is about?

"Not yet, sir. But now that Delgado's with me, we'll find them."

"I hope so. The Marshall boy has taken a turn for the worse."

I shook my head. His attack had been an unnecessary part of the invasion. "We'll get them, sir. You can tell Mr. Marshall that."

Renkin looked at the side of my head. "Is that from the poker game robbery?"

"It is, sir."

"What the hell is going on in this town?" He sat back down after that, and Coop took over.

She held a folder in her hand, which she referred to, then looked at me. "You worked a kidnapping case up north, didn't you? When you were in Philadelphia?"

I gave both of them a sharp look. Something was going on, and I wasn't in on it. I wished I'd gotten a heads-up from Cindy. "I worked two of them. Why? Somebody get snatched?"

Renkin looked to Coop then to me. "Not just somebody. Scott Winthrop's daughter."

"I don't know him."

"Winthrop is CEO of a new biotech firm in The Woodlands. He has an extremely high-profile IPO getting a lot of media attention. We need it handled properly."

"Does he live up there?"

Renkin nodded. "I know what you're thinking—out of our jurisdiction—but we've been asked in."

"Why?"

"They'd rather us handle it quietly, *without* calling in the FBI. This IPO could mean a lot for Houston. Their success could lure other start-ups here. And that is just the kind of business we're looking for—clean, with high-paying jobs." Renkin shot me his famous hard look. "Can you do it?"

"I can, Chief, but I've already got a case. Remember?"

Renkin's eyes narrowed. "Of course I remember. The Marshalls are friends of mine." He got up and paced. "This takes priority. Give the Marshall case to someone else."

"No way." I couldn't let them take the Marshall case, not with Number Three involved. He was *mine*.

"Detective!" Now Renkin *was* pissed. "You'll take whatever case I assign you."

I had to play this right. I took a few deep breaths, calmed myself. "I'll take the kidnapping if you keep me as lead on the Marshall case. Somebody else can run the day-to-day."

Coop was shaking her head before I finished. "No."

"Then give the snatch to the feds. I don't want it."

Renkin glared at me; he was good at that. "You'll take what I assign, Detective."

"I said I'd take it, but you have to let me keep the Marshall case."

"Why?"

"Because they took his *damn* watch," Coop said.

I ignored Coop and looked at Renkin. "What's it going to be, Chief?"

Renkin gave Cooper a sideways glance then reached out his hand to shake mine. "Captain Cooper will give you anything you need. Call me personally if necessary."

After Renkin left, Coop gestured to the chair. "Have a seat, Gino."

"I should go, Coop. We can't afford to delay on kidnapping cases."

She moved some papers around on her desk and stared at me over the top of her glasses. "This will only take a minute, Gino. The priorities on this case may be different than what you're accustomed to."

I sagged in the chair. *Here comes the bullshit.* "Explanation needed."

"We need to catch these kidnappers—true. And we need to bring this girl back alive and unharmed—even more true." She leaned forward and flashed her famous grin. "But we need to keep this quiet—most true of all."

"So you don't want me calling the FBI?"

"Or the reporters, or your dead mother, or anyone else."

I stood. "I think I got the picture. Give me the address and whatever else you've got on this."

She handed me a small folder. I headed for the door. Before leaving, I turned back to her. "I'm going to need help on this. Julie for research, Fat Charlie to chase down leads, and a couple of foot soldiers for leg work. If it gets to a drop, I'll need a lot more."

She took off her glasses and sighed. "Who do you have in mind?"

"Delgado and whoever else you can spare. I'll tell Delgado. Have whoever else you get call me right away. And I want Ramirez and her partner on the Marshall case."

"You can be an ass when you want to be, Cataldi."

"Thanks, Captain. I appreciate the support." I left before she got more pissed off. I figured Renkin forced her to give this to me. I would have preferred Tip on the case, but that would have been pushing it too far.

As I drove up the freeway, I decided to visit Mary. In two days, it would have been our twenty-second anniversary. I figured being a little early wouldn't hurt. I pulled off the freeway, and within ten minutes, entered the cemetery. A short walk had me standing in front of her grave. I knelt. Blessed myself. Something I wouldn't have done a year ago. The rope necklace I'd made lay draped over the headstone, our names formed from knots. Mary loved things made from rope.

"I know you're probably surprised to see me, Mary. Nothing's wrong with Ron, so don't worry about that. He's doing okay…good, actually. Living in a halfway house with a couple of other guys. And I'm doing okay. I don't even know why I stopped. Maybe because I need help. I got put on a kidnapping case."

I lowered my head, searching for the courage to speak the words. "I don't know if I can do another kidnapping. Not the way the others turned out. Maybe I'm not smart enough to work a case like this. So I'm asking for your help to bring this girl home safe."

I shifted my weight from one knee to the other. The ground was damned hard already, and it was only May. By the time summer was over it would be baked concrete hard.

"You remember how bad it was in Philadelphia? How those girls suffered? I can't have that again. I don't think I could make it through that without you. If you can't do anything yourself, see if you can pull some strings, call in favors…anything. I'm counting on you."

I started to get up but remembered the other reason I'd come. "One more thing, Mary. I got this other case I've been working and…" Tears built in my eyes. "They took my watch, baby. The special one you gave me. I'll get it back. Somehow, I will. Let's make a deal. You help on the kidnapping, and I'll take care of the watch."

I stayed for a few more minutes, talking about old times. And about Ron. Then I dried my eyes, leaned down, and kissed the part of the necklace with her name. "I love you, Mary. Happy anniversary."

I blessed myself, got up, and headed to the car. Already I felt better.

It took me forty minutes to get to Scott Winthrop's house. As I drove, I imagined what he'd look like. I played this game often and found out I was wrong more than I was right. But I had nothing else to do; besides, this usually helped me adjust to the scene. If I was wrong, it alerted me to be cognizant of my surroundings—things weren't what they seemed. If I was right, it was like drawing a pair of aces in Texas Hold 'Em. It probably wouldn't happen again for a while—so I had to be alert, cognizant of my surroundings.

Winthrop. The name conjured images of east-coast money and Anglo-Saxon heritage. A name that might figure prominently in the Newport, Rhode Island, white pages. He'd probably be about my height—almost six feet—fit, and immaculately dressed. His nails would be manicured, and he would be clean-shaven, no matter the time of day.

I pulled up to the house, parked in a circular driveway paved in stone, and walked up a stone pathway to the house. The path was meant to resemble an old cobblestone street. Upon closer examination, I realized it *was* an old cobblestone street. He must have paid handsome money to have it dug up from somewhere. The house was a sprawling mansion five families should have shared—five rich families. It was as big as the Marshalls' house but even more…elegant, if that was possible. I rang the doorbell then braced myself for the panicked, grief-stricken father to answer.

The man who answered fit my image almost exactly. He was about six feet, perfectly fit and proportioned, with a warm smile and not a hair out of place.

Almost got it right, I thought, because Scott Winthrop was black. I don't know why that threw me. *Was it the name?* I wondered, or was it because he was living in a mansion? I made a mental note to check my prejudice meter.

I held out my hand. "Mr. Winthrop, I'm Detective Gino Cataldi."

He shook my hand with a firm grip, and then stepped aside. "Please come in."

His manners were impeccable, but he seemed fidgety.

"Has there been any new developments since you called?" I asked.

"Not since I called," he said. "I've tried her cell phone a dozen times with no answer. And she isn't at school, either."

The guy seemed almost *too* composed for a father whose daughter was missing and supposedly kidnapped. But there *was* that edginess under the surface.

"Are we sure this is real?" I asked. "The whole country has had a rash of virtual kidnappings." I looked over at Winthrop, who had taken a seat at the table, which was covered in papers and folders. A computer sat open to his right, displaying a spreadsheet.

Is this guy doing work while his daughter is missing?

"No, I'm not sure," he said. "I—"

"What *exactly* did they say to you?"

Scott sighed. "In short, they said they had my daughter, and that I had forty-eight hours to get them seven million dollars. They said they'd call back with instructions. I have it recorded."

I wondered what kind of man had the presence to record a kidnap call. Or worse, recorded all his calls. "Good. We'll listen to that in a few minutes. About the money. Seven million is a lot. Do you have that kind of money?"

"Not available. I could possibly get it."

"Have you checked with her friends? Do you have relatives nearby? Any place she could, or would, go if—"

"If she what? Ran away?" Scott shook his head. "We're not dealing with that, Detective. I can assure you."

"How so?"

"We're alone in Texas. Her mother is in New York, and my daughter didn't like living there." He got up to get the coffee pot. "The feeling was mutual, so she ended up here." He poured himself a cup of coffee and asked if I wanted any.

"I think I will, thanks." I didn't like his tone, and the way he referred to her as "my daughter" or "she," but I wasn't here to judge Scott Winthrop, just bring his daughter home. I waited until he brought a cup for me, then continued. "What about boyfriends?"

"None that I know of."

None that you know of. She's seventeen, for Christ's sake. You better know if she's got boyfriends.

"Have you spoken to her best friends yet?"

His phone rang. He held up his index finger, as if shushing me. "Hello, this is Scott Winthrop." He smiled after a brief silence. "No, that's okay. Go to Seattle. Make the deal if you can. Yes, exactly as we discussed. And take Nancy with you. They seemed to like her." He listened some more then, "All right. Good. Call me if anything changes. I'll be on my cell."

I was still staring at him when he hung up and turned to me. "Where were we, Detective?"

I had already experienced enough of this arrogant asshole. I stood up and spoke with more attitude than I intended. "We were right about the point where your daughter has been *kidnapped.* Or did you forget?"

A voice sounded from behind me. I turned to see a woman standing in the doorway between the kitchen and the entrance hall.

"Scott, what's going on?" Her voice was forced-meek style, and her outfit was…barely an outfit at all, nothing but a thong underneath a T-shirt.

Scott went to her, and, when she reached up to hug him, her ass cheeks were fully exposed. For decency I wanted to turn away, but I couldn't.

Winthrop broke the embrace. "Jennifer, this is Detective…" He turned to me. "I'm sorry, Detective, I've forgotten your name."

"Detective?" Jennifer said. "What happened?" The way she said *detective* made it sound like *monster.* Panic filled her voice.

"Nothing happened, well not to us, but someone…I don't know where to start."

Nothing happened? This guy is a real head case.

I stepped forward. "Perhaps I can explain." I reached my hand out to introduce myself. "Gino Cataldi, ma'am. Once again I apologize for startling you, but Mr. Winthrop called us earlier. It seems as if someone kidnapped his daughter."

Her hands flew to her gaping mouth. "Kidnapped? Oh my God!" She put her arms around Scott again.

Jennifer had the long dark hair I liked and a hard-earned body, which I *loved.* The smooth tan didn't hurt either.

"Mr. Winthrop, sir, if we can get started. We can't afford to delay."

Scott suggested she go get dressed. "I'm sorry, Detective. I…" He sat in the chair and leaned back. "I'm sure you must think me a supreme ass, but I…I don't know how to deal with this. I've done nothing but work all my life. Faced with something personal, I'm at a complete loss."

The reality of the situation seemed to be hitting him for the first time. Some people were like that, but it didn't make dealing with them any less difficult. "That's all right, Mr. Winthrop, but if we hope to get to the bottom of this we need to get to work unhindered."

"Certainly. What can I do?"

"Other officers will be coming here, and we'll have a few technicians to set your phones up for surveillance. We want to be prepared when they call back."

"Is there a chance this is one of those virtual kidnappings you mentioned?"

I didn't want to dash his hopes, but I needed to keep him real. "This doesn't fit the bill. They gave you forty-eight hours. That eliminates the virtual part unless your daughter was going to be away and out of contact that long."

He nodded his understanding. "I see."

I now officially felt sorry for Mr. Winthrop. For the first time since entering this house, I felt his pain. And the pain wouldn't stop until we found his girl. *If* we did. I shuddered as the memory of the Philadelphia kidnappings came back to me.

CHAPTER 18

COUNTDOWN BEGINS

I asked Scott for a refill. "What kind of coffee is this? It's damn good."

"I get it shipped from a place in the Northwest." He walked to the cabinet by the refrigerator, pulled out a bag of coffee and the grinder. "It's called Martin Henry Coffee Roasters. And yes, it is damn good."

As he brewed, I called Julie. "Coop fill you in?"

"She did, and I'm ready," Julie said.

"I assume you got a copy of the folder. I need you to track any calls to Winthrop's number this morning."

"Won't take long," she said.

"Good." I looked around, whispering, "I also need his financials—personal and business."

"That will take longer, but not too long. He's a public figure."

While I wrote down questions, the thong-panties girl joined Scott. She still hadn't dressed, which made it difficult for me to focus. Almost impossible to focus. Scott soon returned to the table and, fortunately, or not, she left the room. Winthrop was infusing himself with coffee. I doubted if he would sleep tonight. With the amount of coffee I'd be drinking, I doubted I would either.

Winthrop opted to pace instead of sit. "What do we do?"

"Go over details, look at all possibilities, and prepare. There isn't much we *can* do until they contact us again."

"I see," he said, his hands shaking when he lifted the cup to drink.

"Things aren't all bad, Mr. Winthrop. We have reason to feel optimistic."

He didn't look at me, but he lifted his head a little. "Why is that?"

"They didn't tell you not to call the cops until near the end of the conversation, almost as if it was an afterthought or a gentle reminder. It seemed to me they *knew* you would. That means we're not dealing with amateurs."

"Oh God."

"No, that's good. Trouble happens when they don't know what to expect. If they know how the process works, it's good for us. And it's good for your daughter."

He perked up a little. "What else?"

"They gave you forty-eight hours to get the money. They knew it would be too difficult to do it in twenty-four hours. They haven't bothered with instructions yet, knowing that information would be lost during the first call." I patted him on the back, feeling a bit of the hypocrite as I did, but what the hell, if it made him feel better… "I've handled kidnapping cases before. We brought the girls back."

He looked to me with hope in his eyes. "Really?"

"Really," I said. "No shit." My gut roiled. I felt like a scum-sucking prick telling him these half-truths.

He smiled. "I appreciate that, Detective. Thanks."

"Do you have the money?"

He shook his head. "I don't *have* the money, but I can get it."

"Then we'd better get working on it."

"So we're going to…give them the money?"

I fell back on my first impression. Was this guy really deliberating over money versus his daughter? I looked at my watch, which wasn't there. A surge of anger ran through me. "Mr. Winthrop, we don't have a lot of time. They'll probably call first thing in the morning, and they'll want to know if you have the arrangements made." I stared into his eyes. "If you *don't*, it's anybody's guess what they'll do. I'm not trying to scare you, just being honest."

"I'll make some calls," he said. "Let me know if you need anything else."

***

SCOTT CALLED FRED, THE CFO and waited while he got on the line.

"Scott, what the hell is going on? Where are you?"

"My daughter's been kidnapped."

"What!"

"I got the call this morning."

"Dear God, is she…"

"I don't know anything other than that they want a lot of money. That's why I'm calling."

"Sure, tell me what you need."

"I need you to call the bank, or several banks, and arrange for me to pick up seven million dollars tomorrow. All in—"

"Seven million! Good God, these people aren't messing around." Fred paused. "I'm sorry, Scott. What else?"

"The bills are to be hundreds, with no sequence to the serial numbers, no tracers, and no chemicals on the money." Scott waited to let Fred digest this. "This is critical. If they suspect I'm trying to trick them, they'll kill her."

"Got it. I know who I can call." He paused again. "Scott, are you alone?"

"The police are here. Why?"

"Have you called the FBI?"

"No, I thought it better if the police handled it. They agreed to keep it quiet."

Fred lowered his voice. "I know it's not time to discuss this, but remember the 'issues' we spoke of yesterday. What if the IPO doesn't go as planned?"

Scott took a deep breath. "It will, Fred. Don't worry. Just line up the money."

***

WINTHROP LOOKED AS IF he had just fought a battle. For someone who was as wealthy as I'd heard, I wondered what the big deal was. "Problems?"

"Nothing of significance, but as you can imagine, seven million dollars in cash raises a few eyebrows, especially with bankers."

I nodded, but I *couldn't* imagine. If Ron were kidnapped, I might be able to raise seven thousand, but I'd have to sell some things.

It was almost two o'clock. We had to get moving. "Mr. Winthrop, do you have any enemies?"

"I'm sure I have many, but none that would do something like this. My enemies are civilized."

"And your daughter. Does she have enemies?"

Scott laughed. "Detective, what kind of enemies can a seventeen-year old have?"

I didn't join in the laughter. "You'd be surprised. How about boyfriends? She have any now? Before?"

"I told you before, none that I know of."

"How does she get to school?"

"A bus picks her up not three blocks from here."

"When Detective Delgado gets here, I'd like you to show him where the stop is and what route she takes to get to it."

"Detective, surely you don't think—"

"Mr. Winthrop, she was taken from somewhere. Between here and the bus stop would be the most likely."

Scott set his coffee cup on the table. "Strange, Detective. When I said she could live with me, I thought about how safe she'd be here compared to New York. This is like paradise. Then…this happens."

I let it go for a moment. "It can happen anywhere, sir. It *does* happen anywhere. Did you know that Phoenix is the kidnapping capital of the country?"

He looked at me strangely. "Phoenix? As in Arizona?"

I nodded. "Almost four hundred in the past year."

The doorbell rang, and Scott jumped.

"It's probably Delgado," I said.

He ran to the door. I don't know what he expected, but I tried being patient, unable to fathom what he was going through. Half a minute later, he returned with Delgado and Connors, a detective I'd seen around but never worked with. My ex-partner, Tip, said he was good though, so that worked for me.

Delgado nodded to me. "Sorry it took so long. I was tracking leads on the Marshall case."

"Get anywhere?"

"Dead ends. Even Chicky didn't know anything."

"You told him you were working with me on this?"

"He already knew. How's that for connected?"

Chicky was one of the best snitches out there. He was so well-connected he could have made a living from it. I laughed, but I wanted to hit something. If Chicky didn't know anything, these guys were playing it *real* close.

I turned to Scott. "Mr. Winthrop, would you mind getting coffee while I brief them?"

I didn't know if he could tell I wanted him out of the way, but he took the hint like a pro.

"Okay, I know neither one of you has worked a kidnapping before, so listen up. It's time critical, more so than a homicide or anything else." No questions popped up, so I continued. "We've got a seventeen-year-old girl presumably grabbed on her way to school. Scott got the call within the hour. So far, no contact with the victim." I lowered my voice. "That's *not* good, but he doesn't know that."

"Are we calling the FBI?" Connors asked.

"Chief doesn't want to due to publicity, but if we don't make any headway *very* soon, I'm dialing. I'm not fucking with some kid's life."

"What do you need us to do?" Ribs asked.

"Winthrop will show you the route to the bus stop. I want *every* person within view of that route questioned. Did they see anything this morning? If not, any morning for the past week? Anything strange or out of place? A guy walking a dog that they don't know. Cars passing by too often, a cop car, electric company, a jogger…anything."

"Got it."

Winthrop returned with two cups of coffee and handed them to Connors and Delgado. I think this was his fourth cup, maybe my fourth too.

"Ready?" he asked.

Once they left, I called Julie.

"My favorite Philadelphia detective," she said. "Are you looking for information?"

"I hope you got something."

"The call came in on an untraceable line."

I looked behind me to make sure Winthrop hadn't returned. "And Winthrop's finances?"

"Everything is good. And he stands to gain about $80 million more. He owes no one, and he has never had so much as a ticket. The guy may not be a saint, but he hides it well."

"Okay, that eliminates a lot. How about the techs? Charlie send them?"

"They should be there any minute, literally."

"All right, Julie, thanks."

Winthrop came in right after I hung up. "Should we be concerned with the cars out front? What if they—"

"As I said, they knew you'd call the cops. And I doubt if they're watching the house; they already have what they need." I cringed when I said that, realizing how insensitive it sounded. "Sorry, Mr. Winthrop, I didn't mean for it to come out that way."

"I understand, Detective. It's your job. That's something I know about." He sat and looked at his cell phone.

"Thinking about calling her?"

He nodded.

"Don't," I said, then, "How about her friends? Have you called any of them?"

"I don't know their numbers." He paced. "Sad isn't it. I don't even know their names. My daughter is seventeen, and I know nothing about her."

"You don't know any of her friends?"

"I know her best friend's name is Jada, but I don't know the last name."

"That's all right. We can get that from the school." I felt sorry for the guy. "Mr. Winthrop, I don't like to push, but do we have any news on that money? We *will* need an answer for these people in the morning."

The doorbell rang again. It was the technicians. Winthrop steered them to the home phone so they could work their magic.

"Give them your cell phone, too," I told Winthrop. "The kidnappers might decide to call on that."

"They don't have my cell number. Besides, I need it to make calls."

"Is your home number private?"

He seemed shocked. "Yes, it is."

"As I said, these guys are not amateurs."

"Anyone want more coffee?" Scott asked.

"Me," I said. "And if we need to make a run for more, let me know. I'll send someone."

Scott's cell rang. He scrambled to open it. I stopped what I was doing and focused on him. It was probably too early for the kidnappers to be calling, but when dealing with such people, nothing was out of the question. From the look on his face, I presumed it wasn't them. I was too far away to hear the other caller's words, but Scott's side of the conversation was easy enough to follow.

"Hello, this is Scott Winthrop.

"Oh, it's you, Michelle. Who told you, Fred? Thanks. The police are doing everything they can at this point. And, Michelle, please tell Fred that no one else needs to know. In fact, make *sure* that no one knows. Yes, thank you. I'll call when we know something. All right...wait, Michelle. Is Fred there? Can you get him for me?...

"Fred, any news from the bank? They did? Good. Tell Gerard that I will *not* forget this. Thanks, I need the luck. Fred, one more thing. Put me through to Chris, will you?...

"Chris, any news from Sanjay? All right, keep me posted."

Winthrop walked away then, too far for me to hear, but I saw him dialing someone else.

***

SCOTT PUNCHED IN SANJAY'S cell number. It took him half a dozen rings to answer.

"Sanjay speaking."

"This is Scott. Are you alone?"

A pause, then, "Yes, sir."

"Any update on the data?"

"Nothing yet."

"Sanjay, no matter what, we need to delay this information for at least a few weeks."

"But…"

"But nothing. Who gave you the information?"

"Mr. Winthrop, I—"

"I could report you for having it."

Silence.

"Who, Sanjay?"

"My brother."

"Good. If the data comes in as you suspect, see if your brother can…delay things."

"He would never—"

"He already did something that could cost him his job. I'm not asking him to change data or do anything that will affect someone's life. All I'm asking for is a little time. For all of us, Sanjay. Your brother, too."

Sanjay was silent for a long time. "For how long are you talking?"

"At least for a couple of weeks."

"We are treading dangerous ground, Mr. Winthrop."

"It's important. Trust me."

"This data is important too."

"Sanjay, remember your family in India waiting to come over?"

"Yes."

Scott checked to make sure no one was listening. "I'll get them here when this is over. But no one can know about our conversation. Not Chris or Fred. *No one.*"

"Yes, sir. I'll let you know."

***

I KEPT AN EYE on Winthrop. He seemed more relieved. "Good news, Mr. Winthrop?"

"The bank will cooperate on the ransom."

"That *is* good news. It will make our job a lot easier."

"Also, I called the school. Jada isn't in either."

I stopped to give that thought. This *could* be a case of a couple of kids skipping school and someone's idea of a sick prank.

"Out of curiosity, Detective, what would have happened if I couldn't get the money?"

I hoped he wasn't asking out of some greed factor or from second-guessing, but in either case, I didn't want him going off track. "Fortunately, we don't have to worry about that, because it wouldn't be a pretty situation."

A few minutes later, the techs reported they had the home phone ready. "We'll be able to triangulate their position if we can keep them on for more than three minutes."

"How close can you get?"

"If we get all three cell phone towers, we can narrow it down to fifty, maybe one hundred feet."

"So what that means, Mr. Winthrop, is that you have to stall. They will probably time the call to make sure they don't go over, but...we've gotten lucky before. It's worth a shot."

Scott nodded but didn't seem to buy it. As he walked toward his patio, I got a sick feeling in my gut. I didn't want to be in this man's house, and I didn't want this case. I hated kidnappings. In a lot of ways, they were worse than homicides. At least with homicides, the victims were through suffering. No matter what they'd gone through, it was done. Over. Nothing else could hurt them. But with kidnappings—and it was usually a kid, hence the name—the suffering was just beginning. There wasn't much in life I hated more than someone hurting a kid.

Now I had two cases with kids: the Marshall case, where they'd already done their damage; and this one, with a little girl scared shitless. The worst thing was that I knew she'd probably be raped. Maybe killed. Nothing good. An image of Betty Ming from the Philadelphia case returned to haunt me—again.

I can't let that happen to Alexa.

CHAPTER 19

WHAT DO THE NEIGHBORS KNOW

Delgado didn't like leaving Gino alone, even in Winthrop's house. Gino tended to lose control every time he got involved in cases with kids or drugs. Since Mary died, Gino had been angry with the world. Downright pissed off. When Ron got hooked on drugs, it got worse. Rumors on the street said he killed a drug dealer a few months back. Ribs didn't doubt it, didn't mind if he *did* do it. The world didn't need another scum-sucking drug dealer like Rico…but Delgado couldn't let Gino ruin what was left of his life. Blood was blood—even if it was by marriage. Before Mary died, Ribs had promised to keep an eye on Gino. At the time, he hadn't known it would be so damn difficult.

"Where are we going first?" Connors asked.

"May as well start with the neighbors. The friends at school will clam up like New Yorkers once they see we're cops. And they'll see that from a block away."

Delgado and Connors walked across the street to a sprawling ranch house, which sat a couple of hundred feet off the road.

"This is probably our best shot," Delgado said. "Not many trees in the front yard, so maybe they saw something."

A few seconds after ringing the doorbell, a thirty-something blonde with her hair in a ponytail answered. She filled out her jogging suit nicely.

"May I help you?" she asked, her voice a little on the mousy side. Not what Ribs expected.

Delgado held his badge up. "Detective Hector Delgado. This is Detective Connors."

"Is something wrong?"

"We have a few questions, if you don't mind."

"What's this about? Is something wrong with Martin?"

"No, ma'am. It has nothing to do with you, but…and this has to remain confidential. We've had an issue at the Winthrop house across the street. I'm talking to neighbors to see if anyone noticed any unusual activity or strangers in the area."

"You mean *here?* This morning?" She seemed more than surprised, even aghast, at the suggestion that someone had disturbed suburbia. When Delgado didn't answer, she continued. "I was jogging this morning."

"What time?"

"I just got home and showered. I was gone for an hour and a half. No more."

"You're certain of the time?"

"I'm gone for an hour and a half *every* morning, Detective. I go to the gym to work out." She said it as if it were a saintly thing, to work out *every* morning. "Did you see anyone in the neighborhood who didn't belong? Even someone who may seem to—a repair truck, a workman of some kind, a utility person…anyone?"

She chewed on a finger, shifting weight to her left leg. The shift forced Delgado to stare at her legs for perhaps a bit too long. When she cleared her throat to get his attention, he *knew* it had been too long.

"Not today, but a few days ago, I saw a telephone repair truck. Southwestern Bell. The white trucks with their logo."

"You're certain?"

"I know what a phone truck looks like. I remember thinking how long it was out there."

"Where was it?" Connors asked.

She pointed down the street. "Near that bend. It was there when I left to jog, and it was still there when I got back."

Connors took notes while she talked. "Did you see the workers? How many were there? Men or women?"

"I didn't notice. All I remember is one person wearing a yellow hardhat, and, of course, those silly orange cones cluttering up the street."

Delgado waited to see if she'd add anything. He thought about what the neighbor of the Marshalls' had said about a man walking a dog. "How about strangers? See any couples walking around you don't know, or people walking dogs you didn't recognize?"

Her head was shaking before Delgado finished the question. "No. Nothing like that." Her response had been too fast, a sign she was tiring of the questions. It would be better to break it off now and come back later.

"All right, ma'am. Thanks for your time, and please don't mention this to anyone." He handed her a card. "Call us if you think of anything."

As she moved to close the door, she said. "I won't." She blushed. "I mean, I *will* call, but I won't mention it."

Delgado and Connors started toward the next house. "She'll be on the phone calling someone before we hit the end of the driveway," Connors said.

"That's what we're counting on," Delgado said. "She blabs it to enough people, someone might remember seeing something. And they *might* even call us."

"Let's go see what the next neighbor doesn't know," Connors said.

***

I WENT OVER THE details with Scott, hoping to make him feel better, although everything the techs were doing was standard stuff. We could tape incoming calls and we could triangulate the position of the kidnappers, *if* we kept them on the line long enough. It was a long shot, but I knew from my days spent at the racetrack that sometimes long shots came in.

Several times, thong-panties girl came into the kitchen. She hadn't bothered covering up those ass cheeks yet. I wondered if she had clothes to wear or if she just liked teasing me. Maybe she knew I was a widower, and that it had been a *long* time since I'd had sex. A *very* long time. That might explain why my head always felt like it was about to explode.

She bent over to get a pan from the lower cabinet, flashing me those precious cheeks. I couldn't help staring. Now I had two things to worry about exploding. After she stood again, which seemed like forever, and yet, not long enough, I made a mental note to suggest to Scott that she vacate the premises. Or get dressed.

Thong-panties set the pan on the island, poured a glass of milk then threw me a smile that sent a shiver up and down my spine. I normally didn't like shivers. This one, I did. In a very good way. A way that had me reconsidering my mental note to Scott, who was just returning to the kitchen.

He looked upset, and I thought I heard "…and put something on." I expected her to set a quick pace for the stairs; instead, she bent over again and aimed those weapons in my direction.

Scott sat across from me at the table, but before we got into anything, Delgado and Connors returned. I raised my wrist to look at the time, forgetting again that my watch was gone. "Son of a bitch!" A flash of anger raced through me. I vowed once again to get Number Three. It made me want to call Ramirez to see if she had gotten anywhere on the Marshall case.

"What's the matter?" Winthrop asked.

"Nothing. I lost a watch. I keep looking for the time, forgetting the watch is gone."

"Was it valuable?"

Valuable? Did everything come down to money with this guy?

"Not in terms of money, Mr. Winthrop. But to me it was priceless."

Scott nodded as if he'd been there before, but I couldn't imagine anything being more valuable to him than money. Delgado sat next to Winthrop, placing his notepad on the table.

"Anything?" I asked, but assumed the news wouldn't be good.

"Two hours of talking to people, only to find out nobody saw anything. I thought I was in New York."

Winthrop said, "Unfortunately, Detective, this neighborhood doesn't keep much of a watch for trouble. Everyone assumes it's safe. I've lived in places where it *isn't* safe—Mexico City, Bogota, Caracas… When I got here, I thought we'd found paradise."

Delgado turned to me. "We hit every house along the bus route. You want us to expand it?"

Two hours wasted. I shook my head. "I don't think so."

Delgado and Connors filled me in on a few details we needed to follow up on—a telephone repair truck and a strange mystery-woman jogger that a guy at the end of the street mentioned. I didn't put much hope in either.

"How about you and Connors head to the school to see if you can get a list of her friends from the teachers and classmates. Question them. See what they know."

They started to leave when I called them back. "And see if there are any boyfriends."

"You got it," Delgado said.

I looked over to Scott. Thong-panties had gone back upstairs. "Mr. Winthrop, I don't like suggesting this, but…"

"Go on, Detective."

"I think it would be better if Jennifer isn't here while this is going on." I hadn't prepared a reasonable explanation why, so I rushed one out. "It's just—"

Scott smiled. "I already asked her."

"Thanks."

"Kind of distracting, isn't it?"

"What's that, sir?"

"The way she dresses. It's a little distracting."

I'm sure I turned some shade of crimson, but I forced a smile. "Yes, Mr. Winthrop, it is *very* distracting."

One of the techs walked in then. Before he said a word, I remembered something. "Oh, and Mr. Winthrop, how about giving that cell phone to our guys now. If someone calls, they'll let you know."

From the look on his face, you'd have thought I'd asked for his arm or some other appendage. He stared at me, then the tech, then slowly handed over the phone.

The tech pocketed Scott's phone then addressed me. "How many cells are we going to need for the surveillance?"

"A lot of that depends on Coop. Figure a dozen."

"Okay, Gino, thanks." He was off into the back room to do whatever it was techs did.

As we talked, Scott reminded me that he had recorded the conversation with the kidnappers. I could have kicked myself in the ass for forgetting. I planned on waiting for Ribs and Connors, but figured I might as well listen now. "If you can get it ready, Mr. Winthrop."

We listened to the tape. I was going to play it again but opted to wait for Delgado and Connors. About an hour later, the front door opened. I assumed it was Ribs. "How'd it go, Delgado?"

"Dad?"

I got up to see who it was. It definitely wasn't Delgado.

"Dad, what are all the cars about?"

Before I could do anything, or even ask "Who are you," Winthrop flew by me.

"Alexa! My God, are you all right?"

It was obvious that Alexa had no idea what was going on. "Is this your daughter?" I asked.

He nodded and seemed to be holding back tears. "How did you get away?"

She looked at him as if he had just stepped off the Enterprise alongside of Captain Kirk. "What are you talking about?"

I stepped in to cut through the parental red tape. "Alexa, my name is Detective Gino Cataldi. Someone told your father that you had been kidnapped."

She laughed, then got serious. "Oh God, Dad. I'm sorry. I'm fine. Nothing happened to me."

"But we called school, and…"

She lowered her head. "Lisa and I skipped school."

He let the tears go and hugged her. "I don't care. In fact, I'm glad." I let them have their reunion, hugging and crying, then hugging more. Afterward, Scott turned to me. "Detective, I am *so* sorry I put you through this trouble. Thank goodness it was for nothing."

I stared at him as if he were a moron, which he was. "Mr. Winthrop, you don't seem to understand, sir. They might not have *your* daughter, but they have *someone*. And I've got to find her."

He stared at me, dumbfounded.

I didn't like doing this. I could be wrong, and this could all be some sick bastard messing around, but my gut told me no. I liked to follow my gut. Instead of backing off, I stared back and wouldn't let him off the hook. "Now let me hear that tape again."

CHAPTER 20

LOGIC

After Delgado and Connors returned, we listened to the tape. Then I had Winthrop play it again. I listened with pen in hand, jotting down notes.

"Delgado, you and Connors listen to this again."

"Are you ready?" Winthrop asked.

I nodded, and he started it up from the spot where the kidnapper first spoke.

"This isn't Michelle. Listen closely. We have your daughter."
"What? Who is this?"
"I said, we have your daughter. So listen."
"What the hell are you talking about? Is this you, Ted?"
"This is no joke. Get a pen and paper and write this down."
"Mister, I don't know who you are, but—"
"Shut up. Do you hear me? Shut the fuck up, or I kill her."

"Stop it," I said to Winthrop, then turned to Delgado and Connors. "You hear that? The caller was in control until that moment. When Scott challenged him, he lost it. It's almost like he was reading a script." I gestured for Scott to start it up again, explaining that it was him who we were listening to now.

"Okay, I'm listening."
"Do you have something to write with?"
"I'm set. Go ahead."

"You are to get seven million dollars and—"
"What? I don't have that kind of money."
"Mister, we know you don't have it yet, but you can borrow on it."

The man on the phone paused.

"I'm not going to say it again. Shut up and let me finish."
"Okay. Sorry."

I had Winthrop stop it again. "You hear that? He said we *know* you don't have it *yet*, but you can borrow it." I looked at Delgado and Connors. "They knew he had money coming in?" I grabbed my pen and paper and had him start it up again.

"Seven million dollars in non-sequential serial numbers, hundred-dollar bills, no tracers on the money, or in the money. We will know if you try to track us. Have it ready in forty-eight hours. We'll call tomorrow with instructions on the transfer."
"Wait! I need to talk to my daughter."
"The next time we call, you can talk to her."

I got up from the table and walked around the kitchen. Delgado spoke first. "Gino, I hear what you're saying about these guys knowing things, but that leaves a big gaping hole. They got the *wrong person.*"

I shook my head, disgusted at myself. "Goddamn, Delgado, I *am* an asshole. You're right. Everything they said is irrelevant. They thought they were talking to someone else."

"So the question is, who did they *think* they were calling?" Delgado said.

Winthrop traded places with me and sat in my chair. "I need my phone. I've got to call Fred—"

"Whoa!" I said. "We're still going to need your phone. These people are calling tomorrow. They might call your cell."

Winthrop nodded. "Detective, do you think this might be a prank?"

"No, this is real," I said. "Unless these people are practicing for a movie role."

I looked at my empty coffee cup, then at Winthrop's daughter, who'd entered the kitchen.

"Miss, would you mind making us coffee?"

She looked at me as if I had asked her to clean the toilet. What the hell was wrong with kids nowadays?

"I'll get it," Winthrop said.

There's what's wrong.

"Thanks, Winthrop. It looks like we're going to need a lot of coffee." My body would hate me later, and my nerves were already tight as piano wire, but I had a feeling this would be an all-nighter.

Alexa whispered, but not in a very "whispery" way. "They're not staying are they, Dad?"

Scott hesitated, so I answered for him. "Yes, young lady, we *are* staying. A young girl has been kidnapped. We need to find her."

"But *we* didn't have anything to do with it."

I walked toward her, hoping that *something* would make an impact. "No, you didn't have anything to do with the kidnapping, but the kidnappers, for some reason, *think* they have *you*. That's why they called your father. Or they think they called the father of the girl they really have." I handed my empty cup to Scott. "Until we figure this out, we'll be your guests."

***

ALEXA STORMED AWAY, HER cell phone in hand, already dialing. She called Jada twice but got no answer. Next she tried Jason—same thing. Missy was next on the list. She picked up right away. "Missy, you won't believe what happened."

"What?"

"I came home today and there were freakin' cops everywhere. I mean *everywhere*. It was like something out of a movie."

"Oh my God! What happened?"

"Somebody told my dad I was kidnapped."

"What? Did you tell Jada?"

"I can't reach her," Alexa said. "She skipped with Jason. He's not answering either."

"You know what that means."

"You think they're at Uncle Eddy's?"

"You know Jason Rules."

Detective Cataldi's voice came from the other room. "Alexa!"

"Oh shit, Missy. I have to go. That cop wants me."

"Call me."

"Later."

***

ALEXA STOPPED AND TURNED to me. "What?"

"Please hang up the phone."

"Why?"

"Do it!" Scott yelled.

"This is bull," she said.

I tried being nice. "Alexa, this is a serious situation. I have to ask you not to tell *anyone* about this until I say it's okay. Can you do that?"

"Sure."

"Who did you tell?"

"My friend Missy. That's all."

"Please tell her she cannot tell anyone else."

She sighed. "I will."

"Okay, thanks." I went back to Scott to finish up.

"You're convinced that a girl has been taken?" Winthrop asked.

I didn't want to respond this way, but I felt I had to be honest. "I'm not convinced of anything, but we can't afford the risk of assuming they haven't taken someone."

"How could this happen? Who else could it be?" Winthrop brought me back a full cup of coffee then offered some to Delgado and Connors.

Even though it was piping hot, I sipped it. If there was anything I despised, it was lukewarm coffee. I'd rather burn my tongue.

Delgado said, "I hate to bring this up, but we've got to give consideration to the fact that it *could* be somebody with a grudge against Winthrop, and they're just fu…messing with him."

I looked at Winthrop. "What about it? Anybody hate you that bad?"

"I'm certain I have a lot of enemies, although I can't imagine anyone going to these lengths."

I shook my head. "Don't kid yourself. People are sick." I took a big swig of the coffee—damn good—and looked at my notes. "Think of any possibilities and give the names to Connors so he can check them out."

"How about similar names?" Delgado asked.

I nodded. "Get Julie on it. Have her check on Wintrop, Winthorp, and Winthorpe—with an 'e'—Wintrope, Wenthrop… all the spelling variations." I signaled Delgado as he started dialing. "Have her also try the same last name if we've got any. First names don't matter. And tell her to check all North Houston, Spring, The Woodlands, Conroe…all of it."

Connors got up to grab a bottle of water. "Mr. Winthrop, do you have family nearby? Any siblings, cousins…anyone?"

"None in the whole state. I have a few cousins in New Jersey and a sister and niece in Ohio."

"You said you were divorced. Where is—"

"She's in New York."

"I'm sorry. I think you already said that." I checked things off my list as we moved along. "How about volunteer work? Have you been a big brother? Do you do work at a church?" From what I'd seen of Winthrop, these questions weren't worth asking, but I had to cover the bases. I'd been surprised before.

He shook his head, perhaps a little sadly. "Nothing like that, no. And, Detective, how could they get my private number?"

"Your daughter has it, probably her friends, and colleagues at work. With that many people, *anyone* could have it."

He looked as if he wanted to argue the point when the tech walked in. "You have a call on your phone, Mr. Winthrop."

The tech handed him the phone, and Scott left the room. Delgado and I brainstormed with Connors, but when fifteen minutes went by and Winthrop still hadn't returned, I went searching for him.

He was on the back patio, chatting away as if nothing were going on, as if some poor girl wasn't probably bound and gagged and scared to death somewhere. I signaled for him to come inside. I got a scowl and his index finger held in the air gesturing at me to wait. I was half-surprised it wasn't his middle finger.

Instead of doing nothing, we listened to the tape one more time. I wanted to hear the part where he threatened to kill her. I pushed play then fast-forwarded to the part I wanted.

"Mister, I don't know who you are, but—"

"Shut up. Do you hear me? Shut the fuck up, or I kill her."

I rewound it and played it again.

"Shut up. Do you hear me? Shut the fuck up, or I kill her."

I looked over at Connors and then to Delgado, shaking my head. "Someone is getting hurt on this one. I can feel it."

It's going to be Philadelphia all over again.

CHAPTER 21

SEARCHING FOR A VICTIM

Julie called us back in less than half an hour. For a girl with purple hair, multi-colored nails, and *very* weird clothes, she did damn good work. A rock song from the sixties played in the background.

"What have you got for me?"

"I'm glad you gave up on the attempts to call me darlin'. You'll never sound like a Texan."

Thank God for small favors. "Find anything?"

"There are two Winthrops in the whole north area. It's not a very popular name. But there are six variations close enough for someone to easily make a mistake."

"Give the names to Connors. He'll be calling from here." I checked my notes. "Anybody reported missing?"

"Too early for that."

"I know it's early, but if it's a worried parent, they'll call if their kid's been gone an hour."

"And then there are the ones that don't call when they're gone a week," Delgado said.

"Or the ones that *don't know* they're gone after a week," Connors added.

We all nodded with immediate understanding of those situations.

"Julie, anything else you can think of?"

"I was wondering. Suppose somebody just got the number mixed up? I do that sometimes."

My reaction was to dismiss the idea, maybe because it wasn't mine, or maybe because it sounded too simple...but I couldn't. "You may have something. Get Charlie on this. Tell him to check numbers that would be logical mix-ups of Scott Winthrop's."

"I'll get back to you."

I looked for Scott, who had disappeared again. Maybe he was going to the bedroom to visit thong-panties. I couldn't blame him if he was sneaking a little. A moment later, Alexa came back into the kitchen. She seemed *off* from when I'd seen her earlier. I nudged Delgado and gestured toward her, raising my eyebrows as I did.

Delgado got up under the guise of getting more water. She had her head buried in the refrigerator, looking for something to eat. He waited until she pulled some food out and set it on the counter.

"Where is a good sandwich place around here?" he asked.

She mumbled something about a pizza shop by the freeway then went back to fixing herself something to eat, not once offering us any.

Delgado came back, and whispered, "She's on something."

I shot her a glare but didn't say anything. Ever since the problems started with my son, I'd gotten really worked up whenever I saw a kid on drugs. I wanted to grab her, shake her, maybe even beat some sense in her...but this wasn't the time or place. I called Connors over. "Julie suggested they might have mixed the phone numbers up. I got Charlie running possibilities. As soon as he calls, I want you two on it."

"Phone verification?" Delgado asked.

"Unless we get something interesting."

The phone rang. I jumped then realized it was my phone, not Winthrop's. "Gino Cataldi."

"What's going on, Gino?"

"Captain?"

"I expected reports by now. Renkin is pestering me every half hour."

"Coop, I'll call when I get something. Or when I need something. As it is, I've got too much going on for reports."

"So you've got nothing."

I sighed. What I had to tell her would only make things worse. "Coop, whoever was kidnapped wasn't Scott Winthrop's daughter."

"What! How—"

"Because she's sitting in the other room, thirty feet from me."

"So this was a prank?"

"No way. I've listened to the tape four times. These guys have *somebody*. I've got to find out who."

"Like I need this shit. All right. Y'all keep me posted." Coop often slipped into her East Texas accent when she wasn't focusing. It sounded natural on her.

One of the techs came into the kitchen. "Any coffee made?"

"Should be some left in the pot," I said, and then the phone rang. It was Charlie. "What have you got?"

"I ran all the numbers," Charlie said. "They couldn't have mixed up the area code or the exchange. There aren't any other exchanges that would work if mixed up, so it had to be the last four numbers. And usually if there's a mix-up, it's the last two digits that get turned around. I ran the numbers with the last two switched and then with all of them switched. I found twenty-four numbers total. Three aren't assigned, so that leaves us twenty-one working numbers."

"Charlie, you did all right. Can you email me those? I'll get Connors and Delgado on them right away."

"Sure thing. How's it going up there? Y'all gettin' any good food?"

"Good food? Yeah, we were just about to sit down to a seven-course meal."

"I was curious, that's all. You know I've been dieting, and that makes me think about food even more. No sense in gettin' all riled up about it."

"I gotta go, Charlie. Phone's ringing." I hung up with Charlie and answered the other line. "Gino."

"It's Julie. We may have something."

"Spit it out."

"I just spoke with Mrs. Winthorpe. Her daughter never came home from school, and when Mrs. Winthorpe called the school, they said the daughter didn't show up today."

"Shit! Did you tell her—"

"Nothing. She doesn't know why I called. She thinks it has to do with her daughter missing school."

"Where does she live?"

"I've got the address. It's only two miles from you."

"You're the best, Julie. I'm sending Delgado over. If she calls again, patch it through."

I gave Delgado the address. "Take Connors. Call me if you get anything."

I bumped into Winthrop when I turned around.

The tech stepped back, nearly spilling his drink. "Mr. Winthrop, I still need your phone."

He huffed and handed it over. "Don't take long."

The guy hustled out of the kitchen as if it were a war zone.

Winthrop focused on me. "Did I hear right? You found the person who was kidnapped?"

"We're not certain of anything."

"But if you did, I presume you'll be moving your—operations—to their house?"

Scott Winthrop was one cold fuck. If this was what it took to get rich and famous, I didn't want it. "Mr. Winthrop, you don't seem to understand. We need to know who was kidnapped, yes, but what matters more is the kidnappers think they have *your* daughter, or they think you are the father of the girl they have. In either case, I'm staying here until this is over."

"I'm afraid that won't work. I have a business to run. Besides, I have a meeting tomorrow."

I held my breath—and my temper—then spoke slowly, hoping my voice didn't carry the disgust I felt in every muscle. "*Mr. Winthrop,* a girl is being held against her will. She may be suffering. She may be raped at any moment. She may be killed. Those men are calling tomorrow, and *you* need to be here. With *that* in mind, is your meeting so important?"

"We don't know that. This is probably a prank."

"Mr. Winthrop!" I stopped myself before I lost it, took a few deep breaths, and started again, making a point to speak calmly. "I listened to the tape four times. Whoever made that call is holding *someone* hostage. *Somebody's* daughter is in a dark room, or the back of a van, or an abandoned building. She is alone, tied up, gagged, and certainly scared to death."

Winthrop raised himself up—on his haughtiness, probably. "I understand your concern, but my daughter's been through enough already."

It was obvious to me—hell, to anybody—that Winthrop was pissed. I half expected him to take a swing at me. And half of me wanted him to, though it would be a coin toss as to who would win.

"Fine," he said. "Let me call my admin. I'll be available."

"Thanks," I said, but I wanted to smack him.

I called Ramirez; Coop had him filling in on the Marshall case, but she didn't have anything new. "How's the boy?"

"Not good. They ran into complications during surgery."

"What kind of complications?"

"I don't know," Ramirez said. "That's all they told me."

"Keep me posted, Ramirez. And why don't you interview the family again. See if they've thought of anything else. Have someone take a stab at the neighbors again too. Somebody *had* to have seen something."

"We're all over it. I'll get back to you."

I leaned back in the recliner, half asleep, when the phone rang. "Yeah, Delgado, what have you got?"

"We're here. The girl's missing, but we got a bigger problem. I don't think this is it."

"Why not?"

He whispered. "These people are white. No way the kidnappers didn't know what Winthrop looked like."

"He is kind of light-skinned…but you're right. Okay, go through the motions…just in case, then get back here. My guess is the girl shows up before long. Give the woman your cell, though, and tell her to call when they find her."

Just for grins, I thought I'd ask Winthrop's daughter. "Alexa, can you come here please?"

She shuffled in, eyes glazed over. "What?"

The *what* came with an attitude.

"Do you know a girl named Winthorpe?" She goes to your school."

"Kathy? Yeah, I know her. Everyone teases us about our names being so similar."

"Her mother said she didn't come home, and the school says she didn't attend today. You know anything about that?"

She snorted. "Kathy almost never goes to school. More than likely, she's at the mall, hanging out."

"Okay, thanks," I said, and called Delgado. "Check the mall before you come back. And get her cell number from the parents. She may not be answering their calls, but…hang on a minute." I walked to the family room. "Alexa, call Kathy for me. Use *your* cell phone."

A few rings later we had Kathy Winthorpe on the line. I grabbed the phone from Alexa. "This is Detective Cataldi. You need to get home, now."

I hung up, dialed Delgado and filled him in. "Tell the parents where she is, then come back."

I wanted to say this had all been a waste of time, but it hadn't. Delgado had brought up a good point about the white and black thing. "Alexa, who are your black friends?"

"That question is a little racist isn't it?"

"It's just a question." I stared at her, waiting. She glared. Then her father stormed into the room.

"Detective Cataldi, you need to leave the house."

"And what will you do when the kidnappers call tomorrow?"

"I'll tell them they have the wrong person."

I stared at him, doing my best not to kick his arrogant ass. "You'd do that? Leave some little girl out there to die?"

"Like I said before, we don't even know if there *is* a girl."

"You make me sick, Winthrop."

"That's fine. As long as you're out of here before the night is over."

"And this girl, who will likely get killed, what do you want me to tell her parents? That Mr. Scott Winthrop got his feelings hurt, so your daughter had to die?"

He puffed himself up. "You have two hours to get your men and your equipment out of here." With that, he left the room.

One of the techs tapped me on the shoulder. "What do we do now?"

"I don't know. But we're not leaving here. Fuck him if he thinks we are."

I stepped outside and dialed Coop's cell phone, knowing she'd be pissed, but fuck her too. She and Renkin put me on this case; they could share the agony.

"This better be good, Gino."

"I wouldn't be calling if it was, Gladys."

"After calling me Gladys, it better be *real* good."

"I need more men. Lots more. And we've got a problem with the money."

"What kind of problem?"

I wanted to say *think about it, asshole*, but what I said was, "Remember, Captain, I told you this wasn't Winthrop's daughter who was kidnapped. No way he's risking seven million dollars."

"Then you better figure a way to get that girl without any money."

"We need to bring in the Feds."

"Renkin said no."

"I don't care what he said. We can't do this without money."

"I'll see what I can do about the men. And I'll ask Renkin about the FBI, but money is out of the question."

"One more thing, Coop. Winthrop is kicking me out of the house."

"Goddamnit, Cataldi, can't you keep your mouth shut for one fucking night?"

"Sorry."

"Sorry my ass. Figure out how to change his mind. Crawl on your belly or kiss his ass. Do *something* to change his mind. We need to be there for that call tomorrow."

She was right. We had to be here. "Don't worry, we will."

CHAPTER 22

WHERE IS JADA

Lonny Hackett found work for the first time in a few days. Real work, though the pay wasn't much. Nothing like what he made as a bricklayer. And it was tough work, pouring concrete for a barn floor. Hot, sweaty work. Backbreaking work. Lonny loved it. He loved the pain in his lower back and the lactic acid burn in his arms. He even liked the concrete dust lining the inside of his nostrils. And the cement burns on his skin.

He finished troweling the last section of the floor, waited a short while then brushed it with a soft broom. Just enough to take the slipperiness out of the surface.

Can't have slick concrete in a barn. Somebody would fall and bust their damn ass.

Lonny did a final check before cleaning the tools then headed home with the first genuine smile he'd worn in a long time. He almost felt good enough to laugh by the time he got home. "I hope something's cooking, woman. You got a *working* man come home."

Lucia popped her head out from the kitchen, a smile from the old days on her face. "That working man better learn some manners if he wants to eat here," she said, but she set a quick pace to hug him. "Good job?"

"Just a one-day pour. But a broken back never felt so good."

"I might know the remedy for that," Lucia said.

The look on her face told Lonny it was going to be an even better night. "Now you got my appetite going."

"Get a couple of plates. Maybe even pour some wine. Might as well spend that hard-earned money on something good."

"Where are the kids?"

"Mars went to Tommy's house, and Jada went to get a dress with Alexa."

"We're all alone?"

"I guess we are."

"You think dinner can wait?"

Lucia untied her apron and let it drop to the floor, swinging her hips. "I'm not even hungry."

Lonny scooped her up in his arms and headed for the bedroom, her laughing all the way. "Don't go hurting your back and making excuses. I won't have it."

"Don't make me laugh. I'm not as young as I used to be."

"Remember when you carried me up the steps on our honeymoon?"

"It's a good thing we don't have steps," Lonny said, and plopped her on the bed.

As he undressed, Lucia gave him her best mean-faced look. "If you think I'm making love to a sweaty, stinky man covered in cement…" She wrapped her arms around his neck and pulled him to her. "…you're absolutely right."

Two hours later, they finished dinner. Mars came home shortly after that, wanting to try out new jiu-jitsu moves on his father. "Not tonight. I'm a tired old man."

"Worn-out old man is what he is," Lucia said. She started laughing and couldn't stop.

Lonny cleared the table and washed dishes, tossing a towel to Lucia. "You dry."

"Where's Jada?" Mars asked.

"Shopping," Lucia said.

"I'm taking Scooter for a walk," Mars said.

"Take your time," Lonny said then turned to Lucia. "Shouldn't Jada be home by now?"

"Is your memory getting as old as you? She's going to a prom, and you expect her to be home before the stores close?" Lucia laughed more. "Old, old, old."

"You don't take that long."

"When was the last time you went shopping for a dress with me?"

"When was the last time you got a new dress?" He smiled and kissed her. "We're about to fix that. A few more good jobs and—"

"And we might pay the mortgage on time," Lucia said. "Stop talking nonsense." She leaned close and whispered. "Besides, I don't see that you mind so much what I'm wearing."

"I'm calling to see where she is."

Lucia grabbed the phone. "Don't you *dare* spoil her night. We don't need to interrupt her fun." She pinched him on the butt. "You don't like interruptions when you're having fun, do you?"

Lonny pulled her close and hugged her. "When did you get so smart, lady?"

"It's not me. It's you finally catching on." Lucia ran for the bedroom, laughing. Lonny was right behind her.

CHAPTER 23

A FAIR TRADE

The phone rang at 9:30. "This is Gino."

"Are you still there?"

"Yeah, Coop. I'm here. Where the hell did you think I'd be?"

"I wasn't sure. Winthrop must have called everybody he knew, and they all called the chief, and the chief called me." There was a determined pause. "While I was taking a *bath*."

"I didn't need to know that."

"Not what you dream about at night is it, Cataldi? Well, I got news for you, getting calls from the chief about *you* is not what I dream about."

"Yeah, well, screw Winthrop and his pals."

"He wants you out of his house. He wants your badge, too."

"As I said…" I stopped before I got in trouble then said to hell with it. "Coop, this fuckin' guy has a girlfriend not much older than his daughter. And—"

"How old is she?"

"I don't know. Maybe…late twenties, maybe early thirties."

"That's *a lot* older than his daughter."

"Yeah, but she's parading around the house in a goddamn thong."

"Jealous?"

"Maybe."

"Gino, we've got to placate this guy."

"Placate? What the hell, you been playing Scrabble?"

"Get your mind off the girl in the thong, figure out how to placate—yes, *placate*—Winthrop then focus on the case."

I went out front and kicked a few of Winthrop's bushes. "Two can play at this game. You got my back?"

Long pause. "I don't know why I ever put you on this case." Longer pause. "Yes, I've got your back. But Winthrop may have both our asses."

"Don't worry, old girl. I haven't let you down yet."

"I hate the first time."

"Yeah, me too. We'll try to make this different." Coop started to say something, but Delgado was pulling up. "I gotta go. Delgado's here."

"Keep me posted. I don't want to hear bad news from Renkin."

"You got it, Captain."

Delgado and Connors were almost to the door.

"Waste of time there," Delgado said.

"Where was she?"

"Cutting school with a few friends."

I shook my head. "Do any kids go to school anymore?"

"It's springtime, Gino. Time for flowers, and pollen, and cutting school." Delgado lit a smoke. "Anything new?"

"Nothing, unless you want to count Winthrop trying to throw us out of his house."

"What for?"

"He took offense at something I said."

Delgado sucked hard on his cigarette. "Imagine that, someone misinterpreting your words of wisdom."

"Fuck you, too."

"Too? So someone else suggested you're an ass?"

"Maybe."

"Coop?"

"Maybe."

"What are we going to do?"

"I don't know yet." I reached for the doorknob then turned to Delgado and Connors. "But we're not leaving here until this case is over. I don't care if we have to kidnap Winthrop."

Delgado looked at Connors. "I told you this would be an education, amigo."

I decided that Alexa had to know something, even if she didn't know she knew. I got Ribs to lure Scott onto the patio. As soon as they stepped outside, I found Alexa.

"Alexa, I need to talk with you."

"About *what?*"

"About your friends. We've checked all the families with similar names and came up empty. I think it has to be a friend of yours. Is there anyone they could have mistaken for you?"

"Who are they going to mistake for me?" she asked. Then her eyes opened wide as if someone had pried the lids up. "Jada!" She grabbed her phone and hit a speed-dial button.

"Don't!" I said. "Hang up." I grabbed the phone from her.

Alexa yanked it back. "What?"

"If they have your friend, they have her cell. If they see a call coming in from Alexa Winthrop, they'll know they have the wrong person."

"Oh my God, do you think…Daddy, they have Jada!"

I got in front of her, blocking her way to the kitchen. "Let's not jump to conclusions. Calm down and tell me why you think they have Jada."

"She's my best friend. And she's black." She started crying. "And she was here. She spent the night *last* night."

"What? Why *the hell* am I just hearing this?" We might have hit the jackpot, but Alexa was a wreck. "Okay, sit down. Start at the beginning and tell me what happened from the time you got up until you came home."

"After Jada spent the night, we got up and left for school…"

I waited, breathed deeply, trying to relax. I hadn't been at Winthrop's house for long, but it seemed like days.

"A friend picked me up about a block from home. Jada walked to the bus."

Jesus Christ! "Why didn't you mention this earlier? Didn't you wonder where she was?"

"She was supposed to go shopping for a dress with her boyfriend. She told her mom she was going with me. I figured they were just…you know."

"You should have said something. *Goddamn!* A girl's been kidnapped."

Winthrop and Delgado came in from the patio as I was hollering.

"What the hell is going on? Don't talk to my daughter like that. I want you to leave. Now!"

I looked at him with a hard glare. "I'm *not* leaving."

Winthrop raised himself up again. He was good at that. "We'll see about that." He reached for his phone, forgetting the damn tech had it again.

"Do that, and I'll make a few calls myself."

He snickered. "And who would you call?"

"I know a lot of reporters who would love to have a story to disgrace a wealthy, do-gooder black man. A lot of people down here are still like that, Winthrop." I walked over to him. Got face-to-face. "Write that in your diary in case you forget."

"I cannot believe you said that, Detective. I could have your badge."

"Yeah, well, try to get anything you want. But the papers will soon be telling the world that this ultra-clean biotech executive doesn't give a shit about a poor girl about to be raped, or killed, or both." I smiled. "So what do you think? Will those articles earn you much sympathy? Think they'll help your IPO?"

Winthrop shook his head repeatedly. "I cannot believe…"

"That I'd say such things?" I shook my head at him. "I'd say, or *do*, anything to save that girl. Think about *that* why don't you?"

Delgado stepped between us. "Let's everyone remain cool." He glared at me. "*Right*, amigo?"

That was the signal from Delgado telling me to shut up. I did. I was about to apologize to Scott when Alexa wrapped her arms around his waist.

"Daddy, it's Jada. I think that's who they have."

He looked genuinely upset. "What?"

"Jada walked to school by herself. Todd picked me and Lisa up, and we…cut school."

He hugged her, stroking her hair. "Dear God."

"What's her parents' number?" I asked. "Do you know where they live?"

She nodded.

I thought about calling, but that was no way to tell them, assuming the victim was their daughter. "Let's go. You can show me where they live."

CHAPTER 24

MY DAUGHTER IS MISSING

I forced myself to be silent as I drove Alexa to the Hackett's house. I wanted to talk to her about drugs, how she'd ruin her life and her father's life. But I didn't trust myself to maintain control; besides, she said it was only a five- or ten-minute drive to their house. Not enough time to do any good. At least that's what I convinced myself.

We crossed the freeway, took a few turns, went over a set of railroad tracks, and into an older subdivision with a nice, tree-lined drive. A few blocks later, we turned onto their street.

"It's right there," Alexa said. "Number 712."

I parked next to the mailbox, where I noted the car and truck parked in the driveway. "Do you know her parents well?"

She nodded. "They're nice people."

We walked up the sidewalk together, but when we reached the porch, Alexa stood behind me, almost hiding.

A teenage boy answered the door. He was maybe fifteen or sixteen. "Can I help you?"

I held out my badge. "Detective Gino Cataldi. Is your father home?"

He looked nervous, but people—especially kids—usually did when a cop showed up at their house.

"Dad, some cop is here."

Jada's father came to the door, wearing a look I'd seen many times—fear. I'd seen enough people scared of the police to recognize it, and I wondered why he was.

Is this guy a dope dealer? What has he done wrong?

Then I remembered why I was there—their daughter was missing. Maybe, just maybe, the appearance of a cop late at night when your kid was missing could do that. That brought to mind my own situation from not long ago, when Ron was doing drugs. Every time the phone rang, I jumped, certain it was a cop calling to tell me Ron had been busted, or the hospital calling to tell me he'd OD'd. Or was dead.

"May I help you?" Jada's father asked.

"Sir, I'm Detective Gino Cataldi. I—"

"Alexa?" Jada's father said. "Is that you?"

She stepped out from behind me, wrapping her arms around him. "Mr. Hackett. Oh God, Mr. Hackett, I think they got Jada." The tears came pouring out.

I hadn't wanted it to go like this, but now… "Mr. Hackett, may we come inside?"

"Who's got Jada? What's she talking about? Are you holding my girl for something?"

As we entered, his wife came out from the kitchen. "What's going on? Is something wrong?"

I had to get hold of this quickly. "Sir. Ma'am. I didn't want to start the conversation like this, but we have reason to think that your daughter might have been kidnapped."

"What?" Lonny rushed to the table and grabbed his phone, punching in numbers.

I moved quickly toward him. "Mr. Hackett! Please, sir. Don't do that."

He stopped and stared. "I'm calling Jada."

"Sir, if Jada's been kidnapped, it's because they think she is Mr. Winthrop's daughter. We don't want to do anything that could arouse suspicion, including unnecessary phone calls."

Mrs. Hackett was hugging her husband and son both. She had that frightened-parent expression. "What makes you think it's our girl?"

"They called Mr. Winthrop this morning. We thought all along it was Alexa until she came home. Then when she told us that Jada spent the night…"

"I thought she was shopping for a dress with you," Mrs. Hackett said to Alexa.

Alexa shook her head. "That's what she told you, but she was going with Jason."

"Who's Jason?" Mr. Hackett said.

"Some loser," the son said. "The guy she's going to the prom with."

"'Loser'?" I said. "What do you mean by that?" I focused my attention on Hackett's son.

He shrugged. "I don't know. Just…I don't know."

Mr. Hackett grabbed his son and shook him. "This is no time to play games. Tell the man what you know."

I couldn't understand how they must feel, but I tried imagining. "Son, your father is right. Your sister's life may be in danger. Anything you know will help."

He hesitated, looking first at his father, then his, mother, and finally back at me. "He's a punk. Into drugs, gangs. I told her not to go with him."

I thought Mrs. Hackett would lose it. She covered her face with her hands and plopped into a chair. Her body trembled. "Oh God! Mars, why didn't you say something? You should have told us."

"Mom, I can't—"

"All right. Enough!" Mr. Hackett reached his hand out to me. "Detective, my name is Lonny. My wife is Lucia, and that is our son, Morris, but we call him Mars. Let's sit down. Then please tell us what we can do."

While Alexa filled them in on what she knew, I looked the place over. The windows had no curtains—only blinds—and the floor was the standard carpeting that came with small tract houses. The TV was an old tube model. If this guy was a drug dealer, he didn't spend his profits at home.

Alexa told them about Jada walking to the bus stop alone. When she finished, I described the ransom call and what had happened since. "We feel fairly certain it *is* Jada they have."

Lucia was crying again. Lonny looked as if he'd do that same any minute. I figured this was a good time to get them moving. "Mr. Hackett, I know your world has been torn apart, but we need to get back to the Winthrops' house. These people think they have his daughter. They might call, and if they do, I need to be there. Besides, I want you to hear the tape to see if there is anything you can pick up on. I doubt it, but it's worth a try."

"Anything, Detective, let's go."

Lucia grabbed her purse as she headed out the door with Lonny and Mars.

"You should ride with us," I said.

The three of them climbed in the backseat. Alexa sat up front with me. It seemed like two hours to get back to Alexa's house. Lucia cried almost the whole way, with Lonny consoling her. Mars was in a zombie state, silent and rigid as a stone.

"Alexa, do you have this…Jason's number?"

"I've got it."

"Call him. See if he's seen Jada, but don't tell him what's happening."

Alexa made the call. She talked for maybe half a minute. "He thought she was with me."

"But he never called you?"

"He's probably been calling her cell."

I cringed when I heard that, knowing it would bring more tears from Lucia. It did. "Don't worry, ma'am. We'll get her back."

When we got to Alexa's house, the Hacketts sat at the kitchen table while I played the tape.

"I thought they would let her talk," Lonny said afterward.

"This isn't like the movies, Mr. Hackett. These people seem professional, which means they want to control things right from the start. Not letting you talk to her keeps you guessing. They are supposed to call tomorrow. I'd bet we'll hear her then."

"Do you think…" Lucia sounded afraid to put words to her concerns.

I patted her back. "Yes, ma'am. I think she's safe. They are only interested in the money."

No sense in telling her differently.

"What are we going to do?" Lonny asked.

"About?"

"The money. How do we work this?" He stared at me, desperation in his eyes. "You have a plan, don't you?"

"I'm working on it," I said.

"Working on it? You've had all damn day."

I took a few breaths then leaned toward the two of them. "Earlier, when we thought it was Alexa, Mr. Winthrop was going to provide the money."

"And now?" Lonny's voice had a sharp edge to it.

"I've asked my captain if we can do something. I won't know how to approach it until we hear from the kidnappers. The next call will determine a lot."

Lucia patted her husband's hand. "They'll do what they can. Don't worry, the Lord won't let anything happen to her."

I pulled Delgado aside. "Have Connors babysit the druggie while you watch the parents. I've got to get hold of Coop."

"You bringin' in the Feds?" Delgado asked.

"Maybe. I don't like not having the money as a backup."

"That *could* turn it ugly."

"Yeah. And none of us want that."

I called Coop, roused her from bed, and filled her in on the latest development. "And you're sure they have this Hackett girl?" she asked.

"We're not sure of anything. She could be out drinking, could be in a motel with her boyfriend—although he said he hadn't seen her—or she could be taped up and gagged with a bunch of guys who want to do wrong things to her."

"And you feel it's the latter?"

"Pretty damn certain."

"How are the parents?"

"As you would expect. Disbelieving, hoping it's not true. But they know. They'll be worse tomorrow when it's confirmed."

"Did you…"

"*Placate* Winthrop? Yes, I did."

"Good. That's one worry gone. What do you need now?"

"I'm going to need people for surveillance on whatever drop they have planned. I'll need to keep the techs here, and I'll need seven million dollars cash."

Coop coughed between fits of laughter.

"One more thing, Coop. I need a stand-in for Winthrop. He's about six foot, 190 pounds, and he's black. Think Chief Renkin wants the job?"

"I'd ask, but he's noticeably bigger, and blacker, than Winthrop. As for the money, find another way. You're not getting seven million dollars. You won't get seven *hundred*."

"We should call the Feds."

"Chief doesn't want it."

"He made that decision when we thought this was about Winthrop. Now it's some poor sap whose daughter got in the way."

"I'll ask again, but don't count on it. They don't want any controversy surrounding this IPO."

"Captain, this girl's life is on the line."

Coop sighed. "I *know*. Let me work on it."

"At least give me Tip," I said.

"No way am I putting you and Denton on another case together. Get that out of your mind."

I went back inside, trying to figure out what to do next. "Delgado, what time is it?" I cringed having to ask. My blood boiled, reminding me that a guy named Number Three had Mary's watch.

"A little past eleven."

I went to the table and sat next to Lucia, across from Lonny. "I know this isn't a good time, but there are questions that need answering."

Lucia said, "Go on, Detective."

"What do you know about her boyfriend?"

Lucia shook her head. "Nothing. We didn't even know he *was* her boyfriend. She came home the other day saying he asked her to the prom, but other than that…"

"I'll kill that son of a bitch!" Lonny said.

"Hold on, sir. We have no indication that he did anything wrong. It's simply something I have to follow up on. Whenever we—" My phone rang. It was Chief Renkin. "Hey, Chief. What's up?"

"Coop filled me in, Cataldi. I can give you all the manpower you need, but we can't do anything about the money. You'll have to make do."

"I figured that much."

"Anything new on the Marshall case?" Renkin asked.

"I got Ramirez working it with her partner. Last I heard, the Marshall boy wasn't doing well."

"Leads?"

"None yet, but Ramirez is good. We'll get there."

"We better, Detective. That case is getting headlines."

"Yes, sir."

"Keep me informed. On *both* cases."

"Yes, sir. Thanks."

I hung up and dialed Ramirez. She answered right away.

"Ramirez, I'm getting pressure from the chief. What have we got?"

"Nothing new."

"You need to turn up the heat. If that boy dies, they all go down for murder. *Use* that. Find out who was involved and press hard. Start shaking people up. Tongues loosen up when a murder rap's involved."

"Was that the Marshall boy from that home invasion?" Lonny asked.

I nodded. "He's not doing too well." I noticed Lonny had a slight reaction when I mentioned his name. "Why, do you know him?"

"Not personally, but he plays a mean game of football."

"I know him by reputation," Mars said. "He's a *great* football player, and from what the guys on our team say, he's a nice guy."

"He goes to your school?"

"No, he plays for Klein."

"Do you go to the same school as Alexa?"

He looked sheepishly to his mother, then back to me.

"It's not a tough question. You do or you don't."

"He's not supposed to," Lucia said. "But Mr. Winthrop lets us use his address so the children can go to a better school."

"I thought they checked those things out, compared to the tax rolls or something."

Lucia lowered her head. "They do, Detective. But Mr. Winthrop…knows people."

I nodded. I guess money and influence still wielded big sticks. But that did answer one question that had been bugging me. "Does Jada's license have this address on it?"

"Yes, it does. Why?"

"I've been wondering why the kidnappers wouldn't have realized they made a mistake when they saw her license—different name and address— but if the address is the same…"

"Maybe she concocted a story about the name," Lonny said. "That girl can tell a story."

"Let's hope she can maintain that story. It may save her ass."

I turned to Delgado. "Get the boyfriend's number from Alexa. Talk to him. See if you think he's straight."

"You think he has something to do with this?" Lonny asked.

"I don't know *anything* at this point. I'm chasing all angles."

"I see," Lonny said, then he got up to get coffee. "Lucia, you want to sit outside?"

"I'm fine here."

***

LONNY WALKED OUT TO the patio and sat in the chair by a small fountain. He leaned back, closed his eyes, and prayed.

God, I know what I did to deserve this, but please don't take it out on my baby. She's a good girl. She didn't have nothin' to do with my wrongs. If you got to punish someone, take it out on me. Lucia and my girl don't need to suffer.

Lonny got up and walked around then sat on the edge of the fountain, his fingers dipping in the water.

And one more thing. I'm sorry for what we did to that boy and his family. Tears flowed. *Lord, you know how sorry I am about that. Those folks didn't do anything but get rich. And look what we did…Please don't let that boy die, Lord. Please.*

***

I GOT UP UNDER the guise of pouring myself coffee, but I really wanted to see what Lonny was doing. A change had come over him, and I didn't know why. He had dealt with things well until a short while ago. *Something* had changed.

CHAPTER 25

WATCHERS

Boss waited until everyone was there. "I wasn't happy with the call, Number Four. You lost control."

"Goddamn amateur," Number Three said.

"Shut-up, Three. I'd drop both of you if I had time to train more people."

Number Three mumbled something, but a glare from Boss silenced him.

"Maybe *you* should make the next call." That from Number Two.

"I will," Boss said. "And we need to transfer the girl to the motel."

"Why?" Four asked.

Boss sighed. "Don't ask so many questions."

Number Four looked to the others for concurrence, but got nothing. "It's just…if we got her here, why not keep her here?"

"It's not in the plans, Four. She's going to a motel where the clerk wouldn't know if a motorcycle gang rented the rooms or a conclave of Cardinals that were in town to elect a new pope."

"Rooms?"

"We have three. One for her and one on each side." Boss looked to Number Two. "You know what to do?"

"Got it, Boss."

"Take Three with you. I will send Number Five to relieve you by six AM."

"We don't need another person. We could—"

Boss grabbed hold of Three. "I do the thinking around here."

Number Three turned away from Boss. "I don't see why we needed another person, that's all. Less money for us."

"There will be plenty to go around," Boss said, then turned to Number Two. "It's getting late."

***

JADA SAT IN A hard-backed chair, afraid to move. She shivered, and not from cold. She didn't know how long she'd been in this place, but all she'd done since she got here was cry. And shiver.

A spasm seized her arm. She stretched it out, hoping to relieve the pain. Most of her muscles ached, and her legs cramped. They'd already fallen asleep twice, forcing Jada to stand on one leg while she tried shaking it out.

She couldn't see anything, could barely hear anything except an occasional truck rumbling somewhere in the distance. And all she could smell was a dank, musty odor, like the basement at her cousin Anne's house up in Maryland.

A door opened across the room. As she turned her head in that direction, a blast of cool air rushed across her skin, which was wet from sweating. The shivers started again. She didn't hear anyone come in, but she had to try. "Can I have a blanket?" Her voice sounded hollow, not quite an echo but almost.

Footsteps sounded from the direction of the door. Jada focused, listening as they approached. It *was* a big room. "Is someone there?"

A hand patted her hair, making her jump, but then she relaxed. It was a gentle patting, a caress.

"Get ready to go," a woman's voice said. "We're moving you."

"Am I going home?"

The woman stroked her hair more. "Not yet. It won't be long, though."

She heard her purse being opened, someone going through her things.

"Why does your license say Jada *Hackett?* Why isn't it Winthrop?" This was the voice of the man who took her.

Another shiver tortured her. They must think she was Mr. Winthrop's daughter. Jada thought of what she knew about Alexa and her dad. Not much, but maybe enough. "My parents are divorced. I took my stepfather's name. Then I decided I hated him, so I moved back with Dad." It was difficult getting all that out without faltering. She prayed they believed her, and that she was doing the right thing pretending to be Alexa.

"Address is the same as his." This voice was different. It belonged to the woman. She thought it was the one who took her. Jada's stomach churned.

Someone's hands grabbed her face and turned it, as if evaluating her. Fear subsided when she realized it was the woman.

"It's her," the woman said. A slight pause, then, "How did your father get so much money?"

Was this a test? Did they suspect something? They must know about Mr. Winthrop's business. "He *worked* for it." Jada didn't mean for it to come out so harsh. She braced herself for…something. Sensing that the man was about to do something, she took a step away from where she thought he stood.

"Easy, Number Three," the woman said.

So he was *going to do something.*

"It's all right," the woman said. "I'd be pissed off if somebody kidnapped me. Don't try carrying it too far, though." Her voice carried a threat.

Jada nodded, eager to have an ally.

"All right, let's go," the woman said, and took her by the arm.

***

AFTER GATHERING HER THINGS, Number Two and Three loaded Jada in the van. Driver took them to the motel where Boss had rented three rooms. One was rented a week ago, the others, two days ago.

Driver pulled up outside the room, off to the side of the motel and waited to make sure no one was around then unlocked the door to all three rooms before getting back in the van. Number Three got out and went to the room on the left. Number Two took Jada to the room in the center.

Number Two led Jada to the bed, untied her hands and removed the gag, but kept the blindfold on, checking to make sure it was secure. "Do you need to use the bathroom?"

"No."

"Don't say that for spite. If you can go now, you should."

"I said no."

"Suit yourself," Two said. "Lie down. I need to tie your hands."

"What for?"

"Just lie down."

Jada sat on the edge of the bed, then lay on her back. "I think I *do* need to use the bathroom."

Number Two sighed. "Don't make me go through this shit again. Cooperate. It will make things easier for you."

"Okay."

Jada used the bathroom then returned to the bed. "You don't need to tie my hands."

Number Two tied them anyway. Jada cried, big sobs that made her whole body heave. Number Two sat next to her, whispering. "If you do anything stupid, we'll sedate you. Then you'll mess your pants, and none of us will clean it." She placed her hand on Jada's arm, rubbing it gently. "You can make this time go easier, or you can make it really tough."

"Okay."

"I know you have a lot of questions. Ask me. I want you to feel comfortable."

"What are you going to do with me?"

"As long as your father pays us, and you do as we say, we won't hurt you. And I hope you're listening, because that was a really big *if*." Number Two looked around then leaned close and whispered again. "Some of the men are looking at you wrong, if you know what I mean. Don't give them a reason to do anything. Follow orders, and I'll make sure nothing happens."

Jada nodded. "Okay."

"Good. Here are the rules. You signal one of us if you have to use the bathroom. If you need water, same thing. If you hear a noise outside or people talking…" Number Two grabbed her by the cheeks and made Jada face her. Two made sure her own mask was secure then removed Jada's blindfold. "This is *very* important. Do *not* try to attract attention. If you do, they will kill you."

"I understand."

"Good." She smiled at Jada. "I'm putting the gag back in, but I'll leave the blindfold off."

"Thanks," Jada said.

"All right. I'll see you in the morning."

Three walked into the room. "Girls getting cozy, are you?"

Number Two's face twisted into a scowl. "Get back in your room."

Three tried following Number Two into her room, but she stopped him cold.

"We been working together a long time," Number Three said. "No reason to get uptight."

Two nodded to the other room. "You've got your bed. Don't let me see you until morning."

Two watched him go, but she didn't like the way he looked at Jada as he crossed the room. *I should've come alone.*

Number Two took a quick shower then lay on the bed in her panties and a T-shirt. It was going to be a long night. During the middle of a dream about a small cabin in the mountains, muffled sounds jarred Number Two awake. She grabbed the gun from the nightstand and tiptoed to the door, pressing her ear against it. The fan from the air conditioner made it difficult to hear clearly.

Is that stupid girl trying to get out?

Number Two put on her mask and eased the door open. Number Three was hovering over Jada, his hands groping her. He was sitting on her legs so she couldn't kick, and he was about to take his mask off.

Number Two took one small step at a time, never taking her eyes from him. She got behind him and shoved the barrel of the Beretta against the back of his head. "Take off that mask, and I'll kill you."

Three choked up. "Easy, Number Two. I just wanted to show the girl a good time. She's itching for it."

"If you take off your pants, I'll blow your cock off."

He turned to stare at her, hands twitching. "You're a tough bitch, huh? That's all right, I like 'em tough. Maybe after we're done with this job, you and me—"

"Never, Number Three. You got that? Never."

He turned to the girl, a look in his eyes so obvious he might as well have licked his lips.

Two shoved the gun harder against his head. "She's off limits. Don't forget it. If you think I'm tough, you ain't seen shit. Boss will cut your cock off in pieces."

"Okay, okay. You made your point. I'm going to get some sleep."

Number Two waited until Three was gone and then removed the gag.

"Is he gone?" Jada asked, her breathing coming in fear-choked gasps.

Number Two patted her leg. "He's gone. Are you okay?"

Jada cried. "Oh God, I thought he was going to…" She cried more. "I want to go home."

"Don't worry. I won't let anything happen." Number Two started to put the gag back in.

Jada panicked. "Don't leave me. Please? He'll come back. God, please don't."

Two paused, looking around the room. "Here's what I'm going to do. You're going to sleep in my room, and I'll sleep out here."

"Can't you stay in the room with me?"

"I like to sleep alone."

"What if he comes in there? He might…"

"He wouldn't *dare*." She moved Jada, secured her to the bed then took her place in the center room. Number Two put the gun under her pillow, resting her hand next to it. If Number Three tried anything tonight, he'd have a little surprise waiting.

CHAPTER 26

MONEY AND KIDS

Alexa came in from the family room, where she'd been watching television. "I'm going to get a burger. Anybody want anything?"

I didn't like her going, but there wasn't much I could do about it. I doubted the kidnappers were watching the house now. "Not for me," I said.

"Where are you going?" Delgado asked.

"Probably Whataburger."

"I'll take a taquito," Delgado said. "Sausage, egg, cheese and potatoes."

Connors ordered the same. I pulled out a twenty. "Alexa, I changed my mind. Get me the same thing, please."

"Mr. Hackett, Mrs. Hackett, do you want anything to eat?"

"No, but thanks for asking."

"Be back soon," she said.

She returned in about forty-five minutes, setting the food on the kitchen counter. As I helped her unpack it, I noticed the look in her eyes—the zombie stare Ron used to get—and the slurred speech. She'd been gone less than an hour and had gotten *fixed* again. I got away from her quickly, gritting my teeth while I debated whether to tell Winthrop. I didn't want another confrontation, and this wasn't really the time or place to bring it up, but...then I thought about Ron and how I wished someone would have told me about his drug use. Maybe I could have stopped something. Probably not, but maybe.

Delgado must have noticed my focus; he pulled me to the side. "We're not here to bust kids for drugs."

I wanted to ream him out but…he was right. We were here because a girl was kidnapped. Part of me wanted to argue that saving one girl from drugs was just as important as saving another from kidnappers, but that didn't seem right. "Okay, you win."

"It's not about winning. It's what's right."

Alexa handed a taquito to Delgado and one to Connors. "If you're looking for Jason, he was at Whataburger. A bunch of them are hanging out there."

Delgado grabbed a water and tapped Connors on the shoulder. "Let's go, rookie. We got a dude to talk to."

"Go get 'em, Ribs." I grabbed a bottled water from the fridge and took my taquito out to sit on the patio. It was nice out, one of those beautiful pre-summer nights in Houston, before it got so hot you poured sweat at midnight. I tilted my head, staring at a clear sky and pondering my life. For a long time, mine had been the best life a man could want—great son, magnificent wife—then everything went to shit. Mary suffered through years of cancer, and Ron suffered because I didn't know how to deal with it all. Trying to care for Mary and leave enough time for the job and Ron didn't work. He turned to drugs.

"Relaxing, Detective?"

I turned to see Scott approaching, a drink in his hand. "Trying to."

He sat next to me. Both of us were silent for a few minutes. "What happens to the money if you don't catch the kidnappers?"

"We don't have any money."

"But suppose you *did* have the money. And you paid the ransom."

I looked at him. "And we didn't catch them, you mean?"

He nodded.

"Then they get away with it."

I watched Scott go through a process of mulling something over. "I'd be lying if I said I understand. I don't. I can't comprehend losing seven million dollars."

"It's not the money, so much…"

I waited.

"See, I don't really have the money. I arranged a loan with the bank based on the money I'd earn from my company going public."

"And?"

He paused again. "Nothing is ever guaranteed in life. Even this close to an IPO, something could go wrong. If I were to lose this money then *not* get my stock…"

"I understand, sir. No need to say more."

"Don't say anything to the Hacketts, I…"

"I wouldn't do that."

We sat in silence again, him sipping his drink and me staring at the stars. I got the feeling he wanted to talk, but then Lonny popped his head out the door. "Mr. Winthrop, your phone is ringing. Caller ID says it's from a Jennifer…"

He waved. "Thanks. I'll call her back in a minute." I waited for him to face me again. "One thing, Detective. I can't…I don't know how to say this. I can't risk the money. It's—"

"No need to say more, Mr. Winthrop. I don't know anyone who would."

***

SCOTT STAYED OUTSIDE, NEEDING time to think. He had been on a roller coaster ride, and it wasn't over yet. Aside from everything going on at work, he had to figure out how to get his personal life in order. It used to be perfect. Now…now was different.

No matter what happened, his life was ruined. How had it gotten so bad? Not only was he messing with clinical data, he was blackmailing Sanjay and his brother. It seemed like only yesterday he had ethics. He'd taken pride in that, thought nothing in the world could budge him. That was yesterday. What might happen tomorrow?

CHAPTER 27

A LONG NIGHT

I was relaxing in a recliner when Delgado walked in. A quick glance at the clock confirmed it was almost one. It felt like five. I covered my mouth while I yawned. "Get anything from the boyfriend?"

Ribs shook his head. "That boy was so messed up he could barely talk. I have Connors sitting on him in case you want us to take him in."

"Did you *get anything* from him?"

Ribs gave me one of his looks. The kind when there is mixed company, so he can't curse. "As I said, he was so messed up we wanted to take him in. And no, I didn't get anything from him."

"Bring Connors back in." From the corner of my eye, I saw Lonny get out of his seat and move toward the door.

"I'm gonna kill that—" He was about to break protocol with a few choice words before Lucia grabbed his arm.

"Jason's parents can worry over him. We got enough to fret over."

"I guess you're right," Lonny said. He looked at Delgado. "Was that boy with Jada today?"

"Not according to Jason, Mr. Hackett." Delgado flipped open his notepad. "He said they were supposed to go shopping for a dress, but she never showed up at school, and she didn't meet him at the mall like they planned."

"So he goes and gets high? Stinking son of a bitch!"

"Lonny!" Lucia said.

He reached over and patted Lucia's hand. "I'm sorry."

Mars spoke up. "Don't worry, Dad. If Jason did anything to Jada, I'll kick the shit out of him."

A glare from Lucia silenced Mars. Any other night, I'd have bet money on him getting an ass whooping for that slip of the tongue. I got up and sat next to Lonny. "Listen, this kid may not be your idea of a prize for a son-in-law, or even your daughter's friend, but as far as we know, he's done nothing wrong—at least, he had nothing to do with her kidnapping. So hate him all you want for his drug use, or his clothes, or the way he combs his hair, but don't blame him for this."

Lucia nodded the whole time, switching her glare between Mars and Lonny. "Listen to the man. He's talking sense. Like I said, we've got more than plenty to worry over with Jada missing."

Lonny nodded, but he sat on the edge of the seat, cracking big bony knuckles, which made the muscles in his forearms twitch. He looked like a man wanting to hit someone. I wouldn't want him pissed at me; his arms were huge. Not musclebound showy arms like a weightlifter. His were pure muscle, the kind you see on a panther or a lion. I thought about talking to him but opted for letting him cool off on his own.

Delgado slid his chair closer to mine. "Anything from Ramirez on the Marshall case?"

"She went back to Memorial and talked to the neighbors. One of them *might* have remembered a van, though his wife insisted it was a plumber's truck. No other leads."

"She needs to interview the Marshalls again. Maybe they'll remember something."

"Call Ramirez in the morning and get her on that," I said.

We talked for a few more minutes, and then Connors came in.

"Nice night out there," he said.

Delgado gave him a funny look. "Nice night? Did you go on a date with that kid?"

Connors shot Ribs the finger then got a bottled water from the fridge before joining us at the table. "Anything new?"

"Nothing, but now that you're here, we can discuss tomorrow's plans."

Connors looked at Delgado then me. "What's tomorrow? They said two days to get the money."

"But they said they'd call back tomorrow."

"Let's listen to the last part of that tape again," Delgado said.

I looked around. Winthrop was absent, and I liked it that way. Didn't want him or the Hacketts around while we discussed strategy. Especially the Hacketts.

Connors grabbed the tape, pressed play, and navigated to the spot. "Okay, here it is, the part at the end where the kidnapper is telling Mr. Winthrop about the ransom."

"Seven million dollars in non-sequential serial numbers, hundred-dollar bills, no tracers on the money, or in the money. We will know if you try to track us. Have it ready in forty-eight hours. We'll call tomorrow with instructions on the transfer."

"Wait! I need to talk to my daughter."

"The next time we call, you can talk to her."

We listened to it twice. "Seven million is a lot of cash," Delgado said. "But…if it's in hundreds, it won't take up that much room."

I thought about some of the deals we'd done in narcotics, where we had a couple hundred grand stuffed into a briefcase and still had plenty of room. "Seven million would fit in a large duffel bag, or a few backpacks. My guess is there will be more than one of them doing the pickup."

Delgado thought for a moment. "How do they plan on getting away unnoticed?"

"It would have to be someplace private," Connors said.

"And they have got to know we'll be tailing them."

Delgado shook his head. "I'll tell you what I think. These guys believe they can outsmart us. They're planning on losing whatever tail we put on them then driving off into the sunset."

"And they said they'd know if we put tracers in the money or tried to track them," Connors said.

I looked around. "Where are the techs?"

"Watching TV," Delgado said. "I'll get them."

They joined us at the table. "Keep your voices down," I said. "We don't need the Hacketts hearing this."

Delgado whispered. "These guys obviously think they can spot tracers or sensors. How would they do that? What kind of equipment would they need?"

"Can you hide a GPS on Scott's car?" I asked. "And inside the money?"

"We can put a tracer in his car, and in the money, but…"

"What?"

"If they have a device to detect them, nothing will hide it."

I looked at Delgado, already shaking his head. "And if they find them, we're fucked."

"Once they see we have no money, we're fucked anyway," I said.

"The only way this works is if we catch the guy at the drop and convince him to take us to the girl."

I looked around again. "And all before they kill her."

"Everything depends on surveillance," Delgado said. "We need every route covered. Put a fucking net around them so tight their dicks will pop."

I looked at Delgado. "Their dicks will pop? Where the hell did you come up with that?"

"Tip."

"Delgado, I'm going to share some advice. Don't use Tip Denton's sayings. They're old. They're not funny. And half the time, they make no sense."

"Still…we're gonna need that surveillance."

I went in to get some water and shot a look to the other room. Lonny was still on the edge of the seat, literally, and he still looked pissed off. And worried.

"You want anything to drink, Delgado?"

"Nah, I'm good."

"Connors?"

"More water, please."

I handed Connors his drink but didn't sit. "Ribs, how about you keep brainstorming? I'm going to have a chat with Lonny."

I sat in the chair next to Lonny. He was clenching and unclenching his fist in rapid motions. He didn't look up.

"What do you do for a living, Lonny?"

He glanced at me, but didn't answer at first then slowly let it out. "Masonry."

"Masonry? A bricklayer, you mean."

"Bricks, blocks, stone, concrete. About anything that has to do with masonry."

I let that sit for a minute. "I don't envy you. That's hard work. Especially in this heat."

He nodded, the kind that said "how the fuck would you know" but without actually saying it. I pegged him for a guy who might say it under different circumstances, but not with Lucia around. No way.

"My grandfather was a stonemason in Philadelphia," I said. "He liked working stone the best."

A spark came to Lonny's eyes. "Me too. Used to be a lot of stonework. Hardly any now. Maybe a patio or the front of a house now and then." He shook his head. "Hardly no work at all nowadays."

"My pop pop—that's what we called him—he wanted me to take up the trade. At times I wanted to, but he soured me on it with too many summers of hard work when I was young. I came home so tired I couldn't go party, even on Saturday night."

Lonny smiled. "That'll do it to you. Carrying all that stone and mortar."

"And dumping over wheelbarrows full of concrete, 'cause your arms are so tired you can't hold them up straight."

Now he laughed outright. "Yessir, I do remember that myself." He stopped cracking his knuckles and leaned back in the chair. He'd lost the edge.

We continued talking about the trade and how it was dying, like so many others. From behind him, Lucia mouthed "thank you" to me and smiled. It was a tired smile, but warm and loving. She reminded me a lot of Mary.

As Lonny and I talked, she got up, picking some trash off the table where Connors had left it. She started to pick up more but then turned to her son. "Mars, get your sorry self over here and throw this trash away. You too, Alexa. No reason for it to be sitting here with a waste can half empty."

I was willing to bet that was the first time anyone spoke to Princess Alexa that way in all of her long seventeen years. Lucia shot a sideways glance to Connors as she headed toward the sink. He blushed. I thought I heard him whisper, "Sorry, ma'am," but it was so low I couldn't be sure. I made a mental note to rinse my coffee cup.

She grabbed the teapot and filled it with water. "I'm making tea if anyone wants some." She walked down the hall and poked her head in the study. "Mr. Winthrop, do you want tea? Or coffee?"

He came out a few seconds later. "I'll have coffee, thanks. And Lucia, please, it's Scott."

"You go on back in there, Mr. Winthrop. I'll bring it to you."

"I'll have coffee," Lonny said.

"I'm making you tea," she said. "You don't need any more coffee tonight."

I watched as she kept herself busy. A fine woman this was. She got a washcloth and brush and started in on the dishes, doing them by hand even though the dishwasher sat empty. I grabbed a towel and moved in beside her.

She never looked up. "No need for a detective to be doing dishes. I got this little job covered."

I took the cup from her, dried it, and put it away, then grabbed the next one. "I was doing dishes long before I was a detective."

She placed some saucers on the counter then dipped them into the sink full of suds.

"Besides," I said, "if my wife were here, she'd argue that piece about no need for a detective to do dishes."

Lucia smiled. "Call her up. Sounds like a person I could get used to."

I stopped, suddenly choked up, but continued doing my duties.

"Well, Detective, get her over here. I could use some female company. Or is that against the rules?"

"My wife passed away a few years ago." I said it quick, holding back emotion.

She stopped, shaking her head. "I'm sorry. I didn't…"

I took a plate from her and dried it, trying to move on. For a few moments we were silent, and then I thought I heard her say something.

"What's that, ma'am?" I realized too late she was praying—with tears in her eyes.

She shot a quick glance toward Lonny then back to me, whispering, "Is my baby girl gonna be all right?"

I set the towel down and looked her in the eye. "Lucia, I'm working this case like it's my own child out there. And there is nothing I wouldn't do for my child. I can promise you that."

She wiped her eyes, leaned over and kissed me on the cheek. "You're a good man, Detective. I'm gonna trust in you and the Lord to bring my girl home safe."

As I continued drying, I said my own prayer.

I sure hope you're listening, God, because I don't have the first damn clue how we're going to get these guys without the ransom. Whatever happens, don't let them hurt that girl.

CHAPTER 28

EARLY MORNING

I went to sleep about two o'clock, opting for a recliner in the family room. Delgado had the sofa across from me, and his snoring woke me every half hour or so. I made a mental note never to share a room with Delgado again. I was a man who needed sleep.

Sometime between dreaming about Salma Hayek and Scott's girlfriend in the thong panties, I found time to pray we could bring Jada home safe. I also cursed myself for suggesting to Scott that he send the girl home, but the curse must have been vocalized, because Delgado woke, and sat up.

"What did you say, Gino?"

I looked over to him. "Did I say anything?" I hoped I did. I didn't want to think that Delgado and I had the kind of connection that would allow him to hear me think.

"I think you said, 'Why the fuck did I do that?'"

"Go back to sleep."

"You said, 'Why the fuck did I do that?' What were you talking about?"

If I continued arguing, I'd wake up for good, so I spilled my guts. "I was cursing myself for telling Scott to send thong-panties home."

Delgado lay back, pulling a cover over him. "I was already asking myself the same damn thing. Ruin my fuckin' night."

I drifted back off and woke to the smell of bacon, one of the most wonderful things in the world. I always thought someone should make an alarm clock like that. No noise, just the smell of bacon released into the room. It would get my ass up every time. I stumbled into the kitchen to see

Lucia cooking. Sitting next to her was a bowl filled with eggs ready to scramble. Cheese eggs, I hoped.

"Smells good," I said.

"It's gonna be a long day," Lucia said. "We all need nutrition to get through it."

I poured water into the coffee machine then checked to be sure no one else was in the room. "Where do you find the strength, Mrs. Hackett?"

She set the spatula on the counter and looked at me. "I don't have any. This is all fake." She gestured with her head toward the other room. "But that man has been through too much. I'm afraid he'll break if he has to worry about me *and* our girl. I figure I can help him that much."

"Coffee?"

"You go ahead. I'll have tea."

When she was almost done cooking the bacon, she walked to the bottom of the stairs. "Mars. Alexa. Time to eat breakfast." On the way back out, she leaned down and kissed Lonny on the head. "Come on, mister. It's a new day. Gonna be a good day too."

I envied Lonny Hackett. He had a wife like I used to have. A strong woman, full of optimism and goodness. And courage. "I've got to step outside and call my captain," I said. "Be right back."

I dialed Coop's cell as I opened the front door.

"Good morning, Gino. Anything new?"

"I want off, Coop."

"What the hell are you talking about?"

"Call the FBI or give it to someone else."

"Once you start paddling downstream, you can't turn around."

"Don't start, Coop. I'm not in the mood for any damn Texas sayings. I want off."

A long pause followed, then, "Gino, you're the one for this job. Didn't you tell me you solved those cases in Philadelphia? Get another one under your belt. Those people are counting on you."

"Maybe that's what I'm afraid of—them counting on me. These are good people, Captain. I can't let them down."

"Then don't, dammit. Find these sons of bitches!"

I hung up feeling worse than when I'd called. I didn't tell Coop the cases I worked in Philly weren't clean. The victims came back alive, but one had been raped and the other beaten so badly she spent four months in the hospital. On the nights I visited her, she mostly cried and told me how she wished she *had* died. The rape victim said the same thing. The worst part about her was that two years later, she was still saying it. I didn't need another memory like those to keep me awake at night.

***

NUMBER TWO WAS UP at five. She donned her mask, got dressed, and then poked her head in the door to check on Jada. She removed the girl's gag then untied her hands. "You need to use the bathroom?"

Jada nodded. She rubbed her wrists where the rope was, then her ankles. Number Two led her to the bathroom.

When she came out, Number Two led her to the bed and sat her down. "I'll get you some food. *Don't* move." She walked to the other room, where she got some day-old bagels, donuts and a bottle of water. "This is all we've got. It should only be one more day, though. Then you'll be home."

Jada's face lit up, but she said nothing.

"I'll bet you're ready, aren't you?"

Jada finished munching a donut. "What if he doesn't pay? What happens then?"

"Try not to worry. It will be all right."

"I'm just asking."

"Don't."

Jada nodded. "Are you staying with me today?"

"I'll be back tonight. Someone else will be here today."

"Not him!" she said, her voice trembling.

"It won't be him. I made sure of that. It's another guy, but he won't give you trouble."

"You sure?"

"I'm sure. Now finish up. I've got to tie you again."

About an hour later, Numbers Four and Five came to relieve Numbers Two and Three. They called when they arrived, so Three and Two could vacate one of the rooms, leaving them a place to enter and put on the masks, one at a time. When each was done, he entered the center room. "Boss said to go straight to the meeting place. He's making the call soon."

Three started to leave, but Two stopped him. "You get everything you brought? Clean everything?"

"I'm not a rookie," he said and walked into the next room. He alerted Driver that he was coming out.

Two took Five aside. "Some things you should know—"

"Boss already filled me in," he said.

"I've got more to add," she said. "The girl is ransom. You got that? She's not to play with, or torture, or hurt in any way. Treat her as if she were worth *seven million dollars*. She *is*."

Five nodded, but Number Two didn't like the way he looked. "I'll leave you with this, Five. If you hurt her, I'll kill you."

"Guess you bitches all stick together, huh?"

"Us *bitches* live for getting even with pricks like you. Remember that as you while away the hours." Four was just entering the room. "Four, I just filled him in. If the girl gets hurt in any way, I'll kill both of you."

He said nothing.

She waited. "*Got it?*"

"I got it."

Number Two walked into the room, ready to call Driver, but thought better of it. She called Boss. "This is Two. Change of plans. I'm bringing her in."

"Why?"

"I don't like what's going on here. The men can't be trusted."

"Tell Five to stay and guard the rooms. And be careful."

"No need to say that."

She got the girl, making her wear a hoodie and keeping the blindfold on. She called Driver to let him know they were coming. When the way was clear, Two took the girl to the van. After putting on her mask, she got into the back with her. Three was already there. Two took her customary seat by the back door, perched on an old speaker covered in carpet. Jada sat beside her. Four came in a moment later.

Three glared at Two as Driver negotiated the roads. "You think you're pretty tough. I'll show you tough if you ever get out from under Boss' wing."

"I don't need Boss."

"Maybe I'll see you on the street someday, and we'll test that out."

Silence.

"You'd like it; I can tell you that. They all like it from me."

Number Two remained silent. She wanted to take out her gun and plug him…but she didn't. The man was just running his mouth. *Like all men.* He didn't know what she looked like and never would. Once this was over, they'd never see each other again. She'd make sure of that.

They drove for about twenty minutes before Driver announced they were pulling into the meeting place. A tapping sound on the ceiling signaled that they'd arrived. They got out and went inside to see Boss.

"How did it go?" Boss asked.

"No problem," Three said.

"He tried fucking with her," Two said. "If I hadn't stopped him, he'd have raped her."

"Bullshit!"

Two glared at him. "Ask the girl."

Boss threw a lightning-quick jab to Three's face, followed it with a kick to his groin and a massive punch to the left kidney. Three doubled-up on the floor, gasping. Blood dripped from his nose. "Disobey orders again, I'll kill you."

Three stayed on the ground for a moment. When he got back up, he glared at Two. She smiled.

"We're making the call shortly," Boss said.

"Why so soon?" This from Four.

"We moved the timetable," Two said. "They should have the money. No reason not to get it today."

Jada moved toward the sound of Boss' voice with her blindfold still on. "I don't want my dad delivering the money."

"Tough."

"Please, don't let him."

"Why not?" Two asked.

"He's got high blood pressure. And a bad heart."

"A lot of people do. He'll live."

"Wait! He's…he's got a really bad temper. I'm afraid he might try something. And then he'll get hurt."

Boss smiled. "Ah, so now we get to the meat of it. So who would you have deliver it?"

"Uncle Eddy. My mother's brother. He lives here."

Boss looked to Number Two, who shrugged. "I don't care who delivers it, as long as they bring the money."

Boss looked to Three. "What do you say?"

Three held a napkin, dabbing his bloody lip and nose. "I don't give a fuck who does it. Let's just get it over with."

Boss turned back to Jada. "We'll see when we call, but if you try anything, all guarantees are off. I'll give you to these perverts. Understand?"

"I understand," Jada said. She shook when she did.

***

FIVE MINUTES HAD PASSED since Lucia had told Lonny to come eat, but he still hadn't gotten up.

"Lonny, get your sorry self out here and eat. I won't have a hungry man growling at me all day."

Maybe it was the pervasive smell of bacon, or maybe the tone of her voice, but one of them brought Lonny to the kitchen. He took a cup of coffee like a starving man grabs food and situated himself at the end of the table between me and Scott.

"What time you think they'll call?" Lonny asked.

"Could be anytime from now until tonight," I said. "They gave us forty-eight hours to get the money. Today is just to keep us on our toes."

"What have you got planned? You *do* have a plan, don't you?"

"Not much we can do until we get the call. After that, we'll get more men for surveillance. Get resources for tracking the money and the bag. Our techs will plant GPS devices in the car."

Scott cleaned his plate and headed to the patio, already on the phone.

"Excuse me, Lonny," I said.

I caught Scott before he went outside. "Remember, Mr. Winthrop, tell no one anything. And don't stray far. They could call at any time." I went back to the table, not wanting to face Lonny again, but I'd try to assuage his fears.

His coffee cup was empty, but he continued to lift it as if he were sipping it. "So we have no money to give them."

"We've got no money, Lonny. That's right."

"Why—"

"It's policy. It has nothing to do with who you are or who Jada is. The police and FBI *never* pay ransom."

"So how you gonna catch them?"

I didn't want to say I didn't know, which I didn't, but I couldn't outright lie to him. "A lot of what we do depends on what instructions they give us. I can tell you this—we'll have enough men to keep them under surveillance no matter what they do. We'll get them." I started to get up, but he grabbed my arm.

"What about my girl? Am I gonna get to talk to her?"

"They said they'd put her on today." I stared at him. "Understand, though, they think she is Scott's daughter. Somehow Jada has kept them believing that, so you can't talk. Not one word."

"I understand." He looked at Lucia, who had joined us at the table. His expression was almost like he didn't want to ask the next question.

"What is it, Lonny?" I asked.

"How will we know if she's all right?"

I didn't quite know how to answer that. "You can tell a lot through the phone. But remember, she's scared. Scared as hell. And she doesn't know what to expect. She'll sound nervous. She'll probably cry. No matter what happens, though, you have to be quiet. Let Scott do the talking. They know his voice."

Lonny fidgeted. I could tell he wasn't convinced, so I did what I didn't want to. I grabbed hold of Lucia and Lonny by the arms and took them to the other room. "I can't say this strong enough. These people are dangerous. If they suspect something is wrong, they may hurt Jada. I know you don't want that. It may be better for both of you to stay out of the room when they call. We'll have it taped. You can listen afterward."

"No way!" Lonny said. "I'm—"

Lucia took him by the hand and sat him down. "What are you gonna do in that room but worry and get angry?" She paused. "And maybe say something that could get our baby killed?"

I left them alone, convinced he was in good hands. A few minutes later, Lucia came out and said he'd stay in the family room when the call came in.

Scott paraded through the kitchen with his briefcase in hand, heading for the garage.

"Where are you going?" I asked.

"They called from work. We've got some issues I need to look after."

I'd thought that after our talk last night, the man had taken a turn for the good. *Wrong.* "Whoa! Mr. Winthrop." I placed a hand on his shoulder and not so gently steered him into the dining room. "Sir, we need you here in case they call."

"I've got my cell phone. If they call, get hold of my secretary, and she'll patch it through. I've—"

I looked around, made sure no one was near then whispered, "Are you a *fucking* moron? This girl is fighting for her life."

He leaned in close and whispered back, "Detective, I have a job to do. I don't know if you understand this, but I'm taking this company public. That requires a lot of preparation."

I wanted to hit him; instead, I grabbed the keys from his hand. "You're going *nowhere!*" I felt certain this would earn me a suspension, but I didn't give a fuck.

He raised himself up, aggressive. "Detective, give me those keys."

Just then the home phone rang. The tech called from the other room. "Got an unknown caller here."

"That's them!" I grabbed hold of Winthrop and dragged him toward the kitchen. "Get ready. And *don't* fuck this up."

"That's them!" I grabbed hold of Winthrop and dragged him toward the kitchen. "Get ready. And *don't* fuck this up."

CHAPTER 29

ANSWER THE PHONE

On the third ring, Lonny moved toward the kitchen. Lucia intercepted him and took him back to the living room. The tech signaled that he was ready. I instructed Scott to pick up on ring number four. The script we rehearsed lay on the table in front of him.

"Hello."

"Is the money ready, Mr. Winthrop?"

Winthrop looked at me, panicked. I shook my head and pointed to the 48 marked on our sheet.

"You said forty-eight hours."

"But I *know* you have it. Let's do the transaction today. I'm sure you want your little girl back. I *know* she wants to go home."

Scott looked to me for an answer. I scribbled on the pad: 3:00 PM.

"I can probably get it by three."

I pointed to a part of the script we'd rehearsed.

He nodded. "Is my daughter there? I want to speak with her."

Silence.

I pointed to another line of the script.

"I won't do anything unless I know she's all right."

"You've got thirty seconds," the man said. "Clear?"

Scott was being too casual, too businesslike. I jotted some notes down in big letters. *Where's the* emotion? *Earn your OSCAR!*

Jada came on the line. "Daddy! Daddy, is that you?"

I thought Scott was choking up, but he came through. "Jada! Oh God, baby, are you all right? Did they hurt you?"

"Daddy, listen. I don't have much time. I don't want you to deliver the money. Not with your blood pressure and heart. Send Uncle Eddy. You know how calm he is. Even my friends say that about Uncle Eddy."

Scott looked to me with a what-the-fuck-do-I-do-now look. I think I wore one too. I made a quick decision, not knowing whether the kidnappers would approve. If they were smart, they'd know a father would object. I pointed to the paper and wrote *No! I'm doing it.*

Scott nodded. "No way! I'm doing this myself."

"Dad, you're not well enough. Send Uncle Eddy, *please.*"

I nodded.

Scott took a deep breath then said, "Okay. I'll get Eddy to do it…but you stay safe, baby. And don't worry. You'll be home soon."

"It's me again." The kidnapper.

I wrote, *Threaten him.*

"If you hurt her, I swear—"

"Yes, I know. It is natural to worry, but there is no need if you do your job."

"What do you want me to do?"

"Good. A much better attitude. And don't worry—she'll be home soon. Listen carefully. We don't have much time. Get the money. Put it in a duffel bag. You can purchase one at Academy or Walmart if you don't have one. When it's ready, drive to the Denny's restaurant on Research Forest Boulevard. Be there at three o'clock. Park near the back on that same side. Go in and enjoy some coffee and breakfast. I suggest the Grand Slam or the blueberry pancakes with a side of sausage. In any case, do not come out before half an hour is up. That is important. Are we clear?"

"What else?"

"Let's keep it simple. We'll call once you are inside, so make sure your cell phone is with you. And the money, of course. Don't forget that."

I hurriedly wrote. *I don't know if the bank can get it ready.*

Scott nodded. "I haven't checked with the bank. I don't know—"

"They have it ready. Don't mess up."

"Three o'clock?"

"Yes. And tell the police not to try anything. We *will* know." The line went dead.

Scott set the phone down then sat at the table. He was shaking. "Did I do all right? I…"

I patted his back. "You did great."

Lonny ran into the kitchen. "Is it over? Is she all right?"

I led Lonny back to the family room. Lucia looked about to break. "She sounded good, Lonny. Scared, but good."

"Let me hear it."

"Hold on a minute. I've got to call my captain—"

"I want to hear the damn tape."

"Lonny! Time is critical. They want the drop today. I need to get things ready." I made sure he was looking at me, and paying attention. "Sit with Lucia. I'll play the tape when I'm done."

I left the room and called Coop on her cell.

"Cooper."

"Coop, it's me. They want the drop today."

"What!"

"Yeah. Three o'clock."

"What do you need?"

"Seven million dollars, to start with. Assuming you can't do that, lots of surveillance help. Whatever the tech guys need for tracking. I want GPS in the bag, on the car, on Winthrop, everywhere. I need communications so I stay in touch with everybody." I thought for a moment. "I'll send you the tape for analysis. Get that psychologist on it. I think his names's Morris. He might come up with something."

"Can you email it?"

"Hang on." I looked around for Winthrop. "Scott, can we email that tape?"

"Yes, it's digital."

"Okay, Coop, I'll email it to you. Get it to Morris as soon as you can. And make him realize it's imperative that we get an analysis *quickly*."

"Anything else?" Coop asked.

"There's bound to be more. I'll call as I think of it."

"I'll get moving."

"Make it quick, Coop." I was about to hang up when I realized I'd screwed up already. Winthrop wasn't delivering the goods, and we had a genuine okay from the kidnappers to let Uncle Eddy do it. "One more thing. I need someone to stand in for Winthrop."

"I already told you that Renkin is too tall, not to mention too black."

"We couldn't use Renkin anyway. They might recognize him from the news. Get anybody who can handle undercover, as long as they're black."

"I'll call you," Coop said.

When I turned around, Scott Winthrop was staring at me. "I see. We all look alike, huh?"

"Not at all. I'd never mistake Halle Berry for Aretha Franklin."

Winthrop started to walk away, pissed off. I grabbed him. "Hey, I hope you know I'm just shitting about all that. And by the way, thanks for what you did. That *was* an Oscar performance."

"I've got to get ready for work. Call me if you need anything."

I signaled Delgado to join us at the table then called Lonny into the kitchen. "Are you ready to listen?"

He and Lucia clung to each other. Lucia called Mars to join them. He stood behind them, his arms on their shoulders. When Delgado and Connors got there, I played the tape, starting at the beginning.

"Hello."

"Is the money ready, Mr. Winthrop?"

"You said forty-eight hours when you called yesterday."

"But I know you have it. Let's do the transaction today. I'm sure you want your little girl back. I know she wants to go home."

I paused the tape. "This is not the same man who called yesterday. See how nothing bothers this guy? No matter what Scott threw at him, he remained calm." I hit play again.

"I can probably get it by three. Is my daughter there? I want to speak with her. I won't do anything unless I know she's all right."

"You've got thirty seconds. Clear?"

"Oh my God," Lonny said.

"Daddy! Daddy, is that you?"
"Jada! Oh God, baby, are you all right? Did they hurt you?"
"Daddy, listen. I don't have much time. I don't want you coming yourself with the money. Not with your blood pressure and heart. Send Uncle Eddy. You know how calm he is. Even my friends say that about Uncle Eddy."

Lucia was holding on to Lonny's arm and squeezing, her head buried in his shoulders. Mars stood behind them, his arms wrapped around his parents. I thought I saw tears in his eyes.

"No way! I'm doing this myself."
"Dad, you're not well enough. Send Uncle Eddy, please."
"Okay. I'll get Eddy to do it…but you stay safe, baby. And don't worry. You'll be home soon."
"It's me again."
"If you hurt her, I swear—"
"Yes, I know. It is natural to worry, but there is no need if you do your job."
"What do you want me to do?"
"Good. A much better attitude. And don't worry—she'll be home soon. Listen carefully. We don't have much time. Get the money. Put it in a duffel bag. You can purchase one at Academy or Walmart if you don't have one. When it's ready, drive to the Denny's restaurant on Research Forest Boulevard. Be there at three o'clock. Park near the back on that same side. Go in and enjoy some coffee and breakfast. I suggest the Grand Slam or the blueberry pancakes with a side of sausage. In any case, do not come out before half an hour is up. That is important. Are we clear?"
"What else?"
"Let's keep it simple. We'll call once you are inside, so make sure your cell phone is with you. And the money, of course. Don't forget that."
"I haven't checked with the bank. I don't know—"

"They'll have it ready. Don't mess up."

"Three o'clock?"

"Yes. And please tell the police not to try anything. We will know."

I turned off the machine and looked over at the Hacketts. They were a mess. I had planned on asking them questions but figured that could wait a few minutes. "You want anything? Tea or coffee?"

Lonny looked ready to fall down. Mars helped him to a chair in the family room. Lucia sat beside him on the floor. "She's gonna be all right, Lonny. She'll be all right." She repeated it over and over, as if it were a mantra.

Delgado pulled me aside. "What's the plan, Gino? We don't have much time."

I motioned for him and Connors to join me outside. "We need to set up surveillance, and it has to be tight."

Connors looked at me and Delgado. "How are we going to do this without the ransom?"

"It won't be easy. In fact, we're fucked unless we catch them. But we don't want to panic the Hacketts, so when we go back inside, watch what you say."

"Who's Coop sending us?" Delgado asked.

"She said she'd get back to me. I told her to get someone to do the drop too. Worked out good with that Uncle Eddy thing."

"We need to find out about that," Delgado said.

"No time like the present." I opened the door and started back in, Connors and Delgado trailing me. "Scott, do you have a map of the area?"

"He's upstairs," Delgado said. "I'll ask."

Delgado called up. "Mr. Winthrop, do you have a map of this area? A good one?"

"In the study, top drawer of my desk."

Delgado returned a few minutes later with a big fold-out map of North Houston. I quickly pinpointed his address, and we dropped a pin there. Delgado put another one at Denny's.

"We'll need people on I-45, north and south," Delgado said. "And on #242, Research Forest, Woodlands Parkway, Gosling…all the major crossroads they might use to get out of here."

I pointed to the freeway and to #242. "Double teams at each of these spots. We need people in front and behind so they're not spotted."

My phone rang, and I grabbed it. It was Coop. "I got ten uniforms coming your way, Gino. Most of them have good surveillance experience."

"Thanks, Coop. What about somebody for Winthrop?"

"What do you think of Doran?"

"From Narcotics?"

"That's him."

"Perfect. He's done undercover, so he won't crack."

"Glad you think so, 'cause he's on his way."

"Okay, Coop. Gotta go." I hung up and went to the table.

Connors said, "I expected more details of the drop."

Delgado shook his head. "They won't stay on the phone long, and more importantly, they don't want to give us time to plan a defense."

"Smart fuckers, aren't they?" Connors got embarrassed as soon as the word slipped his mouth. He turned to Lucia, just in from the family room. "Sorry, ma'am."

"Detective, that is the *least* of my worries."

Connors blushed. "Of course, ma'am."

Lucia wandered around like a lost child. "Mrs. Hackett," I said, "Would you mind getting me some coffee?"

She brightened. "Of course. Anyone else want any?"

I kicked Delgado's leg. "I'll take some, if you don't mind," he said. Connors chimed in with his request as well.

I leaned in close. "What time is it, Delgado?"

He looked at his watch. "Quarter to nine."

"That gives us six hours until the meet. We need to get our asses busy."

Connors leaned in closer. "Do you think they'll hurt her?"

"Shut up, Connors."

His words brought images of Philadelphia to mind; I didn't need that in my head. Not now. Not ever.

CHAPTER 30

ANALYZE THE CALL

Lonny walked into the kitchen as if he were a zombie. "Detective, about that call."

My phone rang. "Hold on. I'll get with you as soon as I'm done with this." I answered the phone. "Cataldi."

"Detective, this is Dr. Morris."

"Did you listen to the tape?"

"Yes, numerous times. Have you got a moment to go over it?"

I got out my notepad and pen then set the phone on the table. "Ready. And I'm putting you on speaker."

"First let's look at the noise, or perhaps I should say the lack of noise. When I amplified the recording I found no noise in the background. No refrigerator humming or computer whirring or air conditioner running. No clocks chiming or ticking. No outside traffic. No peripheral sounds at all. We could have hit a lull in such sounds, or they could have made it artificially quiet, but I don't think so. Wherever they are is a quiet place."

"How does that help?" I asked.

"Right now, I suppose it doesn't. But if we get closer, that fact could eliminate possible leads."

"What else?"

"The man had a definite Texas accent. From what I could make out, East Texas. He's not a transplant. And he's intelligent, or, at least, has a decent command of grammar. Not uneducated."

So far Morris hadn't given me anything. "Keep going."

"The kidnapper is confident. I sensed no intimidation when Mr. Winthrop threatened him. He made no retaliatory remarks in defense, simply offered a confident response. Also, he didn't argue when the girl suggested a switch in plans. This is a man who can adapt to change. That makes him dangerous."

"Where did you get all this shit from, Doctor?"

"Let's go through the call. I have the recording hooked to the phone."

"Is the money ready, Mr. Winthrop?"

"Notice here that he called him *Mr. Winthrop.* A sign of respect. He didn't try to demean Winthrop. That shows confidence."

"You said forty-eight hours when you called yesterday."

"But I know *you have it. Let's do the transaction today. I'm sure you want your little girl back. I* know *she wants to go home."*

"Notice here he says, 'But I *know* you have it,' and 'I'm sure you want your little girl back.' This is a man who understands emotions and what Mr. Winthrop is going through. He cut right to the chase—he wants his girl back, and she wants to come home. What father isn't going to cave at that point?

"I'm skipping through the part where Jada asks for her uncle to deliver the money." The tape stopped. "Okay, here is where it gets interesting again. Scott threatened the kidnapper. He said, 'If you hurt her, I swear.' That is a normal response from a parent, but the response from the kidnapper is abnormal. He attempts to soothe Scott, being understanding about his threat then assuring him there is no need to worry."

After a slight pause, Morris continued. "When Scott asks what he wants him to do, he *rewards* Scott with a 'Good, much better attitude.' Then the kidnapper once again assures Scott that his daughter will be home soon. What happens after that is classic: he puts the pressure on. 'We don't have much time,' followed by the instructions. He even gives Scott the options of using Walmart or Academy. You would be hard pressed to find a more reasonable man, even to the point of telling him to enjoy a breakfast meal at Denny's, and providing suggestions for what to order. He then closes by asking Scott to 'please' tell the police not to try anything."

"Sounds like a lot of shit, if you ask me," I said.

"Don't be so sure, Detective. As I said, this is an intelligent and dangerous man. He's a man in control."

"So with this analysis, what do you suggest?"

"I have no suggestion, but I *will* warn you. If you think you have this man figured out, be careful. He will fool you. He will do the unexpected."

"Thanks, Morris. I appreciate it."

"Good luck."

I hung up and looked at Lonny. "What's up? You mentioned the call."

He seemed confused. "She said something about Uncle Eddy delivering the money."

"I know. Don't worry. That's a good thing. We're going to have an undercover guy do it."

Lonny shook his head. "You don't understand. She doesn't have an Uncle Eddy."

He had my attention. "How about anybody she calls Uncle Eddy?"

Lucia had come to stand beside Lonny, her hand on his shoulder. She shook her head.

"And there's nobody you know named Eddy?"

"We had a neighbor named Eddy a few years ago, but he moved."

"Anything odd about him, fishy?"

"No, he was a cop."

I looked at Delgado, who seemed to be thinking the same thing I was. "Do you think she's telling us one of them is a cop?"

"Could be," Delgado said. "Might be."

"How would she know that?" Lonny asked.

"I don't know," I said.

Then Connors added, "All of this makes me wonder how they got Jada instead of Mr. Winthrop's daughter."

"If they were watching this house, it could have been an easy mistake," Lucia said. "Jada spends the night here a lot. In fact, last week she told me that Mr. Winthrop drove her to school. Yesterday, she and Alexa walked, but, as you know, Alexa detoured with her boyfriend."

I pondered this for a moment. "So if they happened to be watching the house and saw Scott take Jada to school…it would have been an easy assumption that she was his daughter."

As I thought it over, Scott came down the steps. "I've got to get to work. They—"

"Go ahead. We're good for now." He started to leave, and I went to him. "You did good this morning. Don't worry. She'll be all right."

"Call me if you need something. I'll have my cell phone."

I asked Connors and Delgado to come to the table then suggested to Lonny and Lucia that they keep busy, maybe get Alexa to drive them home so they could change and get their car. I also asked for recent pictures of Jada. I mostly wanted them out of the house so we could make plans for the drop.

"I thought we were going to figure out that shit about Uncle Eddy," Delgado said.

"We will," I said. "But while they're gone, I want to go over some details. The last thing we need is the Hacketts hovering while we discuss options that may not be pleasant."

"Let's do it," Delgado said.

***

LONNY SAT IN THE back seat with Lucia while Alexa drove them home. He held Lucia's hand, her head resting on his shoulder. The whole, time he thought about the phone call. It was Boss; he knew it. The voice, the way he spoke, and the way he said "clear." That was the clincher. It was Boss.

If only I hadn't gotten involved with them.

Would it have made a difference? Had they really made a mistake, or did they somehow know Jada was his daughter, and this was payback? No, he was getting paranoid. It wouldn't make sense to take his daughter. He had no money. And if Lonny knew anything, it was that those redneck crackers were in it for the money. They didn't give two shits about anything *but* money.

He almost told the detective about the whole operation when he heard the voice, thought maybe he had given himself away from the way Gino looked at him. But nothing came of it. Now he wondered whether to turn himself in. What good would it do? How would it help Jada? He didn't know *shit* about these people. Not where they met, not their names. Didn't even know what they looked like.

He should have turned them in from the beginning. They'd be in jail now, and Jada would be safe. But he'd be in jail too.

And Lucia and the kids would have no house. And no food. But Jada would be safe.

It all kept coming back to that. If he had only turned himself in when they hurt that boy, none of this would have happened. *Assuming they caught them.*

This thinking brought to mind the Marshall boy and how Number Three had beaten him. What was he doing to Jada? Lonny fought tears.

God, please don't let him hurt my girl.

CHAPTER 31

SURVEILLANCE

Delgado spread the map across the table. We had already pinned Scott's house and the Denny's restaurant. "We've got ten cars coming from Coop," I said. "We need to figure out what makes sense as far as placing them."

Delgado tapped his finger on the map. "Definitely the Parkway and Gosling. And #242."

"We should have two in each direction on I-45," Connors said. "One in front and one behind, so they can switch."

"Will we have GPS in all the cars?" Delgado asked.

"Coop will have it coordinated downtown. They'll know where we are in relation to Doran at all times. And we'll have GPS devices on him, the phone, the car, everything. We'll be monitored on a grid, like air traffic control."

"Why do you think they picked Denny's? It's right next to the Shenandoah Police Station."

"Maybe to taunt us. Who knows?"

"We could put a survey team on the road," Connors said.

Delgado shook his head. "They'd spot that in a heartbeat. We need someone at the hotel next door. Get a room with a view of Denny's. At least we can see *some* of what goes on there."

"And if everything works, we'll hear it through Doran's second phone."

"You think they'll show?" Connors asked.

"No way are they showing at Denny's," Delgado said. "That's just the first stop. My gut tells me this will be a long chase."

Connors fidgeted with a pen. "When do we take them?"

"As soon as they realize Doran doesn't have the money," I said.

"And we need to take them *alive*," Delgado said, directing the last comment at me.

We were still discussing plans when the Hacketts returned. Lonny came straight to the table and handed me two pictures of Jada. "These are a few months old."

"She's beautiful."

"Yes, she is. Thank you." He stared at the map for a moment. "Anything new?"

"We're making plans for the drop."

"What drop? We've got nothing *to* drop."

"They don't know that."

He started to walk away but came back. "What are they going to do when they find out?"

"We hope to be there so nothing happens to the girl," Connors said.

Lonny bristled. "The *girl's* name is Jada. And she's my daughter."

I closed my eyes and cursed. We weren't used to working around victims. We worked with drug addicts, dealers, and homicide victims. None of them complained about lack of sensitivity. "He didn't mean anything by that. It's how we deal with things."

Lonny nodded. "So how *are* you going to see she's safe? What happens when they don't get the money?"

I sighed. He wasn't going to like it no matter what I told him. "All we can do is buy time and hope they make a mistake. If we can grab one of them, make him talk—"

"*Hope* they make a mistake! These people don't make mistakes." He closed his eyes and raised his head back. "Have they made any mistakes yet? Do you think they'll turn sloppy when it counts most?" Lonny stormed out of the kitchen, brushing past Lucia on his way to the patio.

She looked at me. "He's upset, Detective."

"I understand."

Delgado was staring at me. "He's right, you know. These people *don't* make mistakes."

"They will," I said. "They *have* to."

The door opened, and four of the new surveillance guys came in.

"Techs are right behind us with new equipment," one of them said. "We got half a dozen more cars on the way up."

Quick introductions were made. I got one of the men to run a picture of Jada to Kinko's to get copies. The others joined us at the table.

***

LONNY WALKED SLOWLY AROUND the patio. He wanted to run, hide, hit something, all of those things; instead, he walked. And he worried. What the hell was he going to do? That detective didn't understand who he was dealing with.

Mistakes? That detective is hoping they make mistakes? Lonny knew better.

He sat in a chair by the fountain, struggling to keep his mind focused. Images of Jada squealing when he told her she could get the prom dress popped into his head. Of her laughing with Mars last Christmas. She was a happy girl, always happy. Now Lonny had put her in this terrible situation. Who knows what would happen to her, or if she'd even come out alive. He *had* to do something.

He should turn himself in, tell Gino he *knew* who had Jada. To what end? How could it help Gino find them? Lonny kicked at a loose piece of cement on the flagstone patio. He'd already been through this line of reasoning half an hour ago and came up with the same conclusion.

He wouldn't sit around this house and do nothing. If somebody was going to save his girl, it had to be him. And he knew just how to do it. He'd find Willard, the slimy bastard who put him in touch with Boss to begin with. And once he found him, Lonny would make him talk. If there was one thing he was sure of, that was it: he'd *make* him talk. Lonny picked up his pace as he went inside, heading for the front door.

"Lonny, where are you going?" It was Gino calling.

"Out."

***

I WATCHED HIM LEAVE then shot a glance to Lucia, who hurried to catch him. "Where's he going?" I asked.

"I don't know," she said, and ran for the door, worry etched on her face.

I turned to Connors. "Tail him. I want to know where the fuck he's going."

Connors grabbed one of the new guys and headed out.

"What the hell is that all about?" Delgado asked.

I stared at the door. "I'm wondering the same thing, Ribs."

CHAPTER 32

ONE LAST CHANCE

Jada listened close to see if she could hear where the kidnapper was in the room. They only had one guy with her this time, the one they called Number Five. So far he didn't seem bad. She waited until he went to the other room then rubbed her head against the bed, trying to nudge the blindfold up enough to see. She got it to the point where she could make out a hint of light. The door opened.

She stopped, straightened, and kept still. She heard him walking toward her.

"Won't be long now. Things are happening fast."

Jada didn't know what that meant, but there was no way in hell that her daddy had seven million dollars to give them. Alexa's father wouldn't foot the bill either. She had to do something, and if she'd ever have a chance, it was now, with just him to guard her. She remembered a glass in the bathroom. And a lamp on the table next to her.

She signaled that she had to go to the bathroom. When he spoke, he startled her. She hadn't realized he was that close.

"Got a weak bladder?"

She grunted.

Number Five removed the gag.

"I need to go pretty bad," Jada said, using her most pleading voice.

He untied her feet but left her hands tied. She stood, stretching. "I need my hands free."

"You can go without them."

"I have to…" Jada lowered her head. "Wipe myself." She felt him untying her. "Don't be stupid and try anything."

"I won't."

She felt her way toward the bathroom, feigning a stumble. "Can you help me get there? Please?"

Number Five grabbed her arm, squeezing too hard, and tugged her forward. She almost fell for real this time but managed to keep count of the steps. Five small steps. Once she reached the door, she felt it with her hands and started to close it. "Thanks. I can manage from here."

"Don't lock it," he said.

She closed the door, put her ear to it and listened. The sound of his footsteps faded; he had moved away. Her stomach churned, and her hands shook. She felt for the sink, and carefully searched, finally finding the glass. If she could hit him hard enough to disorient him—even for a moment— she could get the lamp from the table and hit him with that.

Give me strength, Lord.

Jada did her business, gathered her nerves, and pulled her pants up. She only zipped part way and then stuffed the glass in the back of her pants. After taking a big breath, she reached for the door. "I'm ready. Can you help me?"

Number Five grabbed her left arm and moved her toward the bed. Bile rose in her throat, which felt like it was closing. On the fourth step, she reached behind her and grabbed the glass. Estimating where his head was, she swung as hard as she could.

The glass didn't shatter like she hoped, but she caught him on the side of his head. She knew because she felt his ear. Number Five fell sideways.

"You fucking bitch!"

She pushed him, groping for the lamp. She grabbed it with one hand. He still had hold of her other arm. Jada yanked hard to tear out the cord then swung the lamp. She kicked him, hard, and ran, reaching for her blindfold.

Number Five grabbed her leg and yanked it, bringing her down. She screamed, kicked harder, and scrambled to get away, pushing backwards on the floor with her hands while thrashing at him with her feet. She *had* to get away. If he caught her now…

A pillow went over her face, his weight smothering her. Jada kicked and punched, but couldn't budge him. She arched her back, fighting for air. He punched her in the side. Then the pillow was gone. Jada tried getting up. A fist slammed her face, splitting her lip.

She cried. Number Five punched her again, hitting her nose and eyes. "Stop! Please stop."

"You bitch! You whore bitch." He yanked her up and threw her to the bed, face down. Jada didn't move. Number Five put the gag back on. He grabbed hold of her shirt and began undoing it.

She made a feeble attempt to resist. Her bra came next. Then her pants. Her body convulsed. He was going to rape her. She jammed her foot into his gut and pushed with everything she had, fear providing strength. Her effort moved him back, but only a bit. He came back harder.

"You're gonna get what you deserve now, bitch." He ripped her panties off, grabbed her ankles, and dragged her into position.

Jada used all of her strength to fight him, but she had nothing left. She didn't even have the strength to cry. When she felt certain he was going to rape her, he stopped. She waited, silent. Nothing happened for a moment. She could hear him panting, out of breath.

"You're safe for now, bitch. But when this is over…you're mine. I'm going to do things to you that you can't imagine."

Jada inched her way toward the top of the bed. He tied her hands again, and her feet, and left her naked.

"Let's see how you like that. At least the view's a little better."

She fought tears as she lay there, wishing she had never tried to escape. And when she thought things couldn't get any worse, Number Five's next words sent shivers down her body.

"If you think this is bad, just remember, Number Three will be back tonight."

CHAPTER 33

REPLAY THE TAPE

Lucia came back a moment later, tears in her eyes.

"Where did Lonny go?" I asked.

She shook her head. "I don't know. He's very upset."

"What did he say?"

"That he had to get out for a while." She headed for the family room and lay on the sofa, her head buried in the pillow, bawling.

I didn't know whether to go to her or leave. My heart ached for this woman. As the crying grew worse, I risked going to her. I knelt on the floor and stroked her hair. "It's going to be all right, Mrs. Hackett. I won't let anything happen to her." I hated saying that, but I didn't know what else to do. I couldn't stand to see a woman suffer like this.

She shook her head and cried harder. "Things *won't* be all right. They'll *never* be right again."

I fought my own tears. And I fought the urge to grab her and hug her. Assure her that I'd take care of things. Instead, I did what I thought would help the most—bring it back to Lonny. "Why did Lonny leave?"

The heavy tears turned to sobs, then sniffles. She sat up and wiped her eyes on her sleeves. Her voice was shaky, not like the Lucia I had come to know so well in just one day.

"Things have been rough for him. He's been struggling to find enough work to feed us." She shook her head, fighting more tears. "And now this."

She rested her head on my shoulder. I didn't resist. I didn't know if it helped me or her more, but in the end, I think it helped us both. After a moment, I leaned back, stared into her eyes, and did what I always told rookies not to do—I made a promise. "We'll get her back, ma'am. I promise."

She nodded. "Thank you, Gino."

I left Lucia and went to the kitchen. "What time is it, Delgado?"

"Ask me one more time, and I'll kick your ass."

"I'll keep asking until we find Mary's watch. So what time is it?"

"Eleven."

I looked around, did a quick count. Almost everybody was here. The few who weren't could catch up on details later. "Four hours until the drop," I announced. "I want everyone's head in this. Be thinking at all times—what could we do to help this girl? If you have ideas, bring them up. Nobody's going to make fun of you, so don't be afraid to look stupid."

Delgado grabbed a bottled water then came back with the digital recorder. "We've got the last call here. You can listen to it all you want afterward, but right now, I want you to hear one part that's bothering us. What you'll hear is the kidnap victim speaking." He hit play. We already had it set to the part with Jada speaking.

"Daddy, listen. I don't have much time. I don't want you coming yourself with the money. Not with your blood pressure and heart. Send Uncle Eddy. You know how calm he is. Even my friends say that about Uncle Eddy."

"What's bothering you about it?" one of the new guys asked.

"First off, as you all know, this girl is *not* Mr. Winthrop's daughter. But she obviously understands the situation and has somehow managed to convince them she is."

"So she's smart."

I nodded to whoever said it. "No question there. But here's the kicker—there *is no* Uncle Eddy." I looked at my notes. "And her father doesn't have blood pressure or heart problems. The man is a picture of health. Winthrop has none of these problems either."

"Does the family know anybody named Eddy?" that from Sameena, one of the better surveillance experts.

"A former neighbor was named Eddy. He was a cop."

That drew strange looks from a few of them. "You think one of them is a cop?" Sameena asked.

"We're considering it," Delgado said. "But we can't figure out how she'd know that." He looked around, probably to make sure Lucia wasn't in hearing distance. "I can't see a cop giving himself away unless they planned to kill her."

"Why mention her friends?" Delgado said. "She says 'even my friends say that about Uncle Eddy.'" He looked around. "It doesn't fit. Why would she mention either her friends or Uncle Eddy? She wouldn't. This kid is scared shitless, probably wondering if she's going to get killed, or…" He looked around, then whispered, "Or raped. And she brings up what her friends thought about a mysterious Uncle Eddy, who may or may not exist."

Delgado's words struck me hard. It had only been a few hours since the call, so I hadn't had time to digest it. "Delgado is right. Even if she's sending us a signal with Uncle Eddy, why bring her friends into it? Something's wrong."

Delgado looked to the other room. "Only one way to find out."

"Ask her friends," I said, and walked to the bottom of the steps. "Alexa!"

"What?"

"We need you down here."

"Couple of minutes."

"Now!"

***

LONNY HACKETT DROVE HIS old Chevy truck across the freeway and into an old subdivision. Despite the sense of urgency, he drove slow, careful not to attract the attention of the cops hiding on the side of the road, waiting to give someone a ticket. Most tickets were for going a couple of miles over the limit or for not coming to a standstill at a stop sign. You couldn't just stop at the sign; you had to almost put your car in park then shift gears to get going again. Meanwhile, a store was getting robbed somewhere nearby, or a person mugged. Or a house broken into.

Or a girl kidnapped.

He looked at his watch again, resisted the urge to go faster. About two miles later, he pulled into the corner store where he had gotten the phone to arrange that first meet with Boss. The guy inside *must* know something. Lonny parked by the dumpster and walked inside. He got in line behind two customers. The clerk was the same one as the day he got the phone. The same day he called Willard looking for work. He didn't know if it was Willard who had hooked him up. The man had never said he was, and had even denied it. But if he wasn't, how had that person known to call Lonny? And where did he get his number?

It was Willard. I know it.

The first customer left with a newspaper and cigarettes. The guy in front of Lonny got some milk and five Texas Lotto tickets. *Good luck with that.*

Lonny looked at the skinny little prick behind the counter. Some damn foreigner probably come here to do no good. Lonny's arms ached from wanting to hurt this man. He tensed, muscles taut.

Lonny once lifted three bags of cement at the same time and carried them fifty yards. That was almost three hundred pounds. Breaking this little prick into pieces wouldn't be half as hard.

The man in front of Lonny left, leaving him standing at the counter with nothing in his hand. The clerk looked at him, eager to help. "Good morning, what can I get you?"

He grabbed the clerk by the collar and yanked him forward. He slammed his head into the counter. The man yelled. His arm shot toward the back, reaching for something. Lonny tugged harder, pulling him over all the way over the counter. "Where's Willard?"

"Who?"

He punched him in the gut. The man gasped, doubling over.

"Where's Willard. Tell me, or I'll kill you. I swear."

The clerk took a few breaths then leaned against the counter, hands protecting his face. "I don't know any Willard."

"I came here a few weeks ago asking about Willard. You told me to go to the dumpster and get a phone from a bag."

The clerk nodded. "I get calls sometimes. A man I don't know tells me what to do and…and…"

Lonny raised his fist. "And what?"

"He buys my phones and pays me good money."

"Who is he?"

"I don't know."

Lonny punched his face, twice.

The man almost cried. "I swear I don't know."

"How do you get the money?"

"He leaves it in a bag under the dumpster."

Lonny grabbed him by the neck.

"That's all I know. I *swear.*"

"And you don't know anybody named Willard?"

"I never heard the name Willard before you came in today."

Lonny kicked the counter. "Goddamn! Goddamnit."

He shoved the clerk back then walked in a small circle around the store, stopping in front of the clerk. He grabbed a pen from the counter and wrote his cell number on a piece of paper. "If you hear anything from this guy again, or think of any way to reach him, you call. I swear, if I find out different…"

"I'll call you. I will."

Lonny ran from the store, got in his truck and drove off. He looked at his watch—11:15. Not much time left. He stopped at another corner store he had visited the day he got the call, but that guy knew nothing either. Then he went to the spot where people waited for jobs in the morning. Rumors were that notices on the outside board sometimes directed people to get in touch with the mysterious Willard, but Lonny knew it was in code, and he didn't know what the code was. He stopped anyway and asked questions of about ten guys who were waiting on work. Nobody knew anything.

Lonny headed back to the Winthrop's. He didn't want to face Lucia or her questions. Or the detective and his suspicious looks. But he had nowhere else to go, and he was out of ideas.

***

Connors followed Lonny back over the freeway, halfway to Scott's house. When it was obvious where Lonny was going, he called Gino. "It's me," Connors said. "He's on his way back now."

"Where did he go?"

"Nowhere, really—a corner store. Must have stayed in there five minutes or so."

"What did he buy?"

"That's just it—he didn't buy anything, at least nothing he carried out. Guess he could have gotten cigarettes or lottery tickets or something like that, but he had nothing in his hands."

"That's odd. What else?"

"After that, he went to another corner store, but only stayed a few seconds. Nothing purchased there either. Then he went to a spot where day labor waits to get hired. He talked to everybody there, went inside, but again came out with nothing."

"After that?"

"He's on his way back. Pretty damn strange, if you ask me."

"*Very* damn strange. Go back to that first store and find out what he did in there. If they have video, ask to see it."

"But sir, we—"

"I don't give a shit about warrants. Tell whoever is running the place that we've got a kidnapping and need answers. Go, Connors. Go!"

CHAPTER 34

UNCLE EDDY

I hung up with Connors, more puzzled than when Lonny had left. *What the hell is this man doing?* His daughter was being held hostage and he was…what? Running around to corner stores? Why did he go? What did he do?

I thought about asking Lucia again but decided against it. She would blindly support her husband no matter what. She didn't see, or refused to see, his faults. She was a lot like Mary, who never saw my faults. She never complained or griped, even when we had no money.

God, I miss her.

Some nights I dreamed of cloning Mary. I'd bring her back just as she was. Wouldn't change a thing. Not her lazy eye or the extra twenty pounds she always complained about.

I was brought out of my contemplation by the thought of the Uncle Eddy reference. "Alexa!"

"What?" She said as she stormed into the kitchen, Lucia right behind her. Alexa marched to the table, positioned herself with an attitude, and gave me her standard "What?" yet again.

I let her sit for a few seconds. "Who's Uncle Eddy?"

She feigned an I-don't-know-what-you're-talking-about look. It was good.

I wanted to take her pretty little head and bash it into the granite countertop; instead, I asked again. "Who is Uncle Eddy?"

"I already told you. I don't know an *Uncle Eddy*. Who's he supposed to be?" She'd answered too fast. All denial.

Lucia stood close by, intently focused on Alexa.

"Who is he, Alexa?" I asked, raising my voice. "*Who* is Uncle Eddy?"

Lonny walked in the door right then. He looked at me then at Alexa. "What's going on? Why are you asking her?"

"Because she knows something."

"I *told* you."

I grabbed Alexa's arm and dragged her to the other room. She seemed to be struck with that particular kind of fear common among teenagers—the kind they got when dealing with adults. In most cases, no matter how bad things were or how much trouble they're got into, they wouldn't open up to parents or *any* adult. I got as close as I could to her face and whispered.

"Your best friend is in deep shit. If you care *one fucking bit* about her, you better tell me what you know."

She looked at the floor then shot a glance toward the Hacketts. "Not here. On the patio."

I took her outside and sat her down, forcing calm on myself before I continued. "Before you say anything, know that if you need this to be between the two of us, it will stay that way."

"Sure." She said it with the same disgust and sarcasm I had heard from a hundred kids before.

"This is no shit. If I say it stays between us, it does. But I'm telling you now that you'll have to handle the Hacketts on your own. If they ask me, I'll tell them to ask you."

She lifted her head and sighed. "There is no Uncle Eddy."

If I could have hit the girl I would have. "Alexa—"

"No. I mean there *really* isn't an Uncle Eddy, but I know what she means by it."

My blood pumped. "What? Come on. Jada needs this."

"If my dad finds out…"

"He won't unless you tell him." I wanted to say more but felt that silence would work better. It took almost a full minute.

"If the Hacketts are going to find out anyway, I might as well tell you all at once. I don't want to do this twice." She got up and walked inside.

When we got to the kitchen, Lonny pulled me aside. "What's going on?"

"I'll let Alexa tell us."

She stared at the floor and spoke quietly. "Uncle Eddy is not a man. It's our code for a motel."

I listened. Lonny started to say something, but Lucia's hand on his arm stopped him.

"What do you mean, it's for a motel?" I asked.

Her head lowered even more. She wouldn't look at Lonny or Lucia. "It started when one of our friends said the guy at one of the motels looked like her uncle Eddy. After that, whenever we wanted to go fool around with our boyfriends or something, we'd say, let's go to Uncle Eddy's. Or if we wanted to leave a message on a phone, or send an email or text, we'd say I'm going to Uncle Eddy's. Wanna go?"

"Are you telling me Jada is—"

Lucia turned Lonny around to face her. "Does it matter what she did or didn't do right now? We got a lot more to worry about than that girl having sex."

He shook his head.

Lucia went to Alexa and wrapped her arms around her. "Thank you, Alexa. You did right."

I kissed Alexa on the head. "That took courage. I like to see guts in a young person. Thanks. And Alexa, I'm going to need you to give Detective Delgado details on the motels."

She lifted her head. "Don't worry about not telling Dad. I'll tell him myself."

I went back and kissed her head again. "That's even more guts. If you ever want help, let me know."

CHAPTER 35

NOW'S THE TIME

Mars found Alexa sitting outside. She looked as if she needed a friend. He crossed the patio and offered her a smoke. She looked up at him, shocked. "I didn't know you smoked."

"I hardly ever do. Once in a while on weekends or if I'm out with the guys."

She took the cigarette and the light he offered. "Is this all you smoke?"

"I take a hit now and then."

"So what's up? You didn't come out here to give me a smoke."

"You looked like you needed something. This was all I had."

She laughed. "I'm screwed. Dad's gonna find out about everything, including the motels."

Mars sat on the ground next to her. "You're not half as screwed as Jada."

Alexa looked at Mars. "You blame me, don't you?"

"Maybe."

She gave a sarcastic laugh. "*That* didn't take much thought. Your parents probably hate me. And the detectives…"

"Alexa, this isn't about you. Stop trying to be a goddamn martyr and think about Jada." Mars got up and started for the house. "I came out here to make you feel better, but all you did was piss me off."

"Mars, wait."

***

DELGADO WATCHED THE SCENE on the patio from the kitchen window. From the look on Alexa's face, he figured the time might be right to get her talking. He grabbed two bottled waters and headed out.

"Hey, Alexa. Brought you some water. Hot today."

"Yeah, thanks."

He handed it to her and pulled a chair alongside hers. "Gino said you could fill me in on the motels you kids frequented."

"'Frequented?'" She looked at Delgado and shook her head. "We're not whores. We're kids having fun."

Delgado resisted the urge to laugh, recalling some of those same *fun* times. "I didn't intend for it to come out that way. I used to do the same thing when I was your age. We couldn't afford motels, but somebody always had a car, or somebody's parents were away for the weekend. A night would do."

Her first smile appeared. "Even a few hours."

Delgado sipped his water. "I won't tell you about the time I was at my girlfriend's house and we *thought* her father was asleep."

Alexa laughed. "Uh-oh."

"It was worse than 'uh-oh,' señorita. I had to leave through the window."

"You didn't."

"I swear. It's bad enough getting caught by any girl's father, but when she's Mexican…"

Alexa smiled again. Delgado let the comfort level build then lowered his voice. "Alexa, where did you go most of the time? Any particular motel?"

"We went to a lot of them. It depended on how busy they were. We didn't like to go around here, in case our parents spotted our cars. You know, like what is Alexa's car doing at the motel?"

"So where did you go?"

"Everywhere, depending on who was with us. Up to Conroe, down to 1960. Even further down 45."

Delgado took notes. "How far down?"

She thought for a moment. "One time all the way by Beltway 8. I don't think ever farther than that."

"So there wasn't any specific place you referred to as Uncle Eddy's?"

"No, it just meant any motel."

"And were they just motels, or did you stay at hotels too?"

"Never hotels. They cost more, and we were afraid we'd see some of our parents. Who knows, some of them could have been doing the same thing, only with other parents."

Delgado continued taking notes, but inside he smiled. This was no dumb kid. "Now *that* would have been embarrassing."

Alexa was silent for a moment then, "That other cop hates me, doesn't he?"

"Gino? He doesn't hate you."

"He acts like it."

"You just have to understand Gino, that's all."

"I understand him, all right. He hates kids."

Delgado looked at her. He lost his smile. "Let me tell you about Gino Cataldi. He loves kids more than anything. Too much, maybe. That's why he's so tough on them. His boy almost died from drugs. He's out of a rehab now, but every day, Cataldi wonders if today will be the day he gets the call. Every night he puts his phone by the bed and turns up the ringer so he won't miss the call he hopes will never come." Delgado sipped his water and looked at her but didn't wait for her to respond. "Listen, Alexa, I'd like to talk, but we need to find Jada before time runs out."

She looked up at Delgado, real concern on her face. "You think she'll be okay?"

"I don't know. I hope so."

***

LONNY PACED ACROSS THE living room floor. "I can't believe our girl would do that. She—"

Lucia sat in the chair shaking her head. "Listen to yourself. She's seventeen. That's the same age I was on our prom night." She got up and walked to him, made him stop and look at her. "Do you remember *that* night? And where *we* stayed?"

"That was different."

"Different? Why? Did you call me the things you're thinking about her?"

"Lucia, don't go doing that. Don't be putting thoughts in my head that aren't there."

She huffed herself up. "I'm not putting thoughts in that thick head of yours. I'm just trying to show you how wrong your thinking is." Lucia took her seat again. "I don't like it any more than you do, but she's seventeen, for God's sake."

Lonny came and sat next to her. "I guess you're right, baby."

"Again."

He laughed. "Yes, again. As long as we get her home safe. That's all that matters."

Lucia reached over and patted his hand. "When she's here, I'm gonna remember you said that." She sat back in her chair. "Just in case you try to bring up other things, that is."

Lonny laughed some more. "Woman, I love you."

"Of course you do. I knew that the first time you begged me to dance."

"*Me* beggin' *you*? If I remember correctly, it was you admiring my moves that got this whole thing started."

"Huh. This whole *thing* got started because you were tripping over your feet watching me as you danced—or *tried* dancing."

Lonny laughed even harder at that, and then he leaned forward and kissed Lucia. "I truly do love you. Just like the night we met."

"She'll be all right. I know it," Lucia said, and then she held his face and kissed him.

He started crying. He got up, tried hiding it, but she caught him and set him down.

"What's going on?" Lucia said. "Talk to me."

"Nothing. Just…"

"I'm listening."

He took her hands and held them, stared into her deep brown eyes. "Suppose I could trade places. Suppose we could get Jada back in exchange for me."

She laughed. "What would they want with an old out-of-work bricklayer? I sure don't have money for ransom."

"I know, just…well, suppose it could work. Would you do it?"

"Stop talking nonsense. We don't have time for things like that. If you want to do something good, go into that kitchen and listen to what they got planned. Maybe you can contribute something—an idea, or suggestion. Ain't like we got a bunch of expert kidnap rescue men out there. They're just cops. Most of them are used to lots of things, but I don't imagine kidnapping is one of them."

Lonny nodded and got up. "You're right. I know what I'm going to do now." He walked into the kitchen, determined to make a difference. One way or the other, this is how the situation would play out. What was the worst the cops could do to him—put him away for a few years? His family would survive. Somehow.

Now's the time.

He walked up to Gino. "Detective, we need to talk."

***

"Okay, Lonny. One minute."

I called Coop's cell, getting her on the second ring.

"What have you got, Gino?"

"A damn good lead, Captain. They put the girl on today, and she gave us a clue her friend picked up on. We're confident she's being held in a motel, probably on the north side of town."

"A motel. That's all you have? Do you know how many motels there are?"

"Not nearly as many as there are garages, houses, abandoned buildings, small businesses, or any other of the thousands of places she could be if she were *not* in a motel."

Coop took a big sigh. "Gino, I'm going to pretend you thought you were talking to Tip, or Delgado, or some other asshole. Anybody but your *captain*, who is too pissed right now to talk to you."

"But you will, so here's what I need."

"Cataldi, I'm holding my temper for that young girl's sake. When this case is over, we're gonna talk. Now go on."

"SWAT teams. Several of them. I'm putting Delgado in charge of that operation. And we need to get moving on it right away."

"Where do you want them? And when?"

"I'll have Delgado call you. It will depend on what Julie finds out in her research. I'm calling her now."

"Keep me informed."

I hung up and looked over at the group. Some weren't paying attention. "Hey!" I said. "Listen up. Our best shot at bringing this girl home safe is to find her before they know we don't have the money. We've got full support from Renkin, but we don't have much time. What that means is I want every son of a bitch in this room focused on what we're doing. No calling your wives or husbands or anyone else." I'd gotten their silence and their focus, so I continued. "I don't have time to say all this twice, so listen while I talk on the phone."

I called Julie. She already knew about the motels, so Coop must have filled her in.

"Go, Gino. I'm ready."

"I need a list of every motel on the north side first."

"Conroe, too," Delgado yelled to me.

"Including Conroe," I repeated. "Take it down I-45 as far south as Greenspoint and both ways on 1960, say from Hardy Toll Road to 249."

"Gino, that's going to—"

"I know. Just get started. If we strike out, we'll expand the search." I stopped to think. "Julie, coordinate all this with Delgado. He'll be running the show."

She hung up, but I called back right away. "Julie, one more thing. Get a team calling all of the motels. I want ones that have rooms rented in the past three days to people who still haven't checked out. You can scratch the ones who checked in yesterday. These guys would have been better prepared."

"That will still be a lot, Gino."

"I know; do it anyway."

I set the phone on the counter and took a breather. Then I remembered Lonny. I turned to him. "Yeah, Lonny, you wanted to talk to me?"

CHAPTER 36

BAD NEWS

Connors headed back to the corner store where Lonny had spent so much time. When he got inside, he knew there was trouble. The guy behind the counter looked like his nose had been broken. His eye was swollen, and his lip was split. Connors flashed his badge. "Detective Paul Connors," he said. "This is Officer Mirrol. What the hell happened to you?"

"Nothing. This was from yesterday."

The man was either Pakistani or Indian. Connors couldn't tell from looking at him, and he couldn't distinguish the accent, but it was one of the two, he felt sure. "I didn't ask *when* it was from," Connors said. "Who did it?"

"I was at the mall and three young men attacked me."

"That's funny," Connors said. "I was in here early this morning, and you didn't look like that. You don't remember me, do you?"

The man squeezed his hands together, looked around, did anything to avoid eye contact. "It happened yesterday," he said.

Connors pulled his cuffs out. "You're coming downtown with us."

"I have a store to run."

A customer came in, but Mirrol showed him outside.

"I'll only be a minute!" the clerk yelled as the door closed.

"You'll be a lot longer than a minute, sir, if you don't tell me what happened."

The clerk looked around as if someone might be watching. Then he stared at Connors and whispered, "Some man came in asking about someone named Willard. I told him I don't know any Willard. He demanded I tell him. When I repeated myself, he beat me."

He took time to look around again, as if Lonny might come through the door any moment.

"He wouldn't quit," the clerk went on. "He just kept hitting me and hitting me."

"And that's all he asked."

He nodded. "Where's Willard? Where's Willard? He was a madman."

"You want to press charges?"

"No! No charges."

Connors handed him a card. "If he comes back, or if anyone comes back, call me. Especially if you hear from Willard."

"I'm getting a gun that—"

Connors turned and pointed to him. "Sir, I would strongly advise you *not to* get a gun. It wouldn't be a good move. Too many people with guns already." Connors got in the car with Mirrol and started toward Winthrop's house. He dialed Gino as he drove.

"Cataldi."

"Gino, can you talk?"

"Let me call you right back."

***

I FINISHED UP WHAT I was doing then called Connors back, making sure to keep my distance from Lonny so he couldn't hear. "Go ahead."

"I just left the corner store. Lonny beat the shit out of the guy running the place. Bruised him up good. I think he broke his nose."

I made sure not to look in Lonny's direction, instead focusing on the map sitting on the table. "No shit. Why?"

"No clue. The guy said he kept asking where Willard was."

"Where is he now?"

"The guy said he doesn't even know a Willard. He said he told Lonny that, but he wouldn't believe him."

"Hang on, I'm getting a call." I switched over. "Gino Cataldi."

"It's Ramirez."

"Hang on. Let me get off the other line." I clicked over. "Connors, I got to take this. Finish your story when you get here." I clicked back to Ramirez. "Sorry about that. Go ahead."

"The Marshall boy is dead."

My body sagged. I had hoped the boy would be all right. "When?"

"Maybe an hour ago."

I slammed my fist against the door. "Shit! Goddamnit!" I wanted to kick something, but this wasn't my house. "Who's working this with you?"

"Tom Foss."

"Get more help. I want these guys caught. And, Ramirez…no deals for anyone. This is felony murder now. Every *goddamn* one of them is in for murder. And with Marshall's connections, they'll all be going to Huntsville to get a needle in the arm."

"I'm on it. I'll keep you posted."

"Son of a bitch!"

"What's the matter?" Delgado asked.

"The Marshall boy died."

"*Hijo de puta!*"

Lonny headed toward the living room. I'd forgotten he'd asked to talk, and now I sure as shit wanted to talk to him. *What the hell is going on? And who the fuck is Willard?*

"Lonny, you wanted to see me?"

He turned, seemed sheepish all of a sudden. "I gotta see Lucia. I'll be back."

***

LONNY WANTED TO RUN, and not just to the living room. He needed to run for the border or someplace else he could hide—disappear forever. He'd do it, too, if Jada were here. Ten minutes ago, he had made up his mind to tell Gino, figuring he would do time if necessary. But he wasn't going in for felony murder. *No way.* Down here in Texas, they put your ass in the grave for that shit.

Maybe with a high-priced lawyer and a lot of time, he could get off easier, but Lonny didn't have the time, and he sure as shit didn't have the money. As much as he wanted to, there was no way he could tell Gino now. Not when it meant facing the death penalty.

As he searched for Lucia, he ran the possibilities through in his mind again. If he thought he could help Jada, he'd trade his sorry ass in. She was a damn-good girl. But—and he'd been through this a hundred times since yesterday—he didn't see any way that what he had to offer would help her. Besides, maybe Gino would catch them now that they had this motel lead. Maybe they'd find her safe.

Please, Lord, let that be.

***

I LOOKED AROUND FOR Delgado and found him strategizing with Sameena at the table. They had drawn a crowd, probably because Sameena was a looker, *not* because they were all so dedicated.

I tapped Ribs on the shoulder. "You're going to have to move it soon."

He looked at his watch. "I got a few minutes. We're setting up base at a mobile unit by 45 and 1960."

"Starting there?"

"I got three teams. One will start at the beltway on 45 and head north, one will be at 1960 and 249, coming east, and one will start in Conroe, working south. Meanwhile, Julie's working the phones. If she gets anything hot, we switch gears."

I nodded. "At least we have a plan."

"What's the plan?"

"We stall the kidnappers until we find the girl."

"Not much of a plan, cuz."

"Yeah, but it's all we got."

CHAPTER 37

THE DROP

Delgado had been gone a while, but I hadn't heard a thing. I called to see where he was.

"What's up, Gino?"

"It's two fifteen. Is everybody in place?"

"We're good to go. I'm on 45 with Sanchez. She's dressed as one of the cleaning crew."

"She's not going to try anything alone, is she?"

"She'll walk by, see if she can spot anything. How about you—things in place?"

"For all the good it will do, yes, everyone is in place. We've got a guy in the hotel and one in the woods across the street."

"I guess your cynicism means you don't think they'll show."

"Just like you said, Ribs."

"That's what I would do."

"Me too," I said, "and I think these guys are smarter than me."

"I hope not. That would make them almost as smart as me."

"You know, Delgado, one thing's bothering me. They said they'd call once he's inside Denny's, but they didn't ask for Eddy's cell. You think they expected him to take Scott's?"

"Beats me. But I got SWAT here. Gotta go. Keep me informed."

"Me too. *Buona fortuna.*"

"Good luck, *amigo.*"

I looked around for Lonny, hoping he didn't think I was treating this case casually. Sometimes humor was all that kept us going on cases like this. That and the thought of catching pricks and doing evil things to them.

While I went over last-minute details with Doran, Connors brought me more of Scott's good coffee. "I'm nervous. Did we miss anything?"

I shrugged. "I think we're set pretty good on the surveillance. Once Doran leaves the restaurant, we got him covered no matter where he goes."

I walked to Doran and patted his back. "You about ready, Uncle Eddy?"

He smiled. "Eddy's ready."

"Don't forget to leave your wallet here, in case they ask to see a license."

Doran looked at me funny.

I shrugged. "You never know what these guys will do."

Winthrop's home phone rang. On the third ring, the tech came in. "Unknown caller," he said.

"It's all you, Doran. You're Uncle Eddy now."

He took a deep breath and picked up the phone. "Hello."

"Is this Winthrop?"

"No, this is Eddy."

"Ah, the famous Uncle Eddy. Good. We'll be meeting soon enough, so I shall save the pleasantries until then. In the meantime, please go to the mailbox. Inside you will find a phone. Take that with you to Denny's. We will call that number."

"What should—" The line went dead. Doran looked up to me, confused as hell. "They said a phone is in the mailbox."

I pointed to one of the cops near the door. "Check it out."

When he returned, he held a disposable phone. "It was just sitting there," he said. "Should we dust it?"

I shook my head. "No sense. We don't have time, and they wouldn't make that kind of mistake." Now one of my questions was answered—the one Delgado and I had just discussed. "Give the phone to Doran."

I wanted to cover everything one more time with the team before he left. "All right, everyone. This is it. Listen up."

Once they had gathered at the table, I went over the plan. "Remember, the techs will monitor us from downtown. We all have stations. Stay there!

Don't move until you get the signal. As soon as the kidnappers commit to a direction for Doran, we shift gears."

Two guys near the door started talking. I hollered to get their attention. "Keep listening! I know you're all professionals. These instructions aren't meant as an insult. I don't want any cell phones on other than the ones assigned to you. No radios. No reading papers or looking at dirty magazines. No donut runs. If you need to take a piss, take the phone with you or man-dog it. And hurry up." I looked around. "A young girl's life is at stake." I remembered what Lonny said to me not long ago. "Her name is Jada. You've got her picture. Take a look at it. Imagine she is your daughter or niece or sister. That's the goal today—bringing Jada home safe."

Everyone was getting up from the table when one of the younger ones asked, "Excuse my ignorance, sir, but what did you mean by 'man-dog' it?"

I leaned in close. "It means piss on the grass or behind a tree."

"Like a *dog*," one of the older guys said, and laughed like hell.

"Okay. No questions. We're outta here."

I nodded to Doran. "Good luck, Eddy. And don't forget to take your own phone. We need to keep in touch."

The mood was good as they headed out the door. I liked that. It relieved some of the tension.

Before leaving, I went to Lucia and Lonny. She was crying. He looked as if he might too at any time. Mars stood behind them for support. "Keep the faith," I said. "My goal is to bring her back."

"I'll be praying," Lucia said.

"Good. You all should."

***

DORAN DROVE A FEW miles to Denny's, parking near the back as instructed. He went inside, casting glances at all the patrons. As far as he knew, one of the kidnappers might be watching him. He asked the hostess for a booth near the back. She seated him, and then a waitress quickly filled a cup with coffee for him and whipped out an order pad.

"Know what you want, hon?"

"Not yet. Give me a few minutes."

He pretended to scan the menu, but he watched the people around him. He picked up the business section of a newspaper left on the table and started reading, but all the time wondered when the kidnappers would call or contact him. The waitress came back for his order. Doran quickly scanned the menu.

"Still need time?" she asked.

He remembered what the caller had said, and even though he didn't like it, he followed instructions. Maybe it meant something. "Blueberry pancakes with a side of sausage."

"Toast?"

"No thanks."

She scooped up the menu, refreshed the coffee, and headed toward the kitchen. Not a minute later, the phone rang.

"Hello."

"Go to the restroom."

"What?"

"I don't like repeating things. It makes me suspect you of trickery."

"Nothing of the sort. I just—"

"Go to the restroom. In the trash can you will find a cell phone in a brown bag. Pick it up. Stay on the line with me until you get there."

Doran got up and went into the bathroom. As much as he didn't want to, he removed the trashcan lid and opened up a brown paper bag near the top. A cell phone was inside. "Okay, I got it."

"Answer it."

The phone rang, and Doran answered. "Hello."

"Now we're getting somewhere. Take the phone you came in with and place it in the toilet."

"Do what?"

Doran heard a sigh. "I told you I don't like repeating things." The voice on the other end grew louder, more irritated. "Place the original phone in the toilet. Clear?"

Doran dropped it in the bowl. "Now what?"

"Now go back out and eat. We'll be watching. Don't talk to anyone other than the waitress. Don't call anyone. We'll know if you do. One false move, and I will let my sex-starved men have their way with your niece. Clear?"

"Yes."

"Say it."

"What?"

"Say, *clear*. I want to know that you have heard and understood."

Doran wanted nothing more than to get hold of this guy and beat his brains out. "Clear."

"Good. Enjoy your breakfast. Take your time. When you're done, go to your car and we'll call you. I anticipate you should be fifteen more minutes."

While waiting for his food, Doran scanned the restaurant, wondering who might be watching. A cook in the back? One of the customers? Someone outside with binoculars? Or was it a bluff? He wanted to take the other cell and call Gino, fill him in on what happened, but…he couldn't risk it. Not with Jada's life at stake.

Doran sipped the last of the bad coffee, took a few bites of the pancakes and sausage, and paid the check. As he walked across the lot on the way to his car, the new cell phone rang. "Hello."

"Get on 45 heading south."

"Where are we going?"

"Shame on you for asking. Do as I say."

Doran got in, started the car, and soon was on the entrance ramp for 45 South. He reached down and got the spare cell from his boot and started to dial Gino. Just then the other phone rang again.

"I forgot to tell you. Take the Hardy Toll Road when you get to it. Place this phone on the seat beside you. Turn on the speaker and leave it *on*. I want to hear what is going on."

***

CENTRAL PATCHED IN TO all of us. "He's heading south on 45. You need cars in front and behind."

I patched in. "Whoever's on Rayford Road, you're on. He's only a couple of miles away. One of you get on now, get in front. The other one lag on the feeder until we tell you, then pick up the tail."

"He could take Hardy," Central said.

"If he does, the second car will catch him. We have more following. Everyone else is heading that direction."

***

DORAN GOT ON THE Hardy Toll Road entrance and kept in the right lane. Within moments, a voice came over the phone's speaker. "When you see the sign for the Rankin Road exit, pick up the phone."

"Okay."

About two miles before the sign, Doran dialed Scott's number on his second cell phone. He prayed they would be quiet, but just in case, he tucked the phone into his stomach, burying the speaker part.

***

WINTHROP'S HOME PHONE RANG. The tech checked the number and ran to the kitchen. "It's Doran!"

I hollered. "Quiet! Nobody talk. We got Doran calling in."

I listened, but nothing was going on. I could hear the sound of the car running, a little outside noise, but no talking. On the computer screen the techs had set me up with, I could see Doran approaching Rankin Road. I got on the horn to the rest of them. "He's near Rankin. Got that? Doran is at Hardy and Rankin, still heading south."

***

DORAN PICKED UP THE phone from the seat. "Okay, I'm here."

"Take the exit for the airport. Go to terminal C as in Charlie. When you get close, pick up the phone for further instructions."

Doran took the exit for George Bush Intercontinental Airport, making sure to keep to the speed limit. That way, Gino's men could get past him and to the terminal beforehand.

***

"TERMINAL C." I RELAYED the message to everyone. "I want everybody we've got on the way to terminal C. No, on second thought, leave two cars trailing Doran, just in case. The rest of you get there as fast as you can."

I hung up and smiled at Connors as I called Delgado.

"What's up, Gino?"

"I think we got the fuckers, Ribs. They're going to the airport, and we'll have ten cars waiting."

CHAPTER 38

MOTELS

Delgado was on the phone with the team on 45 South. "What have you got, Sanchez? Any dirty rooms?"

"I got *nothing but* dirty rooms in this place. You should get your ass down here."

"Maybe you and me—"

"A big no to you and me anywhere, and a *fucking* big no to me and anybody down here."

"What did the deskman have to say?"

"Only two rooms fit our target, and they both answered the door when I knocked. I didn't go in, but it didn't seem like anything wrong. One guy was old, looked homeless, and the other one was a kid in his underwear. From the way he barely cracked the door, I'm sure he was hiding a girl on the bed."

"And you don't think—"

"If he was eighteen, I'm a virgin."

"Don't you have three kids?"

"Six kids, Delgado. Six hungry kids."

"Okay, move up the line. No way is a kid is involved in this." Delgado checked the map. "There's a motel at—"

"I know where it is. We'll be there in a couple of minutes. How's it going on 1960 and Conroe?"

"Same. We got a lot more to go though. We'll get there."

"How's it going with Gino?"

"Don't know yet, but I gotta go. Call coming in."

Delgado hung up and switched to the new call—Dustin from the Conroe team. "Anything good?"

"Knocked out three already. Got a few junkies, a couple of misfits, and one suspicious couple who claimed they were married, but whose IDs indicated they were *not* married to each other. How about on your end?"

"Thought we had something at Greenspoint, but it busted. Nothing on 1960."

"Find them, Ribs. Bust their asses."

"I'm trying."

Delgado wasn't off three minutes before Julie called. "What have you got for me, *chica*?"

"You must have been talking to Sanchez, because I'm no *chica*."

"But you know I love you. Purple hair and all."

"Well this *chica* might have something for you. I've been calling all the motels, and there *are* a heck of a lot of them."

"I know. What have you found?"

"One guy said they've got a white male in his thirties who checked in with a young black girl yesterday. Said the girl couldn't have been more than 15 or 16."

"And?"

"They are still in the room. But the interesting part is that one of the other patrons said they heard screams from there."

"What! When?"

"Earlier today."

"You should have called us."

"Hold onto your horses, Detective. The manager said he gets complaints like this a lot. Most of them are nothing."

Delgado wanted to scream, but it would do no good. "All right. Give me the details and patch it in to the team."

"It's on 45 North, just south of 1960. It's an America's Best—"

"Used to be the old Lexington, didn't it?" Sanchez asked from her end.

"That's the one."

"I can be there in five minutes, Ribs. Let me have them. I got a niece same age as this girl. I can't bear the thought of something like this happening to her."

"Go for it, *chica*. I'll meet you there with a team."

Delgado rounded up the SWAT team. "Off your asses, *amigos*. We've got a possible situation." Delgado filled them in then looked at his watch. "We leave in five minutes," he said, and called Gino.

"Cataldi."

"You sound like a man in a rush."

"I was going to call you. Why did they pick Terminal C? What the fuck are they doing?"

"I can't think of any one specific reason, but it's not a bad choice. Parking garage is big, crowded, lot of people and cars."

"Yeah, but once they're done, what do they do—exit, pay their ticket and have us pick them up? They *have* to know we're tailing them."

"Did they try to give you the slip?"

"Not once. Straight shot from Denny's to the airport."

"You there?"

"Almost. I stayed at the house until they committed. I'm five minutes away."

"And they didn't take any detours? Change cars? Anything?"

"I'm telling you, Ribs, all they did was give him a new cell phone at the restaurant. From there, he jumped on the freeway and came down Hardy. He should be pulling into C any minute."

"If that's the case, you're fucked."

"Explain."

"These gringos aren't that stupid. They've got something planned. We just don't know it yet."

"Fuck!"

"What?"

"I wanted you to tell me I was wrong. That we got lucky, and they screwed up."

"You forgot your history lessons. Hector Delgado don't lie."

"That was Davy Crockett, asshole."

"Same thing. We both had relatives at the Alamo."

"No, *Davy Crockett* was at the Alamo. You had some tenth cousin of your mother's friend's wife's sister, or some shit like that."

"Like I said, same thing. Blood is blood."

Gino laughed. "That's why I love you. I gotta go. Need to figure out what they're doing."

"Me too. We got a potential lead on a motel. The old Lexington."

"Whew! They're not spending any of that anticipated ransom on comfort are they?"

Delgado hung up and called to his SWAT team. "We're ready."

He climbed into the van with the team. The leader handed him a vest. "Wear it if you're in on this."

"Park at the Ramada Inn just north of the motel. We don't want them to see us."

"Just us?" the leader of the team asked.

"Sanchez is meeting us. Rest of her team is continuing with the other motels."

He got on the phone. "Where are you, Sanchez?"

"Thirty seconds."

"Remember, the Ramada. North side. "We're two minutes behind you." Delgado hung up and made another call. "Julie, call the Ramada next to America's. Tell them we're coming into the parking lot. We don't want any noise or issues. Do whatever you have to."

"Got it, *chico*," she said.

Delgado laughed. He liked that purple-haired, multi-colored-fingernail hippie girl. The van pulled into the Ramada and swung in front of the building. Three muscle-bound macho men and one wiry, tough-as-boar-tusks woman, exploded from the van, vests on and loaded with more guns and ammo than it took to win the war in Granada.

Delgado looked them over, shaking his head. "I feel inadequate."

Sanchez stood a few feet away, a smile on her face that made her look like Howdy Doody from the fifties, but better armed. "You're just recognizing that," she said. "Rosalee told me—"

Delgado put his hand on a gun. "Remember, Sanchez. Sometimes cops get shot in operations like this."

The SWAT leader, Lance, came forward with a rigid posture and an even more rigid expression. Delgado assumed he didn't appreciate the banter. Maybe because he didn't need it. He got to kill the bad guys. Delgado and his teams usually only saw the victims and their families. They worked their ass off to catch the bad guys, only to see them get released early, or worse, get off. That shit made a person crave a drink at night. Some guys took it further, craving it all the time.

Lance was right, though; it was time for action. Delgado got everyone in close. "Sanchez and I go in first. When we exit the office, move into position. I'll signal you from the front of the room."

Sanchez pinched Delgado's ass as they crossed the street, arm in arm.

"What the hell was that about?" he asked.

"Good luck."

"You could have just said *buena suerte*."

She picked up the pace. "Not as much fun."

Delgado and Sanchez entered the lobby, his badge out before he was halfway across the room. "Detectives Delgado and Sanchez."

The clerk was a medium-guy—medium height, weight, and hair color. Not pasty white or tan, just medium all the way around.

"I was expecting you," he said, in a medium-ranged voice. "They're in room #164." He reached for the key. "It's around back."

Delgado took the key. "Who reported the noise?"

"Two rooms down, #168. The rooms on either side are empty. I don't know how #168 could have heard noise from there…unless it was really loud."

Delgado nodded. "Thanks. We're going there now. Make sure no one bothers us. If anyone questions you, say it's police business."

"Don't worry. I want them out of here. This is normally a quiet place."

"I'm sure it is," Delgado said. "Sir, do you think we could borrow a maid's uniform?" He felt certain Sanchez was glaring at him over the comment, but he didn't turn to confirm it. When the clerk gave them a uniform, Delgado grabbed Sanchez by the arm, and they walked outside. "You want to be the maid?" he asked.

"I don't think you'd pass for one," she said.

"Okay, here's what you do—"

Sanchez turned to look at him. "I've got six kids. I *know* how to be a maid." She started around the corner without me, then turned and said, "And I know how to speak Spanish too."

"That's cruel, Sanchez. I'm reporting you."

"To which cousin?"

"That's crueler."

She changed in the manager's office then left with Delgado, setting a fast pace to the room. "Cover me," she said, all humor gone from her tone. Delgado stayed close behind, crouched low.

Sanchez walked up to #164, key in one hand, the other clutching a gun. She took a deep breath then knocked on the door. When no one answered, she knocked again. "*Hola*! Housekeeping."

The curtains moved—just barely, but they moved. One more time, she knocked. "*Hola*! Maid service."

The curtain closed. She reached for the lock with the key, but Delgado shook his head. They'd let Sir Lancelot and the mighty SWAT team handle this.

Delgado let her take the lead back while he brought up the rear, just in case whoever was in there decided to come out. He called Lance on the phone. "Need your special brand of talent, *amigo*. The gentleman in room #164 is not feeling sociable."

By the time Delgado turned the corner, Lance and his crew were there. He didn't know *how* they got there that fast, but they did. "Room #164. And try not to kill the girl."

Lance looked at him. "What do we know for sure?"

"Nothing. This could be a plain old asshole who didn't feel like answering the door because he was getting a piece of tail. Or it could be a wired-up junkie ready to blow his—and your—brains out. Or, it could be the kidnapper with an innocent girl in there. So be careful."

Lance nodded and gave some kind of mysterious hand signal to his men, the kind only Special Forces, and CIA, and FBI, and SWAT team guys—all of the acronym people—do. They moved along the wall like fucking spiders.

They got into position on both sides of the door. The guy from the rear, the one who looked like a couple of trees, moved up with a battering ram that Santa Ana would have paid a bucketful of gold to have had at the Alamo. Delgado presumed Coop knew she would be paying for a few motel doors. Good thing they weren't at the Ritz.

The battering-ram guy swung his tree-trunk arms back then swung what probably *was* a tree into the door. It went down like the houses Delgado used to build out of cards. He rushed to give them backup. Before the door touched the floor, they were inside, and judging from the resulting noise, #168 would have more than a few complaints.

"Down! On the floor! Drop the gun! Drop the gun!"

Delgado heard a shot then several more as he raced through the door, low. A white male lay on the floor, bleeding. More than bleeding, his head was almost blown off. No rush on a bus for him. A gun lay on the floor next to him. Delgado hoped it was actually the guy's gun and not one from the arsenal Lance and his crew had. The girl lay on the bed, face buried in her hands, screaming as if she had a limb severed. Lance and his men cleared the bathroom, closet and under the bed, then announced the area to be secure. Delgado stood, went to the girl on the bed, and sat next to her.

She shrieked and pulled her legs up tight against her. If she could have crawled into the wall, she would have. It wasn't until Sanchez arrived that she showed signs of calming down.

Sanchez turned to Delgado, whispering. "Get them to step outside. I'll see what I can find out."

Delgado got Lance and his men to follow him out. He took out the cell and punched in Gino's number. He wanted to wait for Sanchez, but there was no sense in it. The girl on the bed was *not* Jada Hackett.

CHAPTER 39

TERMINAL C

Doran made the turn from the toll road extension onto JFK. He was fast approaching the airport. He picked up the phone. "I'm on JFK Boulevard."

"What kind of car are you driving?" the kidnapper asked.

The question took Doran by surprise. Did these guys really not know? "I'm in a Ford Flex. Black."

"Good. Listen closely. The next instructions are *very* important. If you fuck them up…well, you don't want to do that. Clear?"

Doran wanted to clear this guy's head out right now. "Clear."

"I am going to give instructions. Take the phone off speaker. I will be whispering, so it may be difficult for you to hear. If the radio is on, turn it off. Turn off the air conditioner too. Do not—I repeat—*do not* repeat what *I* say. *Do not* put the phone back on speaker. *Do not* question anything I say. Clear?"

Doran gritted his teeth. "Clear."

"You will answer me with simple sentences. Yes. No. Okay. Clear. Such as that. Clear?"

"Clear."

"Oh, one more thing. Take the other cell phone you have and drop it out the window now. *Right now.*"

A sickness crept into Doran's stomach. These guys had been fucking with them the whole time. They *knew* he had another cell with him. *How?* He dropped the phone out the window. "Okay."

"Roll up your window."

"Okay."

"Go to the Terminal B parking garage."

The sickness spread throughout Doran's body. Gino would be set up at C. They still had the GPS in the car, and the GPS in his boot, but no communications. He prayed Gino picked up on that.

When the turn came up for Terminal C, Doran went straight then turned left toward B.

Come on, Gino. Look at the GPS. Somebody look.

***

I WAS DOING ALMOST ninety down the Hardy Toll Road when I caught a little slip of the wheels as I negotiated the turn onto JFK. *Watch your ass, Gino. Don't need a wreck.*

The phone rang. By the fourth ring, I straightened up enough to grab it. It was the guy from Central. "Cataldi."

"We lost Doran's phone."

"What?"

"The signal is gone."

"What does that mean? Did he turn it off, or…"

"Even if he turned it off, we'd have a signal."

"So…what?"

"Doesn't matter. We still have the GPS devices in the car and on Doran. The bigger problem is, he's not headed to Terminal C."

"What!"

"He turned toward Terminals A and B. Driving slow."

A or B. Why? They could be making a detour. They might suspect a tail, and if so, the garage would be a good place to spot a tail. No stopping in front of the garage on entrance or exits. I got back on the phone.

"Do we still have the two tails on him?"

"They're still with him."

"All right, they stay. Tell everyone else to stay put. Tell them to stay in range, but if he goes into the garage, *do not* follow him in. Circle and spread out. Try to catch them coming out the other side. If Doran's car stops, we go in." I thought about the layout of the garage, how the kidnappers might work this. "I'm on JFK now. As soon as you know if it's A or B, let me know. I'm sending two cars to provide more cover. I repeat, unless he stops, we *do not* go in."

***

DORAN SLOWED DOWN AS he approached parking for Terminal B. He got his ticket and eased onto the ramp. "I'm on my way up."

Boss's voice came through the phone, smooth and confident. "Good. Continue driving slow. Exit the ramp at the first level." He waited a few seconds. "Turn right and slow down to five miles an hour. Someone will approach the car. *Do not* stop. They will get in. *Do not* stop. Keep going at the same speed."

Doran let off the gas, easing it down to five miles per hour. He could walk this fast. The parking garage was big, and every space he'd seen so far was occupied. He got almost to the end of the lane when the kidnapper spoke.

"Take the left turn at the end and continue at the same rate of speed."

Doran cast a few quick glances to the sides. Their knowledge of his location seemed too close for them to be guessing. They had to be in the garage. As he navigated a turn, a man appeared from behind a car. He wore a mask and pushed a gun against the driver's side window, level with Doran's head.

"Don't stop. Open the doors."

He climbed in the back seat. Through the mirror, Doran could tell that the gun was aimed at his head. "I'm not armed."

"I am. Keep going. Same speed."

***

I STEPPED ON THE gas, kicking it up a notch. When I hit the turn for A and B I slowed so I didn't spin out of control. I'd never been a very good driver, so I couldn't do the shit that other cops did, like take hairpin turns doing eighty, or bob and weave in traffic like they do in movies or on cop shows. I called Central. "What's the news? I haven't heard anything."

"Doran's in the garage at B, but he's still moving. Slowly, but moving."

"Everyone in place?"

"Got three cars circling and one at the exit near the freeways."

"Tell me if he stops. I'm joining them."

***

WITHIN FIFTY YARDS ANOTHER person approached the car, also masked. He got in the front seat. "Where's the money?"

Doran didn't say anything.

The backseat guy put the gun to his head. Pressed firmly.

Front-seat spoke again. "*Where* is the money?"

"They didn't have time to get it. The bank—"

Backseat hit him with the gun, and blood gushed from above his right ear. Doran's head fell to the side, his hand reaching for where he was hit. "Goddamn!"

Backseat said, "Should I kill him?"

Doran spoke with real panic in his voice. "Scott said he can get it tomorrow. That's when you asked for it originally." Doran could tell by the tone and attitude that backseat wouldn't mind killing him.

Front-seat's eyes bored into him. "Why didn't they tell us that on the phone?"

"Scott thought it would be better to tell you in person."

"Scott, my ass," Front-seat said. "Tell Detective Cataldi he made a big mistake."

"He didn't—"

Front-seat leaned toward Doran. "I *know* the money is ready."

This was no bluff. Doran heard it in the guy's voice. "The money was tainted," Doran said. "They put chemical tracers on it. We figured you'd be more pissed if we came with that."

"Tell the detective he will be hearing from us. Soon."

They weren't buying anything Doran said. "I will."

Front-seat eyed him. "Aren't you going to ask how your niece is—*Uncle Eddy?*"

Doran heard the truth in the guy's voice. "I think you know I'm not Uncle Eddy."

"Give me the cell phone," Front-seat said. "Now keep driving at the same speed. *Do not* stop. Go to level two. Repeat the same procedure. Same speed. Someone may approach you again. If not, proceed to level three. Continue until you reach the roof or get new instructions. In any case, do not stop. Clear?"

Doran made sure to get as good a look as he could at the guy—this had to be the top man. "Clear," he said, and noted the man's big hands covered with gloves. For the first time, he realized the man was very large, much bigger than Doran.

Front-seat nodded to the back, and the man with the gun exited, disappearing into a mass of parked cars close to the elevator. When Doran glanced toward Front-seat, the man had a gun. Doran turned down the next aisle at the same monotonous rate. About halfway down, Front-seat opened his door.

"Remember what I said. We'll be watching. And when you talk to Detective Cataldi, tell him it was a *very* big mistake."

In the rearview mirror, Doran saw Front-seat reaching for his mask just as he disappeared behind a minivan. Pretty soon Doran reached the ramp going up to level two. He wanted to speed through this thing, get out of here, and report to Gino. But these guys were too unpredictable. They might be watching. Without Gino's permission, he wouldn't risk that girl's life.

***

BOSS REMOVED HIS MASK and ducked behind the van, watching to make sure the cop followed instructions. When the cop got on the ramp, Boss got in the elevator. He changed out of his jogging pants, turned his shirt inside out, removed his gloves, and tucked everything into a dark plastic bag. When the elevator opened, he walked at a steady pace to the airport entrance, depositing the bag in a garbage can on the way. A long corridor led him to another set of elevators, which he took to the bottom level, and then he got on a tram car bound for Terminal C. If things went according to plan, Number Three was already there, waiting to board a shuttle bus that would take him to long-term parking. Driver would be waiting.

***

I PUNCHED THE SEAT next to me. Too much time had passed. Something was wrong. First Doran's phone disappeared, and now he'd been in the garage driving around for what seemed like half an hour. It might have really been half an hour. I called Sameena, who was in one of the cars tailing Doran. "Anything?"

"Been too long. I know that."

I sighed. "I'm with you. Something is up." I thought for a moment. "Sameena, go in. See what the hell is going on in that garage."

"On my way."

Sameena called back a few minutes later. "I'm on the top level before the roof. Doran's right in front of me, driving real slow."

"Anyone with him? Or in sight?"

"No one but him in the car. I'm checking the lot...got a few people walking, but they've got luggage. None of them fit the role."

What the hell was going on?

"What do you want me to do, Gino?"

"Stop him."

"Sure?"

"Do it."

I waited. It seemed a long time, but I knew it was less than a minute.

"They've been here and gone. Weren't happy about the money."

"Aw fuck!" *What to do? Where would they go?* "Sameena, you and Doran go inside Terminal B. See if he recognizes anyone. I'm splitting everyone else up at the other Terminals."

"What are we looking for?"

I thought about that as I punched the gas pedal. "I have no fucking idea. If Doran thinks of anything, let us know."

From my car, I watched as a mass of people exited Terminal C. One group alone had twenty or more people. I didn't even know what I was looking for or why I was here. No one was coming out holding signs that read, "we're the kidnappers." I felt pretty confident of that.

Maybe I was hiding from the Hacketts, afraid to face them after promising to bring their daughter home. How would I tell Lucia? I got a sick feeling in my gut. Mostly though, I thought of Jada and how frightened she must be. How she must have been counting on us—on *me*—to find her. Now all I could think about was Betty Ming back in Philly, and how she used to tell me over and over that she wished she'd died. I didn't want that happening to Jada. *Couldn't* let that happen to her.

CHAPTER 40

NAKED AND SCARED

Jada lay spread-eagle on the bed, shivering, her hands and feet tied to the four corners. Was he in the room with her? Rope burns had rubbed her ankles raw, and the insides of her thighs had cramped from trying to cover herself. The thought of him looking at her naked made her skin crawl.

She tried thinking of getting back to a normal life, of going home to her family, but that focused her worries in a new direction—on all the things she'd done wrong. Hurtful things she'd said to her mom. The way she'd gotten her dad so upset about the prom dress. The lies she'd told… If she ever got home safe, things would be different.

The uncomfortable feeling of having to pee came again, growing worse every minute. She relaxed her pelvic muscles and focused on squeezing the muscles around the urethra, staving off the inevitable for a few minutes. If she asked to go, he'd watch. Another shiver raced through her body. She felt sick.

Jada tried seeing through the blindfold to see if he was in the room. All she saw was black, the kind of black like when she and Mars used to lock each other in the closets at night and put a towel under the door to see who could stay the longest. She missed Mars, his laughter and jokes, even his teasing. Right now she'd take a lifetime of that. She'd even take a lifetime of helping her mother do the dishes, or of listening to her dad's warnings about boys and the things they wanted from girls.

A noise in the room made her jump. She squeezed her thighs, pushing them closer together. *Please, Lord, get me out of here.*

She listened, trying filtering out sounds to figure out what had made the noise. Silence. *Is he here? Is he watching?*

A car pulled up outside, and a door opened and closed. She heard someone walking, but the footsteps faded. For a moment, she relaxed, but that only increased the pressure on her bladder. As much as she didn't want to, she had to go. The thought of peeing on the bed crossed her mind, but then she'd have to lie in it. And how would he react to that? Instead she moved as much as she could and made grunting sounds, hoping he'd hear.

"Need something?" he whispered in her ear. Very close. Too close.

Jada's muscles tensed. It had only been seconds. *So he was here all the time.*

She nodded then felt the gag being removed. "I have to pee."

He pressed on her stomach, almost forcing it out.

"Please?"

"Don't worry. I don't want you peeing the bed. I might be in there with you soon."

She clenched her teeth. Prayed for someone to rescue her.

He untied her then stepped back. "Try anything like last time, and it will be a lot worse for you. Understand?"

"Yes."

He led her to the door. When she reached to close it, he stopped her. "Oh no."

"I can't go with you watching me."

"Learn."

She sat on the toilet, closed her legs, and covered herself as much as she could. Her shoulders hunched to hide her breasts. She relaxed her muscles and pushed, but nothing came out. She closed her eyes and tried again. Still nothing.

"Hurry up."

"I'm trying. I can't go."

"Get up."

"No! Wait."

"Take a shower. You're filthy. I want you clean…just in case."

"I don't want to shower."

"Take one!"

He sounded closer. In the bathroom. She squeezed her legs tighter together. "Okay."

She heard the water running in the shower. After a moment, he said, "It's ready," then he grabbed her arm and yanked her up.

"You're hurting me!"

His breath was in her ear again. Too close.

"Shut the fuck up," he said.

Jada got in the shower, her hands touching the walls to help her balance. She reached to close the door, but he stopped her. "I've got to take the blindfold off," she said.

"No need to take it off. I'm not concerned about your face being clean."

He grabbed her arm and placed a bar of soap in her hand. "Take all the time you want."

Jada turned her back to him, let the warm water soothe her as much as it could. Her ankles stung from the rope burns. She wanted to rub them, but there was no way she was bending over with him there. As she washed the lower part of her face, she squeezed her legs together and peed, letting it run down her leg so he couldn't see. After that, she cleaned herself with the washcloth and did a quick scrub on the rest of her. "I'm done."

Five led her out of the shower and handed her a towel. "Hurry up."

"Can I get dressed?"

"No!"

There was finality about that answer. She didn't argue.

He led her back to the bed, tied her, then put the gag back in. The room went silent. Had he gone, or was he there watching? Then she felt his finger tracing up her thigh. She tried screaming, thrashing about. He stopped.

"Don't worry, I won't hurt you. You need to be fresh until we get the ransom."

More silence. She waited, tense. Her muscles aching. The sound of a zipper opening startled her. Then she felt the bed sink down. *God, please. No.*

Even with the blindfold on, she squeezed her eyes tighter, trying to shut out the images of him sitting there with his…thing out. The bed shook in short jerky movements. Jada could only imagine one thing doing that. She felt sick, as if she would throw up. The movement continued. His breathing increased. She squeezed her legs tighter, her eyes even more. When she thought she couldn't take it anymore, he got up. Her muscles relaxed, breathing slowed.

Then she felt it. A feeling like aloe vera gel being dropped on her stomach. Jada cringed, tried reaching with her hands to get it off her. Tried turning over. Screaming. She kept it up for as long as she could, the grunting, thrashing, struggling to get free. Finally she surrendered and just lay there.

Why is this happening, God? Why me?

The phone rang. He answered it.

"Everything's fine. Uh huh. So what do you want me to do? Okay."

A faint clicking sound, almost like a camera shutter, and then it was silent.

"That was Boss. Looks like your daddy doesn't love you so much. He didn't pay. I'm just waiting for the word. When it comes—you're *mine*. Or maybe Number Three and I will share you."

CHAPTER 41

CONSEQUENCES

As I exited the airport, I looked at the driver of every car. I had no idea why, other than to slow down traffic. But I did it anyway. Some drivers I glared at. Most glared back with a what-the-fuck-are-you-staring-at look.

The phone rang. It was Delgado. "I hope it was her in that room," I said.

"You got two wishes left."

"No connection, I presume."

"No, but it wasn't all bad. We got another nut off the streets. Lance and his crew made sure he won't push drugs on any young girls again. And we got a runaway to send for treatment somewhere. *If* we can find a house with open beds."

"But no kidnappers."

"No kidnappers." A bit of silence followed, then, "I guess we didn't do any good with Doran."

I didn't answer for a moment, not wanting to vocalize my frustrations or the disappointment I felt. "They made us look like fools."

And me, the biggest one of all.

"We'll get them, Gino. Don't worry."

"I'm heading back to Scott's house. I'm sure we'll be hearing from them soon. Besides, I've got to tell the Hacketts."

"You need me there?"

"Yeah, but I need you checking those motels more. Maybe we'll get lucky."

"I'll call if we do."

It took me about forty minutes to get to Scott's house with the traffic. The delay gave me time to think of what I'd tell Jada's parents. As soon as I walked in, they were all over me—Lucia, Lonny, Mars, and Alexa. Must have been watching out the window, waiting for me to pull in.

"Did you find her? What happened?" That from Lucia.

Lonny stared at me from the back of the room with worried eyes. He had already figured it out, probably knew we'd have called if the news was good. I took hold of Lucia's shoulders, trying to be as calming as possible. "It wasn't her at the motel. And—"

"What happened with the kidnappers? What about the money?"

I shook my head. "I don't know. They said they'd call."

Lonny took hold of Lucia, supporting her as he walked her to the other room. "Call? What they hell are they calling for? We don't have any money."

When they had gone, Alexa came to me. "What's going to happen to Jada?"

It was the first time I'd seen any real concern from the girl since this started. Maybe it took kids longer to accept or believe what was really happening.

"Like I said, Alexa, I don't know." I made sure my voice was low. "Things aren't good. We're going to have to get lucky to catch them. Without a ransom…" I shook my head. "It's just not good."

She nodded and walked away, reaching for her cell. She started to dial.

"Who are you calling?"

"A friend."

"Don't," I said, and went over to her. "I asked you before. *Please* do not tell anyone what you hear in this room. *Nothing.*"

"It's one of our friends. She'll want to know."

I pulled her back into the kitchen so the Hacketts couldn't hear. "Listen. *Someone* is leaking information to the kidnappers. We—"

"It's not *me.* And my friends—"

"I didn't accuse you. But this is how it works. If I am to find out who is doing this, I need to know *absolutely* beyond a shadow of a doubt that it isn't you or your friends. The only way I can do that is if you tell *no one.*"

When she stared at me this time, it wasn't with the rebellious, I-hate-all-adults look she'd used before. This time she might have grasped how important this was.

"I won't tell anyone. Not even Dad."

I smiled and patted her back. "Good. You're helping Jada."

I had time for a few breaths, but that's all before Doran came in. Sameena and a couple of the other guys were with him. I took them to the kitchen table and made sure they knew to keep the talk low.

"Fill me in, Doran."

He told me how they changed locations at the last minute—not a surprise there—and one I should have expected and planned for. Doran had no ID on the men, because they wore gloves and masks.

"The thing is, they knew too much," Doran said. "I tried telling them the money wasn't ready, but he knew. He *knew*."

"You're positive?"

"No doubt. After that, I thought I'd try a different tack. I told him the money was treated, and that Scott thought it would be better not to deliver it that way. He looked at me and said you made a big mistake."

"So he knew the cops made that choice."

"No, I mean *you*. He said, 'Tell Detective Cataldi he made a big mistake.'"

"He actually mentioned me by name?"

Doran nodded. "And he knew I wasn't Uncle Eddy."

"What the fuck is going on?" I paced a moment then turned around. "Anything else?"

"He said you'd be hearing from him soon."

"Shit!"

"What do you think they'll do?" Connors asked.

"Something not good," Sameena said. "You can bet money on that."

I checked to see the Hacketts still a safe distance away then punched my fist into my other palm. "Where the fuck are they getting their information?" I focused on what had to be done. "Connors, you and Sameena get everyone in here. Cops, techs, everybody."

When everyone was seated, I started. "I want each of you to document every call you've made since you came on this job. Every person you've talked to. Anybody who might have overheard you say anything about this job."

"You can't think it's one of us," Connors said.

"I'm past thinking. These kidnappers know way too much about what we're doing. Something's wrong."

A car pulled into the drive. The car door slammed, and then the front door opened, and in walked Winthrop. Considering the circumstances, he wore too big a smile.

"Detective Cataldi, how did things go today?"

"I wondered if you'd ask, sir. But just so you'll know, it went like shit. They said they *knew* the money was ready, and they *knew* that Doran wasn't Uncle Eddy."

He gaped, dumbfounded.

"So my question, Mr. Winthrop, is *how* do they know all this? Have you told people at work what's going on? Who have you talked to?"

He set his briefcase on the kitchen counter then poured himself a drink—scotch on the rocks. Might have been a double. "I haven't told *anyone anything*. I suggest you look inside your own ranks, Detective."

***

SCOTT GRABBED HIS DRINK and went to the patio, plopping into the lounge chair, and setting his drink and cell phone on the table next to his sunglasses. It had been a miserable day and now it looked as if it the night would follow suit.

He took a long sip of Scotch. Work had been a bitch too. Fred pestering about the money, reminding him they could both get in trouble if something went wrong. Scott didn't tell him that Alexa was home safe. The detective had asked him not to tell anyone anything, and he didn't. Now Scott was catching shit on that end too. Cataldi as much as accused him of leaking information.

The sliding door opened. It was Alexa, probably coming to ask for money or to whine about something. Scott drained his glass and got up. "I was just coming inside."

***

SAMEENA LEANED TOWARD THE center of the table and whispered. "Maybe it *is* Winthrop. He's been at work all day. Who knows what he's saying or who he's talking to?"

Despite Winthrop denying it, Sameena had a point. I planned on having a private chat with him. In the meantime, I had to look into my own house, as Winthrop had suggested. "Get busy on it, folks. I'm calling Delgado to make sure all of his people do the same. We've got to eliminate possible leaks one at a time."

Before I had a chance to call Delgado, my phone emitted a shrill beep, alerting me that a new text had arrived. I opened it and almost shit. It was from the kidnappers.

Detective Cataldi, stand by for a Kodak moment.

I looked to Doran. *What the hell?* "Did you give them my cell?"

"Hell no! I wouldn't do that."

"Then how did they get it?" I stared at the group. "How the fuck did this guy get my cell number?"

In the middle of my rage, the tone beeped again. I looked down.

Aw fuck. No!

CHAPTER 42

A LITTLE BIT OF JUSTICE

Boss got the picture from Number Five and opened it on his phone. "This should send him through the roof. If he doesn't pay now, the man has no heart."

"Let me see," Two said.

She looked at the photo. Thought for a moment. Grabbed Boss' phone and checked the timing of the call Boss had made to Five and the one that came back from Five. "That was too quick."

"What?" Boss asked.

"How did Five get her naked and tied again in less than a minute?" She shoved the phone back at Boss. "You called him at 5:09. At 5:10, he sent you back a photo of her naked on the bed. I can only assume she was already naked, which makes me wonder why." Two picked up her own phone and dialed. "Driver, I need a ride," she said, and started for the door.

"Where are *you* going?" Number Three asked.

"To check on Five."

"Who cares what he did to her? I'll take seconds."

Two stopped. Slowly turned her head and glared. "Remember what I told you at the motel, Three. I meant it." Two slammed the door as she left.

***

"WHAT THE HELL WAS that all about, Boss? You gonna let her talk to you like that? Is she calling the shots now?"

Boss shrugged. "It's a woman thing. Best not to interfere with that."

"Woman thing, my ass. I'm gonna fix that bitch when this is all over. Wait and see."

***

NUMBER TWO GOT IN the van and went through the curtains to the back. "Motel," she said. "And you need to wait for me."

Driver pulled into the space closest to the door then tapped the ceiling of the van to let Two know it was okay to get out. "I'm staying in the van, Two. No place for me to go."

Two removed her mask, put it in her pocket and exited through the side door, setting a quick pace to the motel room. She used her key to enter the farthest room on the right, making sure to be quiet then she put on her mask and went in through the adjoining door.

Number Five was sitting on the bed, his hand resting on Jada's leg. He jumped when Two entered. "What are *you* doing here?"

Number Two took the scene in with a glance—Jada naked on the bed, one eye blackened and swollen, her lip puffed out, blood on her. She'd seen the photo. It looked worse in person. "What happened, Five?"

"Bitch tried escaping."

Number Two kept her balance, her left hand in position to draw her gun if necessary. She moved closer, slowly. The nightstand was cocked to the left, and the lamp that used to be on it lay on the floor, broken. The pillowcase under Jada's head was bloody. Number Five's zipper was undone. Two risked a look at Jada and saw the…evidence on her stomach then shifted her gaze back to Five. "We need to be quick. Gather everything."

"What's wrong? Did we get the money?"

"We're doing the switch now."

When Five turned around, Two reached behind her and pulled a specially modified Beretta with a silencer extending from the end of the barrel. Not a piece of pipe stuffed with brillo pads or another makeshift device; this was a professional job. She took two steps toward Five and raised the gun to the side of his head, just above the ear. A small pop sounded, like a balloon breaking. It was followed by a second one. The noise was no cause for concern. Not in this motel.

Five dropped to the floor.

Jada stirred on the bed, trying to wriggle free. Number Two moved to her side, where she untied her hands and feet. "No need to worry. We're going to get you a shower."

Jada shook her head violently.

Two saw the panic in her. "He won't bother you again. I promise. I'll stand guard while you shower."

Two walked her to the bathroom door and removed her gag. "I'm trusting you. Don't let me down."

"I won't."

"All right. Close your eyes. I'm taking your blindfold off, but I want you to keep your eyes closed until the door closes. When you're ready to come out, tell me."

While Jada took a shower, Number Two called Dispatcher.

He answered right away, curiosity apparent in his voice. "Do you want to tell me what's going on. I don't like you calling me. Not a good situation."

"We need a cleanup at the motel."

A sigh followed. "What kind of mess is it?"

"A big mess."

"What else?"

"Tell the cleaners it's room #180."

"Where should the body go?"

"Take it to Boss."

"Anything else?"

"I need another…never mind. I'll take care of it."

Number Two hung up and called Boss. "I need Number Four to babysit."

"What happened to Five?"

"Five is no longer with us."

"What?"

"He broke the rules."

Silence on Boss' end, then, "We'll need Four tomorrow."

"Number Three and I can handle our end. I'm sure you can manage yours."

More silence. "I'll send him over."

"Tell him to use the right door, #182."

"I sent the photo," Boss said.

"Did you scrub it before you sent it?"

"Of course. Nothing but the picture went."

"This will be over tomorrow," Number Two said. "And tell Number Three not to worry. His share just went up."

When Jada was through showering, Number Two put her blindfold back on and led her through the room, careful not to step in the blood seeping into the carpet.

"Where are we going?"

"I'm putting you in the other room."

"What about him?"

"If you mean Number Five, he won't bother you anymore."

"I heard a noise earlier. Is he…"

"I didn't like the way he treated you. I'm getting a replacement sent over."

Number Two felt Jada tense. "Not—"

"No, not Number Three. Someone different."

Number Two put her on the bed in the next room, started tying her. She felt her shaking, heard tears lingering beneath each word.

"What's the matter? You'll be safe. I promise."

"What if you don't get the money?"

"We will."

A lot of hesitation.

"What is it?" Two asked.

"Suppose he doesn't pay? I mean…"

"He will."

Two started to leave but turned back. "When this is all over, you'll have your life back. You won't be able to forget the stuff Five did, but time heals a lot of wounds. Trust me. People like him always pay for it in the end."

Jada started crying, unable to control her tears. "He's not going to pay."

"You mean Number Five, or your father?"

"My father. He won't pay. I know it."

Two sighed. "I'm sure he can be an asshole, but he'll pay." She started to walk away. "He'd better."

***

BOSS GOT OFF THE phone with Number Two then issued instructions for Four to relieve her. Number Three seemed nervous. He paced, moved things around on the desk then paced more.

"What's the matter, Number Three?"

"Suppose he doesn't pay? What are we doing with the girl?"

"He'll pay. Trust me."

"But suppose he doesn't? Two acts like that kid's her own."

Boss got right in his face, inches away. "If he doesn't pay, you can have the girl. But once you're done, she dies."

Three perked up. "What about Two?"

"If she puts up a fight, you can have her, too."

Three rubbed his hands together. "Looks like the shares of this pot keep getting bigger."

Boss grabbed hold of Three and placed a gun to the side of his head. "I said if he *doesn't* pay. Don't get any ideas. Thinking is dangerous for men like you."

Three walked away, mumbling. Boss couldn't hear what he said but got the gist of it from the tone. That was all right; Number Two should be here soon. He'd have to remember to warn her about Three. One way or the other, Boss figured his cut of the ransom had just gone up. Besides, he'd like to see Number Three try to fuck Two.

It would be like a Chihuahua trying to fuck a wolf.

Boss sat at his desk. He changed a few words on the script for the call to Winthrop then fiddled with the final plans for the drop. He didn't like Number Three. He hated to admit it, but the man *did* have a point. Number Two was getting soft on the girl. Boss couldn't have that. If there was one thing he didn't tolerate, it was weakness. He'd have to keep a close eye on them as this project came to a close. He'd already decided it would be his last job with this group. He just wanted to make sure it wasn't his final one.

CHAPTER 43

HELP, DADDY!

I stared at the text they sent—a picture of Jada, naked and tied to a bed. Her face looked as if she'd been beaten. I prayed that was the worst of it.

Bad as that was, the worst part was yet to come. "Lonny, Lucia. You need to come in here."

They ran to the kitchen. Connors stepped aside leaving room for them, and offered a seat to Lucia. She refused it, clutching Lonny's hand so tight I could see the marks on it.

"What is it, Detective?" Her voice was remarkably calm for what I knew she must have felt.

"I want you to stay calm. Perhaps you should sit."

"What's wrong?" Lonny demanded. "Did something happen to Jada?"

"We don't know anything yet, but…they sent this picture." I swallowed hard and showed them the picture. Before long, instinct took over. This picture might have clues for us. "Connors, find me details in this pic. Maybe we can ID the motel. And see if we can get GPS on the pic."

Connors printed a copy and set it on the table. He sent the pic to the techs to analyze. "They didn't give us much. No quilts, no headboard. All we got is a bed. I don't even have wall color here."

I turned to the tech who got the pic. "Anything we can get from this picture?"

"I'll send it downtown, but if they're smart, they took it with an old dumb phone, or they scrubbed it, which means we won't have shit."

"Find something. We've *got* to find something."

I probably let too much desperation show in that statement. Tears flowed out of Lucia as if a faucet had been turned on, hands covering her face as she walked in circles. Soon the cries turned to the keening of a person who's lost everything. The kind you only hear when someone has died. It sent a cold shiver down my spine.

Lonny's arms wrapped around her as he pulled her to him. He rubbed her back and whispered to her, but he was anything but calm. The muscles in his arms flexed; he had the look of a man who wanted to kill someone. I just wished I could put the kidnappers in a cage with him. *That* would be justice.

Mars poked his head in and looked at the picture then went to his parents, doing his best to console both of them. He seemed like a damn good kid. I was almost envious. Maybe I *was* envious. Lonny had a wife who reminded me of Mary and a couple of kids who seemed ideal.

For the millionth time, I wished I hadn't taken this case. I didn't want to be here any more than I had wanted to be with Betty Ming's family when they brought her to the hospital that day so many years ago. The day she looked at me and cried. The words she said to me still haunted me at nights.

"Why didn't you find me yesterday?" she'd said. *"I was still a virgin then."*

I tried blocking my ears so I wouldn't hear Lucia sobbing, anything but that. I fell apart whenever a woman cried. Or a kid. I could do a lot of things—sew myself up with stitches, pack mud in a wound to stop the bleeding, beat a man half to death for things he'd done wrong. I'd done all that and more. Kill a man in cold blood…I could do a lot of things, but listen to a woman suffer…not me. I folded like an old accordion.

Mars led his mother to a seat in the family room and sat next to her. Lonny came into the kitchen. In the ten or twelve steps it took for him to cross the room, I watched his tension build to a critical mass. He grabbed the phone from Connors' hand, stared at the picture then…went berserk. He squeezed the phone, then twisted it, as if he could yank the photo out of there. Or shred it. A growl emerged from him, an animal sound that morphed into words I understood.

"I'm gonna kill that motherfucker!" He grabbed the back of the chair. The veins on the back of his hands bulged. I think he would have broken it if I hadn't intervened, but then I found myself in danger. The man was a beast.

"You hear me? You're dead. I'm gonna find you, and—"

"Calm down, Lonny. Take it easy." I had my arms wrapped around him from behind, but he shrugged me off like I used to do to Ron when he was ten or twelve. "Connors! Anyone."

Connors and one of the other guys came to my rescue, but Lonny was still too much. The chair went down, one of the spindles in the back snapping. I tried moving him away from the table and other things he might break.

Scott came in with Alexa and helped too. Then Lucia was there, her voice subduing him.

"Lonny Hackett!"

He started to settle down then stopped altogether. When she wrapped her arms around him, he fell to the floor in a heap, his head buried in his knees, arms wrapped around his head. "Look what they done to my baby. My fault. It's all my fault."

Lucia sat on the floor next to him. It was her turn to offer comfort. She was good at that.

I empathized with Lonny. Parents blamed themselves when something happened to their kids. It didn't matter if it was truly their fault; they took the blame. I remember blaming myself for Ron's troubles: bad grades, brushes with the law, the drugs.

The drugs most of all. In his case though, it *was* my fault. I wasn't there for him after Mary died, and if ever a kid needs a parent, it's right after they lose one. Not me. I wallowed in self-pity, wondering why God was making me suffer.

I shot a look to Lonny, his head in Lucia's lap, her stroking it. I recalled a strange reaction in him when listening to the original ransom call then his trip to the corner store and his search for the mysterious Willard. Now this. I tried imaging *why* he would blame himself for a kidnapping. *How* could this have been his fault? I didn't have an answer, but I tucked the question in the back of my head. There was too much grief to bring it up now, but sooner or later Lonny had to answer to me for this, especially the Willard thing.

Does Lonny owe him money? Are drugs involved?

I shook my head to refocus. I needed to bring Jada back first…then I'd get to the bottom of the other questions.

"Oh God, Daddy. It's Jada. Look!"

I spun around to see Alexa, the drama queen, staring at the photo. I rushed to her and Scott. "How about we take this outside? They don't need to hear this."

Scott acknowledged my words and led Alexa to the front door.

***

ALEXA HADN'T STOPPED CRYING since she saw the picture. Scott held her, kissing her head. "She'll be all right. Don't worry."

"How will she be all right?"

"I'm sure Detective Cataldi will catch them."

She broke off from the embrace, stared up at her father with hard eyes. "Did you *see* that picture? You know what they probably did? She'll *never* be all right after this."

Scott nodded. There was nothing for him to say.

"Why can't you do something about it, Daddy?"

"Like what?"

"Give them the money."

"That's seven million dollars."

"It's only money. It's not like you don't have enough."

"The money isn't mine. It's—"

"I know. It's the bank's money now, but it'll be yours soon."

Frustrated, Scott started to walk away. "You have no concept of money, or of the work it takes to make it. Everything is given to you." He paced. "Not for long, though. There are going to be changes around here."

Alexa pointed her finger at him. "And you have no concept of what it's like to have a friend. A real friend like Jada. She listens to me. She helps me out when I have problems."

"You should have stayed with your mother."

Alexa was crying again. "I wish I had. At least she cared about my friends."

"Cared about your friends? She didn't even care about *you*. She's the one who called me, begging me to take you."

"You're lying."

"No, Alexa. I'm not. Ask her yourself."

Alexa stared at her father for a few seconds. "Thanks for telling me, Dad. It makes me feel *so* good." Then she burst into tears. She stormed into the house, slamming the door so hard that Scott thought the etched glass might break. Now Scott had one more thing to worry about. He'd thought he was done with the ransom issue, had made up his mind that he couldn't do it. But everyone seemed allied against him—Alexa, the detective, and, of course, the Hacketts. They never said anything specific, but he could see the accusations in their eyes and almost hear it in their voices whenever the subject of the ransom was raised. What the hell did they expect from him? It was seven million dollars.

***

I WATCHED ALEXA STORM by, followed a moment later by Scott. I had no idea what that was about. When parents and kids are involved anything could trigger an argument, from the simplest to the most complex problems. The emotions seemed the same regardless of the degree. The Hacketts were still in the other room, almost in mourning. And I was holding down the fort in the kitchen, armed with coffee—good coffee— and nothing else. No clues. No idea where to go next. And no ransom money. That last hurt the most. I had no idea how we were going to save that girl without the ransom.

Unless we get lucky with the motel.

I looked at the picture again. The text underneath it said.

We'll call soon.

Once again I got that sickening feeling of letting the Hacketts down. I hadn't wanted this case to begin with. I hated kidnappings. Now I'd fucked up good, and that mistake was gonna cost. The longer Jada stayed with the kidnappers, the chances of her being raped or killed soared. It would take a miracle for her to come out of this even close to normal. Lonny Hackett should be blaming me, not himself. And God knew I didn't need this. The nights weren't long enough for me to cram more nightmares into them.

CHAPTER 44

LIKE FATHER, LIKE SON

Mars gritted teeth as he watched his mother fall apart. When his father cried, he turned his head, struggling to control the anger building inside him. He had a lot of his mother's genes, and they worked to keep him focused. Mars said all the right things to his dad, made a few jokes about what Jada was probably thinking, and then insisted that when they caught the bad guys, he'd take care of them.

"You're getting too old, Old Man," he said. "You need to let the young blood handle the tough jobs."

Inside though, anger kept building, and Mars was running out of places to stash it. Sooner or later, he'd have to let it go; he also had a lot of his father's genes in him.

Besides what was happening to his parents, Mars had his own emotions to resolve. Seeing Jada like that... He swore right then that he'd kill the fuckers who did this if he found them. No fancy lawyers would ever get a chance with them.

Once his parents were doing better, he slipped into the kitchen, took the keys from his mother's purse, and slipped out the door. Half a block away, he was already on the phone. The first person he called was Justin, a kid whose allowance was probably more than what Mars' father made in a month, but he did his best to dress like he'd just escaped the slums. And he paid damn good money for that privilege. Justin answered right away. He always did. No one called him.

"S'up, dude?"

"Stop trying to talk like you're black. I don't even talk like that, and I *am* black."

A pause, then, "What's up, Mars?"

"Have you seen Jason Rules today?"

"Jason? The fuck you want him for?"

Mars sighed. "Did you forget the 'what' in that sentence? Have you seen him or not?"

"Down by the mall a little while ago. Him and all his boys."

"Thanks."

"What you want Jason for?"

"I'll tell you later. Gotta go."

On the way to the mall, Mars thought of all the fun times he and Jada had growing up. Of all the things she'd done for him over the years—helping him with homework, teaching him to dance, the crucial advice she gave about girls. She'd always been there for him. It was time for Mars to be there for her.

He pulled into the parking lot where Jason and his crew normally hung out. No sign of them, not even empty beer cans to indicate that they had recently left. Mars headed out the back side of the mall and drove down to Whataburger, another likely hangout. Again, no Jason. He tried a park where they sometimes went, and when that didn't pan out, a strip center that was almost abandoned. Bingo! There was Jason with his whole crew, hanging out and acting tough.

Those detectives had said they'd questioned Jason, but Jason would never tell the cops anything. That wasn't the way he played the game. He and his "boys" dreamed of being gangstas, did everything they could to pretend they already were. The way Mars saw it, they were a bunch of punks living off the adoration of the sheep at school who thought they were cool. Jada and her friends included.

Mars didn't know shit about this detective stuff, but he figured he could ask questions. He pulled alongside of Jason's truck and got out. Jason didn't acknowledge him, but they had never had a friendly relationship, and Mars was almost two years younger.

Mars walked up to him, got to within a few feet of the older boy, and stopped. He nodded. "Jason, have you seen my sister in the last few days?"

From a five- or six-inch height advantage, he sneered down at Mars. "You her dad?"

"She's in trouble. I need to know if you've seen her, or if you know who she was with."

"Cops already been there. I told them I got nothing."

"I know what you told them, but I figured maybe you know *something*. Anything that would help."

Jason didn't look at Mars, but Mars continued. "She stayed at Alexa's night before last. On her way to school, best as we can figure, somebody snatched her. Did you see anything? Talk to her that morning? See any cars or vans or trucks that didn't belong in the neighborhood?"

"Go home, little man. I got no time for you."

"You need to make time. I'm not leaving without answers."

Jason's crew surrounded Mars. He'd seen them do this before, mostly for intimidation. Jason had a tough-ass reputation, but from what Mars could tell, he seldom fought anyone. Never anyone tough.

Jason stepped up to Mars and flicked his cigarette at him. "Me and my boys don't feel like talking. So you go on home. And when your sister comes home, tell her I'm a little hungry for some black meat."

That drew a laugh from everyone but Mars, who grabbed him by the throat and squeezed. Jason broke the hold then pushed back. He threw his fists in the air, ready to fight. "Let's go, motherfucker. You're dead."

"I don't want to hurt you, Jason. Tell me what you know."

Jason came after Mars, throwing a right punch then pushing forward with a left.

Mars grabbed hold of Jason's arm with his left hand, and Jason's collar with his right. As he pulled Jason with his movement, Mars' right foot swept Jason off his feet. He hit the parking lot—hard.

Mars was on top of him in a second. He took hold of Jason's left arm, twisted it then got him in an arm-bar, a jiu-jitsu hold. From there, he could break Jason's arm with one move. The fight was over less than half a minute after it had started. All that remained was getting the information.

"What do you know about Jada?"

"Let go of my fucking arm. You're breaking it."

"It's not broken yet, but if you don't talk, it will be." Mars kept an eye on Jason's boys, but they weren't doing anything. As he figured, the whole bunch of them were pussies. Mars put more pressure on Jason's arm, bringing him to the point where it could break at any moment. He was begging Mars to let him go.

Mars was convinced of two things right now—Jason didn't know where Jada was, and he was a bigger pussy than he'd thought. Mars let go of his arm and got to his feet, waiting for Jason to get up. "Go near Jada again, and I'll take you out for good."

"Who the fuck you think you are?" one of Jason's boys said.

Mars stared him down. "I'm a Hackett." He got into position to fight, shoulders slightly hunched, arms out from his sides. "I got plenty left if you want some."

The boy backed off. "I got no time for little sixteen-year-old punks."

"Just for tonight, how about we pretend I'm eighteen? Come on. Let's do it."

The other guy backed up quickly. The circle that had formed around Mars parted. Mars straightened up, looked at each of them as he went through. "Any of you see anything?"

No one responded until Mars got to his car. One of the boys broke rank and walked over.

"Mars, wait up."

"You got something?"

"I don't know. It's probably nothing, but yesterday morning I'm waiting at my bus stop, and I see this lady drive by three times."

"Where's your bus stop?"

"A couple of blocks from Alexa's house."

"Same lady? You're sure?"

"I *know* it was the same lady. She's a goddamn fox. I park valet over at Kirby's. She came in a few times. I mean a stone-cold fox."

"You know her name or where she lives?"

"I know part of her plate. VNA, then some numbers."

"How the hell do you remember that?"

"When we parked it the first time and she got out, me and my bro couldn't quit staring at her ass. Then he saw the plate and said 'Check it out, VNA—very nice ass.' We laughed about that."

"How old was this woman?"

"I don't know, dude. She was a fox, a cougar, a bobcat, one of them things. All I know is she had a damn nice ass."

Mars tapped him on the shoulder. "Thanks."

"No problem. See you around."

Mars drove to Alexa's house. He had no idea if this information would be any use to the detective, but it was worth a shot. Jason needed his ass kicked anyway.

CHAPTER 45

THE CALL

Tension was high at the Winthrop house. Not a smile was to be found. If someone had dropped a live grenade, it would have been a mad rush to see who could dive on it first to end their misery. It was seven o'clock, but none of us had eaten dinner, living off coffee, a few biscuits left from breakfast, and a bag of pretzels we found in the cupboard.

When the phone rang a few minutes later, it might as well have been a live grenade. Everyone jumped.

One of the techs stepped into the kitchen on the second ring. "Unknown caller!"

I looked around and found Lonny. "Remember, not a word."

Scott stood beside me looking nervous.

"Are you ready for this?" I asked.

He nodded.

"Pick it up on my signal," I said, "and remember, keep looking at this pad. If I need to tell you something, I'll write it down."

We all got our headsets on. On the fifth ring, I gave Scott the go ahead.

"Hello."

"Is this Mr. Winthrop?" It was the same voice as last time, the professional one.

"This is he."

"You messed up sending that cop."

"I'm sorry. I—"

"Bad as that was, though, you *really* fucked up by not sending the money."

I scribbled on the paper. *Blame me.*

"The cop said it was best…"

Money tainted, I wrote.

"He said the money was—"

"Bullshit! Tell Detective Cataldi to stop feeding you lines."

The front door opened, and Mars came in. Sameena got to him before he could say anything. She had him go back with his parents.

Scott did a good job of composing himself. "What do you want?"

"What I wanted all along. Seven million dollars. And you know *how* we want it." A long pause, then, "The problem is, you made a mistake and it's going to cost you. If your daughter was a virgin before, your greed has cost her that."

The first thing I thought of was Lonny going wild. I turned quickly. He was about to react when Lucia's hand went over his mouth.

"Don't you *dare* say a word. They'll kill her."

***

SCOTT HEARD THE WORDS *If she was a virgin before, your greed has cost her that.* He cringed, felt like crawling into a hole. "No!"

The man on the phone said, "It was your greed that did it. You're to blame."

Scott had built his career on making quick, insightful decisions. He hoped his fortune continued, because he was about to make another decision, and he had no time to consult with Gino about it. "I'll pay you an extra hundred-thousand dollars."

"I'm afraid—"

Before the kidnapper finished, a woman's voice from the background interrupted him. "Wait!"

Silence followed then what sounded like arguing before the man came back on the line. "A nice surprise, Mr. Winthrop. We are not unreasonable people. We reward creativity. Make sure you add the new money to the bags."

Scott thought about the decision he'd just made. It could be a life-changing one. Somehow, though, he felt better. Cleaner. "What about my daughter? When will I see her?"

"After we get the money."

"How—"

"Oh, and Mr. Winthrop, come yourself this time. Don't send a cop pretending to be Uncle Eddy."

Detective Cataldi scribbled furiously on the scratch pad. *Don't do it.*

"Don't worry. I'll be there."

"A wise decision. We'll call in the morning, *after* you get the money from the bank. I'll call around ten."

As Scott was about to hang up, the man spoke again. "One more thing. Go to Academy and pick up two Adidas sports bags. You'll need two bags for the money, as it's quite heavy. We've already tested these bags; they're big enough to handle that amount. Each bag will weigh about seventy pounds, but you're a strong man, Winthrop. I'm confident you can manage."

"I'll manage."

"Good."

***

SCOTT HUNG UP, LOOKING as if he'd been victorious. I didn't know if he had or not, but at least we'd bought some time. Before I could gather my thoughts, Lonny rushed into the kitchen.

"What about Jada? Do you think—"

"If you mean do I think they'll molest her, I doubt it. Mr. Winthrop's fast thinking may have saved her from that. I know you're worried, Lonny, but for now, let's focus on bringing her back alive. Everything after that is a bonus."

From behind Lonny, Mars said, "Detective, I may have something for you. I don't know if it's important or not, but…"

"What?"

"A car came by the house several times in the days before they got Jada. A woman was driving, and—"

"How do you know this, Mars?"

"I asked some friends, they—"

I tried to keep the anger from my voice, but I don't think it worked. "What did you say? Who did you talk to?"

Mars seemed nervous now. "Friends, some kids."

"Goddamnit! I told everyone not to say *anything, to anyone.*"

"All I did was—"

Sameena had come over, probably warning me off, but my anger had built to a level where I couldn't keep the tone down. I didn't even try. "What you did was maybe get your sister killed. If they find out they don't have Alexa, your sister's life is nothing to them. Less than nothing."

Mars was crying now, and Lucia had come up to hug him. "Is she gonna be all right?" he asked through the tears. "I was just trying to do something. I couldn't stand just sitting here."

"How the hell do I know if she'll be all right?" I started to settle down.

Crying kids always did that to me. Kids and women. And the tears usually followed one of my rantings. I patted his shoulder. "I'm sorry to upset you, but *please* stay at the house and don't talk to anyone outside."

Scott looked at Mars, then Lonny and Lucia. "Don't worry. Jada will be all right."

I had forgiven Mars already. Scott was another matter. "How the hell do you know that, Mr. Winthrop? Let *me* run this show."

"She'll be all right because I'm giving them the money."

I stopped. Stared. Lucia let go of Mars and ran to Scott, embracing him. Lonny looked as if he'd fall again.

"What?" I said.

Scott hugged Lucia. "I decided to let the Hacketts have the money." He laughed then, one of those cover-up laughs that people do when they don't really mean it. "Of course, I hope you recover it, Detective. I don't want to start my life all over again."

Lonny was beside him now, looking like a kid at a grownup's party, with no idea what to say.

"I'm gonna cook us some dinner," Lucia said. "I *know* I'm hungry, and I'm betting everyone else is too."

Scott laughed, and I realized it was the first genuine laughter in this house all day. "Detective, are you hungry?"

"I'll get something. This is all good news, so good, that I'm going to send everyone home to freshen up for tomorrow." I went to Scott and Lonny. "You both have my cell. If anything happens, call me. Otherwise, I'll see you early in the morning. And remember, don't talk to anyone."

I walked over to Mars my hand extended. "Sorry about blowing up. We're all under pressure, but it's no excuse."

"I shouldn't have done it," Mars said, and shook Cataldi's hand.

"That's okay. Now how about telling me the rest of what happened."

Mars filled me in on the story, including the part about the VNA license plate and how the friend remembered it because the lady had a *very nice ass.* I let him finish his story and thanked him again. Before leaving, I called Connors and the rest of them into the room where the techs had set up. "I want you to go home, get some rest, and be ready for tomorrow. Be here by eight."

"Anything we need to do?" Connors asked.

I looked around. "Yeah, think of ways for us to catch these guys. We've got three things to focus on: catching the kidnappers; getting Winthrop back his money; and most importantly, bringing Jada home safe."

"You don't think they'll let her go when they get the money?" Connors said.

"As far as I'm concerned, there is no way in hell they'll let her go. The fact that they are talking about raping her means they were already thinking about it—at the very least. So put your thinking caps on, people. Tomorrow we've got to be smarter than them."

CHAPTER 46

ANOTHER LONG NIGHT

Delgado stopped by Gino's house on his way home. He tapped on the back door then let himself in. "Hey, Gino. Where are you?"

Gino exited the kitchen and headed toward the bathroom. "I'll be right back. Gotta take a leak."

Delgado took a seat at the kitchen table—actually a poker table with a top that flipped over to make a flat surface. It reminded him of the fun they used to have when Mary was alive. Friday night poker games were a staple at Gino's house. Mary would cook fajitas with homemade tortillas, and there was always an ample supply of Dos Equis to wash it down. Half the guys ended up spending the night after they lost their money to either Delgado or Gino, but they didn't mind. The stakes weren't high, and the food and beer made losing worth it. Laughter was guaranteed. Delgado looked around the house. It hadn't seen laughter since. Even the walls seemed lonely now.

The bathroom door opened, and Gino came out. "What are you doing here, Ribs? Want a beer?"

"Just stopped by to see my cuz. See how the world is treating you."

"I don't know about you, but I'm getting a beer."

When Gino walked by, Delgado saw redness in his eyes. He'd been crying again, and likely about Mary. Or about that little girl the kidnappers had. If anything could make Gino cry, it was Mary, or Ron, or kids in trouble. Especially if he blamed himself.

"Hope you don't have some sweet young honey handcuffed to the bed."

Gino fake laughed. "Yeah, that's what it is. She's in the bathroom now, so if you have to go, step outside and man-dog it."

"You know I can do that."

"Sure you don't want a beer?"

"Dos Equis?"

"Corona."

"Might as well bring me one," Delgado said. "Did we do any good today?"

"A lot better than I figured. Scott coughed up the money."

Delgado whistled, long and low. "You're shitting me."

"Seven million worth of love for his fellow man."

"I never figured Winthrop for that kind of love."

Gino handed Delgado a beer. "Let's go outside. It's a nice night."

Delgado followed him out to the porch. "You need a dog, Gino. Someone to keep you company on nights like this."

"There aren't enough good nights for me to worry about."

"Fuckin' pussy is what you are. Down in Mexico—" Delgado always said *Mexico* the Spanish way, with the X pronounced as an H.

"I know all about it, Ribs. Got to one hundred before noon, right?"

"Before ten."

Gino laughed. "When are you going to stop pretending you're from Mexico?"

Delgado took a long swig of beer and stared up at the stars. "Who knows? In a perfect world…never. In this fucked up world we live in…" He took another swig. "Who knows?"

"Speaking of fucked up, I really let Lucia down on this."

Delgado gave him the crooked glare. "And Lonny."

"What?"

"You said you let Lucia down. I just reminded you that Lonny was part of that too."

"What are you saying?"

"I'm saying you're trying to make her Mary. She's not. She belongs to that other man." Delgado gulped the last of his Corona. "And if you don't mind me citing an observation, that man could snap you in half. Maybe even after you shot him with your gun."

"Did you come by to piss me off?"

"It's my job. I felt obligated."

Gino finished his beer and tossed the bottle into the container. "Next time you feel *obligated*, go home."

Delgado went inside to the fridge and came back out with two more beers. "You've been in a bitchy mood since I got here. Why don't you get some sleep?"

"I can't."

"Okay, you get second prize. Let's bust some motel doors down. We've got plenty of them left."

"What happened to Sanchez?"

Delgado brushed his hand in the air. "That pussy went home. Said something about feeding six kids."

"You're right, she is a pussy."

Delgado sat on the edge of the chair. "So you want to go, or do I have to do this myself?"

The first smile of the night came to Gino's face. "Now you got me excited, cuz."

"So you're finally accepting that blood shit, huh?"

"No, I just like calling you cuz."

Delgado finished his beer in a couple of long gulps. "Let's go. I don't have all night."

***

I KNEW DELGADO WOULDN'T let up until I agreed to go, so…I agreed. "Have you got any leads, or is Rosalee pissed at you?"

"When isn't she?"

I started to get in my car, but Delgado grabbed my keys. "I've seen you drive sober, my man. I'm not getting in there after you've had a couple."

We headed north on I-45, toward Conroe.

"When are you gonna start dating?" Ribs asked.

I didn't bother answering.

"When was the last time you went out with someone?"

"Lay off it."

"I'm asking because I'm tired of Rosalee lining up all of her friends to go out with you, and then you blow it off."

"Ribs, I love your wife, and I love her cooking, but tell Rosalee to mind her own business."

"I'll let you tell her that." Ribs drove in silence for a few miles. He was waiting for me to talk.

"I haven't met anyone who interests me."

He looked at me from the corner of his eye. "No one who interests you? You told Rosalee you didn't want to go out with Mexicans because they reminded you of Mary. No one with dark hair—Mary again. And no brown eyes—Mary." He exited the freeway into Conroe and stayed on the feeder road. "Why don't you see if sweet-boy Chad's got any friends who like big strong cops? His friends won't remind you of Mary."

"You're crossing the line, Ribs."

"Just trying to help."

"I do fine living my life without you."

"Suit yourself, amigo."

I rolled the window down, let the air blow in my face. "Tell me again why we're going to this motel."

"Julie said they had three adjacent rooms rented two days ago."

"Three? Sounds like overkill for our guys. Why three rooms for one girl?"

"Let's find out."

"You got Lance and his crew coming?"

"They went home, but I got a standby if we need it. We'll call it after we see what we got."

"This isn't the old west, you know. I don't want to walk into a goddamn shootout."

"That would be fun though, huh? Just one time, shoot it out with these fuckers instead of arresting them."

"Maybe for you, but I didn't fare too well at the shooting range. I need to get the drop on the bad guys."

"Don't worry, you got me to watch out for you."

"I'd rather have Tip."

"Did you forget I came in fifth in the shooting contest?"

"I know, Ribs, and that's good. But Tip came in first." I didn't add *like he does every year*, but only because Delgado knew it.

"I don't count Tip. He's a mutant." Delgado turned right on #105. "In fact, they shouldn't count him at all. So the way I figure, it I really came in fourth."

"Good by me," I said.

A few blocks later, Ribs pulled into the motel parking lot. We went inside, where we showed the clerk our badges.

"I'm Detective Delgado, and this is Detective Cataldi," Ribs said. "Someone talked to you a short while ago."

The man got nervous as soon as he saw the badges, looking around as if it were a crime to be seen with us. "I told her all there was to tell on the phone."

I knew he was a local from the way he talked. "What rooms are they in?"

"Around the back. First three rooms when you turn the corner."

"You got their information?"

He looked around again. "I don't rightly know if I should…Can I give that out? Isn't that private or something?"

Delgado leaned over the counter, whispering as if it were between the two of them. "It's about as private as your cell's gonna be when I send a team up to see how many underage people you let in here with alcohol and drugs."

He loosened up quite a bit after that. "Far as I recall, the gentleman showed a license from North Carolina." He seemed to focus more on remembering than on worrying about being seen talking to us. "What did these folks do? Nothin' bad, I hope." After hearing the clerk talk more, I not only knew he was local, I figured he might not have ever left the area.

"Did you see the family? You told the woman who called that a family had rented the rooms."

"You know when that young lady called, it got me thinking. I knew something was wrong. These people been here two days, but I haven't heard diddly squat from them. Been here *two* days, and they won't even let the maids go in."

Delgado looked to me, and I nodded. "If you'll give us the keys, sir."

The man fished in a drawer then handed two sets of keys to Delgado. "Here's two of them. Hold on and I'll get the other."

"Don't bother," I said. "These will do."

He followed us out the door, hot on our heels. We couldn't shut the man up. "What in tarnation do you think they're doin' in there? I run a clean establishment. I don't tolerate drugs or women of ill-repute. I'm a God-fearing man. I..."

Delgado pulled out his gun, jammed a fresh clip in then stared at the guy. "I think it would be best if you stayed inside, sir. There could be trouble."

His eyes got about as big as eggs. "What kind of trouble?"

I handed him one of my cards. "If you hear gunshots, call this number and tell them to come. Quickly."

That sent him back inside, probably hiding behind the counter.

"And we're only thirty miles from downtown Houston," I said to Ribs.

"Imagine that."

We came to the corner, both of us with guns drawn. Ribs had a set of keys in one hand and his gun in the other. "Cover me," he said.

"I got it, partner."

"Aren't you even gonna argue over who goes in first? That's the macho thing to do."

"I'm not macho, and besides, you're a better shot."

"That talk doesn't make me feel secure when you're supposed to have my back. You better not shoot me."

"I'll do my best," I said then took a spot behind a parked car, offering a good view of all three rooms.

Ribs stepped quietly up to the first door on the left, looked my way then reached over and knocked. I tensed up, crouched a little lower, and got a good grip on my gun. After a few seconds with no answer, he knocked again. We waited. Still no answer.

Ribs signaled he was going to the next door. Again he knocked, hard. When no one answered, he opened the door with the keys. I moved up beside him, and when he pushed it open, I went in low. Ribs followed up.

"Police!" I shouted as we moved inside.

No one was there. We kept our guns drawn. I cleared the room while Ribs covered me and watched the other two doors. Then we repeated the whole thing to clear the other rooms. No one was there. We searched the rooms but found no sign of anything strange. These were a family's rooms. Suitcases filled with clothes, including kids. They even had a few games, the kind people played on road trips—state capitals, license-plate game—things like that. I shook my head. "I don't think we busted the case on this one."

"I'm getting a complex, Gino. Are these guys too smart for us?"

As Ribs pulled out and got onto the freeway, I gave thought to what he said. "I hope not. For Jada's sake, I hope not."

CHAPTER 47

WHO KNEW WHAT

Ribs headed south on I-45, keeping pace with the traffic. "What's the time, Ribs?"

"Time to catch the guy who stole your watch. Or you could just look at your damn phone to get the time."

"It's easier to ask you," I said, and then, "As to the watch, I'll get the guy. Don't worry about that." I leaned back in the seat, head resting against the window, watching the trees as we rolled by.

"Almost ten," Ribs said.

"What?"

"I said it's almost ten o'clock. What the hell are you thinking about that's got your mind so busy?"

"Sorry." I straightened up. "I haven't had time to think much since this all happened, but there is something strange about what these kidnappers know."

"Like what?"

"First off, they knew Scott's home number."

"Come on, Gino, anybody—"

"Hang on. Let me finish."

I gathered my thoughts again. "His number is private, and yeah, I know that's easy enough to get. But they knew his cell phone too. They knew he would come into money. *Knew* the money was ready at the bank."

"They said that?"

"Yeah. I guess we haven't caught up since the whole thing with Doran. When Doran told them the money wasn't ready, they said 'I *know* the money is ready.'"

"Shit."

"Yeah, and get this—when Doran told them that Scott figured it would be best if we came without the money, they looked at him and said, 'Tell Detective Cataldi he made a big mistake.'"

"Keep talking, Gino. The story's getting interesting."

"Before Doran left, they said they *knew* he wasn't Uncle Eddy."

"What the fuck is going on?"

"I don't know, but stop for coffee. We've got to figure this out."

"Tonight?"

"The drop is tomorrow. When the fuck do you think we're going to do it?"

"Let me call Rosalee." He put his phone on speaker and dialed. "Don't forget to say hi to her, Gino. You know she loves you."

Rosalee answered right away. "Ribs, where are you? It's late."

Even Rosalee called him Ribs. Of course, she'd known him since he was ten, so she grew up with the nickname.

"I'm with Gino, *mi chula*. We picked up some girls and right now we're locked in a motel room. I don't think I'll make it home tonight."

A long silence, then, "Are you and Gino out playing poker again?"

I laughed. "Rosalee, you are the only woman I know who would suspect her husband of playing cards instead of cheating on her."

"I'm the only woman that would put up with his ass, Gino." She laughed, then, "How's Ron?"

"He's doing great ever since rehab."

"I talked to him last week. Did he tell you?"

"He said you called. Thanks. It meant a lot to him."

"I'm taking Marianna to see him next week. She's making tamales."

"He'll love that, Rosalee. I'm gonna give you back to that asshole husband of yours now. You take care."

"Are you really going to be out all night, Ribs?"

"We might be. We're trying to find the kidnapped girl."

"*Dios mio!* I'll be praying for her."

"*Buenas noches, mi amorcita.*"

"*Buenas noches, querido.*"

Ribs hung up and looked over to me. "Where to?"

"Let's get breakfast."

"Denny's?"

"If you've got a better idea, I'll take it. If not…I've got Tums."

Ten minutes later, we slid into a booth at the same Denny's that Doran had been to this morning. That seemed like days ago. The waitress pounced on us. She had coffee cups filled before we said we wanted any. I thought of ordering tea just to piss her off.

She pulled out her order pad with a sparkly green Bic pen attached to it and positioned herself to take our orders.

"We're going to need some time," I said. That sent her away in a huff.

"Treat the lady with kindness," Delgado said. "Or she'll put something in our food."

Delgado always made me laugh. "Okay, Ribs, you win."

"You know, I been thinking since you brought this up. This sounds too familiar, almost like the poker games and the home invasions, where they also knew too much."

I ripped the top off the second container of creamer, dumped it into my coffee, and stirred. "Goddamnit, Ribs. Goddamnit!" I pulled out my cell and looked up Doran's number.

"Who are you calling?"

"Doran."

"It's ten thirty."

"I don't give a shit."

After the fifth ring, he answered. "Doran, it's Gino."

His voice sounded sleepy. I found myself envious. "Detective, what's going on?"

"In the garage today, you said they wore gloves and masks."

"Yeah, both of them."

"Tell me about the gloves. Describe them."

"Latex ones, you know, the kind doctors wear."

Surgeons' gloves. Just like the others. "And they wore masks. What kind?"

"Dark nylons. Why, what's going on?"

"Anything else? Did they say anything to each other? Mention names?"

"No names. One guy called the other one 'boss.' That's all."

I clenched my fist and forced myself to stay calm. "Boss? You're sure about that?"

"I'm sure. Why?"

"I'll fill you in tomorrow. Be there early."

I hung up and turned to Ribs. "These are the same fuckers who did the Marshall house."

"Why do you say that?"

"We can forget the masks and gloves, but Doran said one of them called the other one Boss."

Ribs nodded. "Works for me. Sounds like the kind of organization they use. Structured, disciplined. Masks. Gloves. No mistakes." Ribs sipped his coffee, added another sugar to it then stirred more. "I know you don't want to think about it, but if these are the guys who did the Marshalls' house, it means they're the ones who did the poker games."

I nodded. "I'm way past you. That means they've not only have Jada, they may have Mary's watch."

"It's nice that we figured this out, but the problem is, they don't make mistakes."

"Except one."

"One what?"

"One mistake. They shouldn't have taken that girl."

CHAPTER 48

GINO MAKES A CHART

We finished a greasy breakfast, mopped it up with toast, and chased it down with bad coffee. If there had been hope of sleeping before this, it was gone. On the way to my house, we discussed the best way to crack this case and agreed that we couldn't rely on them letting Jada go. We had to find her. The ransom wouldn't guarantee her safety. It might, however, make it easier to catch the kidnappers.

Delgado went straight to the fridge at my house and got a Corona.

"How can you drink beer after eating that breakfast?"

He put on his best Mexican accent and said, "It's a Corona, amigo."

I laughed again, the second time tonight. "Boil some water. I'm making coffee."

"You know, Gino, I think what's more important than what they know is what they didn't know. That's what we need to focus on."

I got a tablet out and a few pens and drew a chart.

What they knew:	What they didn't know:
~~Knew Scott's home number~~	Too easy to get. Not an issue.
~~Knew Scott's cell number~~	Same
Knew the money was ready at bank	Did not know we didn't have money
Knew Detective Cataldi's name	First time we knew that was at garage
Knew Doran had a cell phone	But didn't say "Don't bring it."
Knew Doran wasn't Uncle Eddy	But not until they got to garage?

Delgado stood over my shoulder, nodding. He grabbed a big red marker and wrote at the bottom:

Biggest one of all—do not know they have wrong girl.

I looked at him and nodded. "You're right about that. That's the biggest mystery. How the *fuck* do they know everything else but not that?"

"That's what we've got to figure out. We do that, and we've got them."

I got up to fix my coffee, and Ribs took my seat. "How about we start by scratching out who knows everything? We can eliminate them."

"To start off with, all the cops know the case, so we can eliminate them."

"What about the support team? We've got Julie, Fat Charlie—"

"Get serious. No way they're leaking anything."

"Gino, they're not the only ones on the support team. They used a dozen people calling motels and gathering information. Any one of them could be a leak."

"I don't buy it. I know it *could* happen, but I don't buy it."

"Okay," Ribs said. "We've got Winthrop, the Hacketts, Alexa, Mars, the techs at the house…"

As he ran down the list, I gave them thought. "No way on the Hacketts. Same for Alexa."

The timer went off for my coffee. I poured it, added cream, and walked back to the table. "No on the techs…"

"That leaves Winthrop," Ribs said.

"And all of the people Winthrop and Alexa have blabbed to. It's no wonder the kidnappers have the information. Half the people in The Woodlands know."

"We need to find out what he told his colleagues."

I sipped the coffee. Shivered. "Ribs, what was the name of that coffee Winthrop had?"

"Martin Henry."

"What?"

"It's comes from Martin Henry Roasters, somewhere in the Northwest."

"Damn, it was good."

"I could get used to it," Ribs said.

I sipped some more coffee. Paced some more. "Okay, so who's giving them information? They knew about the money at the bank being ready. They knew Doran wasn't Uncle Eddy. But they don't know they have the wrong girl. How is that possible? Is it someone from Scott's work? Do the people he works with hate him as much as I do?"

Delgado jotted down more notes. "Their knowing about Doran doesn't bother me that much. They could have made him for a cop. Maybe they had a kid with them. Teenagers can pick a cop out of a crowd by sight, smell, or sound."

Delgado had a point. Something gave us away to kids. It was a lifelong mystery likely to never be solved. "Okay we throw out the Doran issue. That still leaves us with a lot of questions."

"We don't have time for it, Gino. We're gonna need more help."

It didn't take long for me to decide. "I'm calling Tip."

"Captain's not gonna like that."

I dialed Tip's number. After a few rings he picked up.

"Tip Denton, best damn detective in Texas."

It had been a long time since I'd heard that asinine phrase of his. "What happened to 'best in the world'?"

"Today I'm only best in Texas. And what the hell are you doing calling this late? You know I need my beauty sleep."

"I need help, old partner."

"On that home invasion?"

"Kinda. I'm still on that, but the last two days, I've been on a kidnapping. We're pretty sure the same people are involved. And by the way, if you haven't heard, in the home invasion deal, that kid died. It's now felony murder."

"Y'all can count me in on this. What do you need?"

"I got Delgado over at my house. Come over, and we'll plot this out."

Half an hour later, Tip walked in with three cups of coffee and three taquitos. I didn't have the nerve to tell him we'd already eaten; besides, no way I was turning down a taquito. I filled Tip in on everything from the poker games up to tonight's disaster at the motel in Conroe.

He sat still, looking deep in thought. "I'm gonna have to interview that thong-panties girl first. She sounds like the culprit to me. Might take me the rest of the night, but I'll get it done."

Delgado's laughter cranked Tip up. "Delgado, did I ever tell you the one about the midget and the sex-starved Mexican?"

I made more coffee. This was going to be a *very* long night.

"Did you call Coop?" Tip asked.

"I'm calling her now."

"Oh shit."

It rang four times before she answered. "Cataldi, I swear to the Lord in heaven, this better be an emergency."

"I need Tip on this case. We've got too many leads to follow and no time to do it."

"Have you called him yet?"

I opted not to answer that question. "Were you sleeping?"

"I was in the damn tub. Again."

Tip grabbed the phone. "Hey, darlin', can I come over and share that tub with you?"

"Denton, is that you? I knew it. It's starting already." We heard the sounds of water splashing, like she was getting out of the tub. "I better not end up with a bunch of bodies."

"Thanks, Coop. We'll call in the morning."

"It *is* the morning."

After that, we got back to strategizing. The plan was for Tip to go to Scott's work to interview his team and anyone else he came in close contact with. Delgado would pick up where he left off with Lance and his crew of mercenaries, and I would head to the bank with Scott, pick up the money then wait for the kidnappers to call.

Delgado said, "I hope those fuckers forget their smart pills tomorrow, because they sure outfoxed us today."

About four o'clock, I couldn't take it anymore. "I have to catch a few hours of sleep. One of you can crash on the couch, and there's a spare bed in the other room."

"I'll take the couch," Delgado said.

"Wake me early," Tip said. "I'm fixin' to shoot somebody before noon."

"Remember what Coop said, Tip. This ain't Tombstone."

"It was you that shot everybody last time. Not me."

"*Good night,* Tip."

"Night, darlin'."

I heard Delgado laughing as I went to bed.

As I lay in bed, I heard the clock ticking, heard the house creaking, heard goddamn Delgado snoring, even through the walls. It was no wonder I couldn't sleep. Worst of all, I could hear Lucia crying when she saw that picture of Jada naked. I'd *promised* these people I'd bring her home safe. How was I going to do that? These guys had outsmarted me at every turn, and I had no brilliant plans for tomorrow.

For another hour, I lay there, running the whole thing through my head again and again. I pictured the way they handled the drop with Doran, tried to anticipate what they might do tomorrow…today. Then I thought about the motel angle, assuming Alexa's interpretation of Jada's Uncle Eddy comment was correct. I closed my eyes and pictured them in the room, Jada tied to the bed. Suddenly it hit me. What were they doing when the maids come in? I jumped out of bed. "Delgado! Tip! Get up."

"What's going on?" Delgado sat up, rubbing sleep from his eyes.

Tip stumbled into the kitchen. "I said early, but I wanted *some* sleep."

Adrenaline rushed through me. "Ribs, what do they do when the maids come?"

He looked at me as if I were nuts. "What?"

"The maids! Motel rooms are cleaned every day. These guys can't have maids coming in with Jada there."

Delgado jumped up, a light in his eyes. "*Hijo de puta!* A do-not-disturb sign."

"Exactly! So we get Julie to find all the rooms that have had do-not-disturb signs on them for the past two days, and we've got 'em, Ribs. We've got 'em."

"I want in on this," Tip said. "Fuck interviewing a bunch of scientists. I want to shoot somebody."

I grabbed Delgado's cell phone; mine was charging. "Anybody know Julie's number?"

Tip poured water into the coffee pot. "You mean Sixties Julie?"

"That's her."

"It's probably some combination of the astrological chart and a Bob Dylan song."

Delgado was still rubbing his eyes. "What the hell is that supposed to mean?"

"I don't know, but it sounded good."

I shook my head and stared at Ribs. "You see what I mean."

Tip gave me the number, and I called Julie, fully prepared to apologize profusely. She answered on the first ring, sounding every bit like the Sixties Julie she always did. I heard the unmistakable sound of "Sgt Pepper's Lonely Hearts Club Band" in the background. Combined with her chipper voice, I could only assume she had not yet been asleep, which caused me to wonder once again about the contents of the lunch bags that she brought every day—and guarded ferociously.

"Julie, I hate to bother you, but we need help."

"No problem, Gino. What have you got?"

I filled her in on the motel idea and asked if she could get some people on the phones right away.

"I'll leave in a few minutes."

"Thanks. And call Delgado with any news." I started to hang up, then remembered I hadn't run the plates Mars had given me, "One more thing. Get Herb or somebody to run plates that start with VNA. Put the ones registered to women at the top of the list. Check for the usual. And Julie, have him separate the ones that live close to Winthrop."

"Peace, Gino."

She caught me by surprise with that one. "Yeah, uh…peace."

Tip was staring at me with that twisted scar on his face laughing at me. "Peace?"

"Fuck you, Tip."

I regretted it as soon as I said it, forgetting how ridiculous he was.

"Well, all right, but I ain't bending over."

As we walked out the back door, Tip checked his gun. He really *did* want to shoot someone.

CHAPTER 49

KEEPING BUSY

Lucia cooked breakfast for everyone, finding time to even sing a song or two. It wasn't the happiest of times, but things looked good for Jada coming home, and *nothing* could be better than that. Mars and Alexa had gone to the grocery store for food then worked on making coffee and serving people meals. She finished a batch of eggs then walked over to Gino. "Detective, you need to eat something. Coffee by itself won't get you through the day."

Gino smiled at her. "You convinced me. I'll take whatever you've got ready."

Lucia scooped fried potatoes from the pan, added a few pieces of sausage, and plopped a large spoonful of scrambled eggs onto his plate. "Do you want toast?"

He looked at the plate with a sideways glance. "Might as well clog all my arteries."

When breakfast was done, Lucia corralled Mars and Alexa into helping with dishes, while she cleaned counters and swept the floor.

"I've got someone who comes to clean," Scott said. "No need for you to do that."

Lucia looked at him, nodded, but kept sweeping. "No sense in leaving it dirty for them. I got nothing but time, Mr. Winthrop. Besides, sweeping is good work. It keeps me busy and takes my mind off things."

After sweeping, Lucia wiped the ovens clean—both of them. *What's a single man and one girl need two ovens for?* She doubted he used even one.

Probably ate out most of the time. *And paying people to clean his house and take care of his lawn. Person could make a living just taking care of this man.*

She finished the kitchen then worked her way across the tile floors of the family room and onto the patio. Worry pushed her. Worry about her baby girl and what she was going through. Worry over how she'd had hollered at Jada about that darn prom dress. Most of all, worry that it was her fault. *Shouldn't have let her come to school here. Shouldn't have tried getting uppity.*

Lucia stopped sweeping and leaned on the broom as she wiped away tears. How would Lonny deal with all of this on top of everything else he had on his plate? Lucia started sweeping again, moving over the flagstone patio's rough edges and sunken joints. She spotted a few joints that had cracked, the mortar loose.

Be something good for Lonny to do.

She poked her head inside the door. "Lonny, get your tools and get out here."

"What's wrong?"

"Mr. Winthrop's patio is nearly falling apart. I'm surprised you didn't see it."

"Patio? I don't have time to fix a damn patio. Jada's out there somewhere. She's—"

Lucia put her hand to his lips. "She's in the best hands we can hope for. Detective Cataldi is going to find her, and the Lord will watch over her." Lucia kissed him softly. "Let them do their jobs."

Lonny seemed to be fighting something within himself, but eventually he nodded then he stepped outside to take a look. "I can chisel them out, but I don't have any mortar."

"That can come another day. Do what you can. It's the least we can do for the man."

Lucia watched him work for a few minutes before going back inside. Gino met her at the door.

"Smart, what you did."

"About what?"

"Getting Lonny to work on that patio."

"A man sitting around worrying does nobody any good."

"Not many people would know what to do."

Lucia's lips curled in a funny way. "I know my husband, Detective. If nothing else, I do know that."

***

LONNY TOOK OUT HIS Trow and Holden stone chisel, the thin one used for tight joints. He chiseled along the cracks at each edge, careful not to chip the flagstone. With the wooden end of his hammer, he tapped on the stone, listening for hollow sounds, a sure sign of trouble. Two of the large pieces had to come out. He reached in his tool bag, got a piece of yellow chalk, and marked them, then continued with the chiseling.

He could tell by the way the mortar gave so quickly that whoever laid this patio hadn't used a strong enough mortar mixture—too much lime and sand, not enough cement. It had likely saved them money, but would have cost Winthrop a lot to have it fixed. He shook his head as he got back on his knees, a sharpened joint slicker in his hand for prying the loose stuff up.

People don't do their jobs anymore.

He worried about what the world would be like for Mars and Jada when they grew up. Probably more of the same. As he thought about Jada, the worries he had momentarily forgotten returned. What was she doing right now? Had they hurt her? Lonny stopped, rested his butt on his heels. From the way they talked, he felt sure they hadn't raped her, but…what other scars would she have? The image of her naked on that bed sent shivers down his spine. He squeezed the handle of the hammer.

If I ever get hold of them…

CHAPTER 50

THE MONEY

When I arrived at Scott's house, I reminded him again not to mention anything to anybody. "Tell me again, Mr. Winthrop, who did you talk to about this?"

"Some colleagues at work. That's all."

"Do they think it was Alexa who was taken?"

He thought for a moment. "The only people who know of the kidnapping think it was Alexa."

"Don't tell them anything different. If they ask, tell them the police said you can't talk to anyone."

"I'm certain we won't have to worry about it after today, Detective. Once I give them the money, they'll release Jada."

"That's what I'm hoping."

Scott left, heading for the stairs. I began to wonder why he seemed so optimistic. And why he wasn't worried about his seven million dollars. *Seven million, one hundred thousand,* I reminded myself. He almost seemed…relieved. Not the reaction I'd would have expected from a man about to risk his life and all his money for someone who wasn't his daughter.

I went outside and called Julie. I didn't expect her in yet, but she answered on the first ring, chipper as always.

"Hey, Sixties," I said. "How's it going?" The Rolling Stones played in the background, Mick Jagger's unmistakable voice belting out "Mother's Little Helper."

"Hey," she answered.

"Did you ever finish the financials on Winthrop?"

"I gave you what I had. He's solid—nothing late, great credit. And you know about the anticipated windfall."

"Check on his divorce. Find out what his ex got. See if there's a trust fund for the kid. That kind of stuff."

"You think he has something to do with this?"

"I don't know what to think."

"I got a lot to do for Delgado this morning, but I'll get to it."

"You got enough help?"

"Captain Cooper gave me anybody I needed. And she put me in charge."

"Keep it up and you'll have your own research department." I looked at my watch—the one that wasn't there. "Gotta go," I said, and opened the door. "Mr. Winthrop, time to go."

He came out dressed in designer clothes.

"Don't forget the bags," I reminded him.

He returned a minute later with the two Adidas bags, which we tossed in the back of his SUV, and then we headed for the bank. He exited the subdivision, got on The Woodlands Parkway, and then took the exit for I-45 South.

"I'm doing the drop," Scott said.

I laughed. "Like hell."

"It's my responsibility, Detective."

This guy was really out there. "This is dangerous. You can't get involved."

"I already *am* involved. These people have Jada, and they expect *me* to deliver the money. Remember what happened with the Uncle Eddy fiasco."

He had me there. In lieu of an answer, I said nothing.

"So?" he said.

"It's your ass," I said.

"And my money," he added.

"That too. We'll be with you though. I've got even more men, and we'll have you covered all the way, no matter where they take you."

"That's good to know. I'm not trying to sound cocky or arrogant. I *am* scared."

I looked over at him. Winthrop confused the hell out of me, always sending mixed signals. "You should be scared. You do the wrong thing with people like this, and they'll blow your head clean off."

I noticed a few beads of sweat on his forehead. He wiped them off with the back of his hand. "If you're trying to frighten me, Detective, you are doing a damn good job of it."

As we finished the drive to the bank, I thought of Lucia and how worried she must be. That reminded me that I hadn't spoken to Ron in a week or so. I'd thought of calling but hadn't. Sometimes I got afraid to call, fearing something would be wrong. That the phone would ring forever then be picked up by a nurse at an emergency room. Or a cop. I was torn between not wanting to hear from my son—going with the old adage that no news is good news—and wanting to hear from him every day, even if it was a message from him saying, "I'm okay, Dad. No need to worry." I sighed. That's what my life had come to. And every damn bit of it my fault. I vowed right then that I wasn't going to let Lucia—or Lonny—have to worry anymore. They were getting their girl back.

***

DELGADO HAD HIS TEAM assembled and prepped. All they needed was a location from Julie. Ribs looked over at Lance. A vision of an old-time gunfighter came to mind—the sheriff waiting for the bad guy to show up. Or the gunslinger with the pearl-handled guns. Lance was a throwback to the days when no one questioned an officer shooting. If the cop said it was a good shoot—it was. Now…now it was almost better to *get* shot.

Ribs paced, eager for the day to be over. He called Rosalee, faked another upbeat tone, acting as if he had nothing better to do. Despite his bravado, Ribs got scared on cases like this. Not necessarily for himself, but for Rosalee. She wouldn't make it without him. All her life she'd dreamed of being a mother and a housewife. Ribs doubted if she would *want* to survive as anything else. He checked his vest again, then his gun, then paced some more.

The phone rang. "*Buenos dias, amorcita.*" He used his most sexy voice, which Rosalee always reminded him wasn't sexy at all.

"Don't go talkin' that Mexicano shit with me, Delgado. If you're gonna speak a foreign language, speak Texan."

"There's only one person who could say something that stupid. What do you want, Tip?"

"Damn, and after last night, I thought we were sleeping buddies."

Delgado laughed. "What's up?"

"I couldn't reach Gino, so I'm calling to get permission to scare the fuck out of these assholes up here."

"What have you got?"

"Most of them don't know shit, and I mean that literally, if that makes sense—but one guy…"

"What about the one guy?"

"Sorry, I had somebody passing by. So this Sanjay character I talked to, he seems off."

"In what way?"

"He's too nervous. If I take him for a ride, get him outside the comfort of work, I think he'll spill his guts about something."

"Don't hurt him. This isn't some junkie living in a box on Westheimer."

"Hey, Delgado, go catch some fuckin' bad guys and let me do my business."

Delgado heard him laughing as he hung up. The phone rang again. This time he checked caller ID. It was Sixties Julie. "Delgado."

"Get out a pen, my man. I've got you an address."

"You're sure?"

"Motel on FM 1960, not far from you. They rented two adjacent rooms three days ago."

"And?"

"And there's been a do-not-disturb sign on both doors since check-in. They even left special instructions to not be disturbed, promising a bonus to the maids."

"*Hijo de puta!*"

"I don't know what that means, Detective, but I hope it means that you're hurrying on over there."

"We're on our way." Delgado hung up and called Gino. "We got 'em."

"What?"

"Julie found the motel. We're packing up to go there now."

"Goddamn. Keep me informed, Ribs."

"Where are you?" Ribs asked.

"Just pulling into Scott's drive. And we've got a couple of bags full of money."

"What was that about?" Scott asked.

"That was Delgado. He thinks they found the motel rooms. He's on his way there now."

CHAPTER 51

IN THE NICK OF TIME

Number Two sat in the back of the van, mask and gloves on, cell phone to her ear.

"Do you ever put that thing down?" Three asked.

She shot him a look to shut him up and went back to her phone. "Shit!"

"What?"

She frantically dialed a number and put the phone to her ear.

"Yes?" a man's voice said.

"Dispatcher, we need Four and the girl picked up now! Cops are on the way."

"It will take twenty minutes. Have Four take his own car."

Number Two thought. "I don't want the girl seeing his face, but…okay, got no choice. I'm clearing them out."

Number Three sat up, alert. "Why do you have Dispatcher's number?"

"Shut-up, Three. We've got a problem."

She punched in another number. "Four, get out. Now! Cops are on the way."

"What? Where?"

"Take the girl. Get in the car and drive. Go somewhere private. Forget about masks. Just go! Boss will call with more details."

"What if she gives me trouble?" Four asked.

"Undo the gag and put her on the line."

A moment later, the girl got on. "Hello." Her voice was weak and timid.

Number Two said, "You know who I am?"

"I know you."

"Good. Then you know I'm not trying to hurt you. And you know I'm serious. So listen close. You will do everything Number Four asks of you, and you will do it without any fuss. If you make noise or try to escape, he *will* kill you. After that, we will kill your father and your mother." Two paused. "Is that clear?"

"Yes."

Number Two waited. "You don't seem convinced. Perhaps you're thinking that your father is with the cops and your mother is in New York. But if you think that will protect them, you don't understand what is really going on. I know where Lucia lives. And I know about Mars. And I know *all* about your father. Unless you want them to die, do exactly as I say."

Jada's tone of voice shifted to fear. "Okay, okay. I'll do it. I promise."

Two smiled to herself at hearing come through this time. "Good. Put Number Four back on."

A moment later, she heard, "Yeah?"

"She'll cooperate. Hurry up and get out." Two hung up and dialed another number. Boss answered. "Cops are on the way to the motel. Four is evacuating. Call him with a plan. Bring him back to the house if you have to. If we leave him alone on the streets, they'll find him. He's too stupid not to be tailed."

She hung up, put the phone in her pocket, and leaned against the side of the van.

"Is that the way you talk about me when I'm not here?" Three asked.

"I don't talk about you," Two said.

***

FOUR SHUT THE PHONE, put it on vibrate then looked around, heart racing, nerves clenching in his throat. He raced to the bed, took off the girl's blindfold, and moved down to her feet, fumbling with the knots, cursing how tight he'd made them. "Hurry up."

She sat up in bed. "What's going on? Am I going home?"

Four smacked her face. "Hurry and dress."

Despite what Number Two had told him, he had made her sleep with no pants on. She was nice to look at. Now he wished he hadn't. "Forget the underwear. Hurry!"

While she put on her pants, he thought of things he had to do. He'd worn gloves the whole time, so there were no fingerprints except when he touched her and prints didn't show up well on skin. Had he touched anything else? He ripped a pillowcase from the bed and started wiping the room down.

Jada stood, zipping up her pants.

"Hurry, goddamnit!"

As she reached for her blouse, Number Four grabbed her arm and yanked her toward the door.

"I'm not finished dressing," she said, clad only in jeans, no shirt or shoes.

"Bring the top with you. Just before opening the door, he removed his mask. Then he heard a noise outside, one he didn't like.

CHAPTER 52

THE DROP

We weren't in the door five minutes before the call came in. The tech signaled it was them, and I gave Scott the nod. I whispered to Connors to get Lonny and Lucia into the other room.

"Hello," Scott said, his voice carrying the right amount of concern.

"I am glad to hear it is you, Mr. Winthrop, and not that cop pretending to be Uncle Eddy."

"Don't worry. I plan on delivering this myself."

"Are you ready?"

"I'm ready."

"Set your cell phone on the table. Get the money bags ready. I pray for the girl's sake the money isn't tainted. Do not take your cell phone, or any cell phone, with you. I want to find no extra cell phones this time. Do you have paper and pen?"

"Yes."

"Write this down. Make no mistakes. It is imperative that you make no mistakes, as you won't have a phone. If you make a mistake, we will cut off one of her nipples."

"I *won't* make a mistake."

"Head south on I-45. Exit onto the Hardy Toll Road. Go to the airport, Terminal C parking garage."

I looked at Connors. He shrugged. Were they taunting us? Did they think they could get away with this again?

"When you enter the parking garage for Terminal C, park in the first space you find. Take the bags and go inside to ground transportation. Take the shuttle bus to the Four Seasons Hotel." There was a pause. "Am I going too fast, Mr. Winthrop?"

"Hold on," he said, and wrote the last parts of the instructions. I didn't know why; Scott knew we had this taped.

"Tell me when you're ready."

A short pause, then, "I'm ready."

"Talk to no one. Say nothing. If someone speaks to you, ignore them. You *will* be tested. When you get to the hotel, go to the front desk. Ask for a package for Mr. Scott Winthrop. They will require ID. If your ID and picture don't match, we will remove one of Jada's nipples. If we have already removed one, we will remove the other. If Detective Cataldi and his crew get there before you and examine the package, we will know. We will cut off a nipple. If *anything* goes wrong, we will cut off a nipple. If we run out of nipples, we will begin cutting something else. Clear?"

"Clear."

"Good. Inside the package will be further instructions. Follow them exactly. Read them carefully. That is all for now. Go to the restroom if you have to. Take care of any business. I will tell you when to leave."

After hanging up I looked at the tech. "Did we get a location?"

He shook his head. "Not enough time."

Everyone was talking, running through the events. I held up my hands. "Hold on. Before we get off track, does anyone have any ideas on why they want us going back to the airport?"

The tech came by, explaining how he had to get Scott and the bags ready. "We've got a GPS tracker in the car. We're going to put one in each bag, and we've got the special audio GPS for his shoe. It's the newest technology."

I looked at Scott. "We'll have you covered, sir."

"I'm not worried, Detective. I trust you."

I wished I had as much faith in myself as he did. As the techs worked with Scott, I got with the rest of the group. We decided to send six cars to the airport: two to the parking garage, one outside the exit, a woman inside the airport complete with luggage—who would board the shuttle bus with him, and two roamers, in case they got him a message and switched plans.

"We need people at the hotel," Sameena said.

"Sameena, why don't you run that? Take two of your pick and stake it out."

"I'm sure we can place one of our men as an employee."

"Even better," I said.

"What about surveillance?" Connors asked.

"Same as last time. We'll have cars on the freeway, both directions, but slanted toward Hardy Toll Road. I'll post two at Rayford, one on #242, and one on Woodlands Parkway in each direction."

"It sounds good," Sameena said. "I think we've got it covered this time."

I stared around the group. They weren't being creative enough. "Think hard, people! We can't afford to mess this up. Think about *how* they might fool us. *How* they could trick us—again."

For ten minutes, we tossed ideas around. We changed a few plans, but when all was said and done, the plan looked as if we had it covered. We were still discussing it when the phone rang again. The tech popped his head inside the room.

"It's them."

Scott casually picked up the phone. He was getting into this. "Hello."

"Mr. Winthrop, good morning."

"Good morning."

A pause, then, "Mr. Winthrop, you sound very relaxed this morning. I'm glad to hear that; however, I must caution you. If you are counting on Detective Cataldi to get you out of this mess, well…that would be foolish. Ask him what happened in Philadelphia."

Scott shot a 'what the hell is that about' look to Gino. "What do you mean?"

"Just ask."

"Okay."

"Good. Now before I hang up, are all the instructions clear?"

"Yes."

"Good. Are you prepared to go?"

"Yes."

"Good. I want you to leave in *exactly* one minute."

"Okay."

"One more thing, Mr. Winthrop. Take Detective Cataldi's car. Not yours."

The line went dead.

I pounded my fist on the table. "Fuck!"

Connors and Sameena were staring at me; so was everyone else. We hadn't even started, and they had already pulled one on us.

Scott stood there, his hand extended. "Keys, Detective. I've got to go."

I handed him my keys, said good luck, and assured him again that we'd have him covered. I'm sure that guarantee didn't mean as much to him now, but it was all I could offer.

When Scott left, I turned to see Lonny staring at me. "What did he mean by asking you about Philadelphia?"

"Nothing."

"Nothing? You told us you worked a kidnapping case in Philadelphia."

"Yes, Lonny. I worked two of them."

"So what happened? You said you brought those girls back safe."

I didn't answer for a long time, most of the silence spent wondering how the fuck these guys knew about that. When I did respond, it was with regret. I found the courage to stare him in the eyes then I told him, "I said I brought them back *alive,* Lonny. And I did." *Barely.*

"So what did he mean by ask you about it?"

"I guess what he wanted me to tell you, is that the girls were hurt. I assume he wanted that as a warning to follow his instructions."

"Son of a bitch!" Lonny said, and stormed off.

I watched him go but harbored no ill feelings. If I were him, I'd feel the same way. "Call Delgado!" I shouted to Connors. "See if he's got any good news."

Finding that girl in the motel might be our only way to win this one.

CHAPTER 53

BUST DOWN THE DOOR

Number Four cracked the curtains and looked outside. A car pulled into a space at the far end of the lot. Plenty of spaces were closer; why pick that one?

He wants to get a look, Four thought, and continued to watch him. The man walked slowly, his hand conspicuously holding a hotel room key as he went out of his way to look the part of a patron. He didn't look like the kind of man who would stay at a motel; he looked like a cop.

Four grabbed the girl and moved into the room they used for decoys. The maids had already cleaned this morning. He crept in. Looked. The curtains were open. He thought about closing them but opted not to. He took the girl and moved her to the bathroom. To be safe, he gagged her.

Number Four tucked himself against the wall, drew his gun, and checked the clip. No way was he going down for a kidnapping rap. He knew what happened in prison to guys like that.

***

DELGADO GOT EVERYONE ASSEMBLED in front of the motel, with both exits blocked. He showed the manager his badge.

"Samir, we need the keys to the rooms Julie called you about."

He handed over two sets of keys—for rooms #180 and #182. "Please do not ruin the furniture."

"What can you tell me about the rooms on either side? Are people in them now?"

"Number 178 has been rented by a man from Odessa for one week. No trouble. Number 184 has only been since yesterday. An older gentleman."

"Thanks, Samir. We'll try not to disturb anything."

Lance and his crew stood by the van, looking eager for battle. Delgado had no experience in real battle, but this was how he pictured soldiers acting before a conflict—hyped up and itching to pull the trigger. As he got closer, he noticed fear in some of them. That made him comfortable with his own feelings.

Lance looked at Delgado, eyebrows raised. Delgado didn't know if he was missing a secret signal, or if talking aloud was verboten in this line of work. If so, he went ahead and did the unthinkable.

"Let's go, gentlemen. We've got someone to visit in room #180."

As they moved out, Delgado looked at Lance. A smile lit his face. If the man felt fear, he hid it well.

They advanced to the back of the building, careful not to make noise. Lance insisted on an advance man going before them. When he signaled all was clear, Delgado moved forward. As the first of the SWAT team rounded the corner, Delgado thought back to yesterday's mess. One of Yogi Berra's old sayings came to mind: "It's like déjà-vu, all over again." He hoped the results today would be different.

As Delgado passed by #178, he looked through the open curtains and saw a cleaned room, bed made. He imagined the scene in the next room wasn't quite so pretty. Lance knocked on the door for #180, waited a few seconds, then knocked again, harder. With no response, he signaled one of his men to use the key. Lance and two others got in position, and two more stood guard outside room #182. Then they went in.

"Police!" he shouted as they barged through.

Delgado knew what he'd find before he even got there—no gunshots meant an empty room. When he entered, Lance and his crew had already cleared both rooms. No one was there, but the room wasn't quite empty. A pair of socks lay on the floor by the bed. Next to it were a pair of ripped panties and a bra. One of Lance's crew was on the floor examining it.

"Sir, we've got blood."

Delgado stooped to have a look. Someone had tried cleaning the carpet and had done a damn good job, but there were faint signs of blood and from what he could tell, a lot of it.

"Got blood stains on the mattress," another one said.

Lance had the lampshade in his hand. "This lamp has been broken."

Delgado got to his feet. "Don't touch anything else. We're clearing out until forensics gets here."

He looked around the room one more time, not knowing what he expected to see, then got on the phone to request a crime scene unit. Lance and his men waited outside, disappointment etched on their faces like battle scars they wished they had.

"Lance, leave a man in #182 in case they come back."

He looked at Delgado with a scowl.

"I know," Delgado said. "They're gone. But…"

"Bobby!" Lance barked. "Park it in #182."

The walk back to the vehicles seemed a lot slower. Three times Delgado started to dial Gino, and three times he found a reason not to. The man was a bundle of nerves, ready to explode. *But he has to know about this,* Delgado thought, so he punched in the number.

The phone barely rang before Gino answered. "What have you got, Ribs?"

"Nothing."

"Don't tell me that."

"I shouldn't say 'nothing,' but it doesn't look good. We've got blood—lot of it—and we've got her socks…"

"And?"

"And her bra and panties."

"Ah fuck!"

"Even worse, Gino. Her panties are ripped."

There was a short silence, followed by, "Get forensics—"

"Already on the way. I left one of Lance's men, just in case."

Gino didn't say anything.

"If they left that evidence, it means they were in a hurry," Delgado said.

"How the fuck are they doing this, Ribs? How did they know?"

"I hear you on that. And what's bothering me is this: why were her panties and bra off?"

"That's the million-dollar question. And I don't want the answer."

"We'll get them. Sooner or later, we'll get them."

"Somebody has to see these people. They're not fucking ghosts. We need to think harder."

"What's happening up there?" Delgado asked.

"Scott's delivering the money. We're tracking with GPS, and we've got a dozen cars."

"Any more leads?"

"None yet."

"How about you going to the airport? Sameena is going to catch the shuttle to the airport with Scott. See what you can spot from inside."

"I'm on my way. I hope Winthrop is doing okay."

"Me too, Ribs."

***

NUMBER FOUR WAITED UNTIL he heard no sounds then waited some more. When it had been quiet for fifteen or twenty minutes, he stepped silently across the room, motioning to the girl to keep quiet as well. He listened at the door adjoining the next room, the one where they had kept her, and then he looked out the window, both ways. He leaned close to the girl's ear and whispered. "Remember."

As he was about to leave, a van pulled up, and two men got out. *The crime scene unit.* Number Four backed away from the window and grabbed his cell. Boss answered on the third ring. "Need a place to roost, Boss."

"What's going on?"

"I'm stuck. Cops are in the other rooms."

"Where's the girl?"

"Right here."

"Has she seen your face?"

"Yeah, we were on our way out, remember?"

"Stay put no matter what. They have no reason to search that room; it was rented in a different name. If you don't make noise, you should be okay."

"What about—"

"If she gives you trouble, kill her. Use a knife."

"I didn't sign up for that."

"Kidnapping will put you away for the same amount of time. If you have to, do it. It might save your ass."

***

JADA SAW NUMBER FOUR looking at her. She didn't like the look in his eyes.

Who is he talking to? What are they saying?

Inside, she cried, but she didn't dare let it out. It was difficult to stop the sobbing, to stifle the noise. But she had to stay quiet. Her stomach muscles hurt and spasmed, causing her to contort her body to ease the pain. One sob escaped. Number Four glared and moved toward her. She cowered, burying her head in her chest.

This wasn't fair. Why was it happening to her? Yesterday, all she'd feared was getting raped. She was no longer afraid of that with the cops in the next room. But that fear had been replaced by a worse fate. She was going to *die.* She didn't see a way out of that one. She'd seen this guy's face. No way were they letting her live after that.

A SLIGHT INTERRUPTION

Scott left the house carrying two black bags stuffed with money. And no cell phone. He felt naked without it. He felt like he should be carrying a gun along with so much money, or have a contingent of bodyguards. Something. The bags were heavy, as the kidnappers had warned, but nothing he couldn't handle. It would have been more difficult with the full 150 pounds weighing him down on one side. He set the bags down, opened the back door, and lifted the bags onto the seat. Afterward, he climbed behind the wheel, adjusting the seat for his long legs. In thirty minutes or so, he'd be pulling into the airport garage.

Two blocks away, he came to a stop at an intersection. Someone jumped out from behind a van on the side of the road. They wore a mask and had a small placard in one hand. Scott's first reaction was to step on the gas and get the hell out of there, but then he read the writing on the placard.

Don't move, Scott! And don't say a word.

He nodded and swallowed hard. Were they going to kill him?

Another sign flashed.

Roll down the windows.

A second person came from where the van was. He opened the door and removed the bags, then ran toward the van.

Another card: *Stay calm.*

The man removed the bags and dumped the money into the van. He refilled them with paper and magazines then put them back into the car.

The first person handed him a cell phone. A new sign flashed.

This phone is on speaker. Do not talk.

More signs came in rapid succession.

Do not turn off the speaker. Follow all instructions.

Place phone in shirt pocket. Speaker will continue to work.

It will *work in garage. Been tested.*

Do not take the elevator at the airport.

Do not *take the elevator at hotel.*

We will *be listening.*

And *watching.*

After that they got back into the van and pulled next to him. Scott stared, terrified. He looked over and saw the driver wore a mask and was signaling him to move forward. A gun was pointed at his head. He hit the gas and moved through the intersection, perhaps a bit faster than he should have. Scott focused on remembering the instructions on the cards. These people didn't allow for mistakes. He checked his shirt pocket, making sure the phone was on and in no danger of an accidental shut-off.

What else did they say? He recalled the cards, flashing rapidly. He had always been good at remembering things like that; he'd grown up on flashcards.

The garage. That was next. He didn't have to do anything until he reached the garage. Then he had to remember not to take the elevator in the airport.

Easy enough, he thought, and turned right onto The Woodlands Parkway. Now that he had those worries taken care of momentarily, he returned to his *real* troubles. He had not expected the kidnappers to pull this. What if things went wrong? What if he lost the money for good? What if they didn't let Jada go? Things weren't supposed to go like this.

***

I HOVERED OVER THE tech's screen, doing my best to interpret the data, but I had never been good at that stuff.

The tech looked up and smiled. "We've got him, sir. Don't worry."

"Is our tail with him?"

The tech nodded. "Picked him up on the Parkway. He's on the feeder heading south. He should be entering the freeway any second."

I could tell where he was now that I'd been filled in. "If anything changes, anything you feel isn't right—call me."

"Yes, sir."

I dialed Delgado's number. "Scott's getting on 45 now."

"I'll be waiting," Delgado said. "Wish I knew what to look for."

"Suspicious people."

"The airport is full of suspicious people."

"Then look for ones who don't look suspicious. How the hell do I know?"

"I got it, don't worry. You talk to Tip yet?"

"I was about to call him. I missed him earlier."

"You better call. He's about to give Texas a bad name."

"Shit! I knew I shouldn't have sent him. Tip scares the hell out of hardened criminals, not to mention a bunch of white-collar biotech workers who hide their eyes when a couple of kids with baggy pants walk by."

"You know, cuz, we got to find this leak. We don't, and we're gonna lose the money. Maybe the girl too."

"I'm working on it, Ribs. Let me call Tip. I'll get back to you."

Tip answered right away. "I'm not far from you, Gino. I can be there in a few minutes."

"Don't bother. Winthrop's on his way to the airport. I got Sameena and Delgado there. I need you at the hotel."

"I'm on my way," Tip said.

"You do any good at Scott's work?"

"Got one guy who knows something. He didn't talk, but I didn't have a chance to convince him. Give me five minutes alone with him. He'll talk."

"You think he knows something?"

"I *know* he knows something," Tip said. "I just haven't figured out what."

That got me to thinking about what Delgado and I had theorized before, that someone from Scott's workplace was involved. It made sense.

"I'm going to check on some things from this end, Tip. See if Julie or Charlie can dig up some stuff for us."

"Get back to me."

"I will."

I called Charlie first, knowing Julie was swamped with motel stuff. When he answered, he sounded like he was eating. I was going to tell him not to talk with his mouth full, except then he might never talk.

"Charlie, I need information on Winthrop and some of his people from work."

"Gino, y'all got us busier than—"

"No matter how you were going to finish that sentence, I've heard it. So let me tell you what I need."

"Get with it."

"We've got three cases that we feel are connected: the poker games, the home invasions, and the kidnapping. I want everything run for all of them. Things in common, services they used, insurance claims…run all of the addresses through the system."

"We already gave you some of that, remember?"

"I know. But we were focused on the home invasions. I want it all run together. See if we come up with anything new."

"I'll get right on it."

"Thanks, Charlie. I appreciate it." I hung up and went to the tech. "Where is he?"

"Almost to the airport. Got maybe five minutes. Maybe less."

"Let me know if anything changes."

I headed to the coffee pot, craving more caffeine. It was empty. I filled the pot and turned it on. The lack of sleep was making me irritable as hell. Or it could have been the stress. As I waited for the coffee, I wondered again who the hell was leaking information. Somebody close. Had to be. I glanced to the other room and caught Lucia staring at me with a look in her eyes that said she was dying to know what was going on but afraid to ask.

Rightfully so. I got nothing to tell you.

With her stare and sorrowful look, the pressure built in my head until it felt as if it might explode. My gut churned. I *had* to get her girl back. *Had to.* And to do that, I had to find the leak.

Who the fuck is it?

CHAPTER 55

EVERYONE HAS A PLAN

Lonny sat beside Lucia on the sofa, doing everything he could to comfort her. She was a strong woman, a rock. Had been for all these years. But this was too much to ask of any woman. First came the financial pressure, which he'd thought was the worst thing that could happen…but now this. Money didn't seem so important anymore.

He racked his brains all night trying to think of what he could do, but thinking had never been one of Lonny's strong points. Working with his hands, with tools—he shined there. Build a stone wall, pour concrete and make it slicker than cat shit. Those he could do. Hang a door, run electric, fix the toilet. But put his mind to work on a problem like this, and he was lost. It was a God-given wonder the kids did so good in school. Must have got all that from their mother.

Lonny had other talents too. He sometimes helped Lucia with her cooking, not that he could cook, but he could taste the difference in a dish and tell her what was missing, or what it had too much of. And he could smell a sauce or a pot of soup and tell what it was as soon as he entered the door. He had a good sense of place and direction too. But what good did all that do? He'd trade it all for the brains to find Jada. Instead, he was forced to rely on the detective. Gino seemed like a good enough guy, but still…*his* daughter wasn't out there. He didn't have to worry about her when he went home at night. And she sure as hell wouldn't be a flash in his memory six months from now if they never got her back.

Lonny squeezed a little too hard on Lucia's arm. She jumped. "Sorry," he said. "Just nervous."

She offered a forced smile, patted the back of his hand. "We'll get her back."

We'll get her back. That's all Lucia had been saying of late. Lonny worried it might be all she'd ever say if this didn't come out right. He stared at Detective Cataldi, waiting on his coffee with signs of worry etched on his face. Not the same kind of worry, but it was there. He was worried. No doubt.

Lonny lay his head against the back of the sofa. Closed his eyes. If he could only figure out how to find them. Maybe if he had paid more attention when they had picked him up. He shut his eyelids tighter, trying to focus on remembering that first day they had picked him up. He was nervous; he recalled that much. Nerves had been eating at him that day, tearing him up. He'd had a roll of Tums with him, and he'd popped them until they were gone. He remembered coming back up I-45…

Lonny sat up straight. How did he *know* it was I-45? He didn't know *how* he knew, but he *knew.* Maybe it was the smooth ride interrupted by the bump of the joints in the pavement every fifty feet or so. Or maybe it was the sensation of speed. Nowhere else close to where he'd met them that they could have gone that fast, not without the risk of being pulled over. He lay back against the sofa again. If they'd come back by going north on 45, then they had to have gone south to get there—wherever *there* was. Confirming it all in his head made him recall the same sensation on the way down, the smooth ride, the bumps, the speed. And he remembered it being a twenty or twenty-five minute ride. Seemed like he knew more than he thought. Now to get the rest.

In the middle of his train of thought, Lucia tapped his shoulder and said something about tea or lunch. Something unimportant. She got up and went to the kitchen. Lonny tried getting back to the images in his mind but couldn't. He had to get out of here, go where he could focus.

He went to Lucia and whispered, "I'm going out for a drive. Want to come?" He knew she wouldn't.

"Where are you going?"

"Just taking a drive to get my mind off things."

"You go ahead. Be careful."

He tried to look calm as he walked toward the front door, but he wanted to run. Time was running out for his baby girl. He *had* to do something.

***

I WATCHED LONNY GO out the door then looked at Lucia, her gaze still on him as the door closed. He was at it again. "Connors!"

He came over. "What's up?"

"Take over," I said. "I'm following Lonny. Call my cell with anything. And I mean *anything*."

I got halfway to the door before I realized Scott had my car. I turned back to Connors, who already had his keys out. He tossed them to me.

It didn't take me long to fall in behind Lonny. He seemed oblivious. Twice he drifted into the other lane, catching it only when someone beeped their horn at him. I did my best to keep a discreet distance, but I didn't think he looked in his mirror once. Lonny could have had a naked girl on his back bumper and he wouldn't have noticed.

While I drove, I kept thinking about the leak. I had been focusing all this time on *who* it could be. Suppose *it* was a *what,* not a *who.* I called Connors.

"Yeah, Gino?"

"Get the techs to sweep that whole house. I want everything, from the front yard to the toilets."

"You think there's a bug in here?"

"It would explain a lot. Get them going." Next I called Julie. "We find out anything about those plates?"

"I checked every plate in the Houston area that started with VNA. A few had records, but they're still in prison, and yes, we checked. There were six plates in The Woodlands, and we sent an officer to every house. Two were dead ends, and the other four weren't home. He'll be going back again after work."

"Keep me posted," I said, and then followed Lonny off the freeway and into the right lane of the feeder road. I hung back, letting a few cars get between us in case he looked in the mirror, but I wasn't too worried. When Lonny's brake lights came on, I applied mine, matching his speed.

My mind jumped to what I'd told Connors—that a bug would explain a lot. It *would* explain a lot of things, but it wouldn't explain why the kidnappers didn't know they had the wrong girl. That was the biggest puzzler of all, and I had no answer for it.

***

LONNY TURNED OFF THE feeder road into the parking lot at FM 2920. He had mentally counted down the time from when Boss and them would have left the coffee shop. This would have been about the right spot. He parked in the middle of the lot with nothing to block his view, and his gaze swept all directions, searching. Looking for…what? He knew this was a long shot. He was good at travel and distance estimates, but even so, he could have easily been a mile or so off. Or more. Taking that into account, he wouldn't see shit. He didn't even know what he was looking for.

He closed his eyes again and tried to remember anything about where he'd been that first day on the job. The building had the feel of a warehouse—big and empty. There were no windows in the room where he met Boss the first time. No windows in either of the rooms, now that he thought about it. And it was a large building. The image that kept coming back to him were of steel walls, like a warehouse, or a barn.

He tried thinking of smells. Oil, maybe grease. A lot of dust. Yes, dust was the strongest smell. Lonny shifted his focus to sounds. There had been a hollow sound. A slight echo. Something about the sounds haunted him. He recognized one of them and recalled wondering about it at the time, but he had been so nervous that day.

Think, Lonny. Think!

He turned the truck off, rolled up the windows, and closed his eyes. Number Two had been there, off to his left. Number Three in front of him. A desk with a small lamp to the right. Three chairs and a small sofa…

Then it struck him. He'd heard the rumbling sound of a large truck, with the wheels bouncing on a rough road. Maybe a gravel one. And the familiar sound of metal clanging against metal.

Concrete trucks! Lots of them.

Somewhere close by, a crew had been pouring something big. He recalled hearing at least ten or twelve trucks, which meant it was a decent-sized pour. Maybe a hundred plus-yards of concrete. Now Lonny knew what to do and how to find them. He called every dispatcher he knew. Fred Mintz was first—the dispatcher for Superior. They did a lot in this part of town.

"Fred, it's Lonny Hackett."

"Lonny! It's been a long time. Are you keepin' busy?" Fred had a voice that sounded like he had a mouthful of tobacco, which he usually did. He carried an empty can or bottle with him to spit into.

"Not now, I'm not. But that's not why I'm calling. I need your help."

"If it's a job you're lookin' for—"

"No job. I need to know about some pours you might have done a few weeks ago."

"What for?"

Agitation was setting in, but Lonny tried to be patient. "Fred, my girl's in trouble. I can't say much more, but I need to know if you made any big pours, 80–120 yards or more, about two weeks ago. It would have been somewhere up around 2920 and 45. Say within five miles of that, maybe a little more."

"That's a big area, Lonny. Might take me a while to check it."

Lonny gripped his steering wheel and squeezed. He wanted to break something. Still, he maintained his composure. "I know I'm asking a lot, but this is soooo important." There was silence for a moment, and then Lonny thought of something else. "It would have been in the morning. Say between ten and noon."

More silence, then. "Hang on a minute."

Fred put him on hold for what seemed like half an hour. When Lonny checked his watch, it had only been about eight minutes.

"Got two pours that could fit. One came in at about ninety yards, the other at one hundred twelve."

"You got addresses?"

Fred gave Lonny the addresses. One was maybe a mile and a half away. The other more like three. Either one could have been it. Lonny had been in the back of a van with the windows covered and a mask on. Getting within three miles was miracle enough.

"Thanks, Fred. I owe you, man. I mean *really* owe you."

"Just get some work, Lonny. Be nice to hear your voice more often. And good luck."

"I need it."

Three more concrete companies delivered a lot to this area. He got hold of all of them, and after a lot of arm-twisting, got one more address. He wrote it down then studied the three addresses on his piece of paper. All he had to do was check them out and see if the kidnappers were there.

What the hell am I going to do if I find them? I'm no damn Rambo. I'm a bricklayer.

CHAPTER 56

NOT EVERYTHING IS ROSES

As soon as Scott drove off, Driver removed the mask, pulled into the left lane of the parkway, drove a few miles, then headed south on the feeder.

Number Two sat in the back with Three. "Keep watching for tails," she said.

"No one saw us," Three said.

Two pushed the curtain aside at the rear window. "It's possible."

Number Three suddenly laughed, real loud. "Would you look at all of this cash? Seven million."

"A lot of money," Two said. "It turned out to be a good job."

"It would be a lot more money if we didn't have to split it with so many people."

Two turned to glare at him and found herself staring at his gun. She kept her cool and spoke calmly, with a soft voice. "What are you doing, Three? This isn't in the script."

He laughed, the kind that's not really a laugh. "I really hate to do this, but Driver and I decided that splitting it two ways was a lot more profitable."

Two didn't seem fazed. "You have nowhere to clean it. No contacts."

"I'll find a way."

"What about Boss? He's been good to us."

"Fuck boss. And fuck Dispatcher, and Number Four..." Three took hold of the gun with both hands, pointing it at her face. "And fuck you, Number Two."

Two shrugged. "Maybe a three-way split isn't so bad."

"Now you want to partner up with me, is that it?"

"I could do worse."

Three laughed again. "You got that right. None of them know who we are. Have they ever seen your face? Not mine."

Two said nothing.

"Well?"

"I'm thinking on it."

"Think fast, Two. It's not far from here."

"What do you really think of Boss? Wasn't it smart how Boss planned all of this? How would we have ever gotten out of so many jams without Boss? But you still want to betray the one person who helped you get here?"

"If it means an extra two million for each of us. For two million dollars, I'd do anything." Three stared, the gun still focused on Number Two. "Well?"

"I'll go along with it, Three, but before we split the money, let's play a guessing game. Let's see who can come the closest to guessing the real person behind each other's mask."

He laughed. "Winner gets to fuck the other person."

She laughed with him. "All right, I'll agree, but *only*—and this is important—only if the winner wants to."

"I go first," he said.

"We have to establish criteria."

"Like what?"

Number Two thought. "I don't know. Age, weight, nationality, type of house we live in…" She cocked her head in thought. "Let's see…real names…"

"Okay, enough bullshit."

"If you think I'm risking going to bed with you on a few lucky guesses, you're crazy. If you win, that's one thing."

"All right, what else?"

She thought for a moment. Shook her head. "I guess we have enough. Go ahead, you start."

"You are so easy, Two. You gave away too much. By asking the type of house, I already know you live in a house, not an apartment."

"I hadn't thought of that. Good start, Three."

He smiled. "Let's see. You're five feet six. Weigh about...120."

Two raised her eyebrows.

"Lot of muscle on you. I figure I'm close with that." He stared close to her face. "I'd say you are thirty-five, and you're Irish...wait. Didn't commit to that yet." He thought some more. "All right. Irish. You live in a ranch house."

"And the name?" she asked.

"Name? Let me think. I peg you as a...Carla."

She raised her eyebrows again.

"How'd I do?" Three asked.

"Not bad. You've got me a little concerned with how transparent I've become."

"Let's hear it."

"You hit the age, height, and weight right on. Well, close enough. You missed the age by two years, and I weigh 122."

"And?"

"I do, in fact, live in a ranch house, but I'm of German descent, not Irish."

"Only one wrong so far. What about the name?"

"I'll tell you that after I finish."

"Fair enough. Your turn."

She looked at the corners of his eyes, at his neck, and thought some. "I'd say you are thirty-nine. Height—five eleven, weight 185." She watched as his expression went from victory to concern. "Your nationality is likely Bulgarian on your father's side, Belarus on your mother's. And you live in a rat-hole apartment off 59 South." Number Three lost all expression. "Oh, and your name is Dwayne Povich."

His hands shaking, he moved the gun even closer to her, his finger on the trigger. "You whore."

Number Two made a *tsking* sound as if chiding someone. "One more thing, Three. Your gun is empty. I did that this morning."

Three looked at his gun, then at her. He pulled the trigger. Nothing. Before he could do anything else, Two had her gun aimed at his face, the silencer already attached.

"How did you get my information? No one is supposed to have that."

"After the Marshall incident, I decided you were dangerous. I needed to know all there was about you. So I called Dispatcher."

Three looked dumbfounded. "How do you have Dispatcher's number? I thought only Boss did."

Number Two laughed. "You're getting smarter all the time, Dwayne."

Three's brow wrinkled, and his eyes narrowed. Two leaned forward, gripping the gun with both hands, then whispered, "I forgot one part of the game. My name. *I* am Boss. Not that lame-duck asshole you've been taking orders from."

Number Three must have thought of all the times Boss had looked to her before acting on a question or committing to a direction. He might have thought of the time in the motel when she had said Boss wants to do this, or when she had ordered Four to evacuate. There was a lot more he might have thought about, but he didn't have time. She had already pulled the trigger and the bullet was racing toward his head.

Number Two opened the door to the front compartment then poked the gun through the curtain, aimed at the back of Driver's head. "I don't know where you stand on this, Driver, but I'd suggest you abandon any alliance you had with Three. He's dead, and you're no match for me."

Driver nodded. "Where to?"

"The warehouse."

Two emptied Three's pockets, setting his wallet and his cash to the side. She looked at the watch he had in his pants. Unique. She started to put it in the bag with his other things when she noticed an inscription on the back. She got close to the light to read it. A tear formed in her eye. Then another. She wrapped the watch in a cloth they used for wiping down prints then carefully tucked the watch into her pocket.

CHAPTER 57

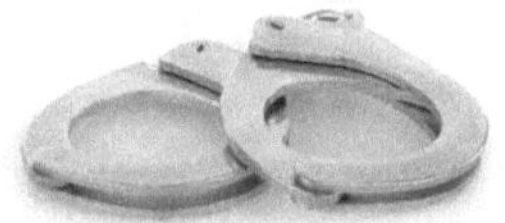

LOGIC

Delgado called and said Scott was on the shuttle bus heading to the hotel. "Did you check with the techs?"

"They still have the bags and GPS in his shoe. Nothing's changed."

I allowed myself a slight sigh. I had been worried something would happen in the airport garage. Now everything depended on the hotel. "Are you going to the hotel, Ribs?"

"Wherever you need me. Sameena is on the shuttle with him. We've got Tip and six other guys at the hotel, and I'm sending everyone from the airport there."

I thought it out for a minute. "I'd rather have you go back to Scott's house. I've got Connors in charge now."

"Connors? Where are you?"

"Lonny left again."

"And you're tailing him?"

"I have to see what he's up to."

"And you're by yourself?"

"Don't worry—"

"Bullshit. Where are you? I'll catch up."

"Hang on. I got a call coming in, and Lonny's moving. Tell you what— I'll call back. It's Charlie."

"You better, Gino. Goddamnit."

I followed Lonny out of the parking lot. He took a right on 2920, heading west. I clicked over to Charlie. "Yeah, Charlie?"

"Any news?"

"Nothing yet. You got anything for me?"

"Some of this you may already know. I took everything Julie had and combined it with what you told me to get. There are still a few things I'm waiting on."

"Give me what you got."

Charlie filled me in on everything they had found. When we hung up, I called Delgado back. "Ribs, I need to put your brain to work. "I'm going all the way back to the games on this stuff. Since we're pretty certain they're all connected, we need to look at it that way. Charlie ran the addresses through the system to see what came up. Two of the poker games had been investigated for gambling in the past year or so, but the cases were dismissed."

"Why?"

"Lack of evidence."

"That could mean almost anything," Delgado said. "Or it could mean that Mayor Rusty Johnson pulled some strings. Remember, he had friends at those games."

"Yeah, we'll go over that later. As far as the home invasions, the Memorial house and the Marshall house both made claims in the past few years."

"Didn't Julie say they weren't the same insurers, though?"

"Right, but Charlie dug deeper and found something interesting. The insurance companies weren't the same, but they used the same investigator."

"So Charlie does do something besides eat."

"I know, for all the shit we give him, he's good." I made a mental note to tell him that more often.

"Who was the investigator?"

"A company called Lone Star Recovery. He's checking them out."

"What about Winthrop? Anything come up on his finances?"

"Julie told Charlie that he's squeaky clean, but she hasn't had time to dig deep enough. On the surface, he looks good."

"And there's still the windfall he'll get from his company."

"I know. That's the killer. There's no logic in him being involved."

"Where are you, Gino? I'm coming up."

"Like hell. I need you at the house. And when you get there, press the techs. These kidnappers are getting information somewhere."

"I'll get on it."

"Ribs, tell them to think about where a bug might be that would pick up *some* information, but not all of it. Something that could explain them not knowing about Jada."

"Got it."

After Ribs hung up, I called Tip. "What's up, Texas?"

"If I were any better, I'd be you."

"You set up?"

"I got David out front working valet parking, Shelby's walking the lobby, looking like a hooker. I'm waiting for somebody to bust her, and then I'll offer her a trade to drop the charges."

"Keep going, Tip."

"Sameena just texted. She said they'd be here in a couple of minutes."

"Keep me posted."

"Don't worry. We'll get the fuckers. What about on your end?"

"I filled him in on the information from Charlie."

"Don't discount that Winthrop guy just yet," Tip said. "I told you there's something wrong at work. All I need to bust it is five minutes with old Sanjay."

"Okay, wrap that up, and I'll give you ten minutes with him. Just make sure you get one of the kidnappers." Before I hung up, I added. "Alive!"

He laughed. "See you, Gino."

I hung up and focused on following Lonny, though it didn't take much. He pulled into a construction site, a strip center with walls framed and a roof on. Not much else.

What the hell is he doing here?

Lonny parked his truck, got out, and walked around. I was about to turn into the lot when I realized there was no place to hide. I drove past, keeping my head turned in the opposite direction. Half a mile later, I made a u-turn and came back, pulling into a car wash across the street. He was still there, walking around and staring at…what? This was nothing but a construction site.

The issue of the wrong girl wouldn't leave me alone. *How did they get the wrong girl?* That stuff didn't happen with pros. If the kidnappers had been bungling idiots, okay, I'd buy it, but not these guys. *Unless they didn't get the wrong girl.* Suppose it was Jada they were after all along. I tried to focus on that.

Why? Who would do that? Who would pay money for her? Scott wasn't going to at first…so what changed his mind?

I remembered thinking how fake it had seemed when he changed his mind, how not worried he'd been about the whole thing. He seemed more worried when he thought he wasn't going to get the money from the bank. Of course, that was when he thought it was Alexa who had been taken… Or was it?

What if he knew all along it was Jada?

I put my hands over my eyes to block out peripheral thoughts. My mind was a jumbled mess, like a fuckin' grasshopper was in there bouncing around.

Think about this, think about that. Missing all that sleep didn't help.

Nothing was connecting, and that made everything worse. I looked across the street at Lonny. I didn't know what he was up to, but I'd had enough of it. I slammed the car into gear. It was time to find out what the fuck Lonny knew.

CHAPTER 58

TIME TO OWN UP

Lonny walked through the building, looking for anything that could be a clue. This could have been the pour the concrete crew did, but if it was, where was the building the kidnappers used as base. He hadn't seen anything useful from outside. If he remembered right, the sounds of the concrete trucks hadn't been far from here. Either way, he was doing no good here. Maybe the next address would pan out. He walked outside, shielding his eyes from the bright sun. And he almost bumped into Detective Cataldi.

***

"Detective Cataldi, I didn't see you."

"Maybe you didn't expect me."

He tried laughing it off, but he was rattled. "Guess not."

"What are you doing here?"

"Just killing time. Taking my mind off things."

"Bullshit!"

Lonny lost his smile, stared at me then tried walking past. I grabbed his arm, that big burly arm full of muscles.

"Not so fast. What are you doing here?"

"I already told you."

"Killing time? While your daughter's being held hostage?"

He turned to glare at me. "What can I do? You tell me."

"That is *exactly* what I want to know. What do you think you can do? You're out here for a reason. Maybe you think you can do something, make a difference, find Jada, find the kidnappers." I let go of his arm and took a step closer. "All of that's fine. I'm a father. I understand. What I *don't* understand is why you came *here*. To *this* spot. What makes you think you can find her when we can't? Do you *know* something?"

He gritted his teeth. His muscles tensed. "I know that some bunch of crazy fuckin' crackers got my girl."

"*Crackers,* you say. Got any reason to think that? Maybe they're black or Latino. Why say *crackers?*"

His edge disappeared again. "Just saying it, that's all."

"Time is running out, Lonny."

"I don't know what you're talking about."

I walked in small circles, trying to figure out how to get through to this guy. I knew he was a good man, but something was wrong. "Lonny, I don't know what's going on, or what you're into, but I've got a gut feeling you know something that will help us bring Jada home alive."

"I don't know shit." His attitude was back, but underneath it, I saw the truth. He was scared. I decided to try a different tactic.

"My son almost died last year. When he was in the hospital, with tubes up his nose and down his throat, barely breathing, his blood pressure hardly registering… I told God I'd trade—straight up—me for my son. I asked Him to take me right then." I paused, hoping some of the story would have an effect. "He did better than that. He delivered both of us."

Now I switched tactics again, grabbing Lonny by the shirt. "Like I said, I don't know what you're into, what kind of trouble, but you have to decide if you're willing to trade for Jada. And you have to do it *now.*"

Lonny remained silent for a long time. He squeezed his hands. Paced. Hung his head low.

"Now, Lonny! They could be raping her while you make up your mind."

Lonny looked at me. His tears had already started. "My wife always said I'm a man who could make the necessary decisions."

"Lucia is a wise woman."

Lonny nodded, head hung even lower. "There was a group of us…"

Once he started spilling his guts, he didn't stop. I absorbed what I could without taking notes; we could go back over it later. I discovered long ago that when a man confesses to something, which all but the worst of them want to do, he's more willing to come back to it later. Unless a lawyer is involved.

As Lonny told me what had happened, it all came rushing into my head. The clues had been there. The way Lonny reacted when the kidnapper said *clear* on the tape. I originally thought it was him responding to the fact Jada was taken; now I knew it was because he recognized the one he called Boss.

And Lonny searching for the mysterious Willard. I made a mental note to follow up on that, see who he was. When Lonny finished, I led him toward the car. "You were at the Marshall house, right? They said there was a black man there."

He nodded.

"And the poker games?" If he answered yes, I might not be able to contain myself.

"No, just the Marshalls' and the house on Memorial."

I wanted to beat his fucking brains out, but right now I needed him to get Jada. "Let's go." I wanted to tell him he'd have to answer for the Marshall boy dying, but I felt certain he knew that. That was probably why he hadn't come forward earlier. "You did the right thing." I had no trouble telling him that. I believed it. Sometimes I didn't believe what I told people. Sometimes I didn't feel right making arrests. Fact is, I was having a tough time keeping to my oath. The longer I was in this job, the more some of the laws irked me. The bad guys got away too often. That, I didn't like.

I had to quit thinking these thoughts. When you tell yourself something isn't wrong enough times, all of a sudden, it's not. That was a dangerous thing in my job. I didn't know if somebody famous had said that. If not, they should have. It was true.

"Detective, where are we going?"

"You said you had three addresses, right?"

He nodded.

"We're going to the next one. I'm not going back to Winthrop's house to face Lucia without Jada."

Relief came over his face. "Just give me five minutes alone with them. Please?"

"You're going to be in the car, mister. This isn't a vigilante run."

Lonny climbed in the front seat next to me. I got on the phone with Charlie. "I need to run some addresses." I looked to Lonny, handed him a pad of paper. "Write them down."

"Hold on," he said, and got out of the car. He went to his truck, returning with a piece of paper. "All right here."

I read Charlie the list. "What I need are any large buildings in the immediate vicinity of these addresses. I need ownership from tax records. Could be a farm with a barn, an abandoned warehouse, a store. Anything like that."

"You got it, Gino. And by the way, Julie pulled up that Lone Star Recovery. It's owned by a woman named…hold on…Susan Masterson. Has been for ten years."

"Anything on her?"

"She used to be a cop. Then she got her PI license."

"Nothing bad, though?"

"Not in the files."

"Okay. Thanks."

"Wait. Julie said for you to call. She has something."

"Transfer me."

He did, and Julie answered.

"Charlie said you had something," I said.

"While I was running addresses, I plugged Winthrop's into the system too. He had a break-in about a year ago."

"When exactly?"

"Hang on," she said, then put me on hold to the sounds of "Mr. Tambourine Man." I was deeply involved with trying to decipher the hidden meaning of it—all songs from that era had hidden meanings— when she came back on. "A little over a year ago."

"Home invasion or—"

"No, a run-of-the-mill burglary. He wasn't home. They took jewelry and small amount of cash. That's about it."

"Okay, thanks. If you get anything else, call." I hung up and called Tip. "What's going on there?"

"*Nada, señor.* Scott came into the hotel, picked up the package, and sat in the lobby reading it, then walked up the stairs. He exited the stairwell on the fourth floor and went into room #424. Haven't seen him since."

"What the hell?"

"Yeah, it's been a while. Something's not right."

"All right. Keep me updated. And hey, Tip, you know an ex-cop named Masterson?"

"Sue Masterson?"

"That's her."

"She's a PI now. Used to do a lot of work for our friend Mayor Rusty Johnson."

"Son of a bitch!"

"Why? Where'd her name pop up?"

I told him about the connection.

"Gino, something's there. Too many coincidences for there not to be."

"I'm on my way." Before I hung up, I said, "And, Tip, don't try to speak Spanish. Stick to Texan or whatever the hell it is you speak."

I made a u-turn in the middle of the road and punched the gas.

"Where the hell are you going?"

"We'll get to those addresses later, Lonny. Right now, this is the better lead."

"What kind of better lead?"

"This might be a person who can lead us to Jada."

CHAPTER 59

THE LAST WITNESS

As I drove down the freeway at almost ninety—close to Tip-Denton speed—I wondered about a lot of things. Mostly though, I wondered how Lucia would take the news that her husband was going to jail for felony murder—if he didn't get the needle. They did that shit in Texas— no messing around.

Twenty minutes later, I exited the freeway, slowing so my tires didn't screech going into the little strip center. I parked out front. There were two doors. One said *Lone Star Recovery*. The other had no text.

"Stay in the car, Lonny. This is no shit. *Stay* in the car."

"Aren't you calling backup or something?"

"If you see me in trouble, call somebody."

I went inside. The receptionist desk was empty, and it looked like it had been for a long time. Dust covered the seat and back of the chair. The keyboard too. No typing had been done on that since the place had opened. I checked my gun then walked slowly toward a door to the right.

"Anyone here?"

No answer.

"This is the police. Is anyone here?"

Again, no answer.

The door was open, so I stepped slowly, balanced on the balls of my feet. Gun in my hand. When I got to the adjoining door, I nudged it open and took a quick peek inside. Nobody. I walked in, checked out possible hiding places, then, when I felt sure it was empty, relaxed a little. In the closet was a large box filled with disposable phones—must have been fifty.

Some had masking tape with names written in marker. I didn't know what the hell that was about, but it couldn't be good.

I stepped back into the office. A large file cabinet sat against the wall behind the desk. I opened it. Empty—no files. I checked the desk drawers and found a few pens, staples, paper clips, and rubber bands, but nothing else. Whoever sat in this office wasn't doing any work. As I continued checking things, I heard a noise—maybe from outside. My muscles grew taut as I moved around the desk, back to the door. I got ready then poked my head around the corner. The noise came again, definitely outside. I moved quicker toward the front door. Lonny wasn't in the car.

Son of a bitch!

The noise came again, this time from the other end of the building. Voices. Someone hollering. I stayed close to the wall, running with quick steps. Quiet steps. I got to the corner, where I heard pleading. I crouched, moved out, and pivoted, gun drawn.

Lonny had a guy against the wall, a gun to his head.

"You got one chance to do the right thing before I blow your fuckin' head off," Lonny said. His whole body shook.

I rose slowly and took two very small steps. I cursed myself a dozen times. How had I not searched him?

"Lonny, you should have told me you had a gun. Put it down. You don't want to do this."

He risked a glance in my direction and shook his head. "Not till he tells me where my girl is."

The man looked at me. "Hey, man get this fucker—" It was the first time he had spoken to me. He looked scared. Real scared. I didn't blame him. Lonny appeared to be a man who just might pull that trigger. When a gun is pressed against your head, it's scary, no matter who it is. I imagined that if it was a man whose daughter you kidnapped, it was a whole lot scarier.

"Put it down, Lonny." I walked closer, slowly, gun pointed at Lonny's chest. "Drop the gun. Now."

The man against the wall talked again. Lonny pressed the gun harder into his head and stood on his toes. He almost looked to be convulsing. "Shut up. Hear me? Shut the fuck up."

I had to diffuse this situation before Lonny lost it. He wouldn't maintain his control for long. "Lonny, who is this? Do you know him?"

"This is Willard, the guy I told you about. The one who recruits people and fences all the goods."

"You're sure?"

"Damn straight, I'm sure. I'd know that voice anywhere. This is the voice that ruined my life."

"Have you ever seen him before?"

"Once. A couple of months ago. It's him. No mistake."

The man against the wall was shaking. I was surprised he hadn't pissed his pants. I fixed him with a glare.

"Are you Willard?"

"I don't know what this lunatic is talking about. If you're a cop, get him off me. I'm gonna sue."

"Lonny, how do you *know* it's him?"

"I just know. Take him to the corner store if you don't believe me. He gives the clerk disposable phones."

I smiled. The man against the wall didn't know it, but Lonny had just sealed this man's fate. "And you say he's the fence?"

"That's what the word is."

Lonny grew calmer. I had hoped talking would calm him. I was almost to him now. I reached my hand out. "Give me the gun."

After going through what looked like an internal struggle, Lonny handed the gun to me. I had been right; Lonny was a good man at heart. "Go back to the car. Stay there this time." Lonny started to say something. "Now! Lonny. Go back now."

After he left, I focused on the man before me. "Face the wall. Spread your legs. You look like a man who knows the drill."

"I'm an ex-cop," he said.

I frisked him and found the holster for his gun—empty. "Where's the gun?"

"That lunatic took it."

That made me feel better; Lonny hadn't come with a gun. "I hope you have a license for it."

"I do."

"So you fence the goods for that crew?"

"I don't know what that crazy man was talking about," he said, and started to turn around.

I grabbed his arm, leading him around front and inside the office. "Which office is yours?"

"That one," he said, gesturing to the left with his head.

We went in. It was like the other office but much bigger. He had his own bathroom, a big closet, furniture. A cinder block wall separated his office from the reception area. If he wasn't the big cheese here, why did he get this office?

"What are all the phones for?"

He didn't bother denying he had them. "I use them with clients so the numbers can't be tracked."

I noted that he'd said *I* not *we*. "Lone Star Recovery. You guys do okay? Keep busy?"

"I do all right. Enough to keep the lights on."

He'd done it again. Answered with *I* not *we*, even when I asked if the company did all right.

"Must have a lot of clients for so many phones."

"Like I said…"

"Yeah. Enough to keep the lights on."

"Tell that maniac I'm pressing charges."

"I'm not sure I'm done with you yet. How about some ID?"

He smirked. "ID. Sure, why not?" He flashed a smirk again.

I looked at his gun license and his driver's license. "Ed Harbough. I know that name."

"I already told you. I'm an ex-cop. I'm sure you've heard my name around."

"Yeah, probably so." I stared him in the eyes. Didn't like what I saw. "About that guy out there. He's a little wound up. His daughter was kidnapped. They've had her two days. Shit like that wears on a man."

"That's not my problem," he said, and gave me yet another smirk.

I had told him about the kidnapping, about the little scared girl, about her parents grieving. What did he do? He smirked. I explained that he was going in. He smirked again, smug in his knowledge that he'd get a high-priced lawyer and likely get off—this man who didn't give a shit about a little girl's life. Or her parents.

I'm not sure what it was that pushed me over. It wasn't the phones. By themselves, they proved little. Not Lonny's ID of the man either. I believed him, but Lonny was emotional and could have made a mistake. It wasn't even the fact that I knew this guy was lying; lots of people lie to cops. Most do. It was the *smirk*. That fuckin' little smirk he put on his face that told me, without any doubt, that he was the one. I didn't need a jury. Juries made mistakes all the time. Smirks didn't. As far as I was concerned, put all the criminals on a stage and accuse them. First one who smirks gets the needle. I hated smirks. Hated it when my kid used to do it when I accused him of using drugs. Hated it when I'd see them on politicians who'd gotten away with something—again. I guess it was fair to say that smirks and me—we didn't get along.

My blow to the kidney dropped him; kidney blows tended to do that. He'd be feeling the residual effects for a day or so. Probably more. He was holding his right side, gasping for air. Despite that, he managed to get out a "What..." before I kicked him in the back. His face slammed into the cinder block wall, blood spewing from his nose.

"You can't—"

I grabbed a handful of hair and yanked him back. Turned him and punched his face, punching that smirk right off his lips. Fuck police brutality. This man had resisted arrest.

***

LONNY WAITED IN THE car, nervous. Agitated. His nerves twitched, and his stomach roiled. He had almost killed that man.

Forgive me, Lord, for what I was about to do.

It seemed as if it had been a long time since Gino had gone in there with Willard. Suppose he disarmed Gino. Suppose he got the advantage on him. Or suppose someone else was in there. That thought scared Lonny. He got out of the car and stepped silently toward the building. He moved inside. Easy. Slow. Sounds of a struggle came from the other room. He looked around, picked up a small lamp from the desk, and went in.

Gino was beating Willard mercilessly. The man's face was streaked with blood. He was doubled up on the floor. "Detective Cataldi. Stop!"

"Get the fuck out of here!" Cataldi said, then went back to beating the man. He kept screaming, "Where's the girl?"

Part of Lonny wanted to jump in and help. The other part wanted to stop Gino. He stepped into the other office and called the Winthrop house. Someone answered on the third ring.

"Who's this?" Lonny asked.

"Who is this?" the voice said.

"This is Lonny."

"Lonny, this is Detective Delgado. What can I do for you?"

"I'm down here with Detective Cataldi. We came to the insurance investigator's office, and he's got some guy. He's beating him something awful. I swear, he's gonna kill this man."

"What are you talking about?"

"I said he's *killing* this guy. You need to get here. Now!"

"Where are you?"

"Down on 45, by Airline Road."

"Too far, Lonny. You're gonna have to stop him."

"Not me. Far as I'm concerned, he can die."

"You're not like that. If you were, you wouldn't have called. Do the right thing."

Silence.

"Lonny, if you won't do it for yourself, do it for Gino. This will ruin his career. He's got a son Jada's age. He needs you. Be there for him."

Lonny hung up and went back inside, where he watched Gino beat that man. This would be good blackmail material. If the detective killed the man, maybe he'd let Lonny go for keeping quiet. He struggled for what seemed like hours, though only a few seconds passed. He was through living in sin. He might have killed that man himself, but he couldn't let Gino ruin his life. Lonny moved up behind Gino and yelled for him to stop.

"Back off!" Gino yelled.

Lonny grabbed him. Wrapped those bear arms around Gino and squeezed. Lifted him off ground. Gino fought the whole time. Lonny squeezed Gino until he gasped for air then set him down maybe ten feet away from the man.

Gino looked up at Lonny. He looked pissed at first. Then his eyes softened. Then he smiled. "Thanks."

Lonny smiled back. "You'd do the same."

***

THE MAN ON THE floor, Ed Harbough, could barely talk. He held his side, dabbing blood from his face with his sleeve, but he had enough wits about him to request a lawyer.

"I'm not arresting you. You don't need a lawyer."

"I'm suing both of you."

"Nah, you won't be doing that, either."

"What are you talking about?"

I dragged him to the door, pulled out my cuffs. I fastened one on his wrist and the other end on the doorknob. Somewhere between smashing his head against the wall and punching his face in, I remembered where I'd heard the name. Ed Harbough was the dirty cop Tip was looking for. Seems he knew something about the man who had killed Tip's mother. At least, Tip thought he did.

I got on the phone and pretended to punch in some numbers. "I got a guy you might want to talk to. Guy by the name of Edgar Harbough. Yeah, that's right. Harbough." I hung up and stared at Ed.

"Who were you talking to?" Harbough asked.

"Guy named Tip Denton. He'll be here in about twenty minutes." I smiled at Ed. "If you have sins you need forgiven, I'd start now."

I looked back at him before I left. Ed finally did piss his pants. I didn't blame him. He knew Tip from the old days, back before the new regime busted up the bare-knuckle fights in jail cells. Back when the Houston police were more like the old Gestapo. I smiled as I left the building, figuring that in ten more minutes, he'd shit himself.

Before I got five feet out, he started screaming, begging me to come back. The bluff had worked. I walked back in. "What?"

"I want to be arrested. I'll confess."

"To what?"

"I brokered the deal for those people to rob the poker games."

A good start, but not what I wanted. "Where's the girl?"

"I have no idea. I don't know what girl you're talking about."

"The same people are doing this deal. Where's their base?"

"I don't know. I've never even seen them. Everything is by phone."

"You know a guy named Scott Winthrop? Rich guy from The Woodlands?"

"Never heard of him."

"How did you know the Marshalls?"

He hesitated. Looked away from me. "I did an insurance claim investigation for the company about a year ago. Their house had been robbed."

"So you gave it to these scum—"

"No, I swear. They must have taken it from my files."

"What files?"

"I was broken into. Check the police reports. Two months ago, someone took all my files."

This fucker was either the best liar in the world, or...I didn't know what the alternative was. I knew he didn't have any files, and had wondered why. Maybe this part was the truth.

"Who's your secretary?"

"She quit."

"When?"

"Right after the robbery." He seemed to give that thought. "Do you think…"

If he hadn't thought of that before, it was no wonder he was a bad cop. I was tired of this guy and had to go.

"See ya' later," I said, and started out.

"Detective! I know what this job can do to you, but if you have any good left in you, listen to me. I don't know where the girl is. I swear. You can't leave me here for Tip Denton. That man *will* kill me."

"If you tell anyone how you got that beating, I'll make sure it's worse when you get inside."

"I won't. I swear. I know the drill."

I stared him down.

"Call off Denton. Call him off, and I'll say I was mugged."

"We'll see," I said, and walked out.

I called a uniform I knew who patrolled the area and asked him to drop by in thirty or forty minutes to take Ed downtown. That would be enough time for Harbough to worry some more.

As I drove up the freeway with Lonny in the passenger seat, my phone rang.

"Have you found what you're looking for yet?"

It was a woman's voice. Not familiar. "Who's this?"

"It doesn't matter. If you haven't found her, go over where you've been."

She had to be talking about Jada. *Where we've been?*

"The motel?"

"There are more than two rooms in a motel."

"Why are you telling me this?"

"The girl reminds me of myself. Besides, if he's in jail, there will be one less person to share the money with."

"Listen, I—"

"Goodbye, Detective." The line went dead.

"Son of a bitch!" I turned to Lonny. "We may have her. Goddamnit, we just might have her."

"Where?"

"Hang on," I said, then called Delgado. "Who do you have at the motel?"

"One of Lance's guys. And I'm sure the crime scene guys are there by now."

"Call Lance's guy. Tell him to watch the rooms on either side of the two you have, but do *not* do anything. I'm ten minutes away."

"What have you got?"

"An anonymous tip. It could be bullshit, but we need to check it out."

"I'm heading your way."

"Stay there, Ribs. I've got this."

"You sure?"

"I'm sure. But get the rest of Lance's crew back to the motel."

CHAPTER 60

NO WITNESSES

Number Two hung up, a smile on her face. It was time to tie up loose ends.

"Is he really dead?" Driver's voice came through the curtains as a muffled sound. Still, Two picked up on the nervousness. And the fear.

"Want to check?"

"No. I just…" Driver was silent a moment, then, "He told me Boss gave him the idea. He said Boss was the one doubting you."

No surprise. Boss had been giving orders for a while now, relaying her orders, but still…put a person in charge, even if it's fake, and they think they're on top of the world. The problem with being on top of the world was that it was a long way to fall. Two slid the curtains back, checking the location. "Where are we?"

"About to exit the freeway. ETA seven minutes."

Driver was playing the game, as if the alliance with Three had never been real, a figment of Two's imagination. She fixed the money bags up the way she wanted them, putting the right amount in each one. The split was different now. Two had tried to build a nice business—professional, organized. But criminals couldn't separate their greed and petty jealousies from business. Too bad. In the long run, it always cost them. Always. Two looked at her watch. One minute to go. She thought of the watch Three had in his pocket. Some things were worth dying for.

The terrain changed from a smooth, paved road to bumpy gravel. The speed slowed considerably. Driver had to navigate potholes. Two zipped up the bags, checked her gun, put her mask on, adjusted her gloves then closed her eyes and breathed deeply. Each breath she took filled her body with life. Each breath out cleansed her soul. A tingling sensation ran through her body, beginning in her arms and extending to her legs and feet.

The van came to a stop. The engine shut off. "Stay in the van, Driver."

"Yes, Boss."

"If you move, I'll kill you."

"Yes, Boss."

Two smiled. *Someone* knew how to follow orders.

She exited through the side door, weighed down by the two bags. One hundred fifty pounds was a lot for most men to carry. The majority of women would never be able to handle it. For Two, it wasn't a problem. Religious workouts assured her of that.

She entered the main area of the "house," as they called it, a bag in each hand, gun in her back waistband. Her mask was intact, her gloves on. Boss stood in the middle of the room, probably alerted by the van pulling in. Number Five's body lay to the side.

"Why is that still here?" Two asked.

"Haven't had time."

"Where did you plan on disposing it?"

"The national park. Up by Crockett. If we bury it shallow up there, the wild hogs and coyotes will get it. They won't leave enough to worry about."

Two nodded. She glanced at Boss then set the bags down, tapping them with her foot. "I love a plan that works."

"That's all of it?"

"See for yourself. And I have to say, money is pretty damn heavy." They both laughed.

Boss knelt and unzipped the bags. "Would you look at this!"

Two stared at Boss. "Three isn't with us anymore." Her hands were in front of her, but they were loose, ready to move.

"What happened?"

"He was having trouble with his math," Two said. "He felt that a split two ways would be better than what we had set up."

"Two?" Boss wore a suspicious frown. "You and him?"

Two shook her head. "Him and Driver."

Boss looked quickly toward the door. "Where is Driver?"

"In the van, but there's no need to worry. Driver is convinced that it was an improper decision."

"Speaking of improper decisions, Number Four is stuck in the motel. They've got cops all over the place."

"No choice," Two said.

Boss frowned. "I told him to kill the girl if it got to that."

"You told him to kill her?"

"She saw his face," Boss said.

"And you told him to kill her?"

Boss must have sensed her irritation. "Only if he had to."

"That was a mistake." She reached behind her, drew the gun, aimed and fired—one shot into the head of the man known as Boss.

Number Two took the IDs from Number Five and Boss, cleaned out their pockets, and got her cell. She dialed Number Four.

He answered in a whispered voice. "What?"

"Status."

"Where's Boss?"

"Dead. You're talking to me."

"I don't take orders from you."

Defiant even to the end. No sense in telling him he had been taking orders from me all along. "I have the money. You *will* take orders from me."

"If I get caught, I'll tell them everything."

"You know nothing."

"I'll…I'll tell them…"

"Calm yourself. Listen to me, and you'll be okay." She waited while he got composed.

"What?" he said.

"You can escape this. But if not, your money will be waiting for you when you get out. Or I will give it to whoever you want if you keep quiet about everything."

"You'd do that? Give me my share?"

"You earned it."

"Okay, what do I do?"

"First, understand that things can still go wrong. No matter what happens, do *not* kill the girl. Do that, and you get the needle. Kidnapping, even with nobody hurt, is bad, but we've got money for lawyers."

"Okay."

"The rest is easy. Stay calm. Make no noise. Same things I told you before."

"All right. Thanks, Number Two."

"Good luck. Now let me talk to the girl. Take her gag off."

"What if she screams?"

"I told her before that I'd kill her parents if she did that. I am going to reinforce the order. Give her the phone."

Jada took the phone. "Yes?" The tone was meek even for a whisper.

"Can he hear me?" Two asked in a low voice.

"No."

"Good. Listen closely. While I'm talking, pretend you're scared. I know you're already scared. Act more scared."

"Okay."

"In ten minutes, ask to go to the bathroom. He will probably have you gagged. Once inside, quickly lock the door. He won't break in for fear of making noise. With the door locked, make all the noise you can. Kick the walls, scream if you can get the gag off, slam the toilet seat up and down. Break something."

"Okay." Jada shivered. There was no need to act. "What about what you said…my dad…"

"Forget what I said before. Do as I say, and you'll be home safe very soon. Now I want you to say the following. 'I won't. I swear. Just don't hurt them.'"

"I won't. I swear. Just don't hurt them."

"Good. Give the phone back to him." Four took the phone, and Two went on. "She won't give you trouble. Remember, stay calm."

Two hung up, started back toward the van then stopped, thinking. She turned, exited through a side door, and crept around to the front of the building, peeking through a window at the van. Driver was not in the front of the van. A quick scan of the room showed Driver pressed against the wall beside the door—waiting to ambush her.

Two went back inside and crouched beside the door. She reached up and opened the door.

Driver made the move, but Two was not where Driver expected. She reached forward and yanked Driver's feet out from under her. After disarming Driver, Two put the body in the van, cracked the side of Driver's head and let the body tumble out onto a pile of metal pipes. She then went to a small room in the back of the warehouse and removed the body of a previous Number Four from a freezer sitting against the wall. She dragged the body to the main room and placed it next to Boss.

This should work just fine.

CHAPTER 61

THE PIECES DON'T FIT

I hadn't gotten half a mile before the phone rang again. "Cataldi."

"Gino, you were right!" It was the tech I had talked to earlier.

"You found the bug?"

"Sort of, but it wasn't really a bug; it was the phone."

"For God's sake, that should have been the first place you looked."

"But it wasn't a bug. They had *spyware* on his cell phone."

"Spyware? What the hell are you talking about?"

"Good, sophisticated stuff—it let them listen to anything, even if the phone was off."

I panicked. "Where is it now?"

"I'm outside. It's in the kitchen, and I let Delgado know about it."

I was pissed now. These fuckers had been listening to us the whole time. "How did you not notice this shit earlier?"

"You need to understand, this stuff is almost impossible to detect. We had to get into the code to find it."

He was getting way over my head now. "How did it get there? Who could have put it on?"

"Anybody who had access to the phone for a few minutes and who knew Winthrop's password and personal information. It's not difficult. And once it's in there, the things they can do with it are amazing—keep track of him with GPS, see who he texts and what he says, listen to calls, listen to conversations near the phone."

"Son of a bitch!"

"Yeah, it's not pretty."

"Put Delgado on."

"I'll have to get him to come outside."

"Okay, hurry up."

I looked over to see Lonny about to go crazy with worry. While I waited for Delgado, I filled Lonny in. "We got a tip that Jada is still at the motel in another room. We also found out that someone had Scott's phone bugged."

He looked more stunned than I was. Delgado got on the line. "Some shit, huh, Gino?"

"Who could have put it there?"

"I've been thinking on it. It could have been Alexa, but that doesn't play out. No reason for it to be Scott. If he wanted to tell the kidnappers something, he could have just told them."

"How about people he works with?"

"Tip said one guy didn't seem right, a guy named Sanjay."

"I remember. We need to go over this later. I need to give Tip a call."

I hung up, but before I dialed Tip's number, I realized the implications of the spyware. That phone had been lying on the kitchen table. No wonder the kidnappers told him to leave it at home. *They were listening to everything we said.* Then it really hit me. They knew every move we were going to make. That's how they knew we were going to the motel. That's how they knew *everything*. There was no way they'd be at the hotel now waiting on Scott and his money. I punched in Tip's number.

"Tip, get in Scott's room now! I'll fill you in later."

"What's going on?" Lonny asked.

"Nothing good."

There was no way the drop would pay off. I prayed that the woman wasn't messing with me about the motel. It would be up to me to find Jada now. Me and Lonny.

Not five minutes passed before Tip called back. "We're fucked!" he said.

"Tell me."

"They got him one block from the goddamn house. They took the money, put a live phone on him, and headed out. We've been on a dead run for hours."

I punched the steering wheel. "Fuck!"

"Yeah. Twice," he said. "I got a description of the van from Scott and I put it out already."

"It's been hours…"

"I know. Fat chance."

I tried gathering my thoughts, but my head was scrambled. "Tip, fill Delgado in. Then go see that guy from Scott's company. Delgado will tell you all about it, but they had some kind of spyware on Winthrop's phone."

"I'm on it."

Shit! I'd almost forgotten about Harbough. "Tip, the guy who was running the insurance investigation firm—it wasn't Masterson, it was Ed Harbough."

Dead silence. "Where is he?"

Tip usually had a semi-dufus, friendly, funny voice. This time his voice was scary.

"On his way downtown."

"You should have let me have him. You owed me that."

"I did it for you."

"The fuck you did."

I felt bad about what I did to Tip. I knew how much he wanted to find his mother's killer, but I also knew he'd have probably killed Harbough. If he had, one of us was going up for it.

I looked in my rearview mirror as I drove. I half expected to see something resembling a spaceship flying by at any minute, piloted by a humanoid who resembled Tip. He'd be pissed as hell at what I did. When he was pissed, he drove fast. And he drove ninety when he was happy.

I called Ribs to pick up where we left off. "Go outside."

"On my way." I waited a few seconds, then he came on again. "What's up?"

"Let's try to figure out who planted the spyware. Do that, and we've got our kidnappers."

"None of us had access to his phone. No reason for Alexa to do it. No reason on earth for Scott to do it."

"So that leaves the people at his work," I said. "They would have access to his phone at various times. And they'd likely know, or suspect, his password. His admin would surely know."

"But *why* would someone from work do this? Don't they all stand to make money from this IPO?"

I didn't have an answer. "Maybe it's a jealousy thing, like that case a while back where the scientist put the carcinogenic stuff in the other guy's nasal spray."

"Cruel shit there."

"So you think somebody could hate Scott that much?"

Delgado laughed. "You tell me."

I thought about it for a moment. "Let's assume it's somebody from work. Why would they not know they had the wrong girl?"

"If their information relied on listening to the phone, maybe we didn't mention her by name when Scott was there."

Delgado got me thinking. "So as long as Scott didn't mention it at work…"

"And you told him not to."

I nodded. "That could explain it. We'll have to ask Scott when I get back."

"You want me to tell him about the spyware and see if he comes up with any suggestions?"

"Yeah. See how he handles it."

I hung up and stared across at Lonny. "I won't tell you not to worry, but we'll get her. I promise."

"Like you promised those people in Philadelphia?"

That was a low blow, but he had a right to say it. I shouldn't have promised. Not them. Not him. We rode in silence for a few moments. I exited the freeway, turned left, headed toward the motel.

CHAPTER 62

LAST ROOM ON THE LEFT

Number Four paced the room, cracking his knuckles and squeezing his hands. The crime scene unit was in the next room, vacuuming, moving furniture, doing God knows what.

When the hell are they going to leave?

He walked to the window. Number Four had the curtains closed again. He didn't see any more cars, but that didn't mean anything. They could have an army around the corner, for all he knew. Why the hell did Boss have to send him here, of all people? He shot a quick glance to the girl, lying on the bed. Number Two must have scared her good. She'd been perfect ever since that phone call.

***

LONNY HAD BEEN ON the phone with Lucia ever since I told him about Jada being in the motel. He hung up as I pulled into the parking lot alongside Lance's van. How Lance had gotten back so fast was beyond me. Maybe he and Tip went to the same driving school. Maybe all Texans did. Lonny and I got out of the car and went to the van.

"Detective," Lance said and nodded.

"Everybody ready?"

"Good to go. Just give the word."

I turned to Lonny. "Stay in the car. Call Lucia. Do *anything*, but stay in the car. I can't be worried about you with Jada's life on the line."

"Lucia's on her way," he said. "Mars is driving her."

"Good. Jada will like that."

I waited for Lonny to get in the car then turned to face Lance. "Consider this a hostage situation. As far as we know, we've got one kidnapper in the room with the girl. He'll be desperate, feeling trapped."

"Not good," Lance said.

"No, it's not." My phone rang. "Hang on, Lance." I answered the phone, assuming it was Delgado but it was her.

"Detective, in a few minutes, you will hear noise from inside room #178—screaming or banging on the wall. The girl will be in the bathroom. That will be your opportunity. Don't miss it."

"How—"

"Goodbye, Detective."

I stared at the phone then looked at Lance. "That was one of the kidnappers. They're in room #178, and the girl will give us a signal when she's out of harm's way."

"When?"

"A few minutes."

"They're giving up their own?"

"Along with the girl," I said.

"What the hell? Why?"

"My guess is she doesn't want any witnesses."

Lance looked at me and shook his head. "'She'?"

"The one who called is a woman. These people are cold, Lance."

"Ice cold," he said. "But it doesn't matter. We're ready."

Gino turned to Lance. "Make sure they are. Have the crime scene unit listening for the signal. And Lance, we want this guy alive. We *need* him alive."

"We'll do our best."

"*Alive!*" I said as he gathered his men.

***

JADA HAD BEEN COUNTING down the minutes, waiting for the right opportunity. She tried judging the time by watching Number Four's mood, but he seemed so…wired. It scared her. Number Two had been insistent though, so Jada figured she'd better make her move. She grunted low to draw his attention.

Number Four turned. "What?" His voice was a harsh whisper.

Jada gestured with her head toward the bathroom.

"You'll have to wait."

She shook her head and indicated again she had to go.

He closed his eyes and sighed. "Can't you wait?"

She shook her head. He grabbed her arm and led her toward the bathroom. When they got to the door, he spoke into her ear with a low voice. "Remember what Number Two told you. Try anything…"

Jada put fear into her eyes. It was easy to do, because she really was scared half to death.

He let go of her arm but stood close to the door. She went in, but he kept watching. She started to close the door, but he stopped it, shaking his head.

Jada unzipped her pants, sat on the toilet, and pretended to try. After a minute or so, she motioned for him to turn his head. She got ready. As soon as he turned his head, she jumped up, slammed the door and twisted the lock.

He banged against the door, but not very hard. Then she heard him threatening her.

"Open this fuckin' door. You know what will happen."

Jada tried getting her gag off, but it was tied too tight. She kicked the wall, once, then more. Her stomach lurched. Number Four was pushing on the door. If he got in, she was dead. She got on her back, stretched her arms back and braced against the tub, and kicked with all she had. She kept kicking, and kicking, even punching holes in the drywall.

Somebody please help me!

***

INSIDE ROOM #180, THE CSU lead heard the noise and called Gino. "We've got a signal. It's a go."

Gino looked to Lance. "Go!"

Lance had men inside #180 and outside of #178. He gave the order to move in.

Number Four heard footsteps. He ran to the window, looked out. They were coming up the steps. He waited for them to get close. Fifteen feet, ten. He fired through the window, taking the lead cop down.

The door from #180 burst open. Two guys rushed in, one low to the ground. The low one fired. The first shot blew out Four's chest. The second ripped a chunk of his head off.

***

LANCE'S GUY WENT DOWN. I prayed his vest covered him. I drew my gun and rushed the room. A shot rang from inside. Then another. Lance's guys busted through the door of #178. I followed them in. The guy on the floor wasn't a pretty sight. Noise was still coming from the bathroom.

"Jada! Open the door, Jada. It's the police. You're safe."

The bathroom door burst open, and Jada flew out. I held my arms open, and she wrapped herself around me, showering me with tears. When I took out the gag, her words couldn't come fast enough.

"Oh my God! Is it over? Oh God."

I patted her back and kissed her head. "It's over, Jada. You're safe."

She couldn't stop crying and wouldn't let go of me.

"Your dad is outside. Probably your mom and Mars, too. How about we go see them?"

She broke off from me. "Oh my God. Are they really here?"

I held her arm and led her through the room, trying to shield her from the gory mess on the floor. She cried all the way out of the room and down the walk. When we turned the corner, she saw Lonny and Lucia. And Mars. Jada broke from me and ran, screaming something incoherent. I took my time getting to them, but it was an easy scene to interpret. A family reunited, sharing in grief and relief. When I got to within about ten feet, they were still crying, even Mars. I felt good inside. This was not how my other kidnappings ended, though there was still a sour note to play out. I felt certain that Lonny hadn't told them of his situation, and I knew that as good as it felt for them to have Jada home safe, it was going to be just as bad to see Lonny go. Maybe worse. For the time being, though, I let them enjoy the moment.

Lucia ran to me, hugging me and spreading more tears on my shirt. "Detective, we can't thank you enough. I knew you'd do it. I *knew* you'd save my baby."

"I'll get an ambulance out here. You can ride to the hospital with her."

Lonny came over, repeating the gratitude. "So what do we do, Detective?"

I knew I shouldn't do what I was about to do, but I did it anyway. "Give me your word that you're not going anywhere, and you can ride with the family to the hospital."

He offered his hand. "No problem there. I owe you for that."

"I'm sending someone to the hospital to ask her questions. I'm going to Winthrop's house. I've got to get these people."

"Get them for Jada."

I let the Hacketts alone and set about wrapping things up so I could get out of there. I called the ambulance and gave Lance instructions for securing the area until someone else arrived. The crime scene unit could handle their own business. Next I called Delgado and told him what had happened, and to keep it quiet for now. Until we figured things out.

It was good to get Jada, but I was still pissed. We had been played like fools through this whole thing, to the point of relying on them to help us save Jada. It was time to get these fuckers. Now!

CHAPTER 63

CHARRED EVIDENCE

I was two miles away when the phone rang. It seemed like all it did was ring. "Cataldi."

"Gino, it's Julie. Those addresses you gave me earlier?"

"Yeah?"

"The fire department just had a call to one of them. There's a big blaze in a building a few blocks away."

Aw shit! "Which address?"

Julie gave it to me. "I'm on it. Call Tip and Delgado for me. Fill them in."

I turned on the siren and punched the gas up to Tip-Denton speed. Fortunately, the traffic was light. From about a mile away, I saw the smoke. As I closed to within half a mile, I saw huge tongues of flames lapping the sky. The end of the road came quicker than I thought, switching from pavement to gravel. The car bounced hard. I thought the shocks broke for a minute. I hit the brakes and got down to a reasonable speed. After a couple hundred feet, woods surrounded me, growing thicker the closer I got. The road skewed right, then left, opening into a small clearing. I hit the brakes. Four fire trucks stood in front of me. I scanned the area. Didn't see anyone but firemen. I got a sick feeling in my gut.

If anyone was in there…

I headed toward the building. A quick glance at the fire made me shiver, despite the heat. I was far away, but my skin prickled. It felt as if the air might explode. I waited a moment then moved forward. Didn't get far before I had to stop, my hands going up to shield my face from the heat. I moved back a step or two. A fireman stood to the left, drinking water. I flashed him my badge and approached.

"What have you got?" I asked.

He shook his head. "Bad one. The place was full of accelerants."

"Arson?"

"Probably."

"Any bodies?"

The fireman put the bottle down. He looked at me. "I know we've got some bodies in there, but we don't know how many yet." He grabbed another bottle of water from a cooler. "We'll know more later. I gotta get back."

I gave him my cell number and asked him to call if he got something. "I'll come back later," I said, and went back to the car. Time to get to Winthrop's house. As I drove, thinking of what to do, the phone rang. It had been ringing so much, it almost pissed me off.

"Yeah!" I said, in a tone I knew was too aggressive.

"Gino, I can barely hear you. You sound pissed off."

"What's going on, Ribs?"

"Scott came back."

"Did you tell him about the spyware?"

"I laid it out nice and pretty. Actually, I had the tech lay it out for him while I watched his reaction."

"How did he take it?"

"I'm not sure. He was baffled, but…something didn't ring true about his reaction. Almost like, 'Okay, that's news to me, but…I'm not surprised.' That type of a reaction. Like if you find out your girlfriend is cheating on you, but you knew she probably would anyway, because she cheated on her old boyfriend with you."

"That's a deep analysis, Dr. Delgado."

"Call me Dr. Ribs."

"Anything else?"

"The oddest part. He hasn't once asked about Jada, and he doesn't know she's safe. All he asked about was whether we had any leads on the van from the description he provided."

"He's worried about his money."

"Guess so."

"And you wondered if people at work could hate him enough to do this?"

"I'm still not buying it, Gino. Ever since this started, I've had a feeling that this guy was involved somehow. That feeling is stronger now."

I didn't say anything, but the same thought had crossed my mind a few times. And I trusted Delgado's instincts. That's what made him a good poker player. He was the best I'd seen when it came to determining if someone was bluffing. "So you *don't* think it was someone from work?"

"As Tip would say, 'That dog don't hunt.'"

I was thinking about how this might have played out when I heard Delgado talking again.

"Hey, Gino, you there?"

"Sorry, Ribs. Let's work this backwards. If it's not anyone from his work, and if we trust your gut and assume Scott had something to do with it…fill in the blanks for me."

"The biggest problem I got with this is that it's his daughter."

"But it's *not*," I said. "This was Hackett's daughter."

"It was *supposed* to be his."

I thought for a moment. "Who said so? Suppose for a minute that this was planned to be Jada from the beginning. If we assume Scott is working with the kidnappers, he can give them whatever information he wants and keep other things out. If they know they have the wrong girl, it doesn't matter."

Ribs sounded frustrated. "None of this works, Gino. Why would he do it? This man stands to make tens of millions. Why risk a kidnapping? For what—to split a few million he has to pay back to the bank?"

We were back to the same place again—no motive. "You're right. Keep thinking. I'm coming back."

When I walked into the house, it seemed empty. No laughter, not even any smiles. Plenty of people, though. I looked around for Scott. He was on the back patio, talking on the phone. I grabbed Delgado's arm. "You told him about the spyware, right?"

"That's another phone," he whispered. "His is on the counter."

I motioned him outside. Once out of earshot of the phone, we revisited the theory regarding Scott Winthrop and his involvement in the kidnapping. As we chatted, Tip pulled up.

"What are you two brain surgeons doing out here?"

"Trying to find motivation for Winthrop doing this."

"Shoot, all you had to do was ask the best damn detective in Texas."

I had nothing in me to laugh. Besides, I'd heard Tip's lines too many times.

"What are you trying to pin on the poor man?"

"We think he could have some kind of involvement, but it doesn't make sense. There's no motivation for him to do it when he's going to be filthy rich in a few months."

"Suppose he's *not* going to be rich," Tip said. "Suppose he's up to his ass in debt."

"But he *will* be rich, and Julie checked him out. His finances look good."

"He's only going to be rich *if* they go public. But if something were to be wrong with their clinical trials, the IPO could fall apart, depending on how damaging the data is. Or, if they do the IPO and the clinical trials look bad, the stock could tank."

I got excited. "Spit it all out, Denton. Don't drag it."

Tip's face twisted a little. His scar twitched. If he had done that to Sanjay, I'm sure it broke him down. "That little weasel Sanjay told me everything. Scott's been blackmailing him to keep quiet, but they've got problems with their drug. Scott *knew* the clinical trials were going bad, but there was nothing he could do about it. The best he was able to do was blackmail Sanjay's brother, who works for the company doing the trials, to delay the results for a few weeks."

"What good would that do?"

"Nothing in the long run," Tip said, "but everything when you think about it in light of the kidnapping. If the data comes out, the IPO is sunk. If he delays it, he has time to arrange a kidnapping and secure a loan against what he'd earn on the IPO."

I gave that some thought. Things were coming together. "So he makes a deal to split the money with the kidnappers, gets the loan, plants the spyware so they know what we're doing at all times…"

"And collects the money when it's done," Ribs said.

I thought more. "The problem is, he still has to pay back the seven million. All he did was get himself a million or two in cash in trade for seven million in debt."

"That's not good math," Tip said.

"We're missing something," Delgado said.

"I'm getting coffee. Anybody want any?"

"Me," Delgado said.

"Tea for me," Tip said.

I racked my brain while I made the coffee and tea. Delgado was right; we had the right idea, but we were missing *something.* I went outside again and handed out the drinks.

"Anybody think of anything?" I asked.

Tip shook his head. "You married into a smart family, Gino."

I turned to look at Delgado. "What? You got something?"

"Remember when we first met Winthrop, the day his daughter was grabbed? Or when we thought it was her?"

"In case you don't remember, that was only two days ago."

"God, you're right. Seems like a long time. Anyway, when we were talking about the neighborhood, he said how safe it was, and how he had lived in so many other places where it wasn't."

"I remember."

"The cities he mentioned, amigo, were Mexico City, Bogota, Caracas…"

"Get to the point, Ribs."

"If he lived in those cities, and he was an executive at the time, I'd bet all of the money I don't have that he had kidnap insurance."

"Kidnap insurance?" I knew that somewhere, maybe in another life, or on TV, or in an article…*somewhere* I had heard of kidnap insurance. But I had no idea what it involved. "How does that help us?"

"It takes away the seven-million-dollar loan he'd have to pay back," Tip said. "Assuming he's got the insurance for that much."

My heart raced. I was rolling with this theory. "So he pays the ransom, collects the insurance, and pays back the loan."

"And splits the money with the kidnappers," Ribs said.

I held up my hands, not wanting to kill the celebration, but... "Whoa, guys. Hold on. I love the enthusiasm, and the thoughts behind it. But a couple of things need to be ironed out. First we need to see if he actually *does* have kidnap insurance; then we've got to see if it is for seven million or more; then we have to figure out how Scott Winthrop, a biotech executive, got in touch with hardened criminals; *then*, one of you brilliant minds has to explain to me how the kidnap insurance would help him when they took the *wrong fucking girl*."

Delgado's dimples faded into his cheeks. Tip's scar twitched and went back to normal. And all of the laughter and celebration disappeared. We were back to square one.

CHAPTER 64

WRAPPING IT UP

I looked at Tip and Delgado. We were all in a state of shock. There isn't much worse than thinking you've got a crime solved, only to discover you were a dumb ass and didn't know shit. "I still think we're on track, but we've got to tie him to the kidnappers, and we've got to figure out the motivation—some way the money would help him."

Something else came to mind. "Tip, you said he was in debt. Julie didn't find any."

"Sanjay says Scott has an interest-free loan from the company. He thought it was for a couple hundred grand."

"I thought Sanjay was in R&D. How does he know about that?"

"He's got a relative in finance."

"Can't anybody keep a secret?"

Tip laughed. Delgado laughed louder.

I called Charlie. "Did we ever finish gathering information on Winthrop?"

"I gave you what I had."

"You mentioned he had a break-in about a year ago. Check it out and see which company it was."

"I'll get on it, Gino. How y'all doin' up there?"

"Not so good, Charlie. One more thing. Is there any way for you to find out what kind of insurance policies Winthrop had?"

"What do you need to know?"

"Whether he had any kind of coverage that would reimburse him for ransom."

"You're talkin' about a K&R policy."

"A what?"

"A kidnap and ransom policy. Pretty common in international work."

Charlie was going and screwing with my meter calibration again. Second time today he proved to know a lot more than I'd thought. "How do you know about that?"

"My sister's husband sells insurance. Every time we get together, he's talking about this policy or that policy. About the most boring man I've ever met. Only reason I go is to eat the food. She's a good cook."

Calibration was fixed now. With Charlie, it always came back to food.

"See what you can find out," I said.

"Probably through his company," Charlie said.

"What?"

"I said, it's probably through his company. Most of those policies are bought by the company to cover all executives. Usually their families too."

"Okay, Charlie. Get back to me."

For the next hour, we brainstormed. Twice I called the fireman I'd met. First time, he didn't answer. When he did the second time, he said they were still battling the blaze but had five confirmed bodies. One female. Said he'd call when they had something else.

"Nothing new?" Delgado asked when I got off.

"Five bodies. One female."

Tip scratched his head. "Five bodies? What the hell! Is this a goddamn kidnap-suicide pact?"

As we puzzled over the implications, Charlie called. "Y'all are gonna owe me for this."

"I already owe you. What have you got?"

"I couldn't get anything from his work other than confirmation that they had a policy and who it was with. Kept citing privacy issues and all that nonsense. So I called my sister's husband—remember, the one who does insurance?" Charlie could drag a story out for days if you let him.

"Yeah, I remember."

"I gave him the information, and he knew somebody over there, so he got the skinny for old Charlie."

I almost laughed. This might be the only time I'd hear the word *skinny* in the same sentence as *Charlie*.

"Not only does he have ransom insurance, but they got him covered like a fresh-gutted deer. Who is this guy Winthrop, anyway? The way they treat him, he must run with the big dogs."

I shook my head and patiently waited. Listening to a Texan tell a story could be painful. Funny sometimes, but painful. "He runs with the big dogs, all right. What did you find?"

"He's covered for ten million."

"More than enough for what we need," I said.

"That's not all. Get your hand off your dick for this one…it covers *guests*."

I must not have gotten my hand off my dick soon enough; in fact, I didn't even know what the hell he meant. "'Covers guests'? What the hell does that mean?"

He laughed. "I like a lot of strawberry cream cheese with my bagels, Gino. Know that before I give you this. *Covers guests* means his policy would cover anyone staying at his house when they were kidnapped. So the Hackett girl is covered."

"Son of a bitch!"

"You betcha." He laughed some more, kind of like a giggle, but from a *really* big belly. "That's not all. Remember when I told y'all about Winthrop's house gettin' broken into? I checked that out some more. Guess who did the claims investigation?"

This was too much to hope for. "Lone Star Recovery?"

"Now *you're* running with the big dogs."

"Charlie, you're the best. You might have earned bagels for life."

"Don't forget to tell Tip what I did for you. He's always bustin' my ass."

"Don't worry, I'll tell him." I cracked the biggest smile I'd worn in days as I looked at Tip and Delgado. "Charlie wrapped it up and put a bow on it."

"Let's hear," Ribs said.

"Winthrop not only has insurance, but it covers guests, so Jada would be covered. And get this—Ed Harbough is the one who investigated the claim Scott had last year."

"*Hijo de puta!* So they didn't take the wrong girl after all. They took exactly who they were supposed to take."

"Right," I said. "Who is going to suspect a guy who's helping his fellow man?"

Delgado paced, running with the excitement of getting close to a bust. "So Winthrop pretends all along not to want to pay—once we know it's not Alexa—then suddenly has a change of heart? Only it's not a change of heart; it's all staged to make us think he's risking seven million for someone else's kid."

"I knew something was wrong when he did, but I couldn't figure it out. Now it fits."

"Sure it fits. Fits even better. Who's going to suspect a guy doing this for another kid?"

"*Hijo de puta!*" Ribs said again. "Jada was the target all along."

"Son of a bitch," I said. "This cocksucker did all this for money. Fuckin' whore."

Tip clenched his fists. "And if Ed Harbough's name came up, he's involved. A lot of nooses hang in that man's family tree."

"He put Scott in touch with the kidnappers," I said.

Tip nodded. "I'd bet ten dollars against every donut Charlie could eat."

I thought about this scenario for a second or two. "So Harbough has been in this all along? The poker games too?"

Tip nodded. "He's always been linked to Rusty. And Rusty had a lot of friends at those poker games."

"So why would Rusty want his friends robbed?" Delgado asked.

"I wouldn't actually call them *friends*," Tip said. "They were 'political acquaintances,' if you get my drift. Rusty is always looking for blackmail material, to put it nicely."

I picked it up. "So the games get busted. Rusty's 'friends' are exposed. He 'arranges' to keep it quiet, and now they owe him a favor."

"Gino, you're getting too good. I expect you could run for office next year."

"Not me, Tip. That's your department."

"Now that we solved this crime in our heads," I said, "how do we pin it on Winthrop?"

"I got an idea," Ribs said. "Get one of the techs."

"What's your idea?" I tended to be leery of anything Delgado came up with, especially in the company of Tip.

"First, we get Harbough out of jail…"

CHAPTER 65

JUST A FEW QUESTIONS

I got a call on the phone. It was the fireman I met at the scene. "Gino Cataldi."

"Detective, this is Steve. The final count is five."

"Are you done there?"

"Not even close, but you can come take a look."

"I'll see you in about an hour."

Delgado looked at me. "What's wrong?"

"That was the fireman. I'm going to look at the bodies, but I want to see Jada first."

"Go on," Tip said. "Delgado and I can handle this."

I shuddered at the thought of those two handling anything except a massacre of some sort. But I had no choice. "After I'm gone, tell Winthrop and the rest of them about Jada being safe. You can even tell them that the kidnappers are dead, or that we think they are, and that the money is gone. But go easy, gentlemen. My badge is on the line too."

I left to the sound of them still laughing—not a confidence builder, but I had to get to Jada. As I drove to the hospital, I thought about how this whole thing unfolded, and I didn't like one bit of it. We'd been outsmarted, outplayed, and outmaneuvered from day one.

I parked the car and ran into Alexa, who was just leaving the hospital. She hugged me.

"I can't believe you got her, Detective."

"How is she?"

Alexa looked as if she'd been crying. "She's okay now. Sort of." She stretched up and kissed my cheek. "Thanks for everything. And I'm sorry I was such an ass."

I smiled. "Get some help, Alexa. You're going to be all right, too."

I didn't know how she was going to take it if we busted her father, but I had no time to worry about that.

The elevator took me to the third floor, and before I knew it, I was standing at the door of the temporary room they had Jada in. The whole Hackett family was celebrating, but you had to look through the tears to find the joy. "I hate to break this up, but I need to hear Jada's story before she talks to too many people."

Lucia hugged her then walked away wrapped in the arms of Lonny and Mars. I sat beside Jada. "How are you?"

"Fine," she said.

"'Fine'? Really?"

She wiped her eyes and gave a short chuckle. "No. I'm scared still. I don't know why…" She started crying again. It made me feel bad, as if I'd caused it.

I handed her a tissue. "Go on. Take your time. Tell me when you're ready."

She blew her nose, wiped the last of her tears, and then sat a little straighter. "I'm ready, Detective. What do you need to know?"

"How about you tell me in your own words what happened? Try to remember anything, not just what you think is important. Later on we can talk about other stuff."

I was afraid to ask if they'd raped her. I didn't want to know. Couldn't know. I didn't want another girl telling me she wished she'd died.

"Okay." She seemed to think for a moment, then started up. She told me about the grab, and how they'd kept her in the motel. How they called each other by numbers, never names. She cringed when she talked about the one we'd killed, saying he kept her naked and watched her.

She covered her face but managed to stifle the cry. "Another one got killed at the motel, too."

"What happened?"

"Number Two killed him."

"Why did Number Two kill him?"

"He tried…" She lowered her head and looked away. "You know."

"Tried raping you?" I hated myself already for bringing this up, but she'd said he *tried*, so I felt we were safe. When she didn't answer, I pried. "*Did* he rape you?"

She shook her head. "He *would* have. He's the one who beat me too. That's why Number Two killed him."

"Number Two? That's the woman?"

She nodded.

"Was she the only woman?"

Again she nodded.

"How many men were there?"

"Four."

I stood to stretch. Jada seemed to have clammed up once I started talking about Number Two. As if she was protecting the woman. I stared at her, astonished. "Jada, she *was* one of the kidnappers. She would have killed you."

She glared at me. "Not her, Detective. She saved my life. Twice!"

I was trying to figure out how, despite theories of Stockholm Syndrome or whatever, that this young girl could have gotten attached to her kidnapper so quickly. Jada answered it for me with her next words.

"Detective Cataldi, she not only saved my life, but she stopped them from raping me. If not for her, those men—*all of them*—would have done it."

Now I understood. I also realized I would get nothing else worthwhile from Jada. Not today. Maybe not ever. "I'll tell you what, Jada. How about you go with your parents? We'll talk more later on or tomorrow. Don't talk to anyone else about the case. Okay?"

She flashed a smile at me. "Thanks, Detective. And I won't. I promise."

I started to walk away, but stopped. I took her hands in mine and looked into her eyes. "Jada, I can't imagine what you felt like these past two days, and I can't imagine what you're going to go after this. The memories won't be good and they won't disappear." She had lowered her head, avoiding eye contact. I gently lifted her chin until I could see her eyes again. "Try to remember that none of this was your fault. Nothing you did, or could have done, would have prevented this."

She faked a smile and said, "Thanks, Detective."

"I'm not good at this, but I meant what I said. And I'll get a counselor to contact you before you leave the hospital."

She squeezed my hand and smiled. "Thanks. For real."

I said goodbye to Jada then searched out the Hacketts. I managed to get Lonny's attention and signaled him over. He wore a somber look.

"Yes, Detective?"

"You know what we've got to do, Lonny."

He nodded. "Can I have a few minutes? I don't know how to tell them."

"Lucia doesn't know?"

His head damn near came off he shook it so hard. "Nobody does."

I sighed. Looked around. Fought with myself. Then I turned back to Lonny. "I'm going to let you go home for the night. I'm walking out on a huge limb here. I could lose my job. I know you understand what that's like. Thing is, if I lose my job for something like this, I can't get one anywhere. I couldn't work at McDonalds. They figure if a cop can't keep his ethics…you see what I mean?"

Lonny looked at me. Sincerity was in his eyes. "Don't worry. I'll be ready in the morning."

"I'm trusting you, Lonny."

He shook my hand. "I won't let you down."

As I watched him walk away, I said to myself. *I'm trusting you.*

I turned down the road leading to the warehouse, smoke still tainting the perfect blue sky, and the smell of burnt things stinging my nose. Burnt things like gasoline, oil, plastic, fabric, and…flesh. That one was unmistakable. Even if you had never smelled burnt flesh, had never singed the hair on your arms, there was no mistaking it. Burnt flesh came with a distinct marker, almost like it sung to you of the vile and putrid nature of its business.

I tried breathing through my mouth, but that only worked for a few seconds. Eventually, I succumbed. After a few big whiffs, I almost puked. It took a moment to get my stomach under control, but when I did, I sought out Steve. He led me to the area where they had the bodies waiting to be shipped off for autopsies.

"Same count?" I asked.

"Four male. One female."

"Anything else you can tell me?"

"Somebody lost a lot of money in there."

"Money? As in cash?"

"I'm talking a *lot* of cash. We've got two bags in the warehouse that looked like they were loaded. Gone now."

We had been walking as he filled me in. I saw the burnt-out shell of the van and made a mental note to have them cancel the APB. "Any ideas yet on how it started?"

"Looks like it may have started with the van. Too early to tell, though. We'll have that later. I'll call you."

"I've got to get going anyway. Call me when you get something."

I filled Delgado in before I left then headed toward Winthrop's house, more confused than when I'd left. I found it impossible to believe that all of them had died in a fire, yet, the numbers added up. Four guys and a woman. Just like Jada said, and Lonny had too.

So what was I missing?

CHAPTER 66

JUST REWARDS

Delgado went to the kitchen, started cleaning up dishes and coffee cups. Lots of those. Some of the other cops stayed to help. Most had gone. The techs were disassembling their equipment, putting phones back in order and unhooking surveillance they had set up out front.

Scott Winthrop grabbed a towel and dried the few cups that didn't fit in the dishwasher. "Leaving, Detective?"

"It's about time, wouldn't you say, sir? I'm just glad it's over and that Jada's safe." Delgado finished scrubbing a knife, one of those nice ones people didn't put in dishwashers. He handed it to Scott to dry.

"Don't forget to clear Mr. Winthrop's phone," he said to a tech passing by.

"Already done, Detective. He's good to go."

"I can't thank you enough," Winthrop said.

"Thank me? We were just doing our jobs. We owe you the thanks, letting us use the house like this. Disrupting your life...I'm just sorry we didn't get the money. I would have liked to have had a few minutes with the kidnappers too."

Winthrop seemed to perk up. "What happened with them again? I didn't get all the information."

Delgado shrugged. "They're all dead. Something happened to the van, we think. A broken fuel line or something. Then it spread to some gas cans, and the whole place went up. Nobody got out alive."

"And the money?"

Delgado hid his smile. He knew the conversation would come around to the money. "The money burnt up in the fire."

Winthrop tensed. "All of it?"

"As far as we can tell. They found both bags and a lot of burned up bills. A *lot*."

Delgado noticed the muscles in Scott's arms tighten. "What are you going to do about that, Mr. Winthrop? You have to pay that back, don't you?"

He seemed lost in thought. "What…oh, yes." He stared out the kitchen window. Gino looked in the same direction, but there was nothing there. "I hadn't counted on losing it all."

Delgado folded the washcloth, dried his hands then gathered his folders from the table. He set a few of them on the seat to the left. "Mind if I take a bottle of water with me?"

"By all means. Whatever you need."

Delgado grabbed a bottle from the fridge and started for the door. Winthrop followed.

"What will happen now?"

Delgado turned. "Now? It's over, Mr. Winthrop. The case is closed." He smiled. "Not officially yet, but it's down to the paperwork. We've got the girl home, and the kidnappers are dead."

"But the money…"

"I know that must be worrisome. More than worrisome, but the money's gone, sir. There's nothing we can do about it." Delgado reached for the doorknob. "Thanks again for the use of the house. Have a great day."

Delgado got in the car and turned left out of the drive. He went only two blocks before he parked on the side of the street. He climbed into a van with Tip and one of the techs. "Anything?"

"Not yet. I suspect it won't be long," Tip said.

About five minutes passed before the tech said, "Got an outgoing call."

Delgado and Tip put on headphones, listening in on the call. It rang four times.

"Lone Star Recovery."

"Harbough, we need to talk."

Scott's voice was a harsh whisper, the kind you hear in old detective movies. Tip raised his thumb up to Delgado, and they high-fived.

"Who is this?"

"You know who it is. The detectives just left. They said all the money's gone."

"I don't know what the hell you're talking about, mister. You must have the wrong number."

"They're gone now. They packed up and left. It's safe for me to talk. What I want to know is who the fuck set the fire? Did you? Do you have the money?"

"*Shut the fuck up!*"

"Did you put that spyware on my phone?"

"What are you talking about?"

"Someone put spyware on my cell phone."

"Are you talking on it now?"

"They already took it off. It's clean now. Where's the money? What happened?"

"Listen, cowboy, I don't know you, so I'm hanging up." The line went dead.

Scott dialed again. This time it rang a dozen times, but no one answered. He tried again, but it went to a machine. He didn't leave a message. Guess he had *some* smarts.

Delgado turned to Tip. "Think that's enough?"

"Enough for what we need," Tip said.

Delgado and Tip headed back to Winthrop's house. Delgado tapped lightly on the door. Scott's expression was full of surprise when he saw them. "Detective, I didn't expect to see you again."

"May we come in, Mr. Winthrop?"

Winthrop hesitated, and Delgado said, "I forgot some files."

He stepped aside. "Of course, forgive me. My mind was wandering. Seems to be doing that a lot of late."

"I understand, sir, with all you've been through." He walked over and picked up the folders, holding them while he studied Winthrop. "We've been trying to figure out who put that spyware on your phone. Do you have any idea?"

"As I said, I have no idea."

"All right, just thought I'd ask." Delgado started to leave then turned again. "I almost forgot. Tip was thinking about the money…"

"Yes?" He perked up again.

"I know you're worried about it, but with your ransom insurance, you don't have to worry. It will be reimbursed."

Winthrop's brow wrinkled. "Ransom insurance?"

Delgado smiled. This guy was good. "And you don't know who put the spyware in your phone?"

"I already said I don't." His frustration was obviously building.

"You're certain it wasn't Mr. Harbough?"

That one hit hard, clearly taking him by surprise. He didn't answer for a few seconds. "Who?"

"Mr. Harbough. Ed Harbough."

He shook his head. "I don't know a Mr. Harbough."

Tip leaned across the table, narrowing his eyes at Scott, getting his mean look going. "You sure? He investigated an insurance claim you had last year."

Scott put on his best expression to imitate deep thought. "Harbough… Was that him? I don't remember. Why? Does it matter?"

"You must have suspected him of the spyware, Mr. Winthrop, because you just called and asked him yourself." Delgado pushed the button on the tape player, which was set to start at the right spot. Winthrop heard his own voice on the recorder:

"Harbough, we need to talk."

"Who is this?"

"You know who it is. The detectives just left here. They said all the money is gone."

"I don't know what the hell you're talking about, mister. You must have the wrong number."

"Look, they're gone now. They packed up and left. It's safe for me to talk. What I want to know is who the fuck set the fire? Did you? Do you have the money?"

"Shut the fuck up!"

"Did you put that spyware on my phone?"

"What are you talking about?"

"Someone put spyware on my cell phone."

"Are you talking on it now?"

"They already took it off. It's clean now. Where's the money? What happened?"

"Listen, cowboy, I don't know you, so I'm hanging up."

Winthrop's face lost every bit of expression. He had nothing left to try. Even his voice failed him. Delgado rewound the tape and sat up straight. "Mr. Winthrop, I think we need to talk."

He nodded then finally found his voice. "Where did you get that?"

"I don't think it matters," Tip said.

He thought for a moment, then, "I don't think you can use that…"

Tip laughed. "You're probably right. I'd bet with a good lawyer this would be thrown out in court, so we're not even gonna try."

Scott shifted his gaze from Tip to Delgado and back. "What are you going to do with it?"

"We just wanted you to understand that we know what is going on. And we want you to cooperate on getting Ed Harbough."

Scott stood. "I need to call my lawyer."

"You could do that," Tip said. "And I could read you your rights, but I'm not."

Winthrop stopped, confused.

"What I'm gonna do is drive over to Lonny Hackett's house and give him this tape. I'm gonna let Lonny read you your rights."

"You wouldn't do that, I'll—"

Tip got right in his face. "You'll what?" He sneered, twisting his scar until Winthrop backed up. "If you can still talk after Lonny's done with you *then* I'll lock your ass up. At that point, you're going in for the full show: felony murder."

"Murder? I never—"

"When you're involved in a kidnapping and someone dies, it's felony murder for all of you. You're new to this great state, so let me fill you in on some little-known facts. Texas puts more criminals to death than any other state. We got a whole damn room full of needles waiting for arms to put them in. We don't much care if it's a black or white arm either. Equal opportunity killing is what we got."

"What if I cooperate?"

"Depends on what you did."

"I told you—I didn't do anything."

Tip read him his rights, and then they sat at the table.

"Start talking," Delgado said. "Start with the fake insurance claim when you met Harbough."

For the next half an hour, Winthrop talked. He told them how his ex-wife had taken him for almost everything. How he needed money. He'd thought he could get away with a fake break-in, so he had one of the people who did his landscaping pawn some of his belongings for him. Harbough investigated and quickly found the stuff, tracing it back to Winthrop's ill-conceived plot. Harbough then offered to split the money with Winthrop. The alternative was getting arrested.

"So I took the money," Winthrop said. "Then I forgot all about him—until a couple of weeks ago. He called and suggested we meet. Over lunch, he proposed the idea for the kidnapping. I don't know how he knew I had kidnap insurance, but he did. He said he would arrange everything. I needed money, so I agreed."

"But you never met any of the kidnappers?"

"Never. I didn't even speak with them until they called."

"And you don't know who they are?"

Scott shook his head. "No idea."

"How did they get the wrong girl?"

Scott sighed. "They didn't. When Harbough first proposed the idea, I wouldn't agree. I didn't want Alexa going through that." He took a sip of water. "After he realized he wouldn't get me to change my mind, even after threatening me, he told me about the guest part of the policy."

Delgado gritted his teeth. He wanted to hit this guy so bad. "So you decided to sacrifice Jada."

"Don't say it like that, Detective. Harbough assured me she would be safe."

Delgado opened one of the folders and pulled out the picture of Jada—naked, beaten and bruised. He set it on the table and slid it in front of Winthrop. "Safe like this?"

Winthrop turned his head. "That wasn't supposed to happen. He promised!"

Delgado and Tip sat silently. Finally Tip said, "You realize you'll have to testify against Harbough in court."

Winthrop nodded. "In exchange…"

"For a lesser charge, yes."

"What kind of lesser charge?"

"I'm willing to bet we can drop felony murder. That will take the needle off the table. You'd still be charged with kidnapping. It will be up to your lawyer to do anything beyond that."

Winthrop was silent for a minute, maybe more. Then he nodded. "I'm ready."

Tip yanked him up. Delgado put the cuffs on.

"Are those really necessary, Detective?"

"Absolutely," Delgado said, and tightened them a little more.

"Where's Alexa?" Scott asked. "I need to see her."

No wonder the girl is so screwed up, Delgado thought. "She went to visit Jada." On the way out the door, he called Gino. "Got him, cuz. We're going downtown."

"What about Harbough?"

"We've got a uniform sitting on him. Tip's going to stop and pick him up."

"No! Send someone else."

"You got it."

CHAPTER 67

ONE LAST NIGHT

Lonny drove the car home, letting Jada and her mother have the back seat. Mars kept him company up front. Lonny was proud of Mars. Jada, too. He had great kids, and now he had to leave them.

Time enough for those worries later. Now was a time to celebrate Jada's return.

"Whatever you want for dinner, young lady, name it, and it's yours."

Lucia laughed. "As long as it doesn't cost more than six dollars."

"And forty-two cents," Mars added. "I'll kick in my bankroll."

Jada leaned forward and kissed her brother's cheek. "I even missed *you*, little bro. Can you believe that?"

They talked and laughed more on the way home, and when they arrived, Lonny announced that he was cooking dinner.

"Lord have mercy," Lucia said. "What on earth are *you* gonna cook?"

He came out of the kitchen wearing Lucia's apron and a chef's hat she'd bought him as a gag gift years ago. "Lonny Hackett's specialty," he said. "Jalapeño hot dogs."

"I should have known," Jada said. "It's the only thing he can cook."

Dinner was full of thanks, prayers, and more laughter. But as the night wore on, Lonny found it difficult to keep a happy face. This was his last night at home. Maybe forever. Several times, Lucia tried saying something to him, but he ducked her. He avoided any situation where he might be caught alone, left to face her questions. After playing a game of Canasta, then a few challenge rounds of Scrabble, Lonny announced he was going to shower.

He went to the bedroom and sat on the bed, wondering what to do. He'd had enough of that dirty money left to get them out of Texas, maybe all the way to Arizona. Or to go the other way to Florida. He'd heard work was good in Florida. And it was warm there. Cops would be after him, but he could change names. A few hundred bucks would take care of that. Get a new ID for all of them, and they could settle down in a growing community. He went to the closet, got a suitcase, and started pulling things out of the drawers, filling it up.

Then he sat on the bed, looking out the front window. He'd promised the detective he'd be here in the morning, and the man had laid his job on the line. The man didn't owe him nothing, but he went out of his way. Lonny let out a big sigh, reached in the suitcase, and started taking clothes back out, setting each one neatly into the drawer where it belonged.

A voice came from behind him. "I'd have gone with you. I hope you know that."

He turned, embarrassed. Lucia stood there, innocent and true. "You know?"

"I know you haven't been the man I married since you lost your job. And I know that all those nights you came home with money, you didn't get it working honest labor."

"How did you know?"

"I didn't smell cement on you, or see stains on your arms."

He sat back on the bed, defeated. "You should have said something."

"Uh-huh. And what would you have done?" She walked over and stood before him.

Lonny looked up at her. "I'm through hiding and doing wrong. But now…"

"What kind of trouble are we in?"

"No *we*. It's *me*. I did some bad things. Now I got to pay for them."

Lucia sat beside him on the bed. Her fingertips traced lines up his big arm. "It will always be *we*. No matter what happens. You remember that."

Lonny kissed her. Her lips weren't soft like they used to be; they quit tasting like honey long ago. But he couldn't let go. Didn't want to let go, not wanting to free his lips for what he had to say.

"I'll be goin' to jail. How long, I don't know." He tried to hold back tears, but they came out in a flood. "What am I gonna tell the kids? All these years of preaching what's right and wrong, and now…now this."

Lucia rubbed his head. Kissed his cheek. "Those kids are old enough. They know you're not perfect. You'll tell them what you did, and why. And then you'll show them how a man handles his business." She kissed him again and stood. "Like you've done all these years."

"They're gonna hate me."

"They might be embarrassed. Maybe even angry. But they'll love you like they always have. Can't take that away."

Lonny stood and looked Lucia in the eyes. "Will you stand with me when I tell them?"

She grabbed his hand and headed for the door. "I've stood with you for eighteen years, Mr. Hackett. I won't step down now."

Lonny talked through the night, telling his kids what he did wrong and helping them figure out how they would live the rest of their lives without him. He'd be gone for most of it, if not all. He didn't tell them he could get the needle. He didn't even want to think of that. He *did* tell them they'd likely be married with grown kids of their own before anyone would even consider letting him out.

When he was done, he took Lucia to the bedroom. They sat on the bed for hours, just holding each other and talking. He was still talking when Detective Cataldi's car pulled into the driveway. He stood, straightened his shirt, took a handkerchief from the drawer, and tucked it into his back pocket. Lonny needed to feel like a gentleman today more than ever.

"Time to go, Lucia." He kissed her, a quick peck, then grabbed a small bag and headed out.

***

I stood in the driveway, waiting. I was both relieved and surprised when Lonny came out. I didn't know if he'd be here. Before I could say anything, Lucia ran out the door. She passed Lonny and ran to me.

"Do you have to take him now?"

"I should have done it last night."

"I know. We all thank you for that. But do you have to take him?"

"If not now, when?"

She stared at me, her huge brown eyes pleading, opening up to let me see her soul. "Never," she said. "He doesn't deserve this."

"Lucia, do you—"

She placed her finger on my lips, shook away tears from her eyes. "Shh. I *know* what he did, Detective. He does too. He did it for his *family*."

Lonny was approaching, but she held up her hand, warning him off, then turned back to me. I loved this strong, wonderful woman. For a brief moment, I envied Lonny.

"Detective, have you ever loved someone so much you would do *anything* to save them? I *know* you loved your wife. I saw it in your eyes that day we did dishes together. She was a lucky woman, your Mary."

She must have seen the look of surprise on my face. "Your necklace, Detective. It's inscribed with her name. That's how I knew."

Lonny came up, opened the car door, and put his stuff in. He went to Lucia and kissed her.

"It's not fair what you're doing," Lonny said. "The man is doing his job and he's been good to us."

She nodded, fighting tears as Lonny got in. The kids came out and surrounded her, waving to Lonny as I backed out of the driveway. I tried focusing on what I had to do that day, but I couldn't get Lucia's eyes out of my head. We drove a couple of miles in silence, and then Lonny looked my way.

"I know it's not fair of me to ask, but would you mind checking in on the kids? They're gonna need some guidance."

"I'm sure Lucia can handle it."

"She pretends to be a rock. But she's gonna break when I'm gone."

"Lonny, I've got my own son. My own problems too."

"I'm sorry. Like I said, it's not fair."

We drove another few miles, heading south on I-45.

"Still, I'm asking," he said.

I pulled off the freeway and into a diner. "You want breakfast?"

"Haven't had any."

I grabbed a booth near the front window, ordered a huge meal then sat there reading the paper. Lonny sat across from me, playing one of those games where you try to leave one peg in the center. All the time, I couldn't get my mind off Lucia and the kids. I drank three cups of coffee and was mopping up eggs-over-easy with white toast, doing anything I could to get the images of Mars and Jada out of my mind. And Lucia.

Lonny had good kids. Real good. I knew how difficult it was to raise good kids. It took a team. Tough enough even then, let alone as a single mother with no money. Putting Lonny away was a sentence for his whole family.

I looked over at him. He was shaking. Scared shitless. I didn't blame him. Going to prison was worse than going to war. All they did was kill you in war. I fought one last time with my conscience—thought about Lucia trying to work and raise those kids. Then I thought about Rico Moreno and what I'd done to him and his family. I owed the world something besides another prisoner in Huntsville.

"You're going home, Lonny."

His eyes opened up real big. "Don't go messing with me, Detective. I'm already shitting my pants. I can't afford no hopes."

I glared at him. "You ever so much as—"

He wiped his mouth, got up, stepped to my side of the booth and picked me up and squeezed. Then he kissed me. Goddamn *kissed* me. Right there in the diner. All I could do was laugh.

I threw a twenty on the table, looked at what I had left—a ten and two ones—and threw them on top of the twenty. Might as well make a few people happy today. "Let's go tell Lucia."

As we rode to his house, I thought of all the lies I'd have to tell Ribs. And Tip. But I brushed that concern aside. Things to worry about another time.

Half an hour later, I pulled into Lonny's drive and unlocked the doors. "Get the fuck out, Hackett. And I swear to God, I better never see you again."

Lucia ran out of the house, followed by Jada and Mars. The whole family stood in the drive, hugging. I couldn't help but smile. I watched for a moment then put the car in reverse.

Lucia came to the car. "Are you coming in for coffee?"

I shook my head. "Thanks anyway."

She leaned in the window next to me. "Get out of that car, mister. And get your butt inside."

I couldn't argue with that. When I stepped out, Lucia grabbed me and squeezed for all she was worth. Then she kissed me, on the lips, soft and warm.

"Detective, if I weren't a married woman, I'd…" She turned her head, embarrassed. "You're a good man, Gino Cataldi. A *damn* good man."

CHAPTER 68

WHERE IS NUMBER TWO

I left the Hacketts and drove slowly down the road. I hadn't reported anything I knew about Lonny, so there was no paperwork to cover up. Delgado and Tip would know, but I could handle them. Delgado was supposed to be getting the wrap-up from the fire department and the preliminaries from the M.E. I called to see if he had any update.

"*Cómo estás, amigo?*" he answered.

"I'll be better if you have good news."

"Depends on what you're looking for."

"Tell me, Ribs."

"Fire department basically confirmed what they suspected. There was a woman on the driver's side of the van with bump on her head on the left side. Almost looks like she fell out the door when the fire started, knocking herself unconscious, and then she burnt up. The fire started with a broken fuel line. Doesn't look like tampering at this point. It spread so fast because there were a lot of empty or half-empty gas cans in there, which made them explode."

I couldn't argue much at that point. "What about the money?"

"They found it in the same kind of bags we sent it out in. It's impossible to tell how much, but enough, they said."

"Enough for what?"

"This wasn't a few hundred-dollar bills, if that's what you're wondering. This was lots—pay-off-your-mortgage-type lots."

"Son of a bitch, are you telling me they all died?"

"The body count is right—four males and the female, just like it was supposed to be."

"That's what bothers me. The 'just like it was supposed to be' shit. Do you buy it?"

"Buy what?"

"That they planned a meticulous kidnapping, pulled it off without a hitch, and then Number Two eliminates her four partners, and as she is getting away the van *happens* to have a fuel-line break. Oh, and lest we forget, she falls out of the van, hits her head, and the whole place blows up, money included." I waited. "You're buying that shit?"

"You know I'm not, but what are we going to do? The lady beat us at every turn. She's probably on her way to a beach in Tahiti by now."

"I'd bet fifty-fifty on that."

"We'll get her. Don't worry."

"Yeah, all right. I'll see you later."

"What happened with Lonny?"

"What about him?"

"That's what I want to know. Something was up with him, going out looking for that guy Willard, leaving again, then him and you seeing Harbough. You tell me."

"Turned out to be nothing," I said.

A long silence followed. "And you want *me* to buy that shit?"

"I'll tell you about it later. I'm going by the Marshalls' house."

I stopped by there and told them we'd gotten the ones who did it. That they were all dead. I didn't like lying, but I couldn't break Lonny's trust. And what good would it do to tell them there might be one left out there. Cause them some more sleepless nights; fuel those fires of vengeance and hatred. I'd been through that myself. No sense in others going through it.

After leaving, I wandered, riding around, not knowing what to do or what I wanted to do. This case had torn me up. I ended up deciding to go to the warehouse. There were things that still bothered me. I parked about fifty feet from the building, still reeking from the fire, then got out and walked around. I didn't go in, but I did walk out back, taking note of the door on that side and the narrow trail leading away from the building. It looked as if it could be wide enough for a car. Only one way to find out.

I drove around the side, keeping to the gravel so the car didn't sink in the wet ground. The trail led to the back section of woods. It grew narrow, but I kept it fully on the road. When I entered the woods, a few branches scratched the sides of the car, probably taking some paint off, but other than that, it wasn't a bad ride. Within two miles, I exited onto a small paved road to the north.

Texas had a lot of small backwoods roads, though most people never drove them, tending to stay on the freeways. This road was new to me. I took it east and followed it for about five miles until it dead-ended into a farm. I headed back and followed it west. The road branched north, then east, ultimately coming out near Conroe on the west side of town.

As I got close to town, traffic became bumper-to-bumper. My eyes wandered as much as my mind. During one of many delays, I found myself staring at a license plate. It started with VNA. It jarred my memory. I'd never gotten those plates from Herb, and they probably never went back to check on them. It was likely nothing, but I had nothing to do. I called Herb.

"Herb, can you send me those plates Julie had you run? The VNA numbers from The Woodlands area."

"Shoot, Gino, I forgot to get that to you."

"How many are there?"

"Hang on." He put me on hold for a few seconds. "In your immediate area, with cars registered to women, six."

"How about texting them to me? Names and addresses."

"Won't be five minutes. You could check with Julie, but I know they already ruled out the last two on the list. Don't know about the others."

I suffered through the rest of the traffic, which miraculously disappeared within a mile or two, and then I got on the freeway heading south. Herb's text came in before I hit the first exit for The Woodlands. I glanced at the names, not recognizing any, and decided to check out the remaining four in order of proximity. The first was off Research Forest Boulevard.

I didn't know what the hell I was going to do when I got to these people or what I was hoping to find, but it was the last clue we had, and I didn't like leaving stones unturned. After parking in the drive of a modest two-story colonial, I made sure my gun was ready and available. I rang the doorbell, keeping my right hand loose. Before long, a woman answered.

"May I help you?" Her accent carried a deep Southern drawl.

"I'm looking for…Martha Kirk," I said, reading it from the list on the phone.

"I'm Martha. What can I do for you, young man?"

I'd struck out. This woman was old. Not a kidnapper. I apologized for bothering her and moved on to the next address. I struck out again. The next woman was large. Very large. She definitely did not fit the "very nice ass" description Mars had told me about. Once again, I packed up and headed to the next house.

It took me almost fifteen minutes to get to the address. I parked in the street and walked up the drive. Damn nice house is what it was—a sprawling ranch with brick and stone exterior, landscaping to win contests, and etched glass in the front door. I stepped onto the front porch and rang the bell. The woman who answered had long dark hair, the kind I liked. She wore glasses, the kind that made a woman look sexy. As I admired her, I got a sick feeling in my gut. It almost made me throw up. Standing before me, smiling as if she had a right to, was the thong-panties girl.

Thoughts ran through my head quickly. *What is she doing here? Didn't she say she lived in the Galleria area?*

I could buy one coincidence. I could buy two under unusual circumstances. *This,* I wasn't buying. Not one bit. I thought I'd try to take her off guard. "Hello, Jennifer. May I come in?"

"Detective Cataldi. You really *are* a detective to have found me. But my name isn't Jennifer. It's Marissa."

"Okay, Marissa, may I come in?"

She stepped aside. "Please."

"Husband home?"

She held out her hand, showing her empty ring finger. "I gave up that habit long ago."

A smile accompanied the statement. I thought it might have contained an invitation.

"I thought Scott introduced you as Jennifer."

"Scott? Scott…Oh, that's right, Winthrop. Yes, he probably did. I don't give out my real name at clubs. That's where we met, you know."

"So he said."

I stood in a marble entrance hall with huge brick arches leading down to a living room on one side and an enormous dining room on the other. The foyer was bigger than my family room. "Nice place."

"I find it comfortable. Would you care for a drink?"

"Since I'm off duty, I'd love one. Whatever you're having."

She walked to a bar that seated six. "I'll make it a surprise," she said and ducked behind the counter.

"Fine by me, Number Two."

I had hoped to draw a reaction. She didn't even turn around. "What did you say, Detective?"

Bitch! "I said you're good, Number Two."

She walked in, drinks in hand. "Number Two? I don't quite understand."

I looked at her. Not a hint of a smirk. Damn good thing. I'd have thrown the cuffs on if she'd smirked. She was good, though. Better than good.

"I've been working a kidnapping case, remember? The Winthrops. One of the kidnappers called themselves Number Two."

She led the way to the living room, where she sat in a large plush chair covered in cotton-white fabric. Her butt sank into the back of it. When she crossed her long legs her skirt rode up high. Way high. I tried not to look but, well, actually I tried looking without getting caught. It was impossible not to look.

"How original," she said. "This was the Winthrop case? Did you finish it?"

"Almost."

"I probably sound callous. Did you bring his daughter home safe?"

"Turns out it wasn't his daughter, but we got the girl. The problem, is one of the kidnappers got away."

"How did he get away?"

"Actually it's a *she*. I'll get her, though."

"I certainly hope so."

I focused on her face. She wasn't gorgeous, but she was attractive. *And very sexy.* Something about the combination of her eyes, her smile, and her body… I forced myself to look away. "I'll have your DNA from the motel," I said while looking out the window. I turned back quickly to judge her reaction.

"*My* DNA? I see, you're role-playing. Okay, I'll go along. Which motel was it?"

"Off the freeway at Ritchie Road."

"Let's see, DNA at the motel. Hmm. Let me think." She mimicked a deep Texas drawl. "Why, Detective, I must have stayed there before. You know they don't clean those rooms often."

"If you did stay there, they'll have records."

"Yes, they *will*. I was coming home from a club and had too much to drink. Rather than risk it, I pulled in and spent the night."

She took me by surprise with that one. *Had she planned it that far in advance?* I made a mental note to check on it but didn't hold much hope.

"We've got your voice on the tape when you okay'ed the extra hundred thousand."

"A voice on a tape? Not conclusive."

"We'll get Harbough's testimony."

"Well, I don't know who this Harbough is, but it sounds like he's a criminal. If he was involved in this, he must be a terrible man. If that's the case, it won't fly. A criminal cutting a deal to turn another one in?" She dropped her accent and laughed. "Come on, he'd incriminate his mother. If we're going to play the game, crank it up a notch."

Obviously, I was getting nothing from this. I stood. "I guess you've got an answer for everything."

She sipped her drink, a smug look on her face. I'd had enough. "This is no *goddamn game*, lady. A girl was kidnapped."

She laughed. Not at me. Just a nice little laugh, like a friend would. "I had fun, Detective, but it looks as if you are losing control." She got up and set her drink on the bar. She didn't formally ask me to leave, but the way she said, "Come by anytime," said as much.

I didn't budge. I stood there staring at her. "The way I figure it, Harbough was the link. Probably busted one of you when he was a cop. Soon enough, you took over, being the smart one." She stayed by the bar, shifting her weight to the right leg. She was listening, wanting to hear what I had to say, I guess.

"The dead lady in the van must have been Harbough's partner—Sue Masterson. I figure she was the one you called Driver. We'll find out when the DNA comes in, but for now, that's how I put it together." I took a sip of my drink and wondered if I would keel over from poisoning. "You had me going for a while with that one. No one knew that the driver was a woman. Pretty clever, the whole thing with the masks and no one seeing each other. I have to take my hat off to you."

Number Two sipped her drink and smiled.

"And the way you planted that spyware—bold. Damn bold. Go right into the guy's house. Kind of cruel though, to play with someone's emotions like that. It's one thing to steal from a person, but that..." I shook my head. "You went a little too far, I think."

She continued to look at me but said nothing.

"And the money. Another clever one. Some people would have been greedy and taken it all. But you were smart. You knew we'd be looking for it forever. So you burned some up, and not just a little. My partner said there was at least a few hundred grand. We'll never know for sure, but you burned enough for a lazy detective to convince himself that the money was gone, burned up in the fire with all the perps." I took another sip, never taking my eyes from her.

"Refill, Detective?"

"What I can't figure out is *why*."

"Why?"

"Yeah, why did you do it? You don't need the money."

Her smile was quick. On and off in a flash. "I see you're back at your game again. I'd like to help you, but I'm afraid I have no answers. Sometimes things don't get wrapped up as nice and neat as we'd like them."

"You sure made an impression on Jada. She won't even talk about you. Was that planned too?"

More silence.

"Either way, Jada said to say thanks for protecting her."

"I'm glad she came back safe."

"Why did you do it? Protect her but kill the others?"

Number Two shifted her stance, sipped her drink. "Detective, I don't know Jada, but if I had to guess, I would imagine that your Number Two person might have had something in her past that caused her to empathize with the girl."

I nodded. "Yeah, I guess you're right. That would do it."

She walked over and pecked me on the cheek then walked to the door. The actions took me by surprise. Shocked is what I was. And now that she was walking away from me, I found myself staring at her ass again. I gulped the last of my drink, said goodbye, and left, the door closing behind me.

As I walked down the sidewalk, the door opened again. I turned and looked back. She stood on the porch. "I had a thought, Detective. If this person really did get away with all the money, I'd imagine they would be done with crime."

"Probably so." I wasn't getting anything out of her unless we got a lot more evidence.

As I started for my car, she called to me again. "I forgot to ask. Did you ever find your watch?"

My fists clenched. Every muscle I had tensed. "What watch?"

"That day I met you, you were saying something to Scott about losing a watch. It sounded expensive."

I relaxed, the memory coming back to me. "No. I never did," I said, and went to the car.

EPILOGUE

I finished the day, got in my car, and headed for home. For two days I had been trying to figure out how to get Number Two. I convicted her ninety-nine times, but I got her off a hundred more. She was a free woman, and I didn't see what I could do to change that. I even questioned myself, thinking maybe that Number Two was *really* lying in that warehouse, burned up like the rest of them. Maybe Number Two *really* did fall out of the van and knock herself unconscious. And maybe the fuel line *really* did break just then and catch the place on fire.

And me finding Jennifer—Marissa, or whatever her name was—all a big coincidence. But somewhere in my mind, in a place I wanted to keep secret, I knew that Jennifer, the thong-panties girl, was Number Two. And I knew how the spyware had gotten onto Scott's phone. It was no accident that she'd met Scott at the club. She'd planned everything down to the smallest detail.

Everything about this case haunted me. I almost ran off the road three times, my mind jumping from that peck on the cheek from Marissa to that warm, grateful kiss on the lips by Lucia. The crazy thing was that both of them excited me. Maybe it was time to think about dating again. I'd have to ask Mary.

I didn't go straight home today; instead, I drove around, wasting time and keeping my mind from breaking. As the sun lost its luster, I finally headed home. I parked in the drive and walked up the sidewalk, surprised to see a FedEx package on my porch. I wasn't expecting a delivery, but I recognized the return address immediately; it was the same as the warehouse that burnt down.

Shit!

I took it inside, wondering if it was an ear or a finger of…God knew who. I opened it and scraped a few of the packaging peanuts from the top—and almost shit. There, lying in the box, surrounded by peanuts—was Mary's watch. No note. Nothing else. Just her watch.

For probably half a minute, all I did was stare. I picked up the watch, then I opened a bottle of wine and went to my bedroom. Tucked under the corner of the bed was a music box I had bought Mary in Sorrento. The top was outlined in ebony, with inlaid pink tulips. It had a rosewood border. I opened the lid and removed an envelope. Inside was a piece of paper folded into a small square. It was heavily creased. I took it to the kitchen then, *very* carefully, I unfolded it and lay it on the table to read.

Dear Gino:

I am dying. God has decided I am needed up there more than here. He must know you'll be good for Ron. I know you will. We had a lot of time together, and every moment was a cherished one. It won't be long until we are together again. That's why I'm giving you this watch.

My love forever,

Mary

I sipped the wine, wiped my eyes, and stared at the watch—a plain black face with only a second-hand showing. It had been lost and now it was found. I flipped it over, staring at the inscription.

Each tick of the clock is one less second we are apart.

I thanked God for letting me save Jada and for keeping her safe.

I thanked Number Two for having the heart to send me this watch. Then I flipped the watch back over and stared at it.

And I counted the seconds until I could be with Mary again.

<<<<>>>>

Thanks for taking the time to read the book. I hope you enjoyed it.
Authors live and die on recommendations and reviews, so if you liked the book, please tell someone about it. And if you have a spare moment, I'd love for you to post a review on Amazon or Goodreads, or Apple or B&N. Connie and Tip will be back again next year. But be sure to sign the mailing list so you hear about all the special sales and new releases. Murder Takes Patience is up next, followed by Old Wounds, another Redemption novel with Gino Cataldi and Ribs Delgado.

Thanks again for your time,
Giacomo

If you would like to be notified of future releases, click here to sign up for my mailing list

http://eepurl.com/kS-IX

If you want to email me about this book, please use: **gg@giacomog.com**

Acknowledgements

The tough part of writing a book is not the writing, it's all the stuff that comes after that. I'll take credit for the writing. For the tough parts I am honor bound to thank the following:

My great copy editor, Annette Lyon.

A fantastic graphic designer, Maria Zannini of Book Cover Diva.

Morgana Gallaway from The Editing Department, for the amazing layout and formatting.

And most importantly the beta readers who helped me get this book into shape: Missy, Aliza, Otto, Chris, Jeanne Haskin, Joe Michalcewicz, Carry Shepherd, Betty Knutson, and Elena Dillon. If I missed someone, please shoot me.

It takes a lot of technical help to write a book like this. I owe a debt of gratitude to Tim Goodnow and Dave Dunn for their guidance on the clinical trials, and huge thanks to Joshua Gold and Brian Giehl for the great information on the insurance angles. If I messed anything up it's my fault, not theirs.

I also want to give special thanks to my niece, Emiliana, for making me laugh on many nights when I needed a laugh, and to Braden and Bella for all the wonderful video chats.

Lastly, to my wife, Mikki.

Ti amo con tutto il mio cuore.

About the Author

I grew up in a large Italian family in the Northeast. No one had money, so for entertainment our family played board games and told stories. I loved the city—the noise, the people—but it was the family get togethers and the storytelling that stuck with me.

I still love storytelling, but now I write the stories instead of telling them.

My wife and I live in Texas, where we run an animal sanctuary with 45 loving "friends." One of them is a crazy wild boar named Dennis, who is my best buddy.

Sometimes I miss the early days, but not much. Now I enjoy the solitude and the noise of the animals.